A DEADLY LIKENESS

Lesley McEvoy was born and bred in Yorkshire and has had a passion for writing in one form or another all her life. The writing took a backseat as Lesley developed her career as a Behavioural Analyst / Profiler and Psychotherapist – setting up her own Consultancy business and therapy practice. She has written and presented extensively around the world for over twenty-five years, specialising in behavioural profiling and training, with a wide variety of organisations. The corporate world provided unexpected sources of writing material when, as Lesley said, she found more psychopaths in business than in prison! Lesley's work in some of the UK's toughest prisons was where she met people whose lives had been characterised by drugs and violence and whose experiences informed the themes she now writes about. Deciding in 2017 to concentrate on her writing again, Lesley produced her debut novel, *The Murder Mile*.

These days she lives in Cheshire with her partner but still manages to lure her two grown-up sons across the Pennines with her other passion – cooking family dinners.

Also by Lesley McEvoy

The Murder Mile
The Killing Song

A DEADLY LIKENESS

By

Lesley McEvoy

ZAFFRE

First published in the UK in 2023 by
ZAFFRE
An imprint of Bonnier Books UK
4th Floor, Victoria House, Bloomsbury Square, London, WC1B 4DA
Owned by Bonnier Books
Sveavägen 56, Stockholm, Sweden

A CIP catalogue record for this book is
available from the British Library.

ISBN: 978-1-83877-656-5

Also available as an ebook and an audiobook

1 3 5 7 9 10 8 6 4 2

Typeset by IDSUK (Data Connection) Ltd
Printed and bound in Great Britain by Clays Ltd, Elcograf S.p.A.

Zaffre is an imprint of Bonnier Books UK
www.bonnierbooks.co.uk

Dorothy Robinson, 4 March 1939–20 September 2022

Dotty – my 'Little Mother', who gave me unconditional love, laughter and fun, and showed me what a childhood should be like.

An 'Apex Predator' is by definition at the very top of the food chain. In its natural habitat, nothing preys upon it.

Therefore, many would say that we are Apex predators.

I know that's not true.

I know *beyond doubt*, we have predators out there, that don't hunt and kill us in order to survive.

They do it because they can.

But the most terrifying of all . . .

do it because they like it.

Chapter One

Thursday Morning, Mid-November, Kingsberry Farm

I threw a stick for my boxer dog, Harvey, and watched as he bounded across the frozen field after it.

We were lucky to live in a place like this, with six acres of my own land to walk across, without seeing another living soul. The isolation up here on the Yorkshire moors suited me, given what I did for a living. But it was easy to get complacent about the scenery when it was an everyday companion.

I turned my face into the watery morning sun, breathing in the crisp air. Jamming my hands into the pockets of my Barbour jacket, I turned down the well-worn track to my woods. Harvey was leading the way as usual.

I felt the mobile vibrate against my palm a second before its shrill tone shattered the rural tranquillity.

'McCready.'

'Finally dragged yourself out of bed then?' I could hear tension in Callum Ferguson's voice, beneath his barely discernible Scottish accent.

'Been up for hours – already out walking.' I climbed a stile, which Harvey took in one leap. 'How come you left so early?'

'Got a call. You were out for the count – didn't want to wake you.' I could picture him at his desk in the CID office in Fordley Police Station. 'Supt. Warner picked up a murder case overnight.'

Detective Superintendent Charlotte Warner headed up a team of specialist detectives in HMET, West Yorkshire Police's Homicide and Major Enquiry Team.

'I'm DCI on it. Going to be putting in all the hours for a while, Jo. This is a bad one.'

I thought about the shock wave from sudden death – destroying everything in its path.

'Aren't they all?'

'Hmm, well this one has extras that I really don't like . . .' He paused but I sensed there was more to come. 'Was hoping you could come and take a look? I really need you to see this.'

'What is it this time? Sick, sadistic or just plain deviant?'

'How did you guess?'

'Because I *only* get called if there's an element of sick or sadistic—'

'Or just plain deviant.' He finished helpfully.

'So . . . Which is it?'

'Thought that's what you did? Read minds.'

'I'm a forensic profiler, not Mystic Meg.' I scooped the stick Harvey had dropped at my feet and launched it for him.

'I know you don't want to get involved in police investigations anymore—'

'I don't.'

'I wouldn't ask if it wasn't important.'

'They're *all* important, Cal – it's not a matter of degree.' Harvey ran back and danced around my legs. 'It's a matter of balance – for me anyway.'

'I know. Last year was a tough one, Jo. Stress wise. I understand that—'

'My case-load is full. Crown Prosecution Service are keeping me busy. I've got offender assessments to do for two upcoming trials.'

'We don't want you in this all the way,' he pressed. 'Just need you to come out and take a look. To give me your opinion. Please?'

'Just today?'

'Absolutely.'

His answer came too fast to be true.

'Warner's authorised your involvement – got a budget code for your time.'

'Already?'

It was unusual for a profiler to be called in at such an early stage, which compounded my uneasy feeling that there was a lot more he wasn't telling me.

He hesitated for just a heartbeat. 'I know you hate seeing them in situ, Jo . . . but it's important for this one.'

Seeing the bodies had never been something I found easy. Even though 'walking the scene' was a process I employed to get into the mind of an offender, to map the events that had led up to whatever atrocity we were dealing with. But usually, it was long after all the physical evidence had been removed. I preferred it that way – for all kinds of reasons.

'I can meet you at the scene.' He pushed again.

Pre-empting my agreement. Nice tactic.

'I don't know, Cal . . .'

'Please, Jo.' His tone was coaxing. 'It's on the Kenley Estate in Fordley. Do you know it?'

I let out a long breath. 'OK,' I said finally. 'I'm walking Harvey, so give me time to get changed.' I glanced at my watch. 'Can be there in an hour?' I still wasn't sure I wanted to do this.

'I'll send you the address.'

Chapter Two

Thursday Morning, Fordley

I drove past rows of identical semi-detached houses on the Kenley Estate. The one I was looking for was in a quiet cul-de-sac of well-maintained gardens, separated by tidy privet hedges.

I remembered the estate being built when I was a teenager. My mother – known to everyone simply as 'Mamma' – dragged me and my father into the show home one Sunday morning.

As an Italian immigrant, arriving in England with my grandparents not long after the Second World War, Mamma had always aspired to living in what she referred to as 'the posh part of town'. My father, a typical Irish-Yorkshireman, was totally unimpressed by this vision of suburbia, and the 'bloody extortionate price' of a new life on the other side of town. Needless to say, we didn't relocate.

I spotted Callum as soon as I turned into the street, even though he was wearing the anonymising white 'scene suit'. The head of silver hair was unmistakable as he leaned against the bonnet of his unmarked BMW. The obligatory face mask pulled down and dangling around his neck.

The women at Fordley nick called him 'The Silver Fox' – though never to his face. In his mid-forties, his hair was an unusual feature, which only made his good looks more striking.

Blue and white police tape marked the outer cordon at the end of the cul-de-sac. A uniformed officer stood guard outside one of the houses halfway down, as crime scene investigators came and went from their van.

This unassuming home had once been the same as all the others. But not anymore. It would now forever be known as the place where a murder happened. Tainted. Different. Changed forever, like everything touched by sudden and violent death.

In a neighbourhood that was just beginning the tentative process of putting up Christmas decorations; festive tinsel and fairy lights were incongruous against the harsh formality of police paraphernalia surrounding a crime scene.

Callum strolled over as I locked my Roadster.

'People think you're a poser, driving that,' he teased.

'Still beats yours out of a bend, any day of the week.'

'Emasculating a man by insulting his car.'

'Then get a decent car,' I said with humour.

'It's the new body shape.'

'You can put lipstick on a pig . . . but it's still a pig.'

Our usual banter – much more fun than a mundane 'good morning'.

We stood apart, feeling suddenly awkward about not touching. But this was work and we'd always kept that distinctly separate from our personal lives.

Everyone in Fordley nick speculated about our on/off relationship, with no one ever quite sure whether we were 'on' or 'off'. After almost two years of dancing around it, I don't think we knew ourselves. Then, just a few months ago, I'd decided to stop holding DCI Callum Ferguson at arm's length. Weighing up the risks of becoming vulnerable against the need to end my self-imposed emotional isolation. But it was still early days, and lately, I'd felt a chill creeping in between us.

'So, what've you got?' I asked, dragging it back to business.

'Barbara Thorpe. Fifty-two years old. Lives alone. Apparently, she let the cat out every night and was up around five every

5

morning to let it in and feed it. But not today. Next-door neighbour heard the cat crying to get inside the house and knocked on.' He gestured next door with a nod of his head. 'She had a key and let herself in around seven o'clock. Found her friend with her throat cut. No sign of forced entry or a struggle, and doesn't look like anything's been taken.'

We both paused as an officer guarding the outer cordon handed me a paper scene suit, gloves, mask and overshoes. Callum leaned against my car and watched as I began to pull them on.

'Still not sure why you need me for this,' I said as I signed the scene log.

'Looks like it might be connected to the Stephen Jones case,' he said, by way of an explanation.

Stephen Jones had been murdered the previous month, in a quiet suburb of Leeds. He'd had his throat cut as he sat watching TV. I'd only read about the Jones case in the newspapers, same as everyone else.

We both stopped to pull up hoods and slip the masks over our faces, before ducking under the tape that marked the inner cordon.

'That's the connection? Both had their throats cut?' I asked. 'Not *that* sick, sadistic or deviant in the grand scheme of things.'

'Not just that.'

'What then?'

His expelled breath was muffled by the mask as he opened the gate and walked me down the path. 'After Jones's murder, we held back certain details.'

'Like what?'

'As well as having his throat cut, he'd had a body part amputated.'

'Has that happened here?'

'Not exactly.'

My legendary lack of patience was being sorely tested. This was like pulling teeth.

'What then?'

'You'll see.'

Chapter Three

There was a hush in the house, despite the level of activity. It was something I'd noticed before. A reverence, I supposed, given that the deceased was still there. That until a few short hours ago, this had been their private space, until a brutal killer had invaded it and taken everything away from them.

To me, being at a crime scene, when the victim was present, had always felt like the ultimate intrusion. Prying into the intimate details of their lives and finally their demise. There was no privacy in death, and in a violent killing, even less.

I followed Callum down the short hallway from the front door and into the living room – careful only to walk on the stepping plates put there by crime scene officers, to avoid people trampling over potential evidence.

Barbara's lounge was what my mother would call 'chintzy'. A three-piece suite with a bold floral pattern that matched the curtains, which were still drawn shut – just as they had been when she was found.

The mantelpiece and sideboard crowded by cheap ornaments and mementos – the kind of thing you'd pick up at the seaside.

A spindly, silver Christmas tree stood in the corner, its bright decorations a stark contrast against the cream-emulsioned Anaglypta wallpaper.

The brassy smell of warm blood still hung heavily in the air – creeping round the edges of my mask, until it felt as though I could taste it.

I stood with Callum, looking down at the victim.

For some reason I looked at her feet first.

I'd always done it that way, maybe because I didn't want to look at their faces, especially the eyes, until I had to.

Barbara was wearing pink fluffy slippers. Her right foot was covered by a cushion that seemed to have fallen off the armchair. Her legs were bare – the skin mottled from sitting too close to the electric fire. Thankfully, someone had turned off the heat – but left the fake 'flickering flame' lights on, which bathed her in a shimmering, unnatural orange glow that did nothing to lessen the surreal horror of the scene.

My gaze took in the heavy pink dressing gown, stained a brighter red from the waist up, where her blood had spilled down the front, from the gaping wound across her throat.

Finally, I looked at her face. Head resting against the back of the armchair, her sightless eyes staring with glassy terror at the ceiling. Her throat had been severed neatly from one side to the other – the fleshy lips of the wound, thick and white and slick, like the gutted belly of a dead fish.

Her mouth was open, as her slackened jaw had dropped in an abruptly silenced scream.

I took a step forward to get a closer look. There was a grey object protruding from between her teeth. At first, I thought it was her tongue.

'It's a thumb,' I said to no one in particular.

I could feel Callum behind me. I half-turned to him. 'You think it's Stephen Jones's?'

'I'm getting Forensics to fast-track it, but I'll be amazed if it isn't.'

I took another look at the wide thumbnail. The severed end was hidden inside her mouth.

'Let me guess,' I said quietly, 'Jones was murdered on a Wednesday night. His killer used secateurs to cut off his thumb, and apart from the wound to his throat, he had no other injuries – no defence wounds either. No sign of forced entry or a struggle?'

'Details of his injuries were never made public ... How do you know?'

'Any connection between Barbara and Jones?' I said, ignoring his question.

'Apart from the fact that she's sucking his thumb?' I felt him shake his head.

I straightened up and took in the whole scene. Behind her chair was the door to the small kitchen at the back of the house. The armchair faced the TV.

A few dark spots of blood marked a path across the room from the armchair to the wall – culminating in an almost artistic arc of red across the pale wallpaper. Like a grotesque abstract painting. What the blood pattern analyst would refer to as 'cast-off blood spatter' – created as the blade was swung, after inflicting the fatal wound.

Her hands rested on the arms of the chair. The fingers curled into claws. Nails digging into the soft material, when they'd clamped in a paroxysm of pain and terror in the split second she'd realised what was happening to her.

'Time of death?'

'Waiting for the pathologist. You know how much they hate being pushed on that – but last night sometime.'

'Wednesday,' I said almost to myself.

I looked down at the cushion covering her right slipper.

'She's had a toe, probably the big one, removed from her right foot ... with secateurs,' I said quietly.

Callum moved away and spoke to one of the CSIs. A moment later, the forensics officer came over and photographed the cushion before gently lifting it to reveal the once-pink, fluffy slipper, which was now stained a dark red.

After taking photographs of it from several angles, she removed the slipper – her latex-clad hands careful not to disturb anything else in the process. It came off Barbara's foot with a soft sucking sound, the congealed blood clinging to the material in dark, sticky molasses-like strings. We all stared at her right foot – missing its big toe.

'How did you know?' he asked again.

'Because I've seen it before . . . fifteen times before.'

Chapter Four

Later Thursday Morning, Fordley Police Station

'The Relay Killer,' Callum said as he poured syrupy-thick coffee from the percolator on the bookshelf in his office.

That was the imaginative sobriquet invented by the press for a killer who slit the throats of his victims, before putting a body part from a previous victim into their mouths.

Fifteen murders over a thirteen-year killing spree throughout the eighties and early nineties. One of the longest manhunts in British criminal history.

'Jacob Malecki.' He sat down and took a sip from his mug. 'Currently serving a whole-life order.'

Life sentences that *really* meant life and only ever handed down to around a hundred prisoners in the UK since they were first introduced in 1983. As far as I knew, there were only sixty-or-so prisoners currently serving such sentences.

'Did you realise when you saw Stephen Jones . . . or Barbara?' I asked.

'Not with Jones. He wasn't one of my cases. Besides, he didn't have a body part in his mouth. There was no reason to make the connection. When this shout came in, Supt. Warner wanted you to see it from the start, so she can justify calling in more resources if we're dealing with a copycat. It was only when you guessed about the toe, we knew for sure. To copy Malecki though . . . bloody hell – he's been banged up for twenty-odd years.'

'Twenty-nine,' I said.

He stretched his long legs under the table – shifting scattered paperwork to find a spot for his mug.

'Our initial theory when Jones was found was that maybe the killer cut off the thumb to torture him. Or Jones had lost it grappling with the blade that was used to cut his throat.'

'So how did you suppose the thumb had gone missing from the scene?'

'It was a couple of days before his body was discovered. His dog was in the room with him the whole time—'

I held up a hand, pulling a revolted face. 'Don't say it. I can imagine . . .'

'It's happened at scenes before . . .'

'I know – bloody gross.'

'It was only when we saw the thumb in Barbara's mouth that we connected the two murders.' He shrugged. 'We still need Forensics to confirm it's Jones's.'

'It will be. Can't be that many amputated thumbs unaccounted for around West Yorkshire.'

'Most of my team were kids when Malecki was locked up. Wouldn't have thought a modern-day psycho would pick him to emulate.'

'You could say Jacob Malecki was a "pet project" of mine . . . back in the day.'

'Before your time, surely?'

'I'd just graduated when he was sentenced.' I was about to elaborate, but thought better of it. My involvement in Malecki's early crimes wasn't public knowledge and I wanted it to stay that way.

There was a lot more I could tell him, about just how obsessed with Malecki I'd become as a student. The horrifying events that

13

connected his life to mine, in ways I couldn't have imagined. But I wasn't ready to share the details with him. It was too painful. Besides, the killer he needed my help with was out there, in the here and now. There was no need to open that Pandora's box of hurt, so it could stay buried, where it belonged.

'He was killing when I was a student,' was all I added. 'Our lecturer, Geoff Perrett, set him as a working case study for us.'

'Get a room full of wannabe forensic psychologists to work the case for free? Clever. I should try that. Save on your fees.' He didn't sound like he was joking.

'Knock yourself out. I'll tell Fordley University to expect your call.'

'Looks like we've got a copycat killer on our patch then.'

'If you have, you can be certain of one thing.'

'What's that?'

'The body count will go up.'

14

Chapter Five

Thursday Afternoon, Kingsberry Farm

Jen, my long-suffering PA and closest friend, looked up from her computer screen.

'Malecki?'

'Yep, everything you can get on him for the last eight years.'

She scratched her greying hair with the end of a pencil. 'Would have thought you already knew everything there was to know about him?'

I shrugged, as I sat at my desk across from hers in our office at the farmhouse. 'Things could have changed. To be fair, he hasn't exactly been at the top of my to-do list since his last murder.'

That had been a doctor at Broadmoor secure psychiatric hospital – eight years before. Killed in an explosion of brutal ferocity, which earned Malecki a transfer to the much harsher environment of HMP Wakefield, a top-security prison in West Yorkshire.

When it hit the headlines, there had been a flurry of news stories and TV debates, sparking renewed interest in a notorious serial killer who had, until then, begun to slip from public memory.

I'd always believed that he should never have been sent to Broadmoor in the first place. That he had was testament to the skill of his expensive defence barrister, presenting a compelling case for Malecki's insanity. A defence accepted by jurors who, naturally, found it difficult to believe that anyone capable of killing fifteen men, women and children without motive or apparent reason could be anything *but* insane.

I'd always held the opinion that he was simply evil.

An old-fashioned concept many found difficult to reconcile in the modern age, where liberal thinkers believed no one was born bad. That such atrocities must be a product of nurture – of an offender's environment. There were plenty of people for whom, sadly, that was the case. An appalling childhood. Abuse. Neglect.

Flouting all the stereotypes, Malecki had suffered none of those things.

Well educated, with an IQ that put him in the Mensa category of a genius, he'd come from a respectable and loving family. A rising star in his chosen profession as an architect. The golden boy. Designer of choice by celebrities from around the world.

Handsome, erudite and wealthy. A polymath. He could have had a successful career as an artist, or anything else he'd set his mind to for that matter. Instead, he declared that painting portraits of the celebrities who commissioned him to design their homes was just a hobby. Until his trial in 1994 revealed that he actually got his jollies by brutally killing and mutilating perfect strangers.

If I'd been practising in the criminal justice system at the time, I may possibly have been called as an expert witness at his trial. As it was, I was fresh out of university and the closest I'd come to Jacob Malecki was creating a profile as part of a class exercise.

'So . . . Callum stayed again last night?' Jen's voice pulled me back.

'Nothing gets past you, does it?' I didn't look up from my notes.

'That's the second time in as many weeks.'

'Didn't know we were counting.'

As the silence stretched out, I looked up to see her watching me. Chin resting on the heel of her hand.

'Well, I am.' She didn't even try to hide her approval.

I opened my mouth, then closed it again, realising I didn't know what to say.

How could I vocalise a half-formed reaction to the changes in Callum's behaviour? Like a glimpse out of the corner of my emotional eye.

But Jen knew me too well, this woman who had taken me under her wing when I was a junior psychologist at Fordley psychiatric hospital.

She had been admin manager in the psychology department back then. Ten years my senior, she decided I needed looking after and somehow adopted me.

'What?' She frowned.

'Nothing . . .'

'But?'

'I don't know . . . he's been a bit "off", somehow.'

'"Off"?' She rolled her eyes. 'Hardly a scientific analysis coming from you.' She studied me for a moment. 'Maybe you're overthinking it?'

The unconscious but ingrained habit of overanalysing every nuance of behaviour and language to reveal hidden meaning. Vital in the job, but lethal in personal relationships.

'Think he's getting cold feet, now you're becoming closer?'

'Maybe.' I shrugged. It was more than that – more than a hesitation to commit. 'It's as if he's building a case, you know?'

'No. You'll have to explain that one.'

I sighed, struggling to put into words what I recognised instinctively in the 'subtext' of our relationship lately.

'He's looking for fault with us ... with *me*.' I wiped a hand across my eyes, tired of going over the same old ground in my head, and reluctant to say it out loud, as that made it more real.

'Even though we're sleeping together, it feels even more casual than it used to. There's a coldness between us somehow that I can't seem to get past. I know he's building a case against us in his head, then looking for evidence to back up the theory, that we won't work as a couple.'

Things he used to find endearing now became a constant source of irritation. Habits and routines he'd never minded before were becoming the cause of petty arguments.

'A radical suggestion I know, but have you tried talking to him about it?' She smiled, but I could see the concern behind those perceptive grey eyes. She knew better than anyone how difficult it was for me to allow someone under my defences.

'We're going out for dinner on Saturday – maybe I'll talk to him then.' But I didn't sound convincing, even to myself.

Chapter Six

Saturday, 5 p.m., Fordley

Joan Rigby had lived next door to Barbara Thorpe on the Kenley estate for the past fifteen years, during which time they'd become good friends. I learned that much as we stood in her small kitchen, waiting for the kettle to boil.

Now, I sat in the lounge, as she set a tray of tea and mince pies on the coffee table.

'I still can't believe it,' she said, as she went to the window, looking at her own reflection in the darkening glass.

There was a net of fairy lights strung across the panes. Her fingers hovered over the switch, then she thought better of it and pulled the curtains instead.

'Doesn't feel right – being festive when she's . . .' She trailed off as her mind shied away from the awful reality. 'I wanted to take the decorations down—' she came to sit in the armchair '—but my daughter persuaded me to keep Christmas, for the grandchildren.' Her smile trembled slightly and she dabbed her eyes with a crumpled tissue.

I smiled. 'You live alone?'

She nodded. 'Since my husband died five years ago.' Her voice faltered and she took a sip of tea.

A black and white cat padded across from the kitchen and rubbed itself against Joan's legs.

'Who's this?'

'Oscar.' She sniffed and wiped her nose with the tissue. 'Barbara's cat.'

I put my hand down and he came to me, sniffing my fingers before curling round my legs, purring loudly. 'You've taken him in?'

She nodded, 'I think Barbara would like that.' Oscar jumped onto her lap.

'Tell me about her.'

'I told the police everything about when I . . .'

They'd been more than just neighbours and the horror of finding her friend, seeing what had been done to her, would haunt this woman for the rest of her life. I wasn't about to make her relive it. Besides, that wasn't the kind of information I was after.

Callum had sanctioned my visit to Joan, to put together the kind of picture I needed. It was a process not easily quantified and certainly not one that neatly fitted into everyday police procedure. But Callum had seen it work before, and trusted it.

'My approach is different, Joan,' I said gently. 'I want to know everything you can tell me about Barbara . . . the person she was.'

Murder defined a person. The act so monstrous that it overshadowed every other aspect of the life that had gone before.

The body itself was a crime scene to be photographed and examined. Even internal organs – removed, weighed and bagged.

But I needed to *know* the person – understand their hopes and aspirations. Hear their words and thoughts echoing from beyond death.

I needed them reanimated. Breathing and moving in my mind's eye, so that I could see what the killer had seen. Because only then could I understand what might have marked her out as a victim.

I needed to see inside *his* mind too – to understand the hungers and motivations that had driven someone to end the life of another human being.

'She was much more than the events of Thursday morning, wasn't she?' I gently prompted.

Joan dabbed her eyes. 'She was to me . . .'

'Tell me how she lived. What she liked and disliked. Her routines and habits?'

'How can *those* things help now?' She frowned.

'It builds up a picture of her life for me.'

And in her life, are clues to her death, I added silently.

'Barbara didn't have any enemies. Everyone liked her . . .'

'She didn't mention anyone bothering her at work, or trouble with a boyfriend?'

'Never had a boyfriend . . . not all the time I've known her. No living relatives either.' She smiled, her eyes welling up again. 'Just a cat for company. Had three or four cats since I've lived here. She could have been my daughter. Twenty years younger than me.' Joan's chin quivered.

I gently replaced my mug. 'Barbara lived here when you moved in?'

'She's *always* been here. Her parents bought the place when the estate was built. When they died, she stayed here.'

'Tell me about her daily routines.'

Joan looked down at the fingers twisting in her lap as Oscar wriggled to get comfortable. 'She worked at a factory in Fordley till it shut last year. Took retirement.'

'Did she have any hobbies? Friends?'

'She was content with her own company. Suppose you'd call her a recluse. But she was happy. Spent most of her time gardening.' She stroked the cat's ears as he slept.

'She used to let Oscar out every night.' I repeated what Callum had told me. 'Then back in for a feed early in the morning?'

'That's how I knew something was wrong. Heard him crying to get in. She was always up early.' She looked at me, her eyes brimming with tears that threatened to spill if she blinked. 'Thought maybe she was ill.'

'Tell me more about her routine with Oscar,' I said, steering her mind away from that morning.

A theory was forming in my mind – fragile . . . hard to grasp, but something I'd learned to trust.

'She was a creature of habit. So is Oscar, aren't you, puss?' She tickled him under the chin. 'Goes out at half six on the dot, then he comes back an hour later for a final feed, then goes out for the night. Barbara used to lock up then, because she knew he wouldn't be back till the morning.'

'Which door did she let him out of?'

'What?' She frowned

'Front or back?'

I watched as her eyes moved up, looking over my right shoulder as she recalled the memory.

'Eye accessing cues' can indicate how a person accesses a memory. Right-handed people, which Joan was, would often look up and to the observer's right when they recalled events.

My stomach grumbled noisily and I considered the mince pies on the plate. Resisting temptation – it was only a couple of hours before I was due to meet Callum at the restaurant in town.

'Front door at half six. Then he'd come round the back and she'd let him in for his feed.' Joan's eyes came back to mine.

'Every night?'

She nodded – certain. 'We'd wave if I was at the kitchen window.'

'Did you wave to her last Wednesday night?'

Joan nodded. Her bottom lip trembled.

'About seven thirty?'

'Yes.' Hesitant, confused by my asking for such minor details. 'If only I'd known then, that it was to be the last time . . .'

'Did she keep the doors locked otherwise, during the day?'

'The front, but not the back, because she'd be in and out of the garden all day . . . we both were.'

We talked more about their friendship, about how much Joan would miss her friend, about grief and loss. Then the final pleasantries as she walked me to the door.

I gave her my card and told her she could call if she ever needed to talk. It wasn't something I did often, but, for some reason, the hollowness of loss in this fragile woman touched me deeply.

As we stood in the open doorway, Oscar slipped past my legs. I glanced at my watch.

Six thirty.

The police officer, standing as scene-guard by the gate at Barbara's house, glanced at us.

The bitter wind blew an empty crisp packet onto the path and Oscar pounced on it, batting it onto the frost-painted grass.

As I turned to go, Joan lightly caught my arm.

'You will find them, won't you? Whoever did this . . .'

I put my hand over hers. Her skin felt parchment-thin and ice-cold beneath mine. 'The police are doing everything possible.'

The usual platitude tripped off my tongue so easily.

I looked into her face, not knowing how to gracefully break away from her pain. Her eyes held mine with a sudden intensity that surprised me.

'Promise me . . .' It was a ragged whisper.

I couldn't avoid the visceral pain, the depth of her anguish – a tangible thing.

'I promise I'll do whatever I can.' It was the best I could say, and the most I dared promise.

Chapter Seven

Saturday, 7 p.m., Fordley

Bombay Spice, a curry house in the centre of Fordley, had once been the Providence Congregational Church, known by the locals simply as 'the Provvy'.

Proud to be the biggest curry house in the country, it felt more like an old town hall than a restaurant. The great hall was a cavernous hangar of a place. Echoing and brightly lit by huge, ornate chandeliers. Despite its origins as a place of worship, it felt soulless to me.

It wouldn't have been my choice, partly because of the charmless atmosphere but mainly because curry was probably my least favourite food. A shameful admission, from someone born in a town that was consistently crowned UK's 'Curry Capital'.

The fabric of my city was inextricably woven with the yarn of exotic spices, brought from India and Pakistan by those who had come to work in the northern textile mills.

Whatever its illustrious history, I didn't regard it as the best venue for a romantic evening à deux. Not that this felt the least bit romantic.

Callum arrived twenty minutes late. His whole demeanour that of a man who'd rather be somewhere else. With a cursory apology, he studied the menu, and then ordered his usual beef madras.

'It'll be a chicken korma for the spice baby,' he said to the waiter with more irritation than humour.

He seemed irritated by a lot of my choices lately.

I handed the menu back with a thin smile that said he was right. As the waiter left, I poured us both water from the jug.

'Not the most intimate venue,' I said.

'Nearest place to the station and I've got to get back.'

'Thought you were coming to mine tonight?'

He shook his head. 'No time.'

'You OK?'

'I've got a serial killer on my patch and DI Wardman, working Jones's murder, is one of the "new breed". Fast-tracked on the direct-entry scheme. His last job was manager in Tesco. Never served any time as a cop on the beat like the rest of us.'

'That won't necessarily make him difficult to work with.'

'No, most of them are pretty good. It's the fact that he's a complete prick that makes him difficult to work with.' He snapped the napkin open and laid it across his knee. 'Can't imagine why I wouldn't be OK.'

'Passive aggressive sarcasm.' I said it with humour, to take the edge off. 'Bit of a clue.'

When he looked at me, his blue eyes were uncharacteristically dark. 'For a behavioural analyst, I suppose it is.'

Bush-beating had never been my strong point. I let out a breath.

'OK, Sherlock . . . you obviously got out of the wrong side of bed this morning, but as it was *my* bed, that gives me the right to ask, what's wrong?'

He raked fingers through his hair – a habit he had when he was irritated – and began toying with his fork.

'I've got a lot on, that's all.'

I took a sip of water. 'Want to try that again?'

He stayed silent.

'Sometimes I think you forget what I do for a living,' I pushed.

He dropped the fork with a clatter. 'I know *exactly* what you do for a living, Jo . . . maybe that's the problem.'

Enough. This was why relationships were such bloody hard work.

I had no patience for game-playing.

'What's brought all this on?'

'*You!*' he snapped. 'You've "brought all this on", by not telling me everything, as usual. Letting me find out the hard way.'

'I haven't got a bloody clue what you're talking about.' I hissed, 'and will you keep the volume down? I'd rather not be the floor show in here tonight, if it's all the same to you?'

'When you told me Jacob Malecki had been a "pet project" of yours as a student, that wasn't quite all, was it?'

'Didn't seem relevant to say any more about it—'

'Really?' he cut across me. 'So, when I applied to the Home Office for an expert to advise us on Malecki's murders, imagine my surprise when *your* name came up.'

'I wasn't to know that you'd—'

'Feel like a complete dick – considering we're supposed to be . . .' He trailed off and looked down. Unable to say the words . . . *in a relationship.*

'I wasn't to know you were applying for an expert, for Christ's sake!' I snapped – my own anger bubbling up to meet his. 'For what it's worth, I've never even *met* Jacob Malecki. I'd only just qualified when they caught him, so I wasn't officially involved with the police investigation back then. Or didn't *they* tell you that either?'

'You might not have been involved *officially*, and it's not in the public domain, but apparently your "amateur" profile at the time helped catch him.'

'There are other "experts" you can use,' I deflected. 'Plenty of people have written books about him.'

'None of them psychologists.' He shot me a withering look. 'Surprised *you* haven't written one, as you know so much about him.'

I flashed him a look that *should* have been a warning, if he'd been in the mood to notice.

'No,' I said quietly. 'But there's a good reason why—'

'Christ, Jo. I think you *enjoy* keeping things from me . . .'

I knew we weren't talking about Jacob Malecki anymore.

Ever since the summer – when I'd stretched the boundaries of our relationship and used my involvement with the police to help a friend who was on the wrong side of the law – I'd dreaded the day he might find out what I'd done. How far I'd *really* gone.

I'd known that he suspected I hadn't told him everything. That I'd deliberately withheld information vital to his case at the time. But he couldn't prove it, so he'd given me the benefit of the doubt.

But it had irrevocably changed things between us in subtle and elusive ways. A shift in our dynamic. An imperceptible shadow hovering over the shoulder of our previous mutual trust.

'Like what?' I asked, not really wanting to know, but needing to hear him say it.

'You tell me?' He said it with the deceptively gentle tone of a dangerous inquisitor.

I resisted the urge to shift in my chair. Guarding my body language. Trying to avoid the razor-sharp edge of his instincts.

'It was just a project . . . a case study when I was Geoff Perrett's student. I told you that.'

'So how did it end up as part of the investigation into Malecki?'

I let my breath out in frustration. 'Forensic profiling wasn't even considered valid by police forces in the UK then. Most cops regarded it as something akin to voodoo, but less scientific.'

'Some still do,' he said tightly.

Two waiters appeared, carrying trays of food and began laying dishes on the table. We both nodded and smiled in polite truce.

As they left, I leaned forward, lowering my voice. 'We were students studying Criminal Psychology and there was a serial killer out there, hunting. The murders fascinated us *all* at the time—'

'But you more than most?'

By the time I'd enrolled at university, there had already been twelve murders, all around the country. Over the next four years, the count rose by another three.

The gap between killings was unusual. Serial killers only stopped if they were caught or died. What made him different? Or were other victims simply not being discovered?

These were things I debated with my friends, sitting on the floor of the communal lounge in our cramped student house – passing around bottles of cheap wine and analysing the psychopathology behind the crimes.

Where my friends' walls were plastered with posters of rock bands, mine was covered in crime scene photographs, cut from newspaper articles and a map of the UK, with coloured pins marking the sites of each murder.

Looking back, it was a mock-up of what I thought a real incident room might look like. In the days when I could only dream of studying serial offenders for a living.

Be careful what you wish for.

Callum, watching me silently across the table.

I didn't feel like eating now.

'How much do you know about Malecki's original victims?' I asked quietly.

He shrugged, spooning madras onto his plate. 'We've got their names, dates they were killed. Putting all our time into Barbara and Stephen's murders.' He glanced at me. 'That's why we applied for an expert. Until we get one, the historical stuff isn't a priority.'

'It should be,' I said, watching him eat. 'Because the degree to which the copycat replicates the original crimes gives you an insight into his mind, how he thinks – what he'll do next.'

'So, I'll ask you again.' His tone was the one he used when interviewing a suspect. I didn't like that he was using it with me, but given his mood, I decided to let it slide. For now. 'If police at the time didn't rate forensic profiling—'

'They didn't.'

'How did your "theoretical exercise" become part of the investigation?'

'His last known killing . . . in 1993,' I said, as if that explained it all.

'Katherine Hutchinson,' he said around a mouthful of food. 'A psychotherapist. Killed in Fordley. Is that why it was significant for you? Because she was in the same profession as you, or because it was your hometown?'

'Neither.'

'What then?'

'Because Kath Hutchinson was Geoff Perrett's wife.'

Callum paused with a piece of naan halfway to his mouth. '*Wife*?'

'She kept her maiden name after they married, because it was on all her accreditations. Her professional name.'

He chewed slowly as he thought about it. 'You didn't draw up your profile *because* of her murder though?'

'No. Geoff set the case study in my first year. She was killed while I was doing my Masters.'

'Do you think that's why Malecki chose her?'

I shook my head. 'There was no way he could have known about my research. It wasn't in the public domain. I was a nobody. We'd *all* worked on the case study. I just carried it on, like a hobby . . .'

'Some hobby.'

I thought back to those dark days after Kath's murder. The horror of it. That a mythical ghoul had reached into the very heart of our small, insulated world and ripped away the life of someone we knew. Simultaneously destroying a man I admired and respected. My mentor and someone who'd since become a lifelong friend.

Coming from a relatively sheltered world, it had been almost too huge for me to comprehend at the time. Traumatising in its viciousness. A brutal baptism into the hard reality of what had, until then, been purely academic.

Theory brought cruelly to life – bringing with it a sudden, shocking comprehension of what my chosen profession might actually look like.

'We were like a family, all the students loved Kath.' I pushed my food around with a fork. 'She was found with an old man's finger in her mouth. Malecki cut off her ear.'

'Is that when you took your profile to the police?'

I shook my head. 'Geoff did. He started banging on doors – trying to get them to take notice. But the investigating officers were suspicious of anything new. It was psychological "mumbo-jumbo" as far as they were concerned.'

'So, how did it get used?'

'Jack Halton. A young DC on the team. Felt sorry for Geoff and took the profile. I didn't think he'd use it.' I took a sip of water to help swallow the lump in my throat. 'My profile didn't catch him, Cal.'

'I know.' He wiped his mouth with the napkin. 'It was good old-fashioned coppering that brought him in.'

In a total fluke, Malecki had come to the attention of the police, six months after Kath's murder.

He'd been driving a rented car one night when a stolen vehicle, driven by local youths, high on drink and drugs, hit him in a head-on collision. Police were called to the scene and found a large quantity of cocaine in the youths' car.

The accident was a bad one. Malecki was unconscious and had to be cut from the wreckage and his car was taken to the police compound. In the boot, under the carpet, where the spare tyre should have been, Jack Halton found a rucksack. The contents identified Malecki as The Relay Killer.

I remembered DC Halton coming to the student house to see me after Malecki's arrest.

'They'll never formally acknowledge your contribution,' he'd said as he drank tea from a chipped mug in our communal kitchen. 'But I can tell you that without it, he might have got away with murder . . . literally. The top brass will never disclose your involvement.' He smiled. 'That would mean admitting that what you do isn't bollocks after all.'

'Thanks.' I'd laughed.

'I was impressed by your profile. It chimed with a lot of what I suspected about our man, and as you know, Malecki *had* come up previously. When I heard his name during the daily briefing, the morning after that car accident, I knew it was a good excuse to take another look at him. To make everyone take another look.' He'd shrugged, leaning back against the Formica-topped kitchen counter. 'I won't lie – it's not done my career any harm. That's why I wanted to come and see you. I didn't tell them I'd read your profile at first. Until I had to justify searching Malecki's car. But you were so spot on about the offender –they couldn't ignore the similarities.'

On the way out, he'd stopped in the dim hallway, his hand on the door handle.

'How did you know?' he asked quietly. 'All those things about him. What we'd find if we searched his car? How he got into Kath's room?'

'By studying the crimes . . . all of them – over and over.'

'We all did that,' he'd answered quietly. 'But didn't come close. What you came up with was uncanny . . . like you knew him.'

'I suppose I did . . . eventually.'

'How?'

There wasn't an easy answer.

'By getting inside his head . . . seeing through his eyes.' I'd struggled to explain it. 'Thinking like him,' I said finally.

The air seemed to still between us. As if he'd held his breath.

'Jesus,' he whispered.

He'd left me standing on the step, shivering, despite the warmth of the day as I watched him drive away.

Chapter Eight

Sunday Morning Briefing, Fordley Police Station

It was 7.am when I walked into the briefing room at Fordley Police Station, slipping in at the back. A few familiar faces turned my way and smiled tired greetings. Most were nursing early-morning coffees as they settled down.

Beth Hastings, a young DC on Callum's team, caught my eye and mouthed a silent 'hello'. We'd met when I'd first worked with the team and we'd become firm friends, despite her being only a few years older than my son.

Supt. Warner was about to address the team. Scanning the room, she acknowledged me with a nod.

I knew it had been her decision to use me as the subject-matter expert. Callum had said as much after rushing through dinner the previous night.

'Briefings at seven,' he'd said as he shrugged on his coat. 'Warner wants you there.'

'But you don't?'

His breath left him in a gust of frustration. 'I called you out on Thursday, didn't I?'

'Then why so irritated about my involvement now?'

'It's just . . .' He frowned. 'Learning about your connection to the earlier case, feels like an ambush somehow.'

'Sorry. That wasn't the intention. It was a difficult time for me too . . . back then. Losing Kath.'

He didn't even look at me as he fished his car keys out of a pocket, muttering, 'Whatever,' as he walked away.

'Thanks for joining us, Jo.' Supt. Warner's voice tugged me back.

'Most of you know Jo. She's agreed to help us with the historical facts on the original crimes, as it looks like this offender might be copying Malecki's murders from the eighties and nineties.'

'Blimey,' Beth piped up, 'I wasn't even born in the eighties.'

'I know. I've got fillings older than you.' It was Frank Heslopp, a gnarled DI.

'Didn't think you still had your own teeth, boss.' Ian Drummond, a DS from Callum's team.

'Yer not funny,' Frank grated.

A ripple of laughter went round the room.

Callum was sitting at the front. A man I didn't recognise was sitting to his left. I assumed it was DI Wardman, in charge of the investigation into Jones's murder. From the body language, there didn't seem to be much good chemistry between them.

Callum deliberately avoided looking in my direction. I felt irritated, but pushed it down – for now.

A whiteboard had been set up with photographs of Jacob Malecki's victims. All aligned in chronological order.

Each photograph was of the person in happier times. Pictures chosen by the families to give to the press. Images of graduations, parties, or family gatherings.

As the banter subsided, Warner went to the front of the room.

'Jo did extensive research into Malecki and his crimes.' She looked over at me and smiled. 'She's modest about it, but her profile, done when she was still a student, played a part in catching him. Jo will go through the Malecki murders and then DI Philip Wardman will bring us up to speed on the Stephen Jones case. Over to you, Jo.'

'Jacob Malecki.' I tapped his mug shot at the top of the board.

Below his picture, a grim pyramid of photos of his victims cascaded down in order of death.

'You'll be familiar with the name, although most of you were probably in school when he committed fifteen murders over a thirteen-year period. Beginning, we think in 1981, in Cambridge. Ending with his arrest, in 1994, in Fordley. His crime spree was the longest in British criminal history. He was sentenced to a whole-life order and is currently in Wakefield prison.'

'He's on a pretty big naughty step, then,' Beth muttered.

'Born in nineteen-sixty-two, in Kent,' I continued. 'Only child. His parents were wealthy and, contrary to everything you've probably heard about serial killers, he had a "normal" and privileged childhood. No issues at school. Played nice with the other kids. Joined the Sea Cadets. His father was a high-ranking naval officer and hoped his son would follow in his footsteps. But Malecki wasn't keen on taking orders. He went to study architecture at Cambridge. At the time of his arrest, he was designing homes for celebrities around the world. A Google search brings up a who's who of the rich and famous. He also received a lot of publicity for his art. A hobby on the side, painting portraits of the celebrities who commissioned him. Some of his work was put up for auction after his arrest and fetched a fortune.'

'Suppose there's always some sick bastard who'd want it on their wall,' DS Ian Drummond said.

'Malecki killed all of his victims by cutting their throats,' I went on. 'He always struck on a Wednesday night, and his MO was to cut off a body part from one victim and then leave it in the mouth of the next. Hence the name 'Relay Killer' . . . invented by some journalist on a London tabloid. Not very catchy, but it stuck.'

I turned to a sea of expectant faces, looking at the whiteboard and its depressing gallery of victims.

'Why did he kill on Wednesdays?' DS Drummond asked.

I thought back to those student days when we'd all pondered the same question.

'At the time, we considered lots of possibilities. Religious dates. Phases of the moon was a favourite, but it didn't fit.' I sat on the corner of the desk. 'I believed that Wednesday was just a significant day for the killer, given his hubris. I speculated it was an anniversary of some kind.'

'And was it?' Drummond asked.

'Yes. Malecki was born on a Wednesday. Although we didn't know that until after his arrest. Eighteenth of July 1962. He stuck to the day of his birth, not the date.'

'I just wanted a pony for *my* birthday,' someone muttered.

'You said, you "think" he began in 1981?' It was Tony Morgan, a DS on Callum's team.

I tapped the first picture.

'Michelle Hatfield. Nineteen years old. Worked in a bar in Cambridge. Left her flat, but never arrived for her shift. It was Wednesday, fifteenth of July. She was reported missing by friends and remained listed as a "misper" until Malecki confessed to her killing. Until then, she wasn't linked to the investigation.'

'He confessed?' DS Drummond asked.

'Only because of his *second* victim,' I tapped the next picture in the sequence. 'Graham Hirst. The owner of a deli in Grant-chester, was found with a finger in his mouth. In 1983, forensics weren't what they are today. DNA profiling wasn't widely available until the late eighties – so the owner of the finger was never identified. All they knew was it was a middle finger from the right hand of a female and that it had been kept frozen at some point. The fingerprint wasn't in the system, and no corpse ever turned up missing a digit. The connection to Michelle was never made. It remained a mystery.'

'Cambridge is a busy city centre,' Beth said, 'surely someone would have seen her that night, or clocked Malecki?'

'This was the Stone Age. No CCTV or ANPR. No passing motorists with dash-cam. None of the technology we rely on today.' I tapped Michelle's photo. 'She had a boyfriend at the time, Mark Lutner. He didn't have an alibi for the night she disappeared and, damningly, he didn't report her missing. They'd had a blazing argument a few days before and he thought that's why he hadn't heard from her. No mobile phones or social media then, so he was waiting for her to knock on his door – unfortunately she never did.'

'So, he would be a person of interest?' someone said.

'He was. The general consensus was that she was dead, but with no body, no sightings and no evidence, all they had was the boyfriend. Even though there was never enough to charge him, it didn't stop the press condemning him.'

'Trial by media,' Heslopp muttered.

I nodded. 'Until Malecki confessed, over a decade later, there were still plenty in the local community who believed Lutner killed her. The only lead came from Lutner himself. He recalled Michelle telling him about a guy who had chatted her up at the bar where she worked – six months before she disappeared.'

'Why so memorable, six months later?' Drummond asked.

'Because when she left the pub, it was one o'clock in the morning. The guy was waiting outside. He offered to walk her home, wouldn't take no for an answer. The conversation was getting heated when a cab came past. The taxi driver remembered, because he said he wouldn't normally do pickups in the street. But the girl was getting some hassle, so he made an exception. Apparently, she was full of it once she was safe in the back seat. Put the rear window down and flipped the guy the finger as they drove away.'

'Any ID from the taxi driver?'

'No. The bloke was down the side of the pub. It was dark and he didn't get a clear look at him. Six months later, Michelle vanished. Beyond confirming the story with the taxi driver, officers hit a brick wall. Just another line of enquiry that never went anywhere.'

Everyone in the room knew that 'no body' murders were notoriously difficult to prove, even with today's advanced forensics. Back then, almost impossible.

'Until Malecki confessed?' Heslopp asked.

'Yes. When Malecki was finally arrested, they asked him about the finger in Hirst's mouth and that's when he told them about Michelle. But he refused to give any more information. Including what he'd done with her body. Unlike all his subsequent victims, she's the only one that's never been found. To this day, he refuses to say what he did with her – despite repeated pleas from her family.'

'Nice guy,' someone muttered.

'From then on,' I continued, 'victims turned up at a rate of one a year, in cities around the UK.' I indicated a map, displaying the markers for each event. 'By then, police knew which murders were linked in the series, because of the calling card of a body part. Investigators had evidence from the various crime scenes. A boot print from one crime scene – size ten. A drop of blood at another, which was type A positive. But never any eyewitnesses.'

'If he did fifteen,' DC Shah Akhtar said, 'from 1981 until his arrest in 1994, that's thirteen . . . he must have done more than one in some years.'

'He did. But there were also periods where there were no killings at all. One killing a year, to December 1985. Then there was a gap of eighteen months, until he kills again in June of 1987.' I indicated the only photograph of a family group. 'This time, he made up for the lull, by killing four people in one night. The Ledlaws. Mum, dad and two children. Daughter aged four and son, eleven years old.'

I stared at their group photograph a moment longer. Their crime scene photographs had been so horrific they'd been kept out of the public domain for almost two decades, until they'd appeared in a TV documentary.

'At the time, the pathologist concluded that the amputations, in the case of the Ledlaws, had been done *before* death. Taking his time to torture the family throughout the night, before finally cutting their throats. He'd swapped body parts between family members. Killing Mr Ledlaw last, after he had watched his whole family being slaughtered. He took his tongue. The trophy he would leave with his next victim, four months later.'

'Bloody hell,' Heslopp said.

'The crime scene photos of all the killings are in your notes, if you've got the stomach for it at this time in the morning.'

There was a shuffling of papers as officers flicked to the photographs presented in court. Those images had stayed with me for over two decades. They were burned into my brain. I didn't need to see them again, but I could remember the impact they'd had on me – the same impact I was seeing on the faces of the people looking at them now.

'Jesus,' someone breathed, to accompanying groans of disgust around the room.

I cleared my throat and took a sip of water.

'The Ledlaw killings were the most violent up to that point. I put the brutality down to the fact that the killer had, for whatever reason, taken a period of abstinence.'

'Making up for lost time?' Beth asked.

I nodded. 'He was hungry. This was a feeding frenzy.'

'Why did he stop?' Beth asked.

'He's never explained. Always refused to cooperate with the police. But once they knew it was Malecki, they could fill in some of the blanks and make educated guesses.'

I walked over to the map, tracing the route of his kill sites with the end of my pencil.

'Cambridge for the first three murders, during the time Malecki was at university. Then he moved to Edinburgh for a twelve-month placement with a firm of architects and the next killing was in Leith. In December 1985, a victim was discovered in North Berwick, and, with hindsight, we know Malecki was still in Edinburgh at that time. Then Malecki went abroad for a series of jobs in New York and Europe. Returning to Newcastle, where the Ledlaws were killed in 1987.'

'The gap's when he was abroad?' Shah said.

'Yes. It was only four months before he killed again, in October 1987. A young man – a waiter in a local restaurant. The shortest time period between kills. I put this down to the typical escalation we often see with serial killers. The period they can sustain themselves between kills often gets shorter.' I tapped the next photograph on the board. 'But, he went against the predicted pattern and didn't strike again for thirteen months. Next victim appeared in Leeds in December of 1988.' I looked at the pretty dark-haired woman smiling happily at me from her picture. 'She was followed just a month later by this man.' I indicated a middle-aged car salesman, killed in January 1989 at his office in Manchester. 'Then came the longest period between kills in the whole of the series. Nothing for three years. Until Malecki struck again in December 1992. He was at the height of his professional success by then. Travelling

41

the world to oversee projects in America, Europe, as well as the UK. No other crimes of this type were ever reported in the places he'd been, although police forces didn't have the computer technology we have today. Nor did forces around the world talk to each other in the way they do now. So, there may have been killings we don't know about.'

'Maybe he was just too busy?' someone suggested.

'I've never been able to accept that he was doing *nothing* during that time. He was too addicted by then.'

That haunting thought had kept me awake at night. The nagging doubt that we'd never know the full extent of Jacob Malecki's crimes.

I pulled myself back to the task at hand.

'In 1992, he killed an elderly couple: Fred and Irene Gordon. Two kills in one night. Again, after a break, the levels of ferocity taken to new heights.'

'Hard to top what he did to the Ledlaws,' someone remarked.

'I'll let you decide.' I indicated their folders. 'Pictures are in there from the bundles presented in court. One juror fainted when she saw them, another threw up.'

'Christ . . .' Beth clasped a hand over her mouth. 'He took their eyes.'

'Finally, he cut off Fred Gordon's index finger. Worse, he did all of that while they were still alive.'

'Bloody hell.'

'Only one good thing came out of this attack,' I continued in the sudden stillness in the room. 'For the first time, Malecki made a mistake . . .'

I rode the silence in the room for just a heartbeat, before telling them.

'He left a surviving witness.'

Chapter Nine

Sunday Morning Briefing, Fordley Police Station

'No one could survive *that*?' Heslopp's voice was almost a whisper.

'The Gordons didn't.'

I pulled a photograph out of my notes and held it up.

'Sophie Adams. The seven-year-old daughter of neighbours. In December 1992, Sophie's mother went into premature labour with her second child. It was snowing a blizzard and a relative, who'd arranged to look after Sophie when the time came, couldn't get to their house. So, they'd asked the Gordons if they'd babysit. Her father dropped her off at the Gordons' house around teatime, then took his wife to hospital.'

'So, she was in the house when *this* happened?' DC Shah Akhtar tapped the photograph in his folder.

The cosy living room of the Gordons, transformed into a slaughterhouse. The elderly couple sitting facing each other, on the high-backed dining chairs they'd been tied to. The injuries transforming their faces into grotesque death masks, hardly recognisable as anything human.

'She'd been upstairs when Malecki broke in. Thankfully, he had no idea she was in the house.' I turned and stuck Sophie's photograph to the board, alongside those of the elderly couple. 'She was woken by the disturbance – stopping part-way down the stairs, watching through the half-open living room door.'

I closed my eyes, pinching the bridge of my nose to ward off the fatigue that suddenly washed over me. Not normal tiredness – more the weariness from staring for too long into the depths of human depravity. A bone-gnawing exhaustion that came from swimming against a seemingly never-ending tide of cruelty.

'She sat on the stairs and watched as Malecki tortured and then killed the Gordons. It was hours before they died.'

'And she never made a sound . . . or moved?' Supt. Warner said quietly. 'Impressive for a seven-year-old, under those circumstances.'

I looked at Sophie's picture. A school photo taken just before the summer holidays. A bright, smiling child with long blonde hair caught in pigtails and tied with ribbon.

'She couldn't move,' I said, more to myself than to the room. 'Literally petrified in the true sense of the word.'

The room of faces, set hard. Experienced officers – sickened, as they each ran the reel of images. Replaying what Sophie Adams must have witnessed that night.

'She was found by her father, rooted to the same spot, the next morning. He turned up, excited to tell them all about the birth of his son and walked into a nightmare.'

'Poor bastard,' someone muttered.

'Sophie was in a catatonic state, she didn't speak for a month. But when she finally did . . .' I pulled out an A4 sheet of a pencil-drawn image of a man's face. 'She was able to put this together with the help of a police artist.' I stuck it up next to Malecki's mugshot.

'Spot on,' Drummond observed.

It was the first image police ever had of the Relay Killer – who, until then, had never been seen by any witnesses. It was only when Malecki was finally caught that everyone realised how accurate little Sophie's description actually was.

'Sophie heard Malecki call himself "Jake". So, for the first time, police had a name, and a face, to go with his shoe size and blood group.'

Supt. Warner cleared her throat, drawing everyone's attention.

'That proved crucial at the time. Police put the photofit image out to every newspaper in the country. Campaigns were run, asking people if they knew anyone by that name who fitted the description, to call a dedicated hotline. Malecki's name came up a couple of times. He was questioned along with hundreds of other men who'd come to our attention from the media campaign, but nothing ever stuck.' She pursed her lips in the way she had when concentrating. 'Until events brought Jo's profile to the attention of the police.'

I briefly explained to the team about my unconventional 'hobby' and the profile.

'But it remained a purely academic exercise,' I said quietly, 'until Malecki's final killing in 1993 changed everything.'

* * *

'When Malecki was involved in the car accident,' Supt. Warner summed up, after I'd gone through the details of Kath Hutchinson's murder, 'things fell into place. DC Halton read Jo's profile and made the connections to little Sophie's photofit, and the fact that she'd heard the killer refer to himself as "Jake".'

I picked up the story.

'Jack Halton searched Malecki's car. He found a rucksack. In it was a knife, maps and notes on his intended target. Most damning – the body part, to leave with his next victim.'

I couldn't bring myself to say it – although it had haunted me for years. That body part had been Kath's ear.

45

'So, he was actually on his way to commit the next murder – the night of the accident?' Shah asked.

I nodded, perching again on the corner of the table. 'A middle-aged man – Dennis Haverley.'

'The one that got away.' Beth said, chewing the end of her pen. 'Imagine, finding out that he was on his way to do you, that night? Enough to make you sleep with one eye open for the rest of your life.'

'Haverley was in therapy for years afterwards,' I said. 'It was the *second* time Malecki had tried to kill him. He told police he'd aborted an attempt the previous month. If it hadn't been for that car accident, Haverley would have died that night, without a doubt.'

'Why didn't he go ahead with it the first time?' Heslopp asked.

'No one knows. He wouldn't say. Haverley wanted his name kept out of it. The whole thing unhinged the poor man. During the court case, he was referred to as "Victim X". Only the investigators, and Malecki, knew about him and what a lucky escape he'd had.'

'Bloody hell,' Shah said. 'He should buy a lottery ticket.'

'After Malecki's arrest, Sophie even picked him out at an identity parade. Astonishing for such a young girl. But that clinched it.'

I walked over to the gallery of Malecki's victims, speaking more to them than to the team.

'After analysing these crimes over so many years, I came to the conclusion that the reason for the gaps wasn't because he *couldn't* kill, but because he was studying his prey. Then taking an even longer period to stalk his victims. Mapping their routines and their lives so that he could choose the exact moment to strike.'

The silence was deafening.

I slowly turned, to see everyone staring at me. Transfixed, as if holding a collective breath.

'I predicted police would find plans or notebooks, and trophies. I'm still convinced he took items from each killing, in addition to the amputated body parts. But police could never prove it. In the rucksack, all they found were things he needed for the killing that night,' I said quietly. 'But I *know* they existed.'

'Could he have destroyed them, after each murder?' Beth asked.

'Maybe,' I murmured, almost to myself. But even as I uttered the words, I didn't believe that – not for a minute.

Chapter Ten

Sunday Morning, Fordley Police Station

The team filed out of the briefing room for a break. As usual, I headed for the kitchen and a much-needed brew.

Ian Drummond fell in step with me. We'd first met when I'd worked with Callum's team on a series of murders a few years before. He had an endearing manner that made him popular with the team, and an infectious humour that could lift the mood in the gloomiest team briefings.

'Bloody hell, Jo ... Kath Hutchinson. Someone you *knew* becoming a victim. Must have been devastating.'

'It was.'

He indicated my thigh with a nod of his head. 'You're limping – leg playing up?'

A few years earlier, while hunting down a killer, I'd been attacked and stabbed in the thigh. A wound that severed the femoral artery. If Callum hadn't applied a makeshift tourniquet, I might have lost my leg – if not my life. The wound had healed long ago, but it had left a bad scar, and a nagging ache, which was worse when I overworked the muscle.

'Good days and bad. Notice it more when it's cold though.'

'You'll be telling me next you can predict the rain.' He laughed.

'That's arthritis – not knife wounds.'

DS Tony Morgan joined us in the corridor. 'You thought any more about signing up for the five-a-side, Ian?'

'Nah. Not sporty, mate. Two left feet. I'd be a liability. You're better off getting someone else.'

Tony looked disappointed. 'We need the numbers. You look fit enough.' He held his flat stomach. 'I've got more of a barrel than a six-pack and I manage. Besides, it's a good laugh.'

'Jogging,' Ian said, 'that's all I do to keep fit. Never had any coordination for sports. I'll join you in the pub after though. I can manage that bit.'

Tony looked at me. 'Not exclusively a male team, Jo, if you fancy it?'

I rolled my eyes. 'You've got to be joking. Chairobics is my event these days.'

'You could always come with me, Jo?' Ian said. 'Think you could run the Fordley 5K?'

'With my leg, the only thing I can run is a bath.'

They were both laughing as they went into the gents.

Beth passed me on the way to the ladies. 'I'll catch you in the kitchen, Jo,' she said over her shoulder. 'Help yourself to one of my tea bags, know how particular you are.'

The 'kitchen' wasn't a room, more an alcove at the end of the corridor which widened out into the open-plan office.

I opened the cupboard over the sink and looked at the selection of mugs. People could be very territorial about their cups. I took one from the top shelf where the 'communal' ones, reserved for visitors, were kept. I found the box of Yorkshire tea bags with Beth's name written on the top and a warning to, *'Keep your sticky mitts off.'*

Reaching for the kettle, my hand found empty space. I scanned the worktop. Toaster, sugar caddy, discarded teaspoons . . .

'First team challenge of the day . . .' a deep voice rumbled behind me. I turned to see a good-looking man leaning against the wall, cup in hand. 'Hunt the kettle.'

'OK.' I smiled back. 'Give me a clue?'

He pushed away from the wall and walked to the sink with an easy grace. The broad chest and thick biceps beneath the crisp linen shirt hinted at regular gym workouts.

I hadn't even noticed the shiny new tap – presumably installed since my last visit.

He put his cup under the tap and depressed the metal collar at its base to get instant boiling water.

'*Et voilà!*' He grinned.

'Ingenious.' I sounded unenthusiastic. 'What's wrong with a good old-fashioned kettle?'

He moved aside as I took my turn.

'Suppose it's space saving.' I pulled a face and looked into startling green eyes that glinted with humour.

'More like time saving.' He sipped scalding black coffee. 'Some jobsworth calculated the length of time people spent standing around, waiting for the kettle to boil.' He indicated the offending article with a nod of his head. 'Reckoned the new gizmo saved on lost man hours.'

I looked longingly at the spot where the kettle used to be.

'But not lost intelligence.'

'What?'

'More information shared round here waiting for the kettle than in a dozen team meetings.'

'True.' He laughed, leaning back against the counter. 'You must be Jo McCready?'

I glanced at him over the rim of my mug, blowing the steam off.

'Didn't think I was so noteworthy.'

'Your reputation precedes you.'

'Really?'

He grinned. 'Even if I hadn't heard you were in this morning, I'd have recognised you from your picture.'

'Picture?'

'On the back of your books. I've read them all.'

'I'm impressed. They're not everyone's idea of bedside reading.'

'I've got eclectic taste.' Those piercing eyes found mine again. 'I'm Ed.' His handshake was firm and I caught the clean scent of an expensive cologne.

'I haven't seen you around here before.' I tried to sound disinterested.

'I'm not a cop.' He said it quickly – as if being one was a bad thing. 'External consultant – pulled in to work on projects, occasionally.'

'You and me both.'

We were interrupted as Beth came in and reached past him to get a mug out of the cupboard.

'Last time I got to sit down and take a proper break was in 2016 ... Sorry.' She suddenly realised we'd been mid-conversation. 'Was I interrupting?'

'No, just going.' Ed smiled. 'Have a good morning, ladies.'

We both watched his retreating back.

'Certainly makes an impression, doesn't he?' She grinned.

'Spill.'

'Eduardo Mazzarelli.' She grabbed a packet of digestives and offered me one. 'The girls in the office call him the "Italian Stallion", not to his face obviously.'

'Obviously.'

'Couldn't help but notice the chemistry when I came in.'

'Only in your imagination.'

She narrowed her eyes as she appraised him – then back to me. 'He's Italian too. Mamma would approve.'

'You're as bad as Jen.' I dunked my biscuit.

'You're beating them off with a stick today.' She grinned over the rim of her mug. 'What perfume are you wearing? . . . Must get some.'

'What?' I was genuinely nonplussed.

'Saw you chatting with Ian in the corridor.'

'So?'

'He still fancies you.'

'For God's sake, Beth, how old are you? Haven't heard that since the school playground.'

'He was going to ask you out in the summer,' she went on, undeterred. 'But bottled it.'

'Yeah, because I'm really that intimidating.'

'Well, you can be . . . sometimes. Only reason he didn't ask you out then was because he heard the rumours about you and the boss.'

'So?' I wasn't entirely sure I was happy with the way this conversation was going, but I let it run just out of curiosity.

'He respects the rank,' she said. 'A relic from his time in the army.'

'Ed was quick to let me know he wasn't a cop.' I changed the subject. 'What's the story?'

'Civilian techy.'

We took our cups and headed back to the briefing. 'Mind you, calling him a techy is like calling Harry Potter a kid who does card tricks.'

'That good?'

'Used to work for Google – owns his own consultancy now. Bit of a tech genius by all accounts. Him, or one of his staff, get called in when we don't have the skills in-house.'

'So, what's he working on?'

'Something for the Cybercrimes unit. Well above my pay grade.'

Further down the corridor, Callum and Supt. Warner were walking back into the briefing room, deep in conversation.

'Everything OK between you and the boss?' Her question took me by surprise.

'Why do you ask?'

She shrugged. 'He's been in a funny mood recently. Just wondered if there was trouble in paradise?'

'Hardly paradise,' I admitted – suddenly and unaccountably feeling the need to share a confidence with another woman who wasn't Jen.

She stopped in the corridor.

'Listen, Jo, I know you both play your cards close and you can tell me to mind my own business—' her teeth caught at her lower lip '—and I don't want to appear disloyal to the boss—'

'But?'

'It's just that, before you came along, he had form . . . you know?'

'No.' I could guess. But I wanted her to spell it out.

'Bit of a player.'

'You trying to tell me he's seeing someone else?'

'I'm not saying that.' This was a conversation she obviously wished she hadn't started. 'But he's got a reputation for enjoying the chase, then sabotages relationships before they get too serious.'

Whatever else she was about to say was cut short when Ian poked his head round the briefing room door.

'Chop-chop, you two – quick or as fast as you like.'

* * *

53

DI Philip Wardman was going through the details of Stephen Jones's murder. The last twenty minutes had been death by PowerPoint. He compounded the sin by reading each slide out loud in a monotone that would have sent a glass eye to sleep.

The circumstances surrounding Stephen Jones's murder had been much the same as Barbara Thorpe.

The crime scene photos showed him sitting on his sofa – head back, throat severed. His right thumb amputated by secateurs. Nothing had been taken and no locks had been forced. But, unlike Barbara's case – where the house had been secure – investigators found an open bathroom window where the killer had probably gained entry.

'Apparently, Jones had complained to the landlord about mould in the bathroom, and been told to keep it ventilated. He left the window on the peg, but it was never locked,' DI Wardman ground on in the same flat tone. It's a bungalow – so the intruder didn't have to climb to get in.'

The usual house-to-house enquiries had been done and the murder squad in Leeds were putting in all the hours, but in the last month, nothing significant had come up, despite hundreds of actions and lines of enquiry.

Thankfully, Warner summed it up before we all fell into a collective coma.

'Jo, if you could finish by telling us what we can expect from our offender?'

I gathered my notes and went to the front of the room. Wishing I had more to give them.

'I know you always approach an offence like this with three main questions: Why this victim? Why here and why now? In the case of a copycat offender, an added consideration is, why have they chosen *this* particular killer to emulate?'

I glanced at the board cataloguing Malecki's trail of destruction.

'Malecki always struck on Wednesday night – alternating between male and female victims. Always cut his victims' throats and amputated a small body part. You have all the same elements here.'

'Any idea as to the "why here?" question?' It was DS Tony Morgan.

I pointed to the map. 'Although Malecki struck all over the country, his last killings moved north. We know he came to Yorkshire. We can't be sure this offender lives here. He could be just picking up where Malecki left off.'

I directed them to the notes I'd put together.

'Malecki killed fifteen people. Our copycat has chosen to replicate this series, so it's doubtful the figure he has in mind will be less. It could be more. Copycats want fame. By picking a notorious case, they piggyback on the legend. Hit the public stage with a bang, cashing in on equal infamy – but, in some cases, they want to exceed what they see as the "achievements" of their idol.'

'Goal setting is good . . .' someone muttered.

'It's early days yet, so we only have a certain amount to draw on, for an initial profile—'

'*Two* not enough for you, Doctor?' DI Wardman cut across me. 'You want this serial killer to come out again, just so your pseudo-science has more material to work with?'

The room became suddenly very still.

Even Callum shot Wardman a look.

'Technically he's not a serial killer until he's done more than two,' I said sweetly. 'I'm surprised a detective of your experience wouldn't know that?'

Wardman opened his mouth, but Warner spoke first.

'Dr McCready is here at my invitation. I, for one, value what she has to say.'

'Copycats fall into the category of "organised" offenders,' I continued. 'Not least because they've studied in intimate detail the crimes they want to emulate.' I tapped a pencil against my teeth. 'They don't strike randomly or impulsively. The victim is usually carefully selected and they bring with them everything they need to commit the crime. They'll often make up a "crime kit" – tape, rope, gloves, mask. Even changes of clothes. Then take everything away afterwards, to minimise forensic evidence. In these recent cases, the murders took place in two different cities. Thirteen miles between Barbara Thorpe in Fordley and Stephen Jones in Leeds. Our offender has access to or owns a vehicle . . .'

'Why not public transport?' Wardman said, without looking up from his notes.

'The crime scenes are in residential estates. The local train stations are several miles away . . .'

'There are buses?' he said, with a thin smile that didn't reach his eyes. 'Even in Leeds.'

'I don't think this offender took the bus.'

'Why not?'

'More witnesses on public transport. All buses and trains have CCTV inside and out. Plus, public transport can be unreliable. Too many things can go wrong. This killer plans meticulously. If he hadn't—' I held his gaze '—you'd have made an arrest by now.'

He stared at me for a moment, before looking down and making a note. His face set.

Heslopp cleared his throat. 'Anything else, Doc?'

'There's a level of maturity in the planning and staging of these murders. So, you're not looking for a young offender. I'd say the age range would be between thirty-five and fifty. He isn't a raving lunatic. No erratic behaviour that will mark him out as different or "odd". To attack in the home of the victim shows a level of self-control and composure. This isn't someone who panics easily. I'd say they're above average intelligence and hold down a steady job. They may even be in a long-term relationship, with a partner or spouse having no idea about the separate life they're leading. The killer will have studied the area. Probably parked a few streets away from the actual scene.'

'We've got teams looking at CCTV and running ANPR checks around both locations.' Tony said.

'SOCO found evidence that someone recently climbed a tree at the bottom of Barbara Thorpe's garden,' someone chipped in. 'Could be that the killer watched the house from there. But there's no CCTV overlooking her yard.'

I ran a finger across Barbara and Stephen's photographs. 'These are blitz attacks, but I don't see anger or rage at these scenes.'

'What then?' Heslopp asked.

'Control,' I said simply. 'But something else . . .'

'What?'

I pursed my lips as I thought about it. 'I don't think this killer shares the same drives as Malecki. He was a sexual sadist – although he never physically had sex with his victims. He derived sexual gratification from the power and control the murders gave him. I get the feeling it's not the same here somehow—'

'A "feeling". Very scientific,' Wardman muttered – just loud enough.

I pretended not to have heard. Staring instead at Malecki's mugshot. Concentrating on his eyes. Deep, dark, like the black eyes of a shark. As if by going there, I could read the monstrous mind that lay behind them.

'Killers develop and improve their technique. In a series, you need to look at the earliest offences, as they're the least practised.' I shot Wardman a look. 'An early learning experience of sorts. Stephen Jones didn't have a body part left in *his* mouth so probably safe to assume *his* was our offender's first killing. So, that's the one where mistakes might have been made. It may be nearer to the killer's home or a workplace. As offenders become more experienced, they often move further afield. If the offences stay local that points to an individual "signature".'

'Victimology?' Beth asked.

'Malecki didn't have a "type",' I said. 'He was an equal opportunities killer. Men, women and children. Ages ranging from four to seventy-four. Mixed ethnicities too.'

I looked at Barbara's picture, but it was Joan Rigby's voice I could hear. Recounting the details of her friend's solitary life.

A familiar 'itch' was there at the back of my mind – something I couldn't quite scratch.

'What was Stephen Jones's back story?' I said to no one in particular.

'Lived alone,' Wardman read from his notes. 'Divorced in 2011. Couple of failed relationships after that. We've interviewed and eliminated the exes. Been single for the past four years. Grown-up kids, both living abroad. No other family.'

'Occupation?' I absently chewed the end of my pencil – still contemplating his photograph – a faint theory echoing in the far recesses of my brain.

'Self-employed design engineer. Clients are mainly small local businesses. He worked from home.'

'How long has he lived at this address?'

'Since 1991,' Wardman supplied.

I directed my remarks to the room, not to Wardman.

'He's choosing people who live alone, rather than busy households. That fits with the need for control and predictability. It's also a departure from Malecki's MO. He didn't feel threatened by numbers. Malecki was confident in his ability to subdue and control multiple victims. So, *this* is an individual signature of our copycat and one that I believe will be repeated in any future attacks. Both of our victims kept regular habits, had set routines. That's what this killer looks for in his targets.'

I wanted to add that we'd only be certain of that if there was another killing. But mindful of Wardman's criticism, I kept that thought to myself.

'Most serial killers escalate. Each attack increases their confidence, but just like drug addiction, their need for a fix becomes shorter as they can't sustain themselves between killings. Stephen and Barbara were killed a month apart. I don't think this offender will have long dormant periods, as Malecki did.'

'So, if you're right—' DI Wardman's tone implied he was far from convinced that I was '—We can expect the next victim to be male. Probably lives alone. That he'll be killed on a Wednesday night by having his throat cut and he'll have a body part amputated. But he could be anyone, any age, anywhere in the country? I have to say, Doctor, that really narrow things down for us.'

'I can narrow it down a little more, Detective.' I smiled. 'With a tiny detail that, for you, might be easy to miss.'

His eyes narrowed a fraction. 'What might that be?'

'He'll have Barbara Thorpe's big toe in his mouth.'

Chapter Eleven

Sunday Morning, Fordley

An icy blast bit into the warmth of my face as I left the police station and headed into town.

I pushed cold hands into coat pockets that weren't deep enough, exposing my wrists to the gnawing north wind. My watch said 11.20. Ten minutes to my brunch date.

Frost glistened on the dark, Yorkshire-stone slabs of the town square, ice crystals crunching under my boots. Warm breath hung suspended in white plumes, advancing ahead of me as I panted with the effort of picking up the pace. An unwelcome reminder, if I needed one, that I wasn't as fit as I'd like to be. As if triggered by the thought, a familiar dull ache began to spread through my left thigh.

As I crossed in front of the town hall, the chiming first notes of a Christmas carol rang out from the ornate Florentine clock tower.

For almost two hundred years, the grand clock had chimed every fifteen minutes and on the hour. A soundscape that had measured out the marching minutes of my life for as long as I could remember. A nostalgic sound I loved, and one that framed the working life of the city.

On the weekends running up to Christmas, the thirteen bells, two hundred feet above the streets, played carols.

The town hall's Italian facade looked down with imperious elegance at the ugly office blocks and pedestrian precincts that had sprung up around it. Still managing to preside regally over a landscape that had changed beyond all recognition since its construction.

McNamara's dominated one of those precincts. There had been a hostelry there since the Romans had created a ford across the River Aire, giving the city its name. Folklore had it that the highwayman Dick Turpin, while making his legendary escape from London to York, on his faithful mare, Black Bess, had stopped there on his way through Fordley. But as the two-hundred-mile journey was supposed to have been done in less than a day, I'd always doubted the veracity of it. Even if it was true, I was certain old Dick wouldn't have had time to stop for a pie and a pint.

For the last two generations, McNamara's had been an Irish pub. I'd lost count of the Sunday lunches we'd spent as a family at the polished wooden tables, listening to my father and his friends spinning tales about the old country. Fascinated as a child by the huge ornate mirrors reflecting the coloured bottles that lined the shelves.

After pushing open the glass-panelled door, I crossed the threshold from crisp cold to the cosy warm smell of food and the bubble of friendly chatter.

'Jo McCready! It's herself,' a voice boomed.

Finn McNamara, my father's old friend, strode over – smile and arms both open wide.

'Let me take yer coat, girl, or you'll not be feeling the benefit when ye go back out.'

My breath was squeezed out in a huge bear hug before he held me at arm's length, looking me up and down.

'Just like yer da,' he concluded, planting a kiss on my cheek before helping me with my coat.

'How you doing, Finn?' I returned his infectious grin.

'Grand, lass, just grand.' He ushered me towards the corner. 'Got your regular table – nice and cosy. Your friend's already here and it'll be your usual, I'm guessing? While you decide what to eat?'

I glanced past him as he led the way, to the elegant redhead sitting at a corner table.

He gallantly pulled my chair out, sliding it back in as I sat. And then he was gone. Weaving his way through the tables, liberally sprinkling entertaining comments over his customers as he went.

'What a welcome,' Elle observed. 'Like being in the company of a rock star.'

'Old family friend – my godfather actually.' I smiled across the table. 'You know how it is?'

'Not really. My parents' friends were crusty old doctors or geriatric lawyers, not half as much fun.'

Doctor Eleanor Richardson was a very young-looking forty. Standing six feet tall, even without her killer stiletto heels, and with supermodel looks. Most people would guess her to be a successful businesswoman, in some glamorous occupation.

They certainly wouldn't expect to find her dressed in scrubs and white wellies in the mortuary, dissecting the cadavers of those unfortunate enough to die of less than natural causes.

Assistant Home Office pathologist in Doctor Tom Llewellyn's department at the local teaching hospital, I'd met her over a decade before in Leeds, at a lecture she was giving at St James' Hospital.

The room – full of police, coroner's officers and criminologists – were held spellbound as she talked us through the finer details of forensic pathology for the non-medically minded.

Since then, our paths crossed often, as we were called to give evidence at various criminal proceedings. Occasionally at the same trial, and sometimes for opposing counsel. But that had never affected the friendship that had grown between us over those years.

'How did your briefing go?' She took a sip from a cappuccino, elegantly managing not to get chocolaty froth all over her top lip.

'Fine.' I distractedly glanced over the menu, although I already knew what I wanted – my stomach had been thinking about it all morning.

'You get to meet our delightful DI Wardman?'

'Hmm. That guy can light up a room, just by leaving it. Made his contempt for my "pseudo-science" quite obvious.'

'Don't take it personally. When I did Stephen Jones's post-mortem, he was a patronising git with me too. Sucked the life right out of the room.'

'Now there's a trick . . . in a morgue.'

'Thinks he has to prove himself. Insecure or something.' She paused as Finn came to the table with a tray of tea. 'There's probably a psychological term for it.'

'There is,' I said, stirring the pot. 'Small prick syndrome.'

'Just love to overhear you professionals at work.' Finn chuckled. 'Decided on food, ladies?'

'Full English, for me.' Elle smiled up at him. 'With extra baked beans, please.'

He looked at me. 'Let me guess . . . colcannon for you, Jo?'

'What else? With your amazing Irish rashers.'

He nodded and left us to it.

'How do you stay so skinny?' I looked at my friend in total amazement. 'You must have the metabolism of a racehorse.'

'I only eat when I see you. The rest of the time, I live on fags and coffee.'

'Carcinogens and caffeine – diet of champions.' I poured my tea. 'You handling the Barbara Thorpe post-mortem?'

'Yes – might as well have the matching pair.' She took a sip of coffee. 'Some of them get to you more than others though.' The cup went back on its saucer with a 'clack'.

'Did Barbara? Get to you?'

'She reminded me of my favourite aunt. Poor woman. Can you imagine? One minute you're watching *Countdown*, the next you're getting your throat cut.'

'What can you tell me?'

'Thought the Boy Scout would have given you everything?'

'Why do you call Callum that?' I heard the defensive note in my voice, but couldn't quite justify it – not lately.

'Because he *is*.' She laughed lightly. 'Such a bloody rule follower, he probably *thinks* in triplicate. You're a maverick. I'm amazed you two get on at all.'

I looked down as I stirred my tea. 'Hmm . . . well, he's being off with me at the moment.'

'Huh, that's men. Reminds me why I don't bother with them.'

'How *is* Rina?'

Elle's partner had been a mentee of mine when she'd graduated. Much younger and, with her Doc Martens and leather biker jacket style, as different from her girlfriend as chalk was from cheese. But it seemed to work for them.

'Fine. Landed that job as a counsellor for the Drug and Alcohol Unit.'

'That's good. So . . .' I nudged her back on topic. 'I haven't seen the preliminary post-mortem report. Callum's not in a sharing mood.'

'Not all the test results are back yet – should get those tomorrow though.'

'And I'm certainly not going to get anything on the Leeds murder from Wardman.'

'He's not cooperating either?'

'Made that perfectly clear at the end of the briefing. Took me to one side and said he didn't want my involvement in the Stephen Jones case. Called it pseudo-science again – just in case I hadn't heard him the first time.'

64

'Tosser.'

'Told him, psychology was still a science, whatever he thought – it would still apply to him. Like gravity.'

She frowned. 'Gravity?'

'Even if he didn't believe in it, if he jumped off a building, he'd hit the ground just the same.'

'You didn't offer to demonstrate?'

'Tempting.'

'So, what's wrong with the Boy Scout?'

'Not sure he wants me involved.'

'But he called you in, didn't he?'

'He wants the historical stuff and a profile on this copycat, but not sure they'll be using me for much more.' I tried to sound matter-of-fact as I added, 'I met Barbara's best friend. The neighbour who found her. Promised her I'd do what I could. Poor woman's heartbroken.' I glanced across at Elle. 'Appreciate anything you can give me?'

'You planning on going off-piste with this one?' It could have sounded disapproving, but her smile took the sting out of it.

'I'm planning to walk the scene – in my own time.'

'Pretty straightforward, really. Throats cut in both cases.'

She stopped as the food arrived. We both waited until the waitress was out of earshot.

'Wounds made from beneath the left ear to the right in a single, slightly upward incision.' She lowered her voice so we wouldn't alarm the locals. 'Inflicted with some force in the case of Stephen Jones. The wound went down to the vertebrae, almost decapitating him.'

'What about Barbara?'

I blocked the images before they could form, as I sliced into a thick rasher of bacon.

'The wound wasn't as deep in her case. Inflicted with less pressure.' She emptied the extra pot of beans onto her crowded plate. 'Amputation of the body parts in both cases was done post-mortem and I'd say the killer used secateurs. A knife was used to cut their throats. Police haven't recovered it.'

'Any ideas on that?'

'Single, long-bladed weapon. But there is an odd shape to the tip of the knife. Not something I've seen before. It's unusual, but it'll make it easy to identify as the murder weapon, once the police have it. I'd also say your killer is right-handed and that the victims were attacked from behind, while they were sitting.'

That caught my interest.

'From behind? Are you sure?'

'Positive.'

'But a cut from left to right could indicate an attack from the front by a right-handed killer, couldn't it?'

She dug into a thick sausage. 'Depending on how the knife was held.' She held her knife in her right hand – palm up, the blade protruding between her thumb and forefinger. 'If it's held *this* way and from the front, then the wound would go left to right, in a vertical incision. But wouldn't travel as high up around the right ear, as these did.'

She changed her grip on the knife. Holding it in her right fist, palm down – knuckles on top.

'Attack from the front *this* way.' She reached across the table – the blade sweeping the air under my chin. 'And *that* would inflict a wound from right to left ... but the depth across the incision would be deeper on the victim's right. More like a stabbing than a slicing action.' She went back to attacking her sausage.

'Thanks, Elle. That's really useful.'

Her eyes were serious when she regarded me across the table. 'They've made the connection to Malecki then?'

'Difficult not to.'

'Must be tough on you.' She put down her knife and reached across, gently touching my wrist. 'Memories of Kath?'

I nodded, suddenly concentrating intently on my plate.

'It must have been a shit time for you?'

'It was. But it taught me a lot.' I stared past her, seeing images I'd not revisited for decades. Like opening the pages of a dusty photo album and getting drawn into the pages all over again – despite the pain they caused.

I'd learned so much.

Not just about death and its aftermath. But about myself.

'That was the first time I ever "walked a scene". In Kath's therapy room – where Malecki had killed her.'

The images spooled out over Elle's shoulder – playing against the ornate mirrors behind the bar. Taking me back in time.

It had been Geoff's idea. A few days after Forensics had released the crime scene, he'd suggested we go there.

'What for?' I'd asked in disbelief. 'Surely you don't want to see . . . I mean it'll still be . . . has it been . . . ?' I didn't know how to say it.

'Cleaned?' he supplied helpfully. 'No, not yet.'

His agony was visceral. It was the first time I'd seen that look, in the eyes of a relative of a murder victim. A mixture of pain, grief and horror as they imagined what their loved one had gone through in their final moments. A reflection of torment and unimaginable loss.

I'd seen it hundreds of times since then and never become used to it. If I ever did, I'd know it was time to quit the job.

'Shouldn't we wait until it has been?'

He shook his head. 'That's the whole point.' He'd held the keys to his wife's office, turning them over in fingers that trembled slightly. 'I want you to see it as it was that night. Want it untouched . . .'

'Why?' I whispered.

He looked at me then – the mist of grief momentarily lifting to reveal the bitterness and rage that flowed underneath.

'I want you to walk in that bastard's footsteps. See what he saw, hear what he heard – everything . . . exactly the same. The physical evidence might show us the sequence of events. You've studied him, Jo. Now you get the chance to get closer to what he did – what he does.'

'*Why?*' I tried to reason with his anguish. 'What purpose will *that* serve?'

'To get inside his head, find out what drives the bastard!' I looked at his fist – the knuckles turned white as he gripped the keys. 'If we work *that* out, it gives us another piece. Another insight. Something that might help catch him.'

I reached out and put a hand over his, stilling his fingers. 'All right, I'll come with you.'

'Tomorrow afternoon?'

I thought about it for just a second. 'No. If we're going to recreate it exactly, then we need the same day, and time. We go tonight. Wednesday.'

I felt his fist relax under my hand and gently prised it open to take the keys.

We both stared as the blood slowly welled up from the gouges in his palm and began to seep between his fingers.

* * *

Finn held our coats, clucking like a mother hen as we bundled up for the weather outside.

'Don't be leaving it so long before ye come again, ladies,' he said cheerily, pulling the door open for us.

We stood together on the pavement as Elle rummaged in her bag for her cigarettes. 'You'll have to come up to the stables sometime. It's ages since we went out for a hack.'

Elle's beautiful stallions, Butch and Sundance, were her passion and a way of decompressing after a stressful day. Horse-riding was a passion we shared but never seemed to have enough time to enjoy together these days.

'How's Rina doing with riding lessons?'

'Considering she can control that beast of a motorbike, she's surprisingly uncomfortable astride a horse. Says she doesn't trust anything that doesn't have brakes.'

As we said our goodbyes, a black BMW I recognised pulled up across the precinct.

I paused mid-sentence as the car swung abruptly into the kerb. A young blonde woman was waiting, hugging herself against the cold. She drew the scarf away from her face and smiled broadly as she pulled open the passenger door.

Elle followed my gaze. 'Someone you know?'

'Callum's car,' I said distractedly.

'And her?'

I shook my head. 'No one I recognise.'

Through the rear window, the silhouette of their heads came together. Were they kissing? I couldn't be sure.

Elle cupped leather-gloved hands around her lighter as she lit a cigarette, tipping her head back to blow a column of smoke straight upward. We both watched Callum's car pull out into traffic.

'Maybe not such a Boy Scout after all,' she murmured, squinting at me through a haze of blue-grey smoke.

Chapter Twelve

Monday Morning, Kingsberry Farm

I flipped the lid on the Aga and put the heavy-bottomed kettle onto the hotplate. Making tea was the first and most important job in my house and a ritual that, for me, soothed frayed nerves after a hectic day, or, in this case, a sleepless night.

Harvey was thundering around the yard after the scent of rabbits who had the audacity to invade his territory. I listened to the sound of his heavy paws skittering across the gravel drive, before he crashed through the hedge into the meadow.

I'd left the door open for him and the bitter cold was whipping through the kitchen. Hugging myself, I leaned back against the welcoming warmth of the stove and thought about the previous day.

After seeing Callum with the mystery blonde, I'd briefly considered calling Beth to ask what she'd been about to tell me in the corridor. But I'd discounted the idea. It wasn't fair to put her on the spot. And besides, there was no way to do it without sounding like some lovesick teenager checking up on a boyfriend.

Boyfriend. Even the term made me shudder. That was for sixteen-year-olds, not a widow with a son in his mid-twenties.

What did I even expect from Callum?

What did we have?

Elle called it a 'situationship'.

An image of the young blonde flashed across my mind, with the accompanying analysis of every expression and gesture that was the curse of my job.

Her broad smile. The way her whole persona became more animated the moment she saw Callum's car. Her body language screaming the very conclusion my instincts didn't want acknowledge, yet one that seemed inevitable.

If Callum *was* seeing someone else, that would account for the way he'd been behaving.

No matter how hard I tried to recapture the warmth we'd once shared, it felt as though he was giving me nothing back. I was having to fight for breadcrumbs.

Harvey barrelled through the porch, skittering to a stop by my legs – panting and looking pleased with himself. I fussed his silky ears and pushed the door shut with my foot.

As usual, when my mind was too full, work was my distraction.

Carrying the tray of tea, I kicked a ball for Harvey down the glass corridor that connected the main house to a barn conversion that was now my office. After the kitchen, probably the place I spent most time.

The room smelled of wood polish and leather-bound books. It wrapped me in a warm hug the minute I walked through the door. I put the tray down on the wide mahogany desk and dumped the files next to my computer.

I looked out of the huge picture window, which afforded spectacular views across open fields and hedgerows that ran to the forest on the edge of my land. It often provided a welcome distraction from work. But today, I didn't want a distraction. I wanted to lose myself.

Harvey settled himself on the Chinese rug in front of my desk, resting his chin on huge paws and for a while the warm silence was only broken by the sounds of his gentle snoring and the mellow tick of my antique grandfather clock.

The crime scene photos from Stephen Jones and Barbara Thorpe were still spread out from the night before.

I looked again at the devastation created by someone who wanted to replicate the crimes of a monster. To emulate the brutality and destruction Jacob Malecki had begun, decades before. And it was my task to unravel why that might be. What had brought someone to savagely take the lives of two innocent people?

In the absence of 'walking the scene' physically, I put my mind into the pictures. Looking through the eyes of a killer. Mind-mapping what had been done – the sequence in which he'd done it. Hoping it would lead me to a 'why'.

I pulled up the report I'd written and read through part of it again.

The offender is probably employed in a role requiring a high degree of precision and attention to detail. Maybe holds a senior position or self-employed, with a high level of autonomy – not closely supervised in work. Maybe local?

Has studied the victims in detail prior to the attacks. Knows their habits and routines – so will have been in the vicinity for several weeks or months prior to committing the offences.

Can gain access to the victims' homes undetected. Physically fit. Has access to or owns a vehicle, which also doesn't stand out or arouse suspicion. Maybe a tradesman's van or vehicle that wouldn't be suspicious parking near to the crime scenes?

The prolonged attacks – over several hours, typical of Malecki's crimes – are not evident here.

In both cases, these victims were killed in a 'blitz' attack, from behind and died instantly. This is a departure from the historic series and is, in itself, a personal 'signature' of this offender, rather than an element of copycatting.

* * *

Most people assume the kind of trophies a serial offender takes are sexual in nature – like an item of underwear. I knew from experience that it was often mundane things which became mementos. Shoes, jewellery, a trinket or ornament from the crime scene.

A physical anchor to the event – cementing that moment in time. Allowing them to recreate the excitement and exhilaration every time they held it. Replaying the scene in all its vivid detail. Often, touching and looking at their trophies would sustain them – until the urge built to unbearable heights, forcing them to act out their fantasies all over again. At huge cost to the next unfortunate victim.

In the case of Kath Hutchinson, it had been several weeks after her death that Geoff Perrett had talked to me about something going missing from her office.

'It's just a paperweight,' he'd said, as we sat in his cottage. 'I didn't even realise it was missing until yesterday.'

He'd poured the tea from a China teapot that I knew he only used when I was visiting.

'A student made it for her as a "thank you" for some free therapy. It was a resin dome with snowdrops inside, her favourite flowers. I was going to keep it on my desk.' He shook his head, looking gaunt and more exhausted than I'd ever seen him. 'When I went to the therapy practice, I couldn't find it.'

'You're sure Kath didn't move it?'

'She always kept it on the table beside her chair.' When he looked up at me, his eyes were haunted. 'In your profile, you said he might be talking trophies.'

'We don't know that for sure, Geoff.'

'Yes, we do . . . *you* do.' He looked down again – not wanting me to see his tears. 'Taking her . . . cutting off her . . . wasn't enough for him, was it? Because he's going to leave that with the next victim. So, he needs something else, to remind him.'

In that moment I didn't want to tell him he was right. The husband of a murder victim shouldn't ever know that the killer would be using that object as a memento for his sick fantasies. That he would hold and caress it as he reran the images of Kath's suffering and death over and over again.

But as we sat in his cottage, in the peaceful village of Haworth, high up on the Yorkshire moors, a million miles away from the horror of it all – we both knew that was the case.

I'd felt it when I'd first walked in the footsteps of a killer. Seeing things through his eyes. Hearing the sounds he heard, breathing the same air. Feeling what he might have felt – until eventually, on that Wednesday night over two decades before, I'd touched the mind of a monster.

Chapter Thirteen

Wednesday Night, 1993, Fordley

Geoff fumbled with the keys to Kath's office. I resisted the urge to take them from his bandaged hand – I knew he wouldn't thank me for the help.

'Can't see the bloody keyhole,' he grumbled, then he pulled out his keys and used the pen torch attached to the key ring.

I studied the street in this quiet part of Fordley. The shops had closed hours before and only a few pedestrians were about. There were no coffee shops or restaurants here, so after office hours it was deserted.

The buildings opposite were in deep shadow – the street light there long since broken.

It would have been like this the night Kath died. A trickle of people scurrying past this indistinct doorway. Oblivious to what was unfolding a few feet away.

Rain slicked the tarmac, the puddles from an earlier shower reflecting the orange glow of the street lamp by the door. A car swished past, its headlights sweeping over the front of the building.

Geoff pushed open the heavy wooden door. The hinges creaking in protest as he went further in and fumbled for the light switch.

No modern office block, this. Just a single flight of stairs leading to a flat, which Kath had taken as her private therapy rooms. The anonymous brown door, sandwiched between a print shop on one side and a dry-cleaner's on the other, offering a discreet entrance to clients wanting to preserve their privacy.

He indicated the intercom.

'Callers have to announce themselves. Kath would release the lock from upstairs.' He leaned against the door, chewing his bottom lip. 'How the hell did he get in? She didn't take "walk-ins". Would never have buzzed in a stranger.'

'Maybe he posed as a delivery man?' I offered.

He shook his head. 'She always got them to leave parcels with the shop next door.'

'Could he have booked an appointment?'

'Kath kept meticulous client records,' he said quietly. 'Police have spoken to the last client that night. She checks out. There was no one else booked into the diary. She keeps all her client records locked in a filing cabinet upstairs. There's no record of anyone new that night – or any night. All regular clients have been eliminated by the police.' He glanced up the short flight of stairs . . . 'So how?'

'What time did she . . . ?' *Die* was what I was going to ask.

He guessed my question.

'Wednesday was her late night. Her last client left at eight.' Glancing at his watch. 'It's just after eight now. They estimate . . . somewhere between ten and midnight.'

Kath hadn't been expecting anyone else. She would have written up her notes, then tidied the office and left for home. Except she never got the chance to do any of those things.

We stood in the cramped space at the bottom of the stairs. Kath's pushbike took up most of the room. Leaning against the wall where she'd left it.

Geoff shifted uneasily. 'How do you want to do this?'

How did I want to do this?

I stared at him for a second, biting back the urge to remind him that this had been *his* idea. Now he was looking at me, as if I had all the answers. Like this was something we'd done a hundred times before.

Until this moment, crimes in general, and murder in particular, had been an academic exercise. Something we analysed in a metaphoric glass jar – in the vacuum of scholastic theory.

Now, I was about to walk into a room where someone I'd known had been murdered.

I'd never felt more out of my depth in my life.

An illogical burden of responsibility threatened to overwhelm me – as if Kath was somehow depending on me not to let her down. And yet I didn't even know what I didn't know. 'Unconscious incompetence'.

I wanted to say this was a bad idea. Tell Geoff we should forget the whole thing. But he was watching me with such an expression of faith – this man I looked up to and admired. I didn't want his belief in me to feel misplaced.

I took in our surroundings.

The stairs to the flat were directly in front of us. To our left, underneath them, was a small alcove, covered by a curtain.

'What's in there?' I asked quietly.

I felt, rather than saw, him shrug. 'Cleaning stuff, I think.'

I pulled back the curtain. It was pitch-black.

'Can I borrow your torch?'

He handed me the key ring. I had to duck my head to look inside the dark, triangular cubbyhole. A sweeping brush and mop in the corner. A metal mop bucket stood upended against the back wall.

I straightened up. 'OK then.' I nodded towards the stairs. 'You go first.'

As he began to go up, I suddenly remembered that the room hadn't been cleaned.

'Don't go in.' My voice sounded too loud – it felt irreverent. 'Just unlock the door – we'll go in together,' I added, more quietly.

He nodded.

I stood at the bottom, watching him go. He looked suddenly much older. Hunched, as if he'd been permanently bent double, by an emotional gut-punch.

I glanced again at the door to the street.

How did you get in?

I imagined the killer watching the office. I knew he watched and waited for weeks – months. Had he broken the street lights opposite, so he could stand, hidden in the shadows? Probably.

He'd know about the intercom. He would have seen clients coming and going. Would know that the old door creaked, announcing to anyone upstairs that someone was in the hallway.

You tailgated a client who was leaving, didn't you?

Earlier, during the afternoon, so you wouldn't be remembered so close to the time of the murder.

Watching a client arrive. Waiting for their allotted sixty-minute session to end, so you would know when they were due out. Easy enough to have your hand on the buzzer as they came through the door into the street . . .

'Oh, sorry . . . was just about to buzz.' An embarrassed laugh. A polite smile as they held the door open for someone they thought was the next client. And you were in.

Closing my eyes, I tried to focus all my senses.

I listened to the tread of Geoff's shoes on the stairs. One of the old boards creaked loudly under his weight.

A stillness settled over me as I controlled my breathing. Finally, there was no more movement. I opened my eyes to see Geoff standing at the top.

I joined him on the landing and silently indicated the door with a nod of my head. Holding my breath, as he opened the door.

78

I didn't know what I expected to see.

The door opened directly into Kath's treatment room. A large sash window overlooked the street.

A high-backed leather chair was to the left of the window. A deep-upholstered armchair to the right, with a coffee table between them.

It was only when Geoff flicked on the light that the scene took on a different texture altogether.

It was then I noticed marks on the carpet. Dark splashes that looked like ink blots, but I knew were nothing so innocent.

The solid surfaces were covered in silver-grey smudges that I guessed were from the aluminium fingerprint powder that had been dusted everywhere by the forensic team.

Geoff gestured for me to go in first. It took a conscious effort to make my legs move, until I stood in the centre of the room – looking around, as if I expected someone to jump out from behind the heavy velvet curtains.

'Take your time.' Geoff's voice was so quiet, I had to strain to hear him.

He looked calmer than he had any right to be. Watching me, as he leaned against the door jamb.

'You've profiled him, Jo. Think about what you already know – about how he's operated before. Tell me what happened.'

I stepped backwards until I could feel Geoff's breath, warm against the back of my neck.

I tuned him out, pretended he wasn't there.

To my left, a door to a narrow kitchen stood open. I walked towards it, stopping to look down at a dark stain on the carpet. Bending down, I touched it. It was sticky. My fingers smelled faintly of coffee. I walked into the kitchen, my feet registering the transition from carpet to linoleum.

A kettle and kitchen jars stood on the worktop beside an old metal sink. A small fridge hummed in the corner.

I walked back into the lounge, my attention focused on the two chairs. The high-backed chair directly in front of me. To the left, between it and the window, was a small occasional table. It had a glass coaster on it. I imagined Kath sitting there. Her coffee cup and perhaps her notes on the table. I moved around it, looking at the armchair opposite. The client's chair.

Stains covered the seat of Kath's chair, turning the leather a darker shade of brown, spilling down the carved wooden legs onto the carpet. I didn't want to see, but I couldn't tear my eyes away. It was a physical reminder of the life that had leaked out of her body.

My fingers brushed the leather arms of her chair, feeling a slight resistance under my skin – a tackiness. I looked at my hands as if they belonged to someone else. There were dark smudges, like faint bruises, from the fingerprint powder.

You taped her wrists to the arms of the chair, didn't you? Gagged her so no one could hear her screams. You took your time with her.

The chair opposite seemed to gloat. A silent witness to what had happened.

In the street below, a few cars went by. The sounds of the city were a distant hum; close enough to hear but too far away to offer any hope.

He'd stood here. The man who called himself 'Jake'. His size ten shoes on this very carpet. Type 'A' blood racing through his veins, injecting a massive shot of adrenaline and cortisol into his body as he'd revelled in the excitement and exhilaration of having a victim – here in this chair where my hand now rested.

Kath would have been able to see out of the window, as people walked below; she would have heard passing cars – knowing

80

no one could hear her, no one could help her. The sounds of a city going about its business while she sat, alone and terrified. Trapped in this room with a monster.

Like everyone else who read a newspaper or watched the news – Kath knew about the Relay Killer. She would have spoken to Geoff about him. Would have known exactly what he was going to do to her.

I swallowed hard, but the realisation of the unimaginable fear and terror she must have felt robbed me of saliva to shift the lump in my throat.

'What was Kath's routine?' I forced the words out. 'In between clients?'

Geoff cleared his throat. 'Uhm ... she always left a thirty-minute gap between sessions. Nip to the loo, make a brew. Then she would write up her notes. She'd seen her last client that night. So, she would have done the same before leaving.' He washed a hand across his face, pinching the bridge of his nose, his eyes still closed. 'I still don't see how he ... even if he'd made it to this door, she wouldn't let a stranger in.'

I turned and walked past Geoff.

'Where are you going?'

'Back downstairs. You be Kath. Close the door and go stand by the window,' I said over my shoulder. 'Then count to ten. Walk into the kitchen and stand by the sink. Run the tap for another count of sixty. Pick up a cup and take it back to Kath's chair. Just as she would have done.'

I reached the bottom and looked back up. He was standing by the door, staring at me.

'OK.' He looked totally bemused.

I was already rounding the bottom of the stairs when I heard him gently close the door.

Look for inconsistencies, Geoff's voice in the lecture hall echoed in my head. *That is where the answers are found.*

I went to the alcove beneath the stairs, using Geoff's pen torch to look again at the mop bucket.

You used the upturned bucket to sit on, didn't you? Hidden behind the curtain. Probably for most of the afternoon, listening to clients come and go – until the last one left.

A few feet above the bucket, there was a small round grease mark on the wall. I reached out instinctively, but pulled my hand back before I touched it. My fingers were trembling.

You sat here – for weeks or months. Enough to leave a mark on the wall, where you leaned your head back.

My heart leaped at the sudden sound of water running through the pipes from above.

I stepped out and took the stairs, the soles of my trainers – soundless.

My breathing was faster as my heart rate began to soar just as the killer's had done. I paused when I reached the stair that creaked. Avoiding it, treading instead on the one above. A thin smile pulled at the corners of my mouth, taking me by surprise. No time to examine that unexpected reaction now – note it for later.

Standing outside the door, I listened, holding my breath before gently turning the handle. The hinges moved soundlessly as the door swung open.

The room ahead was empty.

A glance to the left.

Geoff had his back towards me as he stood at the sink.

A bolt of electricity lifted the hairs along my arms with the adrenaline rush. The muscles in my thighs tensed with an almost unbearable ache that spread all the way into my groin, as I took a step, then another, across to the open kitchen door.

Every sense in my body vibrated as I caught the shimmering glimpse of the terrifying psyche that had conjured up a plan to destroy another human being.

I could feel his presence, hear his excited breathing, feel the anticipation crackling through my veins as it had for him, until my skin tingled with the static of his heightened responses.

I pressed myself flat against the wall just as Geoff's shoulder appeared in the doorway, then I stepped out directly in front of him. My face an inch away from his.

'Jesus!' He jumped back, dropping the empty cup he'd been carrying. It rolled harmlessly between our feet and we both looked down at the coffee stain on the carpet – where Kath had done exactly the same thing.

'That's how,' I whispered.

Chapter Fourteen

Monday Afternoon, Kingsberry Farm

Jen sat at her desk on the other side of our office, peering intently at me over the top of her glasses.

'Don't forget your appointment.'

I glanced at the clock in the corner. 'Shit – lost track of time.' I started to gather up the papers I'd need for my prison visit.

'You don't *have* to go.' She thoughtfully chewed the end of her pencil. 'McGarry's solicitor will have shown him your report.'

'I know, but I want to see him before he's transferred. Could end up serving his sentence at the other end of the country.'

I'd worked with Chris McGarry's solicitor, Joshua Weston, since the very beginning. As I'd set up my private practice several years ago, after too long working the anti-social hours dictated by the NHS.

Joshua had been a well-respected solicitor on the northern circuit, and Chris McGarry had been on his books as a junior offender. Going on to become what Joshua euphemistically referred to as a 'frequent flier' within the criminal justice system.

The McGarry family were well known to the police. Chris's father, brothers and several uncles had crossed the court threshold more times than they could count and Joshua had been their representative of choice for decades.

The role as head of the family business was bequeathed by Chris's gangland patriarch. But times had changed since the days when his father and uncles ran 'protection' for the pubs and clubs around Yorkshire and Chris had inevitably branched out into more lucrative commodities.

Drugs and a profitable arms trading business had secured his 'firm's' place as a major organised crime group. Rumoured to be importing vast amounts of cocaine from Colombian drug lords into the north of England.

The deadly trade made Chris a wealthy and powerful player, and for the most part he'd operated his business at a safe distance from the 'sharp end' of day-to-day activities. Until events a year ago had dragged him into a bitter feud with the family of a rival gang.

Even his influence had been unable to protect him when he'd been tried and found guilty of double murder.

During the trial, his legal team attempted to make the case that their client suffered from a mental disorder and required specialist treatment in a psychiatric unit rather than a prison. I'd been instructed by Joshua Weston to carry out a psychiatric report prior to sentencing.

I'd done the assessment while Chris was being held on remand in Armley Prison and it became evident from the off that the insanity plea was not one he was happy to go along with.

* * *

HMP Leeds, known to the locals simply as Armley Gaol, is a category B, male-only prison on the edge of the city.

Built from locally quarried stone, which has weathered into a grim, brooding black, the castle-like facade, with its twin turrets, dominates the skyline.

Thankfully for Chris McGarry, the Victorian days of execution there were over. I had no doubt that otherwise he would have been making that final walk to the gallows.

The small room assigned for our private visit looked like it could have been in a leisure centre. Only the panic button – a metallic strip running at waist height along the walls – and the fact that the metal legs of the table were bolted to the floor were clues that we were in a prison. The smell too – an unmistakable mixture of sweat, stale coffee and disinfectant.

I stretched as far back as the cheap plastic chair would allow, arching my shoulders to relieve the knots. Then opened the Manilla file and glanced through my report, just as the door opened to the familiar figure of Chris with a prison officer escort, who waited until Chris was seated, before leaving us alone.

The man opposite looked very different to the figure he'd cut at his trial.

Gone, the handmade, silk-lined suit, highly polished Italian shoes and the flashy gold Rolex. Replaced now with a light-grey tracksuit and scuffed trainers. But somehow, Chris still managed to look like he'd just stepped out of the pages of *GQ* magazine.

Long legs stretched out beneath the table, he leaned back to study me – the broad grin only making his handsome features seem more boyish.

'How are you, Chris?'

He shrugged. 'Oh, you know . . . it's not my first rodeo, is it?'

'You've seen the psyche report?'

He nodded. 'Listen, Jo, you don't need to worry. I knew you wouldn't be influenced by what the legal team wanted you to say. Not your style, is it?'

'No.'

'I trust you. You've always been straight with me. You're OK . . . for a shrink.'

'Steady on – no need to gush.'

His laughter echoed from the cinder-block walls. 'You know what I mean. You're one of the good ones in my book, and this is what I wanted.' His piercing blue eyes regarded me. 'But then, you already knew that . . . right?'

'You didn't exactly hide the fact when I did the assessment.'

He ran a hand through the dark hair that flopped across his forehead. 'There's no way I could go along with an insanity plea.' When he glanced across at me, his eyes were hard. 'Might be a lot of things, but I'm not crazy.'

'A lot of people facing what you are would consider a secure psychiatric unit a softer option than prison.'

'I'd rather do honest prison time than go into one of those places.' He visibly shuddered. 'Prison I can handle. But forced medication – the chemical cosh, turning my brains to mush until I end up dribbling in a corner. Having to sit with a shrink every day.' He shot me a glance. 'No offence.'

'None taken.' I smiled.

Chris's easy charm was deceptive. He could switch it on when it suited him, but his reputation as a ruthless gang boss had been earned the hard way.

An astute entrepreneur, he would have been successful in any venture. Fate just happened to dictate that the family business he'd inherited was a criminal one.

He shook his head. 'My brief tried telling me that a secure unit might mean a shorter sentence – you know? Chance of getting out one day, if I could convince the doctors I was "cured".' His perceptive eyes held my gaze across the Formica-topped table. 'But we both know, I'm never getting out. The cops were just waiting for a chance like this. I always knew they'd throw away the key – so I might as well do the kind of time I can handle . . . right?'

87

His sentence had already been handed down. Life – with a minimum term of twenty-five years, for the double killing of a rival drug dealer and his 'business partner'. Chris had shot them both in the back of the head at point-blank range – execution-style.

'Can you? Handle it?'

He shrugged. 'I made my choice when I accepted this life. High risk – rich rewards. I've done time before.'

'That doesn't answer the question.'

He studied me for a second. 'I've got people in every prison from Barlinnie to Parkhurst. Screws on the payroll as well. Makes the time easier. I'll be OK.'

'You've got family inside. Uncles and a brother?'

He nodded. 'Business as usual. Just conducted from whichever big house they send me to. The firm's in good hands. Sarah and the boys are well taken care of for life.'

'But they won't have you.'

'Didn't have a choice. That crew were getting out of hand – there's a code . . . even for us.'

I already knew what his motive had been. It formed the basis of his legal team's defence, that the balance of his mind had been affected when he'd killed the two men and then gone out to dinner as if nothing had happened.

'You think your family will be safe now?'

'If I hadn't taken care of it, they wouldn't be. Hurting my wife, trying to snatch the boys on the school run . . .' He shook his head, sucking his teeth. 'A move too far. I had to send a message – end it right there.'

Something behind his eyes made me shiver.

I shifted in my chair. 'Do you know which prison you'll be transferred to?'

'Not yet. The legal team have requested somewhere accessible, for the boys and Sarah. If they want to be bastards about it, could be the Isle of Wight. Should know soon. I'll put your number on my PIN, if that's OK?'

'Of course.'

To make phone calls, prisoners were given a PIN number and a form to list the people they wanted to call.

Our visiting time was ticking down. I needed to move things along.

'I've got some good news for you – about Red.'

'I know, his mum wrote to me. I owe you one.'

Jimmy Wilcox, aka 'Red', was a member of Chris's 'firm'.

Jimmy had learning difficulties and a shock of ginger hair, which earned him his nickname, and had attended the same school as the McGarry brothers.

Throughout his youth, the archetypal gentle giant was used as a drugs courier and gopher. Devoted to his handicapped mother and fiercely loyal to the gangland family who looked after him.

Inevitably, Red, like the rest of the gang, had spent his fair share of time in young offenders' institutions. But eventually it led to time in an adult prison, which, for someone like him was a whole different ball game. His was a typical case of someone who needed treatment, not prison.

His elderly mother was desperate as she watched her son's mental health deteriorate and finally asked Chris for help. He'd paid Joshua Weston to apply for Jimmy to be assessed by a psychologist. That's where I'd come in.

'His mum said you'd managed to get him transferred,' Chris was saying.

'Yes, to a "step-down service" – like a halfway house. He's getting guidance and daily therapy. They'll help him transition from prison, back into society. Eventually, he'll be back home with his mum.'

'Like I said, I owe you one. Red wouldn't have survived much longer on the wing.'

'You've paid my fees, Chris, we're even.'

His expression was shrewd. 'Joshua said you didn't charge half what it cost you in man hours so the tab's still open as far as I'm concerned.'

'We're good.'

'I mean it. If ever you need anything—'

We both looked up as the door opened. The prison officer nodded to indicate time was up.

Chapter Fifteen

Tuesday Afternoon, Kingsberry Farm

Jen had taken the afternoon off to do some Christmas shopping, leaving plenty to keep me occupied.

There was a 'Malecki' file on my desk and a book she'd ordered to complete the fact-find. It was the biography written about him.

The picture of the author on the back cover gazed out at me. Tom Hannah had been the crime correspondent for the *Fordley Express*, before finding success as an author of true crime and leaving journalism to cash in on his thirty years as a crime reporter.

Jen had compiled a list of galleries that had hosted exhibitions of Malecki's paintings over the years. Before his arrest, his famous clients had held glittering charity galas, attended by the great and the good from film and television, as well as a panoply of stars from the sporting world. Malecki had gifted portraits to his famous clients, many of whom auctioned the work and donated the proceeds to charity. Most had quickly offloaded them after their artist 'friend' was discovered to be one of the most vicious serial killers ever brought to trial.

In typically meticulous fashion, Jen had listed the amount each sale of his work had fetched. Some figures were truly eye-watering. Surprisingly, there had even been an auction during his trial. I raised an eyebrow at the amount raised during that one. The largest figure on the list. Some people were happy to have his artwork on their walls. Maybe it made for a good talking point at dinner parties.

There were news articles about Malecki's professed remorse and desire to pay back to society. He'd appointed a manager to oversee his exhibitions and founded a charitable trust, with profits going to Rebuild, a charity that supported reconstruction in the wake of natural disasters around the world.

I sipped some tea and settled down on the Chesterfield sofa in my office.

I decided to start by reading the book – something I'd avoided when it was first published. The title that deterred me then still irritated me now.

Repentance – Contrition of a Killer.

I very much doubted it.

* * *

I jerked awake, my heart jumping.

I sat up, looking for my mobile – finally finding it under a cushion.

'McCready.'

'Jo? It's Ron . . . from the *Express*.'

I straightened up, rubbing my eyes into focus. The clock said 6 p.m.

'I was just reading something by your old boss.'

'Let me guess – the Malecki bio?'

I had a natural caution around the press, forged by bitter previous experience, but Ron Wallis was one of the few I had time for.

Tom Hannah's young apprentice had carved out a name for himself with the local media, while at the same time gaining a reputation with West Yorkshire Police as one journalist who could be trusted to play fair.

I rode his uncharacteristic silence, knowing that a question might give away more than I should. I didn't have long to wait.

'Heard you'd been pulled in to advise on the recent double murders. I guessed it would be your knowledge of Malecki that made you useful.'

'Who told you I'd been advising?'

'You know how it is, Jo . . . sources. Fordley nick's got more holes in it than a leaky colander.'

'If you're ringing for an inside track, you know I can't, Ron.'

'Actually, it's the other way round. I'm ringing to give *you* a heads-up. The police asked the press to keep the coverage low-key for the next couple of weeks – we all agreed . . .'

'But?'

'It's about to break early.'

'How come?'

'Before I say, I want you to know that I'm giving you this first, Jo.'

'Why?'

'I scratch your back . . .' He let the inference dangle.

'Go on,' I hedged – not actually promising anything.

'I received a letter today, at the office. It contained information I really can't sit on.'

'Who from?'

He paused, before delivering the punchline.

'The killer.'

Chapter Sixteen

Wednesday Morning, Kingsberry Farm

'Why the hell did he come to you first?' I could almost hear Callum's teeth grinding over the phone.

'Suppose he thought I'd return the favour with some insider info.'

'Hope you told him to bugger off?'

'Not in so many words.'

'Jo . . . ?'

'Calm down, you should know I wouldn't. Besides, I've nothing to tell him, have I?'

'Not the point.'

I was beyond trying to hide my irritation. 'It was *me* who persuaded Ron to give you the letter before they ran it. If I hadn't, you'd be reading it for the first time in the *Fordley Express*.'

'Small mercies then.'

I bit back the response that he was being a complete arse.

'Or did he come to you, because that's the arrangement you have with him?'

'What?' I couldn't hide my shock. 'You can't be serious?' I could feel a pulse behind my eyes, as my blood pressure began to rise. 'How can you believe for a minute that I'd—'

'I'm not sure what I believe anymore. Just when I think I know you, I learn about something else you haven't told me—'

'*I* could say the same!'

Cue-card images of the blonde.

There was a slight pause – enough to know I'd hit a nerve. 'What's that supposed to mean?'

I wanted to say, but instinct cautioned me not to.

'I'm sure you don't tell *me* everything?' I said instead.

'That's rich . . .'

'Why are you being such an arsehole?'

'You know what's in the letter?' he said, ignoring the insult and changing the subject.

'Yes.'

'It could only have been written by the killer. We withheld details about severed body parts and secateurs.'

'Copycats want the notoriety. This letter guarantees it,' I said.

'The *Express* is running it today. By tomorrow the media will be on meltdown.' He made it sound like an accusation.

'Today's Wednesday, and—'

'Think we don't know that?' he snapped.

Enough!

'Jesus, Cal, what *is* wrong with you? We're on the same side . . . remember?'

The silence stretched out. It was a technique he used that drove me nuts – going quiet to prod the uninitiated into filling the space and probably saying more than they intended. Despite knowing it was a tactic, I happily fell into it.

'What's changed, Cal?'

Another silence, and then, 'Are we done here?'

'Sounds like we might be done permanently.'

'Fine.'

I stared at the phone in my hand as it went dead.

* * *

95

Stinging from my argument with Callum, I buried myself in work. I was vaguely aware of Jen answering the office phone as I reread the killer's letter.

Jacob Malecki, made killing an artform. His work was good, but mine is better!

I left Stephen Jones's thumb in Barbara's mouth. Sucking his thumb. Ha ha . . . that spinster never had a man in her mouth in her life! Thought she deserved a treat.

Two down — more to go. How many more?? The police are keeping it quiet because they can't catch me.

They won't be quiet for long. This is just the start.

I watch. I wait. I've already chosen my next and my secateurs are nice and sharp.

F.O.W.

Jen touched my shoulder. I looked up as she held out the phone.

'It's Joan Rigby,' she whispered.

'Hello, Joan.'

'I've seen that letter in the paper.' There was a tremble in her voice. 'Is it true – what he did to Barbara?'

'Don't believe everything you read, Joan.'

'I can't bear . . . to think it.'

A killer's cruelty – the gift that keeps on giving.

'It could be just some crank writing this.' I tried to deflect her away from the gruesome details and silently cursed the author of the letter.

'He says they can't catch him, that he's going to keep doing this?' A sob caught in her throat.

I washed a hand across my face. 'They will get him, Joan. But these things take time.'

'The victims don't have time though, do they?' Her panic was rising. 'This is going to happen to someone else . . . someone like my Barbara. You said you'd catch him, Doctor McCready.' Her voice went up an octave.

'That's the job of the police. I said I'd do everything I could and I have.'

She jumped on the past tense. '*Have*. Is that the end of it? Have you given up too?'

'No one's given up, Joan. The police are working round the clock – they won't stop until they catch whoever did this.'

'But what about you? Are you not working with them now?'

'It's not my decision—'

'No one cares, do they?' She cut across me. 'People like us . . . we're not important.'

'It's not—'

'Barbara doesn't have anyone to fight for her. No family. No one to make sure she's not forgotten . . . except me. But I thought *you* cared. I believed in you.'

She'd inadvertently hit that weak spot, making me feel I had a responsibility to the victims. That somehow, they'd trusted me with the intimate details of their death and I owed it to them to finish what I'd started.

I let out a long breath. 'It's complicated.'

'It doesn't seem complicated to me.' She sniffed heavily and I could imagine her wiping her nose with a tissue. 'Either you're still helping, like you promised, or you're not?'

'I haven't given up on Barbara and I won't.'

'Do you believe that?' Jen asked when I put the phone down. 'That a crank wrote the letter?'

'No. Just trying to take some of the horror away from her.'

'Why a letter?' Jen pushed her reading glasses into her hair. 'Why not just email it to the *Express*?'

'Old school. Harder for the police to trace.'

I looked at the image of the envelope that Ron had sent. A smudged postmark. 'The address, like the letter – typed, then printed off. So, no clues from handwriting either.'

'Well, no one said they were supposed to make it easy.' She walked across to my desk and collected our mugs. 'Cuppa?'

'Please.' When she didn't move, I dragged my attention from the computer and looked up at her.

'What are you going to do about Joan Rigby? It's obvious Callum doesn't want you involved anymore. They haven't sent another budget code either. So, unless you're working for free, looks like that's it.'

'Wouldn't be the first time I've not been paid, would it?'

'So, what now?'

'You know my motto, Jen – it's better to beg forgiveness than ask permission.'

'Not easy to go it alone though.'

'You know as well as I do, if I ask to walk both crime scenes, Callum won't agree – not with the mood he's in. And as for Philip Wardman – he wouldn't give me the steam off his tea.'

'I agree, you can't just walk away. But Callum will go ballistic if he finds out.'

'He's pissed off with me whatever I do these days. May as well get hung for a sheep, as they say.'

'So, you'll be proceeding until apprehended then?'

I smiled at her. 'Exactly.'

Chapter Seventeen

Wednesday Night, Rawdon, Leeds

The small semi-detached bungalow looked like any other on this seventies housing estate. Except it wasn't, because this was the house where Stephen Jones's life had come to a brutal and premature full stop.

I sat in my car and studied the house.

It was only five o'clock, but at this time of year, dark already. The lights were on – curtains open, giving me a clear view into the small lounge. There was a Christmas tree in the corner. Its flashing fairy lights pulsing bright splinters of colour across the ceiling. The family was sitting on the sofa. A young couple and two small children – illuminated in the blue flickering light of the TV.

I wondered whether the landlord had told them what happened in that very room. Or had he kept quiet when he'd relet the place?

How many other houses had a dark history the occupants were blissfully unaware of? Probably more than was comfortable to contemplate. I dragged my thoughts away from my own two-hundred-year-old farmhouse and studied this one instead.

It was on the end of a row, with a large, fenced corner plot to the right and a wooden gate leading to the back of the property.

I got out of the car, pulling my scarf tighter against the bitter cold and burying my nose in it to breathe some warmth onto my face.

The street was quiet as I walked to the end of the block and turned left. At the end of the boundary wall, there was a snicket – a small path that ran along the back of the houses.

To my right, another road branched off from this one. Cars parked along the kerb. No driveways here – just on-street parking.

The heels of my boots rang on the icy pavement as I turned into the snicket. The gardens on my left were higher – the trees hanging over the towering walls – throwing the footpath into deep purple shadow. No windows overlooked the route. No chance of being spotted by neighbours.

Stephen Jones's gate opened under the slightest pressure. I stepped onto the softly-frosted grass. Light from the kitchen window spilled across the enclosed yard, illuminating a bright orange plastic swing, creaking lazily in the breeze.

The windowpane beside the back door was frosted-glass. Obviously, the bathroom. I could see, even before I reached it, that it was partially open.

Glancing around. No CCTV cameras here or on any of the properties that overlooked it.

I ran a gloved hand along the bottom of the window, feeling the handle inside. One flick of my finger and the handle popped off the peg, allowing the window to swing out.

I peered inside the small bathroom, listening to the muted sounds of the TV in the next room.

That's how a killer climbed into your home? Didn't they tell you?

Or do you know, and simply believe lightning won't strike twice?

I replaced the handle on its peg – just as I'd found it.

I retraced my steps, walked to the end of the snicket and looked around – considering the killer's options.

100

If I were you?

I walked down the street opposite. Past lines of parked cars and gardens illuminated by fairy lights strung along hedges or draped in the branches of trees.

CCTV, doorbell cameras and security lights. Most houses had them. It would be impossible to park here and not be picked up by some kind of surveillance.

Plastic snowmen and resin reindeers watched with unseeing eyes from wintery gardens. Un-curtained windows, allowing glimpses into not-so-private lives as people went about their business, oblivious to the light show they were putting on for prying eyes.

Two hundred yards along, a 'T' sign indicated a dead end for vehicles. I carried on, past the last of the houses and the final street lights, until the road became more of an unmade track, bordered by hedges, into unlit fields. At the end was a metal gate to an allotment.

It was dark here. The night-time skulking out of reach of the street lights. The hard ground under my boots was cracked by tree roots breaking through to coil over uneven stones. Grass verges churned into ice-hardened, rutted tyre tracks where vehicles had turned around in the gateway.

I looked back the way I'd come, hearing nothing but the steady rhythm of my own breathing. I was just five minutes' walk from Stephen Jones's house.

In the dark.

Inconspicuous.

Hidden, but close enough.

A perfect place to park a vehicle . . . if I were you.

* * *

Wednesday Night, Fordley

The drive from Stephen Jones's house back to Fordley took less than half an hour. I parked a block away, along a road where the street light was broken. The glass from it crunched under my feet as I locked my car.

I walked towards Kenley Avenue, stopping often, to watch and listen. There was no one around, despite it being just after six o'clock. In the rabbit warren of side streets that all looked the same in the thickening darkness, there was no traffic either.

This was a quiet neighbourhood, where people were safely tucked up in bed by eleven most nights. During the winter months, when the nights drew in, the curtains were pulled and the doors locked much earlier, as people hunkered down.

A sharp gust of wind whipped stinging hair across my face. I tucked it inside my scarf and turned up the collar of my coat.

Barbara Thorpe's house was in a part of the estate that seemed even more remote than the rest. Sitting in a quiet corner of the cul-de-sac. No short cut or rat run. Any stranger walking round here would be noticed.

Standing on the corner, I could see Barbara's gate, surprised there was no police officer standing out front, guarding the property.

Was it only a week ago? How could a life be airbrushed from existence in such a short space of time?

Forensics hadn't released the crime scene yet as the blue and white 'police' tape still fluttered around the perimeter.

A police car was parked opposite the house. The PC had his head down as he studied his phone, his features sharply lit by the glow of the screen. Obviously opting for the warmth of his vehicle rather than stand in the bitter cold as he should have been.

A gust of wind shifted through the bushes, carrying with it a half-heard sound. A door opened down Kenley Avenue. I glanced at my watch. Six thirty.

Right on time, Oscar.

The cat stopped and briefly looked back as Joan Rigby closed the door, cutting off his runway of light. He sniffed the air and looked in my direction, sensing I was there. We stared at each other in silent recognition for a moment before he turned away, heading off on his own night manoeuvres.

I walked back, towards the street that ran along the back gardens of Barbara and Joan's row of houses. The neat backyards all enclosed behind high fences. Each one had tall gates with the numbers displayed. There was no police presence at the back of the house, either. Things were obviously being stepped down as investigators were finishing up at the scene.

I hugged the line of the buildings, staying in the shadows until I reached Barbara's gate – easily identified by the blue and white cordon of tape tied to the gateposts. I pressed the latch. It stubbornly resisted – bolted from the inside. But on this night, a week ago, it wouldn't have been.

Joan's voice echoed in my head. Barbara only locked up once Oscar was out for the night.

Oscar was habitual, because Barbara had trained him to be. *Her* routines had become his.

Lethal predictability – that played into the hands of a predatory killer who exploited routine. Making the kill easier.

'*Sit-and-wait predators*'. *The definition scrolled through my mind.* '*Animals that capture prey by stealth or strategy*'.

Walking a few paces to Joan's gate, I tried the latch. The gate swung open easily.

I stepped inside, avoiding a row of recycling bins. Gently pushing the gate closed. I waited – becoming still as I studied the surroundings.

A row of slabs, like stepping stones across the lawn, to the back door. The kitchen light spilling across flower beds and pots of spiky, grey, dormant lavender.

Joan, illuminated against the bright backdrop of the kitchen, standing at the sink. Unable to see beyond her own reflection in the dark glass, as she did the washing up.

I stood in the dark, listening to the water gurgling down the drain as she let it out. After wiping her hands on a tea towel, she went back to the lounge.

The floorplan of her house was an exact replica of the one next door. Barbara's home. A sanctuary easily violated because of her predictable routines. Routines Joan had adopted to accommodate Oscar, who now lived with her. Routines that had cost Barbara her life.

My footsteps were hushed by the grass as I went to press myself against the wall beside the kitchen door. I cautiously risked a glance through the glass, listening to the muffled sound of the TV coming from the lounge.

Opposite the window, a short hallway led directly to the front door. To the right of that, I could see the edge of the stairs to the bedrooms.

The door was unlocked when I tried it.

I closed it again with a barely audible 'click'.

There was no need to go in. To silently walk across the kitchen, down the hall and up the stairs to hide in one of the bedrooms.

No need to wait for Oscar to return, for his final feed.

No need to listen as Joan took out the bin – maybe even peering at her from behind the edge of the curtain in the back bedroom, watching as she locked the gate. Before coming inside to settle in front of the TV – oblivious to the dark figure silently creeping down the stairs towards the lounge. To stand behind her armchair, with a long-bladed knife held in a gloved hand.

In my mind's eye, the shimmering image of a killer walked through Joan's house, as clear to me as if he were there in person, just as it had happened a week earlier in the house next door.

The boundary fence between the two neighbours was lower than the one to the street. Easy enough to climb – even for me.

I dropped down over the fence into Barbara's garden. The unoccupied house was in total darkness. All the curtains and blinds shut, to prevent press photographers with long lenses breaching the tenuous privacy of the dead.

The only sound was the soft creak of tree branches moving in the wind.

Gravel in the narrow border crunched beneath my boots. I walked to stand by the tree at the bottom of the garden and look back at the house.

My breath frosted the air. I pulled the scarf away from my face and took a deep lungful.

This was where you stood, waiting until the time was right to go into Barbara's house.

I suddenly had the unsettling feeling there were eyes on me.

Unbidden statistics ran through my mind about how often murderers returned to the scene of the crime.

The wind moaned through the swaying branches and lifted the dead leaves on the path, sending them swirling angrily around my feet, as if the very air was screaming at me to leave.

I was acutely aware of how isolated I was.

A sixth sense I'd long ago learned to trust jangled somewhere deep inside.

It felt as though the shadows were moving. A sense of foreboding trailed icy fingers down my spine, and in that moment, I knew with terrifying certainty that I wasn't alone.

My amygdala – that small cluster of cells at the base of the brain – suddenly fired the starting pistol on a flight response.

Run . . . NOW!

I began to move just a second before I felt his hot breath on the back of my neck.

I turned, but not fast enough to avoid the strong hands that grabbed me from behind.

Chapter Eighteen

Late Wednesday Night, Fordley Police Station

'What the hell were you thinking?' Callum rounded on me in his office. 'Breaching the cordon at a crime scene?'

I was tempted to suggest that if his officer had been guarding the house, instead of sitting in the car to keep warm, it might not have been so easy for me to get past him.

'I was walking the scene—'

He was in no mood to listen. 'Don't you think I have enough on my plate, without *you* trampling all over a live murder enquiry?'

'Trampling' – that stung as much as he'd intended it to.

He paced in front of the desk. 'You of all people should know better than to go there without authorisation. Potentially contaminating evidence—'

'I wanted to see the scenes on the same night, at exactly the same time.' He opened his mouth to cut me off. I spoke faster, unwilling to concede. 'To see things as the killer had. Same people – everything. Just as it was then—'

His eyes widened at the significance of what I'd just said.

'Scenes? Plural? Fuck's sake – don't tell me you've been to Stephen Jones's place too?'

My answer was a shrug, which probably looked more sheepish than defiant.

'Christ. Wardman's going to have a fit.'

'That's just a happy bonus.'

'Not funny.' He glowered.

'I won't tell him if you don't.'

'Your little escapade tonight was recorded in the scene log so he's bound to find out about it.' The volume went up.

'If it happens, I'll deal with it—'

'That's just the point,' he snapped. 'It won't be *you* who gets the flack, will it? Because *I* brought you in on this, it'll be *my* cock on the block.'

I decided now might not be a good time to point out that I didn't actually *have* a cock to offer up for sacrifice, even if I'd felt like being so noble.

'I'll take the blame,' was the best I could do.

'Damn right you will.' He was still pacing – displacement for anger that had nowhere to go, except towards me.

'Do you want to know what I learned?' I was struggling to keep the volume of my own voice down, knowing that my rising anger would only feed his. 'Or are you going to let the fact that you're pissed off with me get in the way of finding out more about your killer?'

It felt like his eyes were boring into my skull. 'It better be good – to justify this fuck-up.'

In an effort to interrupt his escalating anger, I walked over to the percolator on the bookshelf behind his desk and poured a mug of syrupy coffee for him. He took the proffered mug, begrudgingly.

I sat on the edge of his desk and pulled my phone out of the back pocket of my jeans. Studying Google Maps to find what I was looking for.

'Stephen Jones's street,' I said, tilting the phone so he could see it. 'This road opposite—' I swiped my finger along the map '—goes down to an allotment.'

'So?'

'It takes three minutes to walk there from Jones's house. There are no street lights there and no CCTV. The chain on the allotment gate is held by an old padlock that isn't locked. I checked. A track runs through the allotment, straight to the main road on the other side of the estate. The plots are pretty much deserted by dusk.'

The muscles were tight in his jaw as he studied my phone.

'If I was the killer,' I said, 'I'd get onto the estate through that allotment, so as not to be picked up entering or leaving. Then I'd park either somewhere in the allotment, or by the gate.'

'And we all know how easy it is for you to think like them . . . don't we?'

'I'll take that as a compliment.' Although I knew from his tone, it wasn't meant to be.

He straightened up and took a mouthful of coffee. 'Wardman's team have checked for vehicles entering or leaving the estate on the night Jones was killed.'

'What if our man left his vehicle on the allotment a day or so *before*? Outside that timeline? Then crossed the allotments on foot rather than appearing again on the street?'

'Possibly.'

'The vehicle wouldn't have had to go anywhere near Jones's house. Not even on that estate. Would they have picked *that* up as easily?'

'Like to think *I* would.'

'Wardman's not you.'

I waited for him to say something. He let out a slow breath, raking frustrated fingers through his hair. 'OK, I'll get it checked. Anything else?' His tone was ice-cold.

'I know how the killer got into Barbara's house without her knowledge, or forced entry.'

He simply raised one eyebrow in a silent question. He really wasn't making this easy, but I'd given my word to Joan and a silent promise to Barbara. In that moment, I didn't want to let either of them down.

So, I told him about Barbara's routine with Oscar. That I believed the killer had studied her long enough to know her habits. How he might have slipped into the house and hidden upstairs, just as I could have done tonight, if I'd wanted to replicate the method.

He listened in silence.

I held up my phone to show him where I'd parked.

'The street lights have been smashed, which is why I chose it. You might want to check with the local council to see if anyone reported the damage.'

'Not the first time a killer's done that.'

'Malecki did.'

'Anything else you're willing to share . . . or do I have to find out from third parties as usual?'

I ignored the dig. 'The killer's letter.'

'What about it?'

'The way he signs it?'

Two could play at being difficult. I'd make him work for it.

'F.O.W.' He frowned. 'Initials maybe?'

I shook my head. 'An obscure reference to the fact that Malecki always killed on Wednesdays. He's letting you know he's going to replicate that element of the original series.'

He raised his eyebrow but said nothing. I let the stillness stretch, before putting him out of his misery.

'From the nursery rhyme . . . "Monday's Child?"' He still looked nonplussed. 'Monday's child is fair of face, Tuesday's child is full of grace?' I explained how it went. 'Wednesday's child is full of woe. F.O.W.'

'Is that everything?' He made a note, determined not to sound impressed.

His tone was so dismissive I felt any willingness to share evaporating fast. If my suspicions were right, I owed him nothing. Even if I *had* broken the rules in our professional lives, *he* was guilty of a far more personal betrayal.

I was suddenly tired of the games.

My innards felt constricted as I took a tight breath.

'You've changed, Cal.' It wasn't a question – though there were plenty I could have asked. It was a simple statement, giving him room to answer in whatever way he chose.

Words.

They can be used to heal or wound. Build up or tear down. Lead or mislead. They represent our inner world. The clues I followed into the minds of others.

Sometimes one word inadvertently gives away far more than intended.

'I don't think you feel the same way about me, either,' he said.

And there it was, the one word that changed the whole emotional landscape between us. *Either.*

I stared at him, feeling like I'd been punched in the guts.

'You feel differently about me?'

'Maybe we've just been through *too* much, Jo.' His tone was less angry, which made his words even more painful.

'It was good – until recently,' I said quietly.

I could hear the hope in my voice and I hated myself for the weakness of it. I'd closed myself off to feelings like this. To the possibility of pain like this. I should never have let Callum breach those carefully constructed defences. Never have allowed myself to love someone again.

Thank God, I'd never told him that.

'We *were* good,' he was saying – the past tense just another knife-twist. 'But our timing never was. If we'd met under different circumstances, a different time . . .' He spread his hands in a defeated gesture. 'Feels like there's too much debris getting in the way now.'

He was right. Even though I didn't want to admit it. We reminded each other of too much shared pain and trauma. There were too many unresolved questions. Subjects we didn't dare discuss. Events that were too painful or dangerous, for me at least, to share openly with him. Lies and secrets that lay between us like a minefield in an emotional no-man's land.

During our last case together, Callum had suspected I'd crossed boundaries. Committed a crime . . . more than one, to protect a friend. Without hard evidence, he couldn't prove it. But it had changed things. Injected a caution into his dealings with me that tainted everything. Elle was right – he *was* a Boy Scout and that ingrained nature to follow the rules would lie between us like an unbridgeable chasm. And tonight's events hadn't helped.

I could deal with his anger easier than this. But the resignation in his voice, echoing the hopelessness of our situation, made me feel more alone than ever.

He was looking at me with an expression of regret. 'I never promised you a sunset, Jo. No "happily ever after".'

'I never expected that. Don't believe in those things anyway,' I said quietly. 'But I *did* believe in you. My mistake.'

'Cuts both ways.'

I stared at him – unable to believe he could be this cold. But his expression was giving me nothing back. Whatever we might have had was gone. That much was obvious and, in that moment, I simply didn't have the emotional energy for the fight.

'Looks like we have nowhere left to go then, doesn't it?' I snatched my bag from the chair.

His breath left him in exasperation. 'Going off-piste tonight doesn't help – running with your own agenda, as usual.' He was winding himself up again. 'Getting the heads-up from a third party, instead of from you. Always wondering what else you're keeping from me?' His eyes were like shards of glass. 'I can't be in a relationship like that – not in my job, Jo.'

I stopped and turned back, my hand resting on the door handle. Something he'd said hitting a wrong note.

'A heads-up about what? About tonight?'

A micro-expression flashed across his face. A lightning-fast 'tell', but like the professional he was, he masked it faster than most.

'I've got a murder enquiry to run. If we're done here?'

'Oh, we're done all right.'

I strode through the main office, ignoring Callum's shout to close the door on my way out. Studiously avoiding the eyes of the team, who watched me with a humiliating mixture of curiosity and sympathy.

Chapter Nineteen

Thursday Morning, Kingsberry Farm

Jen and I sat in companiable silence in the office. As usual, the TV was switched to twenty-four-hour news, with the sound muted. The press had gone into meltdown since the *Express* published the killer's letter and Ron Wallis was making the most of his fifteen-minutes of fame. His face looking out at me from every news channel.

The only saving grace was that so far there hadn't been any news of a third victim.

It felt as if the whole city held a collective breath from sunset last night until dawn today – fearing the Wednesday-night killer might strike again. Like a medieval village in the grip of a vampire, terrified of the night. The modern-day equivalent of garlic around the door was the reported soaring sales of security systems as people fortified their houses against an invisible evil stalking the streets.

Jen nodded towards the TV. 'This has all the makings of a new nightmare.'

'Not my problem now, is it?'

'You don't mean that?'

I took a sip of my, now cold, tea. 'Callum made it perfectly clear last night that he doesn't want my involvement.'

'Never stopped you before.' She left a silence I knew I was supposed to fill.

'I've given up, Jen.'

'On Callum in particular . . . or relationships in general?'

'Both.'

'Well don't.' Her expression suddenly softened. 'For what it's worth, I'm surprised at him. Thought he was one of the good ones.'

'Story of my life, Jen.' I was trying to sound matter-of-fact, to throw her off the scent. Her sympathy would unravel me and I really couldn't go there. Not today. 'Kissed a prince, who turned into a bloody frog.'

Thankfully I was saved from any more when my mobile rang.

'McCready.'

'I've seen the news . . .' Geoff Perrett's voice exploded down the phone. 'Christ, Jo, he's back.'

I massaged my temple to ward off the beginning of a headache. 'No, he's not, Geoff. He's still banged up in Wakefield nick.'

'You know what I mean.' I could hear him pacing. 'Christ!' he said again.

'I know . . .'

'Why didn't you tell me?'

'I couldn't—'

'It says in the *Express* you were called in as an advisor a week ago. You should have told me, Jo. I really didn't need a trigger like this over my cornflakes.'

The headache was beginning to eat through my eyeballs.

'I couldn't say anything, Geoff. Confidentiality—'

'Bollocks! It's *me* you're talking to. Of *all* people, don't you think I have a right to know if there's another sick bastard out there, trying to resurrect those crimes, bringing *him* back into our lives?'

'Yes, and I *was* going to tell you.' I glanced at the TV. '*Before* it broke in the media, but they went with it early. Took us all by surprise.'

'No shit!'

'Can we meet?'

'What about confidentiality?' The sarcasm was evident.

'I'm done with the case,' I said tightly. 'Besides, it's *you* I'm talking to, right?'

'OK, touché.'

My office line began ringing. I was vaguely aware of Jen fielding the call.

When I got off the phone, she held out a message slip. 'Supt. Warner. Wants you down at Fordley Police Station. There's a meeting this afternoon. She needs to speak with you first. I said you could make it—' she glanced at her watch '—in an hour.'

I didn't hide my annoyance. 'Callum more or less threw me out of his office last night, and now I'm supposed to walk back in there the minute they snap their fingers?'

'Callum's the arsehole, Jo, not Warner and *she* wants you involved—'

'And what if *I* don't want to be involved? What then?'

She pursed her lips in that way she had when I was trying her patience. 'You made a promise, remember?'

Her expression told me it was pointless to argue. Besides, I knew she was right. I washed a hand across my eyes.

'Great. Only ten o'clock and already my day's going to rat-shit.'

Chapter Twenty

Thursday Morning, Fordley Police Station

Supt. Warner watched as I read over the notes she'd pushed across the desk.

'DCI Ferguson briefed the team on what you found during your nocturnal adventures.'

I looked up, bracing myself for another bollocking. She smiled and waved a hand to show she wasn't going to make an issue of it.

'That's not why I asked you in. There's a meeting this afternoon with the assistant chief constable, the press office and the SIOs. We need to agree a strategy for handling the media.' She paused, waiting for me to say something. When I didn't, she took a sip of black coffee. 'Unfortunate that Ron Wallis saw fit to run the killer's letter.'

The inference wasn't lost and my hackles were already up.

'I'm getting pissed off, having to defend myself where that's concerned. It was only because of me you got a preview.'

'If I believed otherwise, you wouldn't be here,' she said simply.

'Cold comfort.'

'Look, Jo, I'm sorry if things are . . . tense with Callum. If it helps, you can report directly to me on this.'

She was trying to save my embarrassment, but the fact that she knew about the previous night was cringeworthy enough.

'Thought you didn't need me on this anymore?'

'That was before the *Express* published the note. I'd like you to be at this meeting.'

'Wardman and Ferguson have both made it clear they don't want me involved.'

'I'm in charge, and I *do*.'

'I'll be about as welcome as a turd on a picnic table. Wardman, especially, will just take a contrary stance to anything I contribute – it'll only make your job more difficult.'

'I understand. Can't order you to do it, you're not on the payroll.' She smiled, but I knew she was only half-joking. 'At least, could you help me put something together? We need to understand how the press coverage might affect the killer's behaviour.'

'Assuming the media cooperate.'

She let her breath out in a long sigh. 'This latest development is a game-changer.' She indicated the killer's letter. 'The sensationalist elements in the press can't resist it.'

'I can imagine.'

'Our phonelines have been jammed. Mostly members of the public wanting to help. Some might provide useful leads, but we're attracting all the usual cranks and attention-seekers.'

'What do you need from me?'

'Apart from the signature "Full of Woe", can you get anything else from it?'

'The fact that he talks about Barbara being a spinster, with no physical experience of men. Shows he's studied his victims in detail. Far more than he needed to know, to carry out the kill.'

I looked again at the killer's letter.

'"His work was good, but mine is better." Tells us he's in competition with his idol. I think he wants to improve on Malecki's body count.'

'Jesus . . .'

'"Two down – more to go." He's not going to stop until you catch him.'

'Before I go into this meeting, I want to understand how media coverage like this might affect our killer? You studied Malecki.'

'But we're not dealing with Malecki. And the motivations of this copycat might be very different. In fact, the more I study these killings, the more convinced of that I am.'

'In what way?'

'Malecki tortured his victims. Spent a lot of time with them – in some cases overnight. That didn't happen with either Stephen Jones or Barbara Thorpe.'

'Perhaps he's working up to it? He's already hinting at more victims. Maybe we'll see those things as he escalates?'

'I don't think so. If the motivation was sadistic control, as it was for Malecki, those elements would be displayed already. Even if these two murders were practice runs, there would be some evidence of sadism or a need for control. But I'm not seeing that. No hesitation wounds or attempts at bondage.'

'What if he's still developing those things?'

'Fantasies like this begin young, often in early adolescence. If this person had been developing fetishes around Malecki's crimes, then those factors would be fully formed by the time he'd worked up the confidence to act them out on a real victim.'

There was something else bothering me – something that had struck me from the moment I'd seen Barbara Thorpe's body.

'There's no real *rage*. It's Malecki's by numbers, without the same primal emotion behind it.' I was struggling to explain something that I simply knew instinctively.

119

'If our man wants press attention, do we give it, or starve him of it?'

I paused, to gain thinking time.

'Both are risky,' I finally said. 'We know that media attention in a particular type of crime can be an influencing factor. "Platforming". Giving the offender air time creates celebrity status. That creates "fandom", without which we wouldn't get copycats, like this one.'

She got up and went to stand at the window. Resting her fists on the windowsill. 'DI Wardman is arguing the case for depriving the killer of oxygen the publicity might generate.'

'He would.'

She turned to look at me. 'Does he have a point?'

'It's an option. But, in my opinion, the riskiest one.'

'OK. Why?'

I hated doing analysis 'on the fly'. But Warner was under time pressure – time I knew we didn't have.

'This killer wants attention. Not just police, but the public at large. Sending this letter guarantees it. If you impose a press blackout, he'll up the ante until it's impossible to ignore him.' I glanced up into shrewd eyes that were studying me with an intensity that was borderline uncomfortable. 'And that means someone else dies – maybe multiple murders in one night, like Malecki did. The public outcry would be unprecedented and the media would feed the fire.'

She snorted. 'We're wrong even when we're right.'

In that moment, I was glad the ultimate decision wasn't mine to take.

'Which way do you want to play it?' I asked.

She stared out of the window in silence, then finally came to sit back behind her desk.

120

'I'm with you.' She regarded me across the table. 'I think we can get the media on board. But I'll have to put forward a convincing argument in this afternoon's meeting.'

'You can use clues in the note to make your case.' I pulled it towards me and pointed to specific lines.

'This bit about you keeping it quiet is a direct reference to the first press blackout. Obviously, that pissed him off. For what it's worth, I think that would escalate him. The taunt, *"The police are keeping it quiet because they can't catch me"*, is an amateur attempt to force your hand and *not* keep quiet. It's a win-win for him because he knows when *that's* published, it feeds the outcry about police incompetence. Designed to rile up public opinion – get them calling for more visible policing. That's political, which puts him front and centre of the news agenda.'

'It's already happening.' She pushed the file away. 'There's an organised protest at the weekend. Groups on social media are calling for people to gather at Fordley Park before marching through the city to police headquarters. A killer who targets victims in their own homes means people no longer feel safe. They want more community policing. The list goes on.'

'So, he's choreographing things.' I tapped the file with my pen. 'Wouldn't be surprised if he isn't contributing to social media himself – pulling strings behind the scenes.'

'The digital equivalent of a killer injecting himself into the enquiry,' she agreed.

'Is it possible to track the social media groups? Look at the instigators. See if anyone flags up?'

'Cyber unit are already on it.' She pursed her lips. 'Can you put together the things we've just discussed – make the case for me, to take to the meeting?'

'Of course.'

'Good. Can you work from here this morning?'

I'd rather stick pins in my eyes.

'Er . . .'

'Great stuff. We can give you some desk space for a few hours. Really appreciate this. Thanks, Jo.'

Wonderful. This day just gets better and better.

Chapter Twenty-One

They found space for me in an empty office along the corridor from the incident room. I was grateful I wasn't on a desk with the rest of the team. At least here I had some privacy, despite the glass-walled cubicle opening onto the hallway leading to the kitchen.

After half an hour, I forgot to be distracted by the figures walking past, and became absorbed by the work.

The press office would have to walk a fine line.

Get it wrong and the killer could either up his game, with deadly consequences for some unfortunate victim, or go to ground, which meant not catching him.

'How's it going?'

I looked up to see Ian Drummond peering round the edge of the glass door.

'I did knock—' he grinned '—but you were miles away.'

'Sorry.' I dropped my pen onto the notepad and rubbed my temples. 'Got to finish this—' I glanced at the clock '—in just under an hour.'

He stepped into the room, holding the door open with his foot. 'Would a cuppa help?'

My smile felt weary, even to me. 'Always.'

His looked concerned. 'You OK?'

'Headache, that's all – can't shift it.'

'Tea then. Maybe I can pinch a biscuit – I'll see what there is.'

I could hear him whistling as he disappeared.

Before I could pick up the loose thread of my thoughts, the door opened and Beth stuck her head in. 'Heard you were here.' She let the door swing shut behind her. 'How you doing?'

She'd been in the incident room the previous night. I'd caught a glimpse of her expression – a mixture of shock and concern – as I'd strode past the team on my way out of Callum's office.

'Been better.'

She perched on the corner of the desk. 'You don't look well, mate.'

'Tired, that's all. Not been sleeping.'

She pulled a face. 'I'd offer to get you a brew, but Ian beat me to it.' She rested her hand on my arm. 'Don't know what happened between you and the boss last night, but you looked gutted when you walked out.'

'Think you could be right, that he's seeing someone else.'

She sounded genuinely surprised. 'You sure?'

'Not totally.' I took a long breath. 'But whatever's going on with him, it looks like we're done.'

'I'm sorry.' She sounded like she meant it. 'Is that what you argued about?'

'He found out I'd visited the crime scenes last night – lost his shit over that. It kind of went from there.'

'I heard about the cordon breach.' She grimaced. 'If it's any consolation, looks like it generated a lead, though.'

'Oh?'

'You didn't hear it from me, but they've identified a vehicle – a white van. It was parked down by one of the vacant allotments. Local dog walker said it'd been there over a week. They thought it belonged to someone renting the vacant plot, so didn't think anything of it.'

'Where on the allotment?'

'Other end, furthest away from the estate, near the main road. Techies are reviewing CCTV and ANPR around both crime scenes to see if it we can pick it up.'

'Did your dog walker get a registration number?'

'No, but it had some distinctive markings on the side, as if a logo had been removed. The suggestion to check out reports of damage to the street lights on the Kenley estate – that was you too, wasn't it?'

I simply nodded, trying to save my throat from more punishment.

'That fell to me. Wardman's had a roasting from upstairs for not doing that initially.' She rolled her eyes. 'Lack of experience. Anyway, I've been on to Fordley council. They've had complaints from residents, going back a month before Barbara's murder.'

'A month.' The words came out like a croak. 'That fits with our man stalking her.'

'Nice call, Jo.'

She slipped off the corner of the desk and left when Ian came back with a mug of tea. He waved a chocolate Hobnob like the spoils of war. 'From the team's private stash – don't think anyone will mind, seeing as it's you.'

'Thanks.'

He hovered at my elbow. 'I'm off duty in an hour, fancy grabbing some lunch?'

'Sorry.' I ran a hand across my eyes. 'Not feeling too great. Maybe next time? Thanks for the brew though.'

'No problem.'

* * *

125

I finished the report with ten minutes to spare.

I could hear the team banter coming from the main office, while I washed my cup in the kitchen.

'Part-timer.' DI Frank Heslopp's unmistakable voice boomed across the sea of desks. 'How come you're not working through lunch, like the rest of us?' Even when he was trying to sound humorous, he never quite managed it.

'I'm not screwing overtime out of the system like you lot.' I recognised Eduardo Mazzarelli's deeper voice.

'Butty box for the rest of us,' someone remarked. 'Suppose we could always call Deliveroo – tempt you to stay on for a pizza?'

Eduardo was packing his laptop into a backpack when I emerged from the kitchen. 'Wouldn't be as good as Mamma used to make.' He put on an exaggerated Italian accent.

'Where you from anyway, Pizza Boy?' Heslopp prodded.

'Fordley.'

'No – I mean, where's your family from, originally?'

'Halifax.' Eduardo shrugged into his jacket. 'Enjoy your butty box delights.' He swung the backpack over one shoulder and headed for the door.

We both reached the lift at the same time.

'Going my way?' he said as the door opened.

'Looks like it.'

The doors closed, leaving us together in a suddenly intimate space.

'"Pizza Boy"? That's discrimination.' I smiled – only half-joking.

'I've had worse.' He leaned against the mirrored back wall, grinning down at me. 'Not a bad suggestion though . . .'

'What?'

'Pizza for lunch. Fancy joining me?'

I was about to say no. My head was pounding and my throat felt like I'd been gargling with razor blades, but then the doors slid open to reveal Callum and DI Wardman waiting for the lift. They both stood aside to let us out.

'You not attending the meeting, Doctor?' Wardman's smirk said he already knew I wasn't, and the reasons why.

I stepped past him avoiding Callum's stare, turning instead to Eduardo. 'Yes, lunch would be lovely. Thank you.'

'Great.' Eduardo grinned, holding the lift door open for them. 'Enjoy your meeting, gentlemen.'

Callum's scowl could have soured milk.

Chapter Twenty-Two

Flurries of snow greeted us as we stepped out of the warmth of Fordley Police Station. I didn't need much encouragement to take Eduardo's car, rather than make the thirty-minute walk to the restaurant.

'I'll drop you back here after lunch.' He pressed the remote to unlock a sleek black Range Rover. It looked like a monster parked next to my Roadster in the police car park.

'Thanks, Eduardo.'

'Please, call me Ed. I only get my Sunday name when I'm in trouble.'

We listened to the radio as Ed negotiated traffic on the five-minute drive through town.

Bella Napoli was a small authentic restaurant in the heart of Fordley's Little Italy. An area named after the Italian immigrants who'd populated the community in the 1800s, to work in the woollen mills.

What had once been a centre of industry was now lined with restaurants and bars along the old cobbled streets. Breathing new life into a part of town that had been neglected for years.

Despite the Range Rover's heated seats, my body was starting to ache and I was shivering when we walked into the restaurant. The sensible thing to do would be to decline lunch and go home, to nurse what was obviously the start of a stinking cold. But I'd never been good at listening to my own advice.

The waiter greeted Eduardo like a long-lost brother, slapping him on the back as they exchanged a man-hug. Their rapid Italian chatter washed over me as we were led to a table, then the waiter left us with some menus.

'I can recommend just about everything.' Ed smiled at me over the top of a huge cardboard menu.

'Come here often?' I smiled at my own cliché.

'Got to support the family business.'

I raised an eyebrow. 'You own a restaurant, as well as an IT company? I *am* impressed.'

'It's my uncle's place.' He nodded to the waiter who was making his way to our table. 'Gino's my cousin.'

Gino poured water from a carafe, which I accepted with a thin smile. I looked again at the list of food, none of which I felt like eating. Finally, I handed the menu to him. 'Just minestrone soup for me, please.'

'Pizza for the "Pizza Boy",' Ed said with a smile. 'My usual, *per piacere*, Gino.'

He watched his cousin leave, before turning his attention back to me. 'Are you sure it's worth it? Given that you really don't look well.'

'What?' I frowned.

'Accepting my offer of lunch, just to make Ferguson jealous.' Emerald eyes glinted with humour, taking the sting out of his words.

I opened my mouth to offer a rebuttal, but decided against it.

'You're right, I was going to go home to a hot bath and a hot toddy – not necessarily in that order. But when I saw him in reception, I just . . .' The words tailed off as I realised how immature they would sound.

'Wanted to piss him off. Yeah, I get that.' He laughed.

'Sorry.' I straightened the linen napkin over my knee. 'Not fair to you.'

'Not at all. From what I heard, he was a total prick last night.'

I wasn't sure that made me feel any better – knowing what happened had travelled the length of the office grapevine.

'Is it true? What they say about you two?' he asked.

'Depends what *they* say?'

'That you're in a relationship.'

I looked at him for a moment, considering my answer – which veered between an expletive and a straight-out denial. In the end, it was neither.

'It's never been that straightforward between us. Kind of on–off, if you know what I mean?'

He nodded. 'But after last night, more "off" than "on", I'd guess?'

'Looks like it.' I paused, debating whether to say more. 'It's the job – the things we've been through. Callum has a certain way of doing things, and it's very different from mine. It causes problems.'

He ran a finger round the rim of his glass. 'He's by-the-book. What you do is more . . . esoteric.'

'But no one complains when it gets the results they want.'

'I get it. What I do isn't mainstream either. Which gives me currency with the police. We both operate on the fringes; in those dark edges they can't explore without us. We don't fit the neat framework of their rule book, do we? Anyway, heard you generated a good lead. They should be grateful.'

'You seem to hear quite a lot, considering you're not attached to the investigation.' That sounded more critical than I'd intended. But if he felt the sting, he didn't let it show.

He took a thick wedge of focaccia from the bread basket. 'Like any office, you pick up a lot of chatter when you're around day after day.' He shrugged. 'Won't be there much now though. My project is finished, so I'll be back to the day job.'

'Shame.' It was out of my mouth before I could stop it. Having a head full of cotton wool had a lot to answer for.

'Oh? Why's that?' His tone was playful, even though the question was loaded.

'Just means I won't see you around, I suppose.'

Lame, McCready . . . very lame.

'Could always take a chance and meet me outside of work?' His eyes twinkled with humour. 'Unless of course, it's not as much fun as pissing Ferguson off?'

Thankfully, I was saved from having to answer, as Gino came back with our food.

The soup soothed the lining of my throat, which felt like raw meat. My discomfort wasn't lost on Ed, who frowned at me around a slice of pizza. 'You OK?'

'Sore throat,' I croaked, already starting to lose my voice.

'You should be sipping brandy, not cold water.'

'God, that sounds tempting. But I can't. Have to drive back home.'

He was already gesturing for Gino. 'No, you don't. Your car's safe enough in the police car park. I'll drive you home.'

'No, that's OK.'

'It's no trouble, and the brandy will help.' Gino was already standing by his elbow. 'Vecchia Romagna, Gino. *Tiepido, grazie.*'

'My favourite brandy.'

'Really? Most people outside of Italy have never heard of it.'

'My mother's Italian. Family used to bring bottles over when they came to visit.'

'And the McCready bit?'

131

'Dad was Irish. Came to Yorkshire and met my mother. The rest is history, as they say.'

'Hmm – Irish *and* Italian. Interesting mix.'

'It's been remarked upon before.'

'Accounts for the short fuse,' he teased.

'Guilty as charged.'

'You speak Italian?'

'Badly.'

'Can't imagine you doing anything badly. Lucky I didn't say anything inappropriate to Gino when we came in.' He laughed.

I took a spoonful of soup, grimacing as it stung the back of my throat. As if on cue, the brandy arrived.

'Warmed too.' I smiled as I took an appreciative sip. 'You think of everything.'

'I try. Unfortunately, they don't offer hot baths here, but I can at least provide the hot toddy.'

'So, tell me about these "dark edges" you explore for the police?'

'We get called in when they don't have the expertise in-house. Their cyber unit is actually pretty good – so it doesn't happen often.'

'What kind of expertise?'

'Following cryptocurrency exchanges, that kind of thing,' he said, cautiously vague.

'On the dark web?' I said, my voice just a hoarse whisper now.

Some of the cases I'd been involved with had included offenders who operated on the more anonymous version of the internet. Dealing in child pornography, weapons or drugs. Chris McGarry and his organised crime group had traded on this 'darknet', beneath the surface and away from the scrutiny of the law.

'Saying that makes it sound like I have a level of knowledge that I actually don't,' I confessed.

'Each to his own. I couldn't begin to navigate the human psyche.'

I took a sip of brandy, welcoming its honeyed warmth as it travelled down my throat.

'Brandy helping?' He smiled.

'Absolutely.'

Before I realised, he was waving the ever-attentive Gino over to our table and ordering another Vecchia – a double. And this time, I didn't object at all.

Chapter Twenty-Three

Friday, Kingsberry Farm

I woke late, which was unusual, but I put it down to a soporific combination of high fever and the warm brandies at lunch the day before.

Ed had brought me home, as promised.

His humour and easy-going nature felt somehow comforting at a time when everything else was conspiring to make me feel decidedly low.

Inherent caution had made me question the wisdom of bringing him back to the private space I was so protective of. But I was exhausted with the emotional effort of constantly building barriers.

I'd created a self-imposed isolation that no longer suited me and I knew that was down to Callum. He'd become my 'go-to'. A best friend, long before he'd become a lover.

Already there was an empty ache where his familiar presence used to be. I felt it most in the early hours of the morning – when I'd lie awake, replaying those moments that had seemed so precious. Looking back, it was obvious that sex was the only way we'd ever communicated those deeper feelings. Now, even those memories felt tainted.

Maybe that was why I'd allowed Ed here.

Harvey had no such reservations. Jumping up excitedly at the prospect of a new playmate, as we came into the kitchen.

Harvey almost knocked him over in his enthusiasm. 'You didn't tell me you lived with the Hound of the Baskervilles.'

'Hound of the Biscuit Barrels, more like.' I'd shooed Harvey outside to let him run off some energy.

Ed stood in the doorway, filling the space. He seemed too large for the room and he held himself in a way that reminded me of a rugby player about to go into a scrum.

I couldn't resist the question. 'Ever played rugby?'

'Random – but yes. Local team.'

'What position?'

'Half back. Why?'

'No reason. Fancy a coffee?'

He shook his head. 'Won't stay. Not being funny, but you look like hell.'

'Smooth-talking charmer.' I smiled wearily.

'Could be the start of the flu.' He frowned. 'You don't need to be playing hostess to me.'

I dumped my bag on the long kitchen table and leaned back against the warm Aga, hugging myself in an effort to get warm. But the chill was in my bones.

'You need to get that hot bath.' He looked genuinely concerned. He took both my hands in his and my skin felt like frozen parchment against his warmth.

'Thanks for today. Really enjoyed lunch.'

'Me too.'

He gave me a peck on the cheek before handing me a card. 'My number.' He called over his shoulder as he went out of the door, 'Phone me. Let me know how you're doing, or if you need anything? I do house deliveries of medicinal Vecchia Romagna.'

After the bath, I'd gone to bed and slept the clock round. I vaguely remembered waking in the early hours and squinting at the time, amazed that twelve hours had passed. Then slipped back into a deep sleep until late-morning, when the sounds of a raging storm battering the house woke me.

Knowing I was awake, Harvey padded upstairs, nudging my bedroom door open with his huge head. A second later, his wet nose found its way through the folds in my duvet and he nuzzled my face.

'OK . . . OK – I give in.'

I got up, with Harvey following me around to make sure I didn't sneak back into bed.

The wind howled down the chimneys, into my open fireplaces, and rattled the latches on the internal doors, making me shiver despite the central heating. I pulled on tracksuit bottoms and an oversized sweater that had belonged to my dad, hugging the long sleeves around myself as we went downstairs.

I called Jen and told her to take the day off. She was worried about me and offered to come and play nursemaid. But when I felt this bad, I preferred to hunker down and get through it on my own.

A gust of wind, loaded with stinging sleet, ripped the heavy oak door out of my hand when I went to let Harvey out. He stood on the step as the icy northern wind flapped his ears back, making him look like a forlorn seal, before he braved it for a quick 'splash-and-dash' pee on the grass.

I emptied the postbox beside the door, as Harvey ran back inside – shaking water all over the stone flags, looking pleased at the mess he'd created.

The kitchen felt mercifully warm after the hailstorm. I flipped the lid on the Aga and put the kettle on the hotplate, then dropped the pile of soggy envelopes onto the table as I waited for the kettle to boil.

The habitual notepad and pen were on the counter and I began to doodle. My thoughts drifted back to the last encounter in Callum's office. His whole demeanour had been different and I knew it was down to more than personal tension between us.

Words.

I replayed our conversation – grateful for the gift of auditory recall that meant I could retrieve dialogue almost verbatim. An inherent skill I'd had since childhood.

The audio equivalent of a 'photographic memory'. One of the reasons words had always chimed intuitively for me. Or jarred, as they had in Callum's office.

Hailstones hammered against the windows, sounding like handfuls of gravel being thrown at the glass. The storm seemed to be clawing to get inside the house. But this farmhouse had stood for hundreds of years. Its foot-thick walls built to withstand the conditions, high up here on the wild Yorkshire moors.

I closed my eyes, tuning out the sound of the raging weather, concentrating on Callum's words. Letting my pen wander over the page as I jotted down the phrases that didn't seem quite right. Not just *what* he had said . . . but *how* he'd said it.

After a minute, the whistling kettle pulled me back. I glanced at what I'd written and circled a phrase – the most discordant of all.

Off-piste.

It was a skiing term and not one Callum used. That's why it jarred when he said it. I'd heard it only a few days before. Part of the lexicon of someone who *did* ski, and used it often.

Elle – over lunch in McNamara's. *'You going off-piste with this one?'*

Coincidence? Maybe. But experience meant I didn't believe in coincidences.

* * *

137

I'd built a huge log fire in the grate, preferring to work in the lounge today. Candles created flickering shadows that danced across the walls, as the fireplace crackled.

As Harvey snored on the rug, I reached for a bottle of paracetamols while I waited for my emails to download. I struggled with the child-proof top and cursed as the lid came off with a 'pop' and tablets spilled all over the rug. I picked up two and took them with a mouthful of tea as a 'ping' alerted me to incoming mail.

As if my thoughts had conjured her up, the first email was from Elle, asking for dates for a ride out. I thought about that as I began to open the post. Distractedly, ripping open damp envelopes.

Being caught in Barbara Thorpe's garden hadn't been random. Someone had tipped Callum off that I would be looking at the case in my own time. Anyone who knew me, would know that meant walking the scene – preferably on the same day and time as the original crime.

I could imagine Callum calling the scene guard to make sure he was being thorough. Enough to make the officer think twice about sitting in the warm patrol car.

Callum had known – I'd heard it in his voice.

'Getting the heads-up from a third party, instead of from you . . .'

Had that third party been Elle?

How did it make me feel, to think that one of my closest friends could have been briefing Callum behind my back? More to the point – why would she?

I threw the post onto the table in frustration then stared at the one on top of the pile.

The HM Prisons logo was unmistakable.

I picked up the letter and froze with the cup halfway to my lips.

The wind moaned outside, the ghostly sound, as much as the words on the page, making the hair stand up on the back of my neck.

'Jesus,' I breathed.

Whatever I'd expected, it hadn't been this.

Chapter Twenty-Four

I reached for my mobile and punched out a familiar number. There was only one person who would understand the impact of this.

It was answered almost immediately. The gruff voice on the other end sounding annoyed at the interruption. No small-talk, which was typical of the man.

'Thought we'd agreed to meet tomorrow?'

'Geoff, I . . .' My words trailed away – swallowed by the enormity of what I was looking at. A thousand thoughts were jostling for position.

Trouble must have crackled through my tone. 'Jo, what's wrong?'

'I . . . could you . . .' I stumbled, until finally taking a steadying breath. 'Can't explain over the phone. Can you come to the farm?'

Ordinarily, *that* request would have met with a curmudgeonly growl that in such foul weather, *I* should be the one going to him. But he could already tell that whatever this was, it was far from ordinary.

'Give me an hour,' he said, before abruptly hanging up.

* * *

'What the fuck?' Geoff stared at the prison visiting order I'd received.

I poured him a mug of tea from the teapot that sat on the low table between us.

He'd arrived ten minutes earlier – dripping and cursing as he shrugged off his waterproof and wellingtons in my porch.

Even Harvey was subdued, seeming to sense the tension as he followed us into the sitting room.

'And you had no idea this was coming?' He glanced at me over the top of his heavy, dark-rimmed spectacles.

I raised my eyebrows. 'Of course not – why would I? I've never met the man.'

He dropped the order back onto the table, and we both stared at the name on it.

Jacob Malecki.

'Looks like you're going to meet him now.' He was studying me closely. 'If you want to?'

I slumped back against the sofa's thick cushions and ran fingers through my hair – as if untangling the knots would do the same for my thoughts.

'I don't know.'

'Don't know whether you want to deal with him ... or whether you're going to go?' His eyes were those of a psychologist, rather than a friend in that moment.

'Is there a difference?'

He took a sip of his tea. 'You can engage with him, to find out what he wants, without meeting him.'

'Everything Malecki does is calculated.' My eyes never left the visiting order. As if it was a reptile that might uncoil and strike at any minute.

'Indirectly, you helped put him away,' he said quietly.

A log cracked loudly in the grate, sending a shower of sparks up the chimney. Casting an amber glow over Geoff's face as he watched me.

'How would *you* feel about it?' I asked. 'If I went to see him?' I looked into hazel eyes, which, despite age and the weariness, had lost none of their shrewd intensity.

'How do I feel about you sitting opposite the man who tortured and killed my Kathy?'

I waited, trying to fathom the emotion flickering behind his glasses.

He ran a hand over the stubble on his chin. 'Truth is, I couldn't do it.' I glimpsed again the hatred I'd seen, after Kath's death. 'If I was in the same room as that bastard, I'd want to kill him.' He shook his head. 'Whatever he wants, it's a chance to learn something, Jo. An opportunity to examine that twisted specimen up close.'

I knew what he meant. Like scientists researching the possibility of aliens – to suddenly be presented with a live specimen. To get answers to unfathomable questions was a prize too good to pass up. Despite the danger that exposure to such a creature might present.

For us, Malecki was the Rosetta Stone in the study of psychopathy. An essential key that could unlock a treasure trove of knowledge in a field that was ever-changing, like shifting sand beneath our feet.

'Whatever he *thinks* he's getting out of it,' Geoff was saying, 'he's underestimating your ability to get inside his head. You could get more out of him than he anticipates.'

I stared into the fire, watching the flames slowly roiling around the logs.

'And what if I can't?'

'I don't believe that for a minute. But even if it happens, you've lost nothing. You get to stare into the abyss, and from *that* alone, you'll learn.' I felt his eyes on me. 'But the danger is, he'll get to stare into you.'

Chapter Twenty-Five

Saturday Morning, Kingsberry Farm

Jen sat at her desk, peering at me over the top of her glasses.

'So, you're going?'

I read the visiting order again, as if today's date on it could change, or the letters might suddenly evaporate, like invisible ink.

'Yes.' I sounded more certain than I felt.

'But we have no idea what he wants.'

'Only one way to find out.'

'Don't you think you should let Callum know?'

'No.' I snorted.

'Supt. Warner then?'

I ran a hand across my eyes. 'No point, at this stage – until I know what Malecki wants.'

'Why risk being told no, you mean? You don't want them to interfere. Or worse, forbid the visit. I know you, Jo.'

I gestured to the email I'd received the day before from Warner's office. 'It says here, my services are no longer required. They have my offender profile and unless something else crops up, they don't need me.'

'And visiting Jacob Malecki *isn't* getting involved?'

I was saved by the doorbell.

'Expecting someone?'

'No.'

I hadn't heard a car coming down the gravel drive, but it was still blowing a hooley. The sleet had stopped to be replaced by thick frost – painting the trees and transforming the landscape into a glistening winter wonderland.

I walked into the kitchen, followed by Jen, in time to see Ed, stamping snow off his boots.

'Hi.' He grinned, holding out a carrier bag. 'I come bearing gifts.'

Jen glanced from him to me, raising her eyebrows in a silent question.

'Jen, this is Eduardo Mazzarelli. He's an IT consultant. Been working with the police.' I took the carrier bag from him. 'Ed, Jen, my PA.'

They shook hands, the formality seeming incongruous in my kitchen. Jen broke the awkward moment by putting the kettle on.

'Hope you don't mind my dropping in?' Ed stood by the oven, hugging himself to get warm. 'But I thought you might need help retrieving your car?'

Jen's look was one of undiluted, salacious interest. I told her about going to lunch with Ed, trying not to make too much of it, though I knew *she* would.

'The medicinal brandy meant Jo had to leave the car in Fordley,' Ed supplied helpfully. 'But it made me think this might come in handy.' He delved into the carrier bag, producing a bottle of Vecchia, a couple of lemons and a jar of Yorkshire honey. 'Hot toddy kit.'

'That's really thoughtful.' I was genuinely touched.

'How is the throat?'

'Still not great – so the toddy will help. Thanks.'

Jen was grinning at me over Ed's shoulder, finding this highly amusing. 'Well, I suppose I should get back to the office – things to do.'

I ignored her expression, which told me I was going to get interrogated the minute she had me alone.

'Thought your company worked weekends,' I said, once she'd gone.

'Being the boss has its perks.' He stretched his long legs out as he leaned against the Aga, watching me pour scalding water into the teapot. 'Not treated yourself to an instant hot-water tap then?'

I pulled a face. 'Certainly not. Haven't even got an electric kettle.' I stirred the pot. 'There's something about the ritual of brewing up that I like. Besides, it's a sin to make tea in the cup – it tastes better from a teapot.'

'If you say so.' He took the cup from me. 'Can't say I'm an aficionado. Like any good Italian, I prefer coffee.'

'I'm not a good Italian, then. Obviously more of a Yorkshire girl. Sorry, I should've asked what you preferred.'

'This is fine. I'm a stickler for the blend of beans, so tea is OK otherwise.'

A warm silence wrapped itself around us, and for a moment, we just stood by the stove, drinking tea, listening to the wind outside.

'What do you want to do about your car?' he finally asked, breaking the intimate stillness.

'I have to go to Wakefield. Would be helpful if you could drop me at the car park.'

* * *

'You going into the police station while you're there?' Ed asked, trying to make it sound like casual small talk as we drove into Fordley.

'No. Doubt I'll be going in, for the foreseeable.'

145

That drew a glance. 'Why not?'

'I'm benched.'

'While this nutter's still out there? Got to be more you can add to their investigation, surely?'

I stared out of the window. The scenery had changed, from the crystalline winterscape of the countryside around the farm to city roads, crunchy with salt. Dirt-grey snow piled along the edges of the kerb, where the gritters had cleared the main arteries into town.

'Callum doesn't want me involved.'

My reflection in the glass looked tired. Long blonde hair escaping from the folds in my scarf. Dark-ringed brown eyes that looked back at me with a cynical weariness.

I risked a glance at Ed. He was frowning. 'Warner rates you. Wouldn't have thought she'd want you on the outside.'

'If she needs me, she knows where I am.'

'You're not going to leave it? I mean, if I'm heavily invested in a problem, I'll work it in my own time. Even if the client runs out of budget. Like an itch I can't scratch. I think you're the same.'

I turned in my seat to look at him. Shrewd jade eyes regarded me with a perceptiveness I hadn't expected.

'You don't really know me.'

'Know your reputation.' He shrugged. 'And now we've spent a little time together, I'm getting to see the person behind the myth.'

'Hardly mythical.'

'You're impressive.' He said it in a way that really had no edge. 'Strength of character and intelligence – a compelling mix.'

'Bet you say that to all the girls.' I was making light of it, but his remarks suddenly and unaccountably meant a lot. 'This isn't an Agatha Christie novel and I'm not Miss Marple. If the investigation team aren't sharing, I'm out in the cold. There's only so much I can do on my own.'

'You're not on your own.'

'No?'

He slowly shook his head. 'I'm in the information business, remember?'

'I'm talking about confidential data.'

'The kind I like best.'

'You'd jeopardise your relationship with the police if you did anything like that.' I was choosing my words carefully.

'I'm a gamekeeper these days, but poaching was always much more fun.'

'Poaching?'

He turned his attention back to the road as the lights went to green. 'How do you think I got into this business? As a teenager, I was a bloody good hacker. One of the best. Had a lot of harmless fun – until I broke into a server at the Ministry of Defence—'

'You're shitting me?'

He laughed. 'I shit you not. My parents had a fit. Thought I was going to get thrown in jail.'

'Obviously you didn't?'

'No, but it was a close-run thing. Only avoided it because the department in question wanted to know how I'd done it. I offered to help them design a firewall to keep people like me out.'

'In exchange for them not throwing away the key?'

'Something like that. Built a lucrative business, being paid by companies to test their cyber security – mostly by breaching it. Setting one to catch one.' He shot me a look. 'A bit like you.'

'I'm not a serial killer.' *That* sounded more defensive than was comfortable.

147

'Thankfully not,' he conceded. 'But I've read the articles about you. They say your talent is being able to think like them. That you have a gift.'

'More of a curse.'

'You shouldn't see it like that. *I'm* paid the big bucks because I think like a cyber crook. Being able to think like them, doesn't make you one. If things had been different, I could easily have taken another path – the temptation was there.'

'Do you see yourself as a "black hat" or a "white hat" these days?' I asked, only half-joking.

'Hmmm . . . grey hat, maybe.'

'You've never regretted not going over to the dark side?'

'I could ask you the same. On second thoughts, don't answer that. It'd give me nightmares.' He laughed. 'Sometimes I do, if I'm honest. Would have had more fun and probably made a lot more money.'

'Looks like you're doing OK.'

'Yeah, but could've had my private island by now.'

'With the false lake that slides back to reveal your Bond villain's lair?'

'Absolutely. No white cat though. More of a dog man myself.'

'Harvey would approve.'

'He can join us on Mazzarelli Island.'

We were both laughing now.

'Seriously though,' he said, 'I work in a shadowland like yours. There's a sick bastard out there, killing innocent people, Jo. What you do can help stop him, and if you need access to information to help with that, you know where I am.'

'Yeah, on your island . . . with my dog.'

Chapter Twenty-Six

Saturday Afternoon, Wakefield

Five Love Lane, Wakefield, could be a charming address. It could be, but it's not. It's the location of one of Britain's most infamous prisons.

His Majesty's Prison, Wakefield. Doesn't sound too bad either. But, because of the above average population of high-risk sex offenders, terrorists and murderers held there, it's known colloquially as the 'Monster Mansion'.

In 1594, the former house of correction held both male and female prisoners. In the exercise yard was a mulberry tree, around which female prisoners would dance for daily exercise. Forever immortalised in the children's nursery rhyme 'Here We Go Round the Mulberry Bush'.

Sadly, the eponymous bush died in 2019, but I was reliably informed that efforts were being made to regrow it. Though I doubted contemporary prisoners would feel like doing much dancing.

Today, Wakefield is a Category A all-male prison, housing some of the most violent and dangerous offenders in the British penal system. One of the UK's elite 'Supermax' facilities, designated for those deemed an extreme threat to the public, police or national security and home to Jacob Malecki for the past eight years.

After driving around the slush-covered side streets of the city centre, I finally managed to find a parking space in the Wakefield

Westgate train station. From there it was just a few hundred yards walk, beneath the railway bridge, to the prison.

There were the customary security procedures to go through. My passport and ID were scrutinised and the visiting order checked. The name on it drawing a curious glance and raised eyebrows from the officer behind the bulletproof screen in reception.

I faced the camera to have my image captured, then my thumbprint was required on the electronic fingerprint scanner.

A system of doors – worryingly reminiscent of airlocks, where one had to be locked behind me before another could open – led into a room where all my belongings were placed in a locker.

Nothing was allowed that could even remotely be used by a prisoner to fashion a weapon or a means of escape. No pens, keys, coins or even so much as a paperclip. There were airport style security scanners to walk through, shoes to be removed while I stood on a box, arms outstretched to be swept with an electronic wand. Then I was sniffed by a drugs dog, with an enthusiastically wagging tail.

Even though I'd gone through all of this before, it never ceased to cause a shiver. A cautionary reminder of the environment I was about to enter.

The well-practised security measures existed because behind these heavy metal doors were men who had committed the most appalling acts of terrorism, or had raped, tortured and murdered their way into a stay at the Monster Mansion.

The slightest slip in vigilance by the officers who managed them could result in brutal explosions of savagery by inmates on hair triggers, who could kick off at an often-imagined insult.

I passed through the security foyer under the scrutiny of prison governors, whose framed photographs adorned the walls, and into a small waiting room, with an old church bench against one wall, where I was told to wait until my escort arrived.

The hard seat was uncomfortable and I shifted my position, flexing the muscles in my left thigh, which had begun to ache.

There were colourful posters along the walls, put there in a failed attempt to brighten the place up. I read them, half-listening to the banter of officers on shift change, putting radios on charge and depositing their keys.

Eventually, a young prison officer stood in front of me – his feet planted slightly apart like a sailor on a tilting deck.

'Doctor McCready? The governor has asked to see you before your visit. If you'd like to come with me?'

Unexpected.

I covered my surprise and followed him to a metal turnstile, which was unlocked as he pressed his thumb onto the glass scanner, then through another door that led outside into the yard.

The cold air hit my face like a slap, but was perversely welcome after the claustrophobic atmosphere inside. We walked across the yard, where secure prisoner-transport buses – known to inmates as 'sweat boxes' – would come through the huge gates to deliver new arrivals, or transferees from other prisons.

The train station, where I'd parked my car, was just on the other side of the perimeter wall. The sound of announcements coming from the platforms could be heard as we walked across the yard. The automated female voice, broadcasting the departures and arrivals in a very plummy, un-Yorkshire accent.

To those locked away inside, it must have been a perversely cruel reminder of freedom so tantalisingly close.

My escort nodded in the direction of the station.

'Come here to get away from the sound of the missus, then get Sonia in my earhole all bloody day.'

'Sonia?'

'That's what we call the voice – because she gets *Sonia* nerves.' He laughed. 'Get it?'

'Hmm,' I said, distracted by keeping a wary eye on the dog handlers across the yard.

Grim and forbidding as most of these institutions were, what always struck me about *this* place was the overt presence of the dogs. Land-sharks on leads, continually patrolling the perimeter. Straining to test the strength of their handlers, who looked only too prepared to release them, should the need arise.

The incessant barking overlaid the cacophony of metal doors clanging, keys rattling, radio chatter and the distant shouts of prisoners. The discordant sound of prison life, once heard, never forgotten.

My escort stopped at a white metal fence, looking up into the ever-seeing eye of the security camera mounted above the gate. He stated his name and collar number.

'Escorting Dr Jo McCready to the governor's office.'

He indicated for me to step forward and show my ID and state my name, after which a click announced the unlocking of the gate.

I looked up at the imposing facade of the main prison. Wide steps leading to large, old-fashioned polished wooden doors, complete with brass handles – a remnant of the original Victorian building, which looked more like an old town hall.

Our boots rang on the flight of grey stone steps that led to the governor's offices. If only the stone could talk, what stories would it be able to tell of the feet that had climbed these same stairs over the centuries?

At the top, carpet replaced stone, in a dark-wood panelled corridor. The smell reminded me of museums I'd visited as a child with my parents, on rainy Sunday afternoons.

A heavy wooden door creaked open and a tall woman, in an elegant wool suit, greeted us.

'Dr McCready.' She extended a slim hand and shook mine. 'I'm Emma, the governor's secretary.'

My escort left us and I followed her into an office, dominated by a cream marble fireplace and a couple of black leather sofas. An ornate desk was set back with a huge window behind it that overlooked the main yard.

'Can I get you a coffee?'

'I prefer tea – if that's OK?'

'No problem.' She smiled.

As the door closed softly behind her, I went to stand by the window and looked down over the grounds.

There was an energy in this place that crackled. Like the buzz from high-voltage cables. The hum of a dangerous current that had to be carefully monitored and contained.

Muted sounds drifted across from the main accommodation block. The hubbub of prisoners milling about in recreation; the raised voices of officers – all to the backing track of Sonia's platform announcements and the rhythmic clatter of the trains.

I turned as the door opened and a tall, athletic-looking man breezed into the room, bringing with him a gust of cold air. He extended a hand as he came round the sofa.

'Dr McCready.' He sounded out of breath. 'Good to meet you – my name's Rob Harding. Sorry to keep you waiting. Won't you take a seat?' He indicated a leather sofa and sat on the one opposite.

'I wasn't expecting this meeting,' I confessed.

'No.' Dark fringe flopped across his forehead and he swept it back with his hand. 'In view of his status, VOs for Jacob Malecki usually pass across my desk.'

153

'Do you meet *all* his visitors?'

'Not ordinarily.' He flicked an imaginary piece of lint from his trousers. 'But I'm sure you can understand why *your* visit would raise some questions, particularly at the moment?'

He paused as the door opened and Emma came in carrying a tray, which she put on the coffee table and left. We went through the polite ritual of pouring tea, then he sat back.

'Jacob Malecki is *the* most high-profile prisoner, in a population where infamy is the norm. He gets love letters – even proposals of marriage from men and women alike.'

'After all these years?'

'Admittedly not as much these days,' he conceded. 'Like any other kind of fame, unless it's fed, it begins to wane. More newsworthy characters come along to steal the headlines and, I suppose, he slipped from public attention in recent years. Not in the prison system though. He holds rock-star status with some offenders in here.'

'Only some?'

'That same status makes him a target for others.' His smile didn't reach his eyes. 'It's something we have to manage – for his own safety.'

'And you think my visit might upset the equilibrium?'

'One celebrity visiting another won't go unnoticed in a place like this. Some of the inmates might resent the attention he's getting. Men get stabbed in here for less.'

'I'm hardly a celebrity, Governor . . .'

'Please – call me Rob.'

'I'm here at Malecki's request.'

'And you have no idea *why* that might be?'

'None.'

'Feelings on the outside are running high at the moment. There's a protest march through Fordley later today.'

'And you think Malecki sending me a VO for the same week-end isn't a coincidence?'

'Let's just say, it's my job to make sure that whatever he has in mind doesn't translate to problems in my prison.'

'Can we cut to the chase, and you tell me what this is really about?'

'There's a lot of scrutiny around his offences at the moment. We feel your meeting should be kept as low-key as possible.'

'You could have prevented the visit.'

'Unfortunately, that would have violated his human rights. They do have them . . . Even in here.'

He shifted slightly in his seat and I waited, knowing that whatever was coming next was the *real* reason I'd been invited for tea in the governor's office.

'We don't allow the media access.'

And there it was.

'You think I'm here for a story?' My tone was incredulous.

'The journalist who received the letter from the killer sent it to you first.'

'And I shared it with the police.'

'Journalists are going to extraordinary lengths to get to Jacob, or anyone here who has dealings with him—'

My legendary thin patience was being overstretched.

'Let me stop you right there . . . Rob.' I put my cup down like a full stop. 'I'm a forensic psychologist, not a journalist.'

'I appreciate that, but—'

'And I'm certainly not interested in selling an exclusive to the press.'

'You have written books about criminals—'

'If I'd wanted to write a book about Malecki, I could have done years ago. Believe me, it's not something I'm interested in. Not then and certainly not now.'

He sat back and regarded me for a second.

'I'm glad to hear it.'

'I was engaged by the police to create a profile of this copycat. Malecki sent me the VO. The *only* reason I agreed to come is to find out anything that might help this investigation.'

Chapter Twenty-Seven

Rob Harding seemed satisfied. 'You can understand my caution. Jacob enjoys . . . even encourages, his celebrity status. But as far as I'm concerned, he's just another prisoner – here to serve his sentence, with as little drama as possible on my watch. I need to keep a lid on things.'

'The media can be relentless – I know.'

'That's putting it mildly. We've been under siege. My officers have been doorstepped by reporters wanting access to anyone working on the Exceptional Risk Unit. They all know not to talk to the press. Obviously, I can't prevent authors writing books about him on the outside, though.'

'Like Tom Hannah?'

'Do you know him?' A caution crept into his tone.

'Not personally. I've read his book.' I took a sip of tea as a thought occurred to me. 'If you don't allow journalists access, how did Hannah manage it?'

'It was before my time as governor. Hannah applied as a friend of Jacob. The visits were listed as "personal". Hannah had quit his job as a journalist then, hadn't been on the media scene for quite a while. So, the visits went ahead. It was only when his debut was published that people realised what they'd been working on. As you can imagine, the victims' families were appalled. They tried to have the book banned. There was a public outcry and demands that neither of them profited from it.'

'But Hannah did. That was his springboard into a publishing career.'

'Jacob didn't. He asked that his share of the royalties go to the victims' families. They all refused.'

'I'm not surprised.'

'Under the Proceeds of Crime Act, he never received anything. Any money went to his charity.'

I recalled my impression of Hannah's book. It read like a 'soft-ball' interview that seemed at best superficial and at worst an exercise in stroking Malecki's ego.

If I was being generous, Hannah wasn't a psychologist, and at a push, I could excuse the lack of theories into Malecki's motivations. But even as a crime reporter it lacked the depth I would have expected. It covered Malecki's childhood, and early life. An absentee father who spent too much time at work, and a mother whose love and attention morphed into overcompensation and almost suffocating devotion.

I could almost hear Malecki dictating the narrative. A thinly disguised attempt by a manipulative narcissist to blame his parents.

The book concentrated on his glittering career. His impressive skill as a painter and the exhibitions that had brought him praise and attention from the artworld.

As to the murders, it documented only what was already in the public domain. Failing to fill in the tantalising gaps that Malecki had always refused to provide. Such as the details surrounding Michelle Hatfield's disappearance, and more importantly for her family, the whereabouts of her body.

'Does Malecki still paint?' I asked.

'Yes, as a form of therapy,' Harding said. 'His last exhibition was a few years ago, but it was poorly attended and only sold a

158

couple of paintings. He's actually been producing more in the past six months than he has for a while.'

'What do you do with the canvasses?'

'Send them to his art agent in Saltaire.'

There was a soft knock on the door and Emma appeared.

'Your next appointment is here, Governor.'

'Thank you. Can you arrange for an officer to escort Dr McCready to her visit with Jacob.'

Harding turned his attention back to me.

'One more thing, before you go.' We both stood. 'Jacob isn't like any other prisoner I've ever dealt with.'

'In what way?'

'He's been in prison for over two decades, Doctor. He's not the same man.'

'Oh?'

'I suppose you could say, he's mellowed.' He smiled. 'But that's not a psychological term, is it?'

'In Broadmoor, he scored the top percentile of the PCL-R.' I recalled.

The Psychopathy Checklist – Revised was an assessment tool, used to determine whether offenders in the criminal justice system had psychopathic traits.

'And psychopathy doesn't "mellow",' I said.

'The condition may not, but the person can, surely?'

I considered for a moment. 'Some psychopaths stop killing, simply because they physically can't, or they're in prison. But their minds . . . the way they're wired, doesn't change.'

'Don't underestimate the effect prison can have on a man. Malecki's been at the sharp end of the system for a long time. When he was first sentenced, he had an arrogance that made him a target. Not just with inmates – staff too. It was a very different regime in those days. He was brutalised. Some of the things he experienced were cruel. Vindictive even.'

'Are you surprised? Given the nature of his crimes.'

'You think he deserved that?'

An answer sprang to mind, but I didn't voice it.

'You believe those experiences changed him?' was what I actually said.

'You haven't worked with him, I have. All I can say is that since he transferred here, he's different. He's not segregated from other prisoners on his wing. He works in the library and has been a model prisoner.' The thin smile was almost regretful as he added, 'I'd like to say that's down to our more enlightened regime. But, in truth, I think the system has simply chipped the edges off the man. He knows he's going to die in prison, he just wants to see out the remaining time in peace.'

Chapter Twenty-Eight

The governor's precautions were evident from the moment I left his office.

I was escorted by a silent prison officer, through a warren of corridors with whitewashed walls and green-painted metal doors. Then outside, skirting round the accommodation block and recreation areas to avoid being seen by the other prisoners.

I now found myself in F Wing. Separated from the main prison and home to the most dangerous of the most dangerous.

At the heart of this supermax facility, security here was as tight as it got. A meeting here would be well away from the prying eyes of the general population.

We were allocated a room down in the segregation unit – the 'Seg'. Twenty-one single cells where prisoners were held in solitary confinement for up to twenty-three hours a day as a punishment for breaking prison rules.

On our way, I'd caught glimpses of Victorian high-arched ceilings with the paint peeling off in quivering sheets. Metal landings with nets strung across them, to prevent prisoners from jumping – or, more likely, being thrown over the railings.

The first thing you notice as you're led down into the Seg is the cold. Not crisp and clean, but dank and musty, like a cave. The kind of cold that seeps into your bones and makes you ache.

Here, the corridors were separated by rows of bars, like the cells in the sheriff's office in old Western movies – reminding me of cages.

Harsh strip lights over each cell door, to facilitate constant night-watch on these close-supervision units, and separate facilities, ensuring that prisoners could be catered for in complete isolation.

The interview room was plain, with cinder-block walls, painted an insipid pale green. A floor-to-ceiling perspex screen divided the room, enabling the occupants to see each other, but to have no physical contact.

The only furniture was a small table against the partition with a single chair bolted to the floor. The whole dismal scene illuminated by a mesh-enclosed strip light.

'OK?' the officer asked as I sat down.

I nodded.

'I'll be just outside. The door has to be closed.' He pointed to a metal strip that ran at waist height along the wall. 'That's the panic button – press that and the cavalry comes running.'

'OK.'

'Malecki will be brought in through the door on his side.' He gestured to the partition. 'The screen doesn't look much, but he'd need a sledgehammer to make a dent. Safe enough . . .' Then added ominously, 'As long as you're on this side of it.'

The metal door behind me clanged shut as he left.

Now alone, a heavy isolation descended, wrapping around my shoulders like a weighted blanket and I wondered how it would feel to be locked away down here, in the bowels of this place, for more than the duration of a visit. Like being trapped in a pothole with a mile of rock over your head. Suddenly, it felt claustrophobic and I straightened my spine and took a deep breath.

I glanced at the door opposite, checking in with myself to realise that my heartbeat had increased and my breathing had become shallower. Non-verbal signals I was determined to control before Malecki walked through that door.

162

Anxiety – brought on by the almost theatrical build-up of the Malecki myth.

He's just a man.

I took a steadying breath.

You've dealt with people like this a hundred times before.

No. That inner voice persisted. *Not like this.*

This is the man who mutilated and killed your friend.

I jumped when the door suddenly opened and I stared into the black void beyond.

A prison officer came into the room first. His key still in the lock – suspended by the chain on his belt.

Then the darkness behind him shifted and another figure filled the space.

* * *

Jacob Malecki stood in the doorway, until the officer removed the key and gestured him inside.

Malecki sat on the chair as his escort backed out of the room.

Contrary to popular belief, inmates in UK prisons aren't shackled hand and foot. Nor do they have their wrists cuffed to metal rings on the table in interview rooms, like they do in American cop shows. The toughened security panel was all that separated us.

I didn't know what I'd expected him to look like – never having seen him in the flesh. Only photos of him from the time of his trial and from Hannah's book – all of which were taken in his younger years.

The press at the time had made much of his film star looks. The millionaire architect with the playboy lifestyle. In the minds of the women who flocked to court to get a glimpse of him during the trial, his handsome features seemed to grant some kind of absolution, or at least convinced them that a man who looked so wholesome could never have committed such ugly offences.

So, I studied him, in silence. This man, whose bloody crimes had dripped without consent, into my life, all those decades ago.

Dark-brown eyes considered me across the divide. His fair hair still thick, making him look younger than his sixty years. He'd obviously made use of the prison gym. The full biceps as he folded his arms across a broad chest giving a hint of the power beneath the grey, prison sweatshirt. He almost looked the picture of health, if it hadn't been for his 'prison tan' – the pallor of someone deprived of sunlight.

'Welcome to the Monster Mansion, Dr McCready.' I hadn't expected his voice to be so warm. 'Or may I call you, Jo?'

'No. McCready is fine.'

He smiled. 'I'm glad you came. I wasn't sure you would.'

'Well, here I am. Want to tell me why?'

His laugh was a short, soft sound, barely audible through the toughened partition. 'I'd heard you were direct. Good . . . that's good.' He nodded to himself. 'So, I won't beat about our famous mulberry bush.' He tugged the leg of the grey sweatpants, as if adjusting expensive suit trousers before crossing his legs. 'It appears you have a copycat killer on the loose, Doctor.'

'And?'

'I don't like it,' he said simply.

He was appraising me – gauging my responses in the same way I was doing to him. And I was reminded, not for the first time, that predators like Malecki were the most natural profilers of all.

No classes or textbooks had taught him how to read people at an advanced level. It was instinctive. A predatory ability that gave him an edge when hunting.

I kept my hands folded in my lap; legs crossed to mirror his relaxed pose. Marshalling my body language to give him no clues.

'I'm sure the killer will be filled with remorse at the very thought of pissing you off.' I met his eyes with a steady gaze of my own. 'But that still doesn't explain why I'm here.'

'Because I'm going to help you catch him.'

Chapter Twenty-Nine

Whatever I'd expected, it wasn't that.

'Talk to the police. Why ask to see me?'

'Because you're working with them on the case.'

'Who told you that?'

'It's hardly a secret, Dr McCready. We do get the news . . . even in here.'

'Same question – why me?'

He smiled. 'Maybe I like the irony of it. Working with the person who profiled me – to catch *my* copycat.'

'Is that what this is to you? A game to feed your ego. Like some second-rate re-enactment of Hannibal meets Clarice?'

He watched me silently for a moment, then shifted in his chair, clasping his hands around one knee, before exhaling a breath that sounded like the sigh of an impatient parent.

'This is *not* about ego, Doctor.'

'Then what? Don't tell me this killer offends your moral code?'

'He offends my sense of originality. I object to my art being copied.'

'You regard what you did as *art*?'

'I did, once. A long time ago.'

'But not now?'

'I know you won't believe me when I say that I've changed.'

'You're right, I don't.'

'But it's a fact, whether you believe it or not. My motives for wanting to help are genuine.'

'And what might they be?' I could hear the scepticism in my own voice. Not the tone of the impartial clinician it should have been. But I couldn't maintain the 'unconditional positive regard' that my profession demanded. Not with this man.

'This killer is copying what I did. If he continues, more people will die. I don't want that.'

'You're a serial killer. I wouldn't have thought an escalating body count would keep you awake at night.'

'The classification of "serial killer" is overused.'

'What would you prefer? "Multiple murderer"? "Monster"?' I was needling him. Trying to puncture his composure, for reasons I wasn't quite sure of. Perhaps his demeanour had taken me by surprise.

I didn't really know how I'd expected him to behave. But it wasn't like this.

He spoke quietly. Tilting his head, to study me. 'Psychologists feel better if they can label a problem. But what happens when you encounter someone who doesn't fit your classifications? What then?'

'You think you're beyond explanation?'

'Not these days. But back then, when I couldn't control those impulses, I didn't understand it myself.'

'You do now?'

He nodded slowly. 'I've come to . . . over the years. I wish I'd had that level of understanding then. If I'd been able to keep those urges in my fantasies, instead of acting them out, no one would have died.'

'But fifteen people did.'

'Yes.' He looked down at the hands clasped in his lap. 'A burden I carry every day.'

I followed his gaze, looking at those strong fingers and couldn't help picturing what they'd done.

'If I'd killed for rage, or jealousy or profit, people may have understood it. But to know it was simply my nature was incomprehensible. Unless I'm mad – drooling at the mouth. An unhinged lunatic is acceptable, pitied even. But an educated professional. That made me a puzzle . . . don't you think?'

'Sounds like you have all the answers. So why don't you tell me what made you do it?'

'Nothing *made* me do it . . . I was just *made*.' He lifted his shoulders in a slight shrug and his eyes were filled with something like regret.

This was what I'd wanted . . . wasn't it? An invitation into Malecki's psyche.

Now I was standing on the threshold, I was no longer sure I wanted to go inside.

'Nature versus nurture,' he went on, 'the age-old debate. Are psychopaths born or made? I don't fit the stereotypical background. No childhood abuse. I didn't torture animals, set fires or wet the bed into my teenage years. So, what other explanation would you have?'

'I believe psychopathy's innate. But there are non-offending psychopaths, whose brains are wired differently from birth. They don't feel emotion like the rest of us, but they don't get their kicks from killing innocent people either.' I met his unflinching gaze. 'So why did you?'

'At the time, I didn't stop to analyse it, and even if I had, I wouldn't have understood.'

'So, what conclusions have you come to – with this new-found insight?'

'You're sceptical, Doctor. I understand that. But I was a young man then. My urges and drives were wrapped up with a powerful sexuality that I couldn't control and wouldn't have wanted to. I've grown old in prison. The temptations that fed my hungers then are not present. I don't have the libido of that hungry young man anymore. Prison has changed me, mentally and physically. Torture clears the mind.'

'Torture?'

He took a long breath, then lifted his sweatshirt, to reveal scars covering his torso.

Like a living depiction of Dorian Gray's portrait. His face, flawless and handsome, while his body bore the scars.

He traced a line of puckered flesh with his fingertips. 'A jugging,' he said.

'Jugging' was prison slang for an attack using a jug filled with boiling water to throw over a victim. Lacing it with sugar intensified the burns.

'My first year at Broadmoor, I was getting a lot of love letters,' he continued. 'One of the other patients decided to make me . . . er, less attractive.'

'There was no mention of it in the press.'

'I didn't want it made public. Even I have a right to privacy.' He shifted in his seat. 'This was the worst. But there have been many other attacks over the years.'

The muscles bunched in his jaw, revealing a tension. A surprising chink in his otherwise unruffled demeanour. Somehow it made him seem more human – vulnerable even.

'Being on the receiving end of violence was a new experience. I was used to being in control. To lose that was a shock. It began to reshape my thinking. The greatest leveller of all is physical agony.' He indicated my leg with a nod of his head. 'You've experienced torture yourself.'

If I was surprised that he knew about that, I didn't let it show. I said nothing.

169

'I was sorry to read about what happened to you.'

'Really?'

'I know what pain can do to the mind, as well as the body.'

'You'll forgive me if I find it hard to sympathise.'

'I don't want sympathy. I'm simply trying to explain how I've changed from a person driven by sadism to someone no longer aroused by inflicting pain in others.'

'What were your motivations . . . back then?'

'I love detail. Even as a youngster, I didn't play like other children. I had projects. Collected things obsessively. Cataloguing and listing albums of stamps, or coins, or whatever it was in that particular phase. I have an exceptional IQ and was easily bored. When I discovered art, painting became a constant striving for perfection that I could never achieve. No matter how good I was, I could look at the Old Masters, and feel inadequate. That pursuit of excellence stimulated me – engaged me. I never tired of it.'

'You killed because you were bored?'

'You asked what drove my offending. It was that same endeavour. To work out the most efficient way to perform the kill. *That*, Doctor, is an artform as much as any of my paintings. I wouldn't appreciate anyone forging those either.'

'You regard this copycat as a forger?'

'A poor one at that – which is even worse.' He spread his hands. 'So, do you want my help, or not?'

I recalled Geoff Perrett's words. *Ask questions he's never answered. Find out what drove him.*

'That depends.'

'On what?'

'Why you want to help?'

'*Pentimento*.'

170

'Repentance?'

'You speak Italian? Oh, but of course, your mother is Italian.'

'Repentance for your crimes?'

'Yes. Ever since my imprisonment, I've tried to repay my debt to society.'

'I'm sure that's a constant source of comfort to the families of your victims.'

He sighed wearily. 'What would you have me do, Doctor? Write heartfelt notes of regret to them all? Believe me, I tried that, but they don't want to hear from me. I also tried to give them the proceeds from my art, or the book, but they refused. So, I decided to pay back in more practical ways.'

'Through a charity that funds reconstruction of buildings? Hardly a donation to the widows and orphans, is it?'

'I hate the destruction of beautiful architecture.'

'But happy to destroy human life?'

'Your insistence in pointing out my lack of conscience all those decades ago isn't helpful. I struggle with what I did every day. Try to make sense of what happened and look for any good that can come out of it.'

'What can you salvage from what you did?'

'Sadly, not much. Except that perhaps people like me serve a purpose. No one really believes in the Devil these days. So, the cold-blooded killer takes his place in the popular imagination. People need monsters. It makes them feel better about themselves. Even their worst failings don't seem so bad, when they measure against someone like me.'

I simply stared at him. So many responses sprang to mind, but none of them would have been helpful. I composed a more moderate reply.

'And that level of understanding helps us how, exactly?'

'By giving you an insight into how this killer thinks.'

'Do *my* job for me?'

'Give you another resource. Another dimension to your expertise.'

'And if I refuse to play . . . What then?'

'Unless you are involved then neither am I.'

'I thought you were driven by remorse? That shouldn't come with conditions.'

'"On much speaking cometh repentance, but in silence is safety."'

'William Drummond – Scottish poet.'

'You recognise the quote, excellent. It's nice to have an intellectual to talk to . . . They're in short supply around here.'

'What's your point?'

'Sharing information has consequences in here.'

'How does dealing with me protect you?'

'Police officers coming to see me wouldn't go unnoticed, even with Governor Harding's precautions. Even some prison officers would like to see my guts spilled in the shower block. They're not above letting people know if I were to help the police. Even in the Monster Mansion, a grass is regarded as a lower form of life than a paedophile. Phone calls are equally risky. But over the years, I've lost count of the psychologists visiting to probe my brain. That is much easier to explain away. Who knows—' he smiled '—when this is all over, perhaps we could write a book together? That really would be something special, don't you agree?'

Dangling the bait of a bestseller was pretty transparent as tactics went, but I pretended not to see through it.

'And if the police don't agree to you dealing through me?'

'I'm sure you can persuade them.'

'Supposing I can, how exactly do you see this working?'

172

'You share the details with me. Crime scene photographs, post-mortem reports . . . intelligence. And I'll give you the benefit of my unique experience.'

And let you get off on the details? Live vicariously through the eyes of another killer. There's more chance of finding a one-ended stick than anyone going along with this.

'What's in it for you?' was what I actually said. 'Don't tell me . . . "a window, where you can see a tree, or even water"?'

That barely-heard laugh again. 'You really can't let that analogy go, can you?'

He was trying to get a bite. I simply gave him my silence.

'Are you afraid of me, Jo McCready?'

'No.'

'Good. You have no need to be. But I bring out your insecurities, don't I? That little student who wrote her rudimentary profile. Wanting to be accepted by the players in a grown-up game.'

'The rudimentary profile that helped put you in here for life.'

His smile was almost rueful. 'These days, I've come to see that in a more positive light.'

'How?'

'I played a part in propelling you into this career. Putting the most notorious criminal in British history behind bars, when you were just a student, can't have hurt your CV.'

'You want me to thank you?'

'I'm grateful. Your work protects innocents from people like me.'

'Really?' I was unconvinced.

'You save lives.' He was undaunted, leaning forward as he spoke. His face animated. His eyes alive with a genuine conviction that was hard to fake. 'That pays back a small portion of my debt. I've followed your career over the years, with a sense of gratitude, at what I feel I helped create. If there's any good to salvage from what I did, it's that.'

That caught me off guard and for a split second, despite myself, I felt my emotions leaning in to the sentiment.

A thirst for approval that had never been quenched, by the one person in every child's life who *should* have. My mother's impossibly high standards and constant reminders that I failed to reach them all through my life left an aching void – even now.

As an analyst, I understood it. A sense of never being good enough had been hard-wired in those vital formative years, and that meant the hollow longing for love and approval could be managed, but never eradicated.

'Cut to the chase,' I deflected, to cover my misstep. 'If you're serious, you have to offer me something.'

'I'm offering my expertise, and my time.'

'Time is something you have too much of. It's not exactly a hardship for you to give any of it away, is it?'

'So, what *do* you want?'

'Answers.'

There was a long pause as he seemed to consider it. 'Ask,' he said simply.

'Do you know who this copycat killer is?'

'No.'

'Do you have any suspicions? Ex-inmates . . . someone who did time with you here, or in Broadmoor, who's on the outside now?'

'I have a lot of admirers. It's conceivable one of them has decided to copy my work.'

'That doesn't answer my question.'

'I may be able to come up with a list. You'll have to come back for that though.'

'Is that what this is? A way of getting visits to break up the monotony?'

'I admit, I *do* want to see you again. But I can also help catch your killer. Surely that's worth a few hours of your time?'

'Why me?' I still wasn't sure.

'Because something connects you to me. Something we need to resolve.'

I felt a sudden dread at what was coming.

'What?'

'Your friend . . . Kath Hutchinson.'

The air seemed to get trapped somewhere deep in my chest.

His eyes instantly went to my throat and I knew that he hadn't missed the change in my breathing. His sensory acuity was sharper than razor-wire and I cursed the momentary lapse that had given away my feelings.

'I need to prove to you that I *am* truly sorry for what I did to her.'

'Did you know who she was?' My voice sounded like it was coming from a distant place. I felt suddenly dissociated, like an observer in a stranger's nightmare.

'You mean, did I know she was Perrett's wife? Yes. That's why I chose her.' He paused, waiting for me to say something. When I didn't, he leaned back in the chair. 'Did I know about the profiling project he'd set his students? Yes. But, more importantly, I knew about *you*.'

'How?' My mind was racing. 'I was just—'

'A nobody. My point exactly – about elevating you in this profession.'

'How could you know about the project?'

'Synchronicity,' he said simply. 'Described by Carl Jung as "meaningful coincidences which seem beyond the probability

175

of chance". The universe giving me an opportunity. So fortuitous it seemed preordained.'

'How?'

'My work brought me to the North in the late eighties.'

'You killed in Leeds in 1988 and Manchester the following year. But then a gap of three years which you never explained?'

'There's no mystery. I was moving between overseas projects and work I had in the north of England. In 1992, I had an invitation to go back to my old university – to make a speech at the graduation ceremony, as the celebrity ex-student.' He smiled. 'At the dinner afterwards, the conversation turned to the murder of the Gordons. It had been front-page news and someone at the table mentioned a psychology professor he knew, who had set the profiling of the "Relay Killer" as an exercise for his students. He mentioned one student in particular . . . a prodigy. And there it was – synchronicity. So, I did some research, even travelled to Fordley when my work brought me close enough. I considered Perrett, but then Kath presented herself as a better project.'

Red-hot rage rocketed through my brain. 'Don't *ever* say her name.'

The words were out before I could bite them back. A bereaved friend in that moment, not a psychologist. I broke eye contact, struggling to regain some composure.

'I'm sorry.' He sounded genuinely regretful. 'Believe me, if I could turn the clock back, I would. That sounds trite and you have no reason to trust it. But I'm a different person to the one who did those things. I've had nothing but time to reflect on it all. I can't change what I did, but I *can* try to give you answers now.'

A silence began to penetrate and I looked up to see him regarding me.

'I even watched *you* for a while.' He said it with shame, like a whispered secret.

'What?'

'I considered taking you next.'

I forced myself to meet his intense gaze. 'Why didn't you?'

'I met your father.'

Chapter Thirty

My brain froze. The enormity of what he'd just said was too much.

I watched his eyes – expecting, at any moment, for him to laugh and tell me it was a sick joke. But he continued to regard me, with an unnerving stillness.

'No,' I croaked, trying to dislodge his words.

'While I was in Fordley.' He spoke softly. 'I wanted to see this tutor's protégé. I watched your student house. One afternoon, your parents visited.'

I didn't want to hear this, but was compelled to listen. I stared at my hands, watching my knuckles turn white as I held on throughout the whole horrific litany.

The forensic psychologist in me knew what was unfolding.

The clinician's questions scrolled like ticker tape through my brain. But exploring the scenarios that I *knew* would have propelled him towards his next victim seemed impossible when those involved were the people I loved.

He'd robbed me of my objectivity; I had to regain it. Either that, or get up and leave. As fast as that thought occurred, I dismissed it.

Christ, McCready, take control.

I took a long breath. 'You "studied" my parents?'

'Study'. Malecki's word for choosing his victims.

'Your father was a creature of habit. He drank in McNamara's on Saturday afternoons. So, I went there. Sat at the next table.'

'Did you speak to him?'

'No. But I listened to him talking to the landlord. They were obviously friends. He spoke about how proud he was of you.'

That was like a precious message from the grave. I shifted in my seat, clearing my throat to dislodge the lump.

'Sentiment wouldn't have stopped you making me a victim, Malecki. In fact, given your psychopathology, it would have made me a prime target.'

'You're right. Back then, I wasn't soft-hearted or sentimental.'

'What then?'

'Curious. I saw something in you. Something I felt should be preserved. You were too interesting to remove from the board. Perversely, I wanted to see how the tutor's pet-profiler would shape up. In much the same way your father wanted to see what you would make of your life.' He tilted his head to one side, studying me carefully. 'He must be very proud.'

'He passed away.'

'I'm sorry. I know how close you were.'

'No,' I snapped, 'you don't!'

'I heard the way he spoke about you,' he said gently. 'Just because I can't *feel* love, Doctor, doesn't mean I don't recognise the emotion in others.'

'And so, you chose Kath instead of me?'

He nodded, gauging my reaction. 'That probably doesn't make you feel any better.'

Damn right.

'Worse, I imagine. But sadly it's the truth.'

This is what you wanted. The still, quiet voice in my subconscious whispered, *Is it worth it?*

'You say you want to help catch this killer. What's your impression of him?'

If he registered the shift in topic, he didn't let it show.

'The very fact he's a copycat tells us he wants recognition. Killing gives him a status he doesn't have in reality. He feels close to me when he replicates my kills. Wants my fame. He thinks emulating me will give him that.'

'Did you ever discuss this with anyone – encourage their interest?'

'Believe me, they don't *need* encouragement. People find violence exciting, as long as they're not on the receiving end of it. People who commit violent acts hold a certain fascination. These days, being famous means you *matter*. It's immaterial what you're famous for. People want to be close to those society has deemed special. They're drawn to frightening experiences – to get the adrenaline flowing. The perception of danger, even of death, makes them feel alive.'

'Is that how it made *you* feel?'

He leaned back in his chair. 'I enjoyed tapping into those primitive fears. I even waited under the bed of some of my victims.' He frowned at the memory. 'I'm not proud to say, the sheer terror as my hand grabbed their ankle, knowing I was their childhood horror come to life, fed something inside me.'

I shuddered as I thought of that. An intruder, in what should have been the safest of places. A hand appearing from under the bed – like the sudden, unexpected strike of a rattlesnake.

'At the time, I believed I was giving my victims something precious. Something they could only experience once.'

'What?'

'Feeling more alive than they ever had, in the moment of their death.'

'Does this killer believe he's giving *his* victims a gift?'

'Whoever he is, I doubt he has that level of insight. I think it makes *him* feel more alive than anything else in his pathetic existence though.'

'Is that why you did it?'

'I already had all of that through my work.'

'Then why?'

The million-dollar question. The one he'd never answered. Not in court; not to psychiatrists; not his biographer. I almost held my breath.

He paused, then said simply, 'For the challenge.'

I hesitated, trying to choose the right words, but what was there to say when someone reduced the slaughter of fifteen human beings to a personal 'challenge'? Like increasing his daily step count.

'Explain that.' Was all I could manage. The clinician's tone in my voice was reassuring – anchoring me in professional mode, when every fibre inside me was screaming.

He shrugged. 'I was easily bored and had an insatiable curiosity. I'd accomplished everything I wanted. Academic achievement, wealth – wasn't enough. I felt restless . . . hungry, but I didn't know why or for what.'

'So, you woke up one day and decided to kill?'

'My first kill was an accident. But after that . . . I realised.'

'What?'

'That I liked it.'

Chapter Thirty-One

'It's a shocking admission, but I said I'd be honest so, there it is. I realised I was aroused . . . stimulated by taking another's life. It was a drug, and the challenge I'd been looking for. To hunt the ultimate prey and evade capture myself.'

'Murdering Michelle Hatfield gave you a taste for it?'

He simply nodded. Leaning back in his chair, arms folded as he regarded me through the glass.

'I knew I could be as successful at killing as I was at everything else. I began to make notes – to plan the ultimate killing.'

'While you were at university?'

'Yes. My degree didn't tax me much. So, I set myself the task of researching why other killers I'd read about made such senseless mistakes. I knew I wouldn't.'

'What was your conclusion?'

'No impulse control.' He sounded like a professor in a criminology class. 'The thrill they get from killing is addictive. The gap between fixes becomes shorter. That kind of frenzy makes them careless.'

'That's what made your offences unique.' I fed him the line. 'The long gap between killings was rare. Was it a de-escalation of arousal? A time out when you returned to normal life?'

In the case of Malecki, I'd never believed that. But I hoped he wouldn't be able to resist correcting my error.

He pursed his lips, like a tutor assessing my reasoning.

'For me, it was never a reduction in arousal.'

'Then what?'

'The courtship period. Foreplay before actual consummation.'

His words sent a prickle of electricity across the back of my neck.

'I found killing an anticlimax. The process leading up to it was the ultimate fulfilment, for me anyway.'

'The cooling-off period was the planning phase?' My tone was clinical.

He shook his head, like an exasperated teacher with a slow student. 'Anything but "cooling off". A time that heightened the senses. Searching for my next victim. Choosing the right prey, the perfect location. All the circumstances had to be exactly right.'

'Is that why you didn't kill Dennis Haverley the first time? Because something wasn't *exactly* right?'

'If I'd killed Haverley as originally planned, I would never have been caught.'

'Why did you abort the first attempt?'

'Because of the rain.'

I thought I'd misheard. 'What?'

'I'd planned every detail, but I couldn't legislate for the weather. Torrential rain overwhelmed the drains and flooded his neighbourhood. On the date I'd planned for him, the Water Board had workmen manning a pump right outside his house. I heard them tell a neighbour they'd be there through the night.' He lifted his shoulders in a slight shrug. 'I'd planned on a fine day for him to die.'

'How did you choose him?'

'I passed him as I was driving. It was the same with all of them. I could notice them in an airport, at a station . . . or hear about them over dinner,' he added, with a faint smile. 'Something about

183

them would draw my attention and I'd follow them. Decide whether they were right. If not, I let them get on with their lives.'

The matter-of-fact way he said that struck a terrifying chord deep inside me. The realisation that it was so simple. That someone could meet the most horrific death at this man's hands, just because they came to his attention in the street.

I'd always known that people like Malecki walked among us. Thankfully most never followed through with their sick fantasies. They kept them as that. Fictional desires to be played out in their own imaginations, to satisfy some deviant urge. But every so often, just occasionally, nature created an aberration.

A fracture in the veneer of normality that a monster like Jacob Malecki could crawl out of. Becoming a terrifying reality, to prowl among the blissfully unaware. Crashing into someone's life – to torture and kill them, just for the thrill of it.

'You satisfied yourself between kills by planning the next one?' I asked.

'For months, sometimes *years*. I used the body parts I'd taken to satisfy myself, until the next time.'

'To prevent the "frenzy"?'

'Would you rather I'd indulged my passion more often?' He clucked his tongue against his teeth. 'The ability to sustain myself saved lives. You should be grateful I learned to contain those baser instincts, or *you* wouldn't be sitting here right now.'

I'd heard the twisted logic of violent offenders before. But *this* was on another level.

I kept my tone matter-of-fact, as if we were still discussing the weather. 'Did you take other trophies? Apart from the body parts?'

'No.'

His breathing rate changed and his skin tone flushed slightly. He'd just lied.

184

I sidestepped the evasion and continued with the questions.

'Tell me about Michelle Hatfield.'

'Is that the golden nugget that earns your trust?'

'It's a start.'

'"He who does not trust enough, will not be trusted."' He tilted his head to one side. 'Do you know who said that?'

'Lao Tzu.'

'Well done—'

'I prefer: "Don't trust the person who has broken faith once."'

'Shakespeare. Touché. Do you know your IQ score, Doctor?'

One hundred and sixty.

'No,' I lied.

'I'm one hundred and seventy. Higher than Einstein.'

'Then you should find my questions easy. So, tell me, where's Michelle's body?'

'If I tell you that, you have no need to come back.'

'We still have a copycat to catch.'

'And when he's caught, I'll tell you.'

'Why not now? Prove you've changed. Give her parents some peace.'

He nodded slowly. 'When our business is concluded, Doctor. You have my word.'

185

Chapter Thirty-Two

Saturday Afternoon

'The word of a serial killer?' Jen's disembodied voice came through the Bluetooth in my car as I negotiated the traffic out of Wakefield.

'He's using Michelle as a bargaining chip.'

'Bastard! Obviously doesn't give a damn about her parents.'

'Narcissists don't give a damn about *anybody*, except themselves.'

'Think he *will* provide anything useful?'

My reflection in the misty windscreen regarded me, thoughtfully. 'Maybe. He knows if he doesn't, the police will lose interest. But getting insights into the way he thinks teaches us something.'

I thought back to what he'd said about Kath. About me. My knuckles turned white on the steering wheel.

'So, what now?' Jen was saying.

'I'll tell Supt. Warner about my visit. Hand it over to her. If he provides any names, the team will follow them up.'

'But?'

'I don't know, Jen. The governor said Malecki's changed. That his repentance is genuine. He certainly comes across that way. But the thought that someone like him can do a complete one-hundred-and-eighty?'

'You've seen offenders turn their lives around before.'

'He's eking it out,' I said, almost to myself. 'Dangling bait, like a trail of breadcrumbs.'

'Then don't follow.'

'Can't afford not to and he bloody well knows it. He's giving us things he knows we want . . . *I* want.'

I met your father . . . Killed Kath instead of you.

I wasn't going to drop that bombshell on Jen just yet. I had to process it myself first.

'We ran out of time today.' I stopped as a light held me at red. 'Said he'd send another VO.'

'What are you going to do?'

'Right now? Scrub my skin off under a very long, very hot shower.'

I could wash the smell of the Monster Mansion out of my clothes, but doubted I could cleanse my mind of Malecki as easily.

'You don't do showers.'

'Can't stand the thought of him sitting in the bathwater with me,' I said. 'Want to watch him go down the drain.'

'I can imagine.'

'In the meantime, I want to fact-check things he told me, about Michelle. I don't believe his version of it.'

'Which bit?' Jen snorted. 'Can't imagine much of what he says is reliable.'

'Said killing her was an accident.'

'That doesn't apply to the others though, does it? Ooops, fifteen accidents!'

'I believe Michelle was his first kill. That's where mistakes are made. By looking at hers, we might find something he wants to keep hidden. The fact that he's never said what he did with her body, while he displays all the others, makes me think it's a key to more.'

'Anything I can do?'

'I need you to find someone for me.'

I could hear the shuffling of paper. 'Fire away.'

Chapter Thirty-Three

Sunday Afternoon

I relaxed back in the saddle and took a deep lungful of crisp air, happy to soak up the view across the moor, while I waited for Elle to catch up.

The invitation for a Sunday hack across open country was a welcome one, but I'd been waiting for the right moment to ask her about Callum and whether she'd been the one to tip him off about my visit to the crime scenes.

Not yet though. For now, I was enjoying the freedom and the scenery.

Butch – the chestnut gelding I'd borrowed from her – snorted and tossed his head, the breath pluming from his nostrils to hang suspended in the cold air.

We were high up, on moorland that formed the boundary between Lancashire and West Yorkshire, just a few miles from the village of Wycoller. A sleepy hamlet that had been there since medieval times. Just four miles from the Lancashire town of Colne, and handy for us, sitting along the Pennine Bridleway.

I loved it up here, especially in winter. With no Sunday picnickers and fewer walkers, the snow and ice gave it to us – like a secret gift all to ourselves.

The land rolled away to the horizon, in a seemingly endless white carpet, dotted with ice crystals that formed a shimmering diamond crust on the snow.

I always found this landscape healing. Something about the ancient timelessness of it was a touchstone – grounding me.

Giving me a foothold in what sometimes felt like an overwhelming sea of human cruelty that I dealt with on a daily basis.

I heard Elle come up the track. She nudged her horse, Sundance, alongside and we sat together and breathed in the view.

'Nothing beats Yorkshire scenery, does it?' she said.

'Says the woman who technically lives in Lancashire.' I laughed.

'Only just. Could almost spit across the border.'

Sundance was eager to go. Elle tapped her heels against his sides, urging him to walk on, letting him find his own way. Butch dutifully followed, their hooves disappearing hock-deep in the freshly drifted snow.

After a few minutes of companionable silence, I decided to grasp the nettle.

'I wanted to ask you something.'

'What?'

'Did you mention to Callum that I was planning on walking the scene at Barbara Thorpe's place?'

She turned in the saddle to look back at me, as Sundance carried on walking. 'No. Why?'

'Get the feeling being caught there wasn't just bad luck.'

She lightly lifted the reins, stopping us all on the narrow track.

'And you think I tipped him off?' Her tone had no edge to it, but I knew she was pissed off.

'Just something he said. Made me think perhaps you'd spoken.'

She took a long breath before turning to look back across the valley. 'Well, I didn't. Surprised you'd think I'd drop you in it.' She lightly tapped her stirrups into Sundance's sides and he began walking – the awkward silence between us only broken by the sound of creaking leather and the chinking of metal tack.

'Sorry. But you and Jen were the only ones I mentioned it to.'

'And you've asked Jen the same question?'

'Yes,' I lied.

'Well, for future reference, me and the Boy Scout don't share confidences, so it must've been just shit luck.'

We stopped at the top of a rise to take in the view.

In the distance, watery afternoon sunlight glinted off the Atom Panopticon. A contemporary sculpture that resembled a space capsule, above Wycoller. A shelter from the weather and a favourite stopping place for walkers and birdwatchers. Beyond it, in the far distance was Pendle Hill – made famous by the Pendle Witch Trials in the seventeenth century.

History never felt far away on these moors. Local folklore, born in the rugged terrain and nurtured by fierce weather, had fired the imagination of writers and artists for centuries.

The dark line of dry-stone walls that dissected the landscape like grey scars only added to the air of bleakness and desolation – which far from being depressing, made my problems feel insignificant in the grand scheme of nature and gave me a perspective I often needed.

'Come to think of it,' Elle said over her shoulder as we rode down the hill, 'I *did* mention that you might be looking into the Thorpe case in your own time. While I was conducting Barbara's post-mortem.' She steered Sundance around a large ice-covered pothole in the track. Butch had no compunction about crashing through the ice. That's why I always chose to ride him, rather than his more well-mannered stable mate. His hooves shattered the surface into glass-like shards and he shook his head and snickered like a naughty schoolboy.

'I told Gus you'd made a promise to her friend to follow it up.'

Angus, better known as Gus, was Elle's mortuary assistant. As much a part of the place as the autopsy table he washed

190

down between examinations. He'd been on Elle's team for as long anyone could remember. A friendly, but solitary young man who wore Marvel-comic T-shirts under his scrubs, and smoked cannabis at the weekends.

'He'd said he felt sorry for her – not having a family,' Elle said.

'Can't see Gus telling Callum.'

'Me neither, but that's the only time I mentioned it. A passing remark. Just chat to pass the time.'

I couldn't imagine wanting to indulge in idle banter over a corpse on a mortuary slab, but I knew that's how it was down there. Chatter, gossip and endless cups of tea. A way to maintain a sense of normality in what was a most abnormal place to spend your working day.

'And there was no one else present?' I pressed.

'Only the police officer, sent to observe.'

'Remember who it was?'

'Young girl. DC in HMET. Pleasant enough. Liz . . . or Bet?'

'Beth?'

'Could be. Ask Gus. He'll check the duty log.'

My stomach suddenly felt hollow. I'd eliminated the possibility of one friend being treacherous, only to replace her with another. I wasn't sure which felt worse. But Beth made more sense. A cop, on Callum's team.

As we rode down the hill, back into the valley, we passed outcrops of large flat stone slabs, rising out of the snow like irregular rows of ancient teeth.

Called 'wolf stones', by some locals. The ancient 'vaccary walls' were medieval cattle enclosures. Another reminder, if one were needed, of the timelessness of this place. I pulled up the collar of my waxed jacket and marvelled at the resilience of people who'd carved a living out of this unforgiving environment.

'Did you say I was planning on going "off-piste" by any chance?'

'Can't remember. Wasn't expecting to be cross-examined about the exact words I used in a casual conversation.'

'Sorry. It's a term you use. Callum repeated it. Made me think of you, that's all.'

'Well, at the risk of being predictable, I'll use it now.' She halted Sundance at the top of a wide, open stretch of moorland.

Across the valley, I could see her house. A large grey-stone farmhouse nestled in a natural dip in the moorland, and surrounded by trees. 'Fancy going off-piste?'

Sundance sidestepped impatiently beneath her, knowing this was their usual place for a gallop.

'Race you.'

Sundance sprang forward, lunging, breakneck across the smooth snow.

Butch stomped the ground, tossing his head, eager to follow. I leaned over and patted his neck, then urged him on. He launched us both down the hill – hind legs kicking back, almost bucking in pleasure at the sudden, reckless freedom.

Chapter Thirty-Four

Monday Morning, Fordley

I drove down the street, trying to make out the house numbers along the row. Slowing to look at the address written in Jen's neat script.

A net curtain falling back into place told me I'd found what I was looking for.

By the time I pulled into a space in front of the house, the door was being opened by a man I recognised – even though I hadn't seen him for over twenty years.

Jack Halton hadn't changed much. Now in his mid-fifties, he was a little thicker around the middle and had a few more lines. Unusually for winter, the salt-and-pepper in his dark hair was offset by a deep suntan.

He smiled as he held open the door to usher me in to the neat semi-detached house on the outskirts of Fordley.

'I daren't even count the years,' he said over his shoulder as I followed him down the hall.

'You look just the same,' I said as he showed me into the lounge.

'Liar.' He laughed. 'You look good on it though.' He shifted a pile of books from the armchair for me to sit. 'I'll get the kettle on. Tea OK?'

'Always.'

I stood admiring a wall of framed certificates and commendations presented to him over thirty-years of policing. 'Impressive.'

'The wife called it the "Wailing Wall".' He laughed as he went into the kitchen. 'That's how she saw the job. Nothing but misery for her.'

'Do you miss it?' I called.

'Only every minute of every day,' came the disembodied reply.

Coloured lights on the Christmas tree flickered across silver picture frames on the sideboard and mantelpiece. Family snaps of him and his wife, and a handsome young man in military uniform.

I sat in the armchair as he came in with the tea. 'Your son?' I asked, nodding at the photo.

'Yes. Marines. He's out now. Works with me these days. I set up a security consultancy when I retired. Closest I could get to the job, I suppose.' He took a sip of tea. 'Keeps the wolf from the door – that and the police pension. Some of the lads I used to work with joined us. Mostly overseas contracts. Just got back from a job in the Middle East, as it happens.'

That accounts for the tan.

'And your wife?'

'She passed away – five years ago. Cancer.'

'I'm sorry.'

He sat back on the sofa, his demeanour signalling an end to our small talk. 'Your secretary called. It's him, isn't it? Malecki – the reason you're here?'

I nodded, putting my cup on the coffee table. I told him about the unexpected VO and my visit to Wakefield.

'Thought he'd died in prison. Or maybe I just hoped he had. You know, in all my years as a copper, I never believed in the concept of evil – not until the day I looked into Malecki's eyes.'

'Did you interview him after his arrest?'

He shook his head. 'Wasn't high enough up the food chain, even though it was my find in his car that caught him. I actually got a bollocking for that.'

194

'What happened?'

'After the media campaign, we were inundated with names. Malecki was one of them – especially after the photofit was released. I'd even brought him in, earlier in the investigation. I told the SIO I liked him for it, but it never panned out. Then I read your profile and so much about him fitted, but when I passed *that* on, the bosses regarded it as hokum.' He shot me a glance. 'No offence.'

I smiled. 'None taken.'

'It was at a morning briefing that I heard about the accident. Malecki's car was in the police compound. It was too good an opportunity to pass up.'

'Synchronicity,' I murmured.

'Jackpot. A murder kit hidden in the boot. Everything we needed – right there on a plate. But technically, the search was illegal, because I didn't have a warrant. Malecki's lawyers tried to have it disregarded and I got hauled over the coals for it.'

'You're kidding.'

'Thankfully the judge ruled it admissible, because it was compelling and pivotal to the case.'

'Common sense prevailed then.'

'Some days it felt like the system wasn't on our side, but that day it was, for once.'

I cut to the chase. 'Malecki gave me an account of what happened with Michelle Hatfield. I don't believe his version. Was hoping you could fill in the gaps?'

'I was a junior officer in CID, then. Doing the legwork. Trace, interview, eliminate. Not sure how helpful I can be.'

'He said that after he tried chatting her up, when they argued in the street, he'd gone back to the pub to try again a week later.'

'And?'

195

'She agreed to go out with him. They dated a couple of times, but she'd been jealous of the attention he was getting from other girls. An argument about it got out of hand and he killed her by accident.'

He shook his head. 'She had a boyfriend at the time of her disappearance and it wasn't Malecki.'

'Mark Lutner,' I said.

He nodded. 'Poor bastard. Newspapers crucified him, but they weren't as quick to come back with a public apology once Malecki was charged.'

'What happened to him?'

'The family moved away. Who can blame them?'

'Was Malecki asked about the incident with the taxi driver?'

Jack nodded. 'Said he started stalking Michelle. Became obsessed, by his own admission. Admitted kidnapping and killing her, but wouldn't say what he'd done with the body. Don't know why he'd say she was his girlfriend – that's cobblers.'

I'd come across this kind of 'twisted narrative' more times than I cared to count. Many offenders, even the worst, seemed blind to their own nature. Most tried to justify what they'd done. Create a story they could live with. Or there were elements of the offence that they wouldn't or couldn't acknowledge. Not to investigators, or their families – even to themselves.

For those imprisoned for sex offences, this 'altered truth' was an attempt to protect themselves from retribution. Their crimes were seen as the lowest of the low in the prison hierarchy, where offences are stratified by inmates.

Maybe Malecki altered the truth about Michelle, after his jugging in Broadmoor? Or to prevent more attacks once he was sent to Wakefield?

'When we found out she'd flicked him the finger,' Jack was saying, 'we wondered if that's why he cut it off.'

'What did he say?'

'Nothing. It was a kind of control for him, I suppose.' He took another mouthful of tea. 'He did shed light on one thing, though.'

'Oh?'

'The date of her disappearance . . .'

'Fifteenth of July?'

'Three days before his nineteenth birthday. Said she was a birthday present to himself.'

Something occurred to me, as I jotted notes in my pad. 'Do you know what he did on his *actual* birthday?'

'Went back home. His parents had a party for him that weekend. I remember, because the mother tried to alibi him for the time Michelle disappeared.'

'Even though he'd confessed?'

He nodded. 'Mother was a right domineering bitch. Would argue black was white where her darling son was concerned. She tried telling us that Malecki was at her place on Wednesday, so couldn't have kidnapped Michelle. But the car company records told a different story. He'd picked the car up on Wednesday afternoon and drove home the next day. The father remembered events more clearly – even after all those years – because it hit him in the pocket.'

'How do you mean?'

'They'd hired the car and the father was pissed off because Malecki had exceeded the mileage charges. Think they argued the toss with the company, but ended up paying.'

'Malecki always used hire cars, never his own, when he killed.'

Jack nodded. 'He'd passed his test and the parents offered to buy him a car. But he said he didn't need one. Lived within walking distance of university and a short cycle ride to his part-time job in Grantchester.'

'Where Graham Hirst was killed.'

'That's obviously where their paths crossed. Why he picked him, is anyone's guess.'

Sometimes I just see them in the street . . .

He studied me for a moment, before asking, 'Why the pre-occupation with Malecki? Surely the focus is on catching this latest copycat?'

'It could be someone known to Malecki. An ex-con. Or someone who writes to him in prison. Is there anything you can remember, from those days, that might tie in?'

He sat forward, resting elbows on his knees. 'I had my sources on the streets. All good cops did. I drank in a local pub where hacks from the press hung out. Crime reporter for the *Express* was a regular.'

'Tom Hannah?'

'That's him. There were a few whispers that he got a bit too cosy with his subjects . . .'

'In what way?'

He shrugged. 'It was all rumour, but word was, some seri-ous villains on our patch used him to grass up rivals. Would give him tip-offs about what the others were up to – he'd get an exclusive and the competition would be put away. Win-win.'

'Suppose he was helping you in a weird way,' I mused.

Jack didn't look convinced. 'I got a few collars from his intel, so I can't complain. But I used to wonder more about the stuff he *didn't* tell us.'

'How do you mean?'

'There were some things a crime reporter would have been all over, but he'd seem less enthusiastic than he should.' He shrugged. 'Those were the ones I felt he'd been told to leave alone, by the people who had him in their pockets.'

'Such as?'

'The worst incident was a fire. Flat on Manchester Road. Guy who lived there, Dave Finch, was killed and we had it down as arson. I was due to work it, but got pulled off to help on Malecki's last murder.'

'Kath?'

'Hmm, you see why I'd remember it. Anyway, word was Finch owed serious money to some big boys. His trade was selling pirated Disney movies. The latest blockbusters. He'd film them in the cinema the week they came out, then run copies to sell on market stalls.'

I smiled at the memory. 'Used to go round to my friend's house to watch those. You'd get distracted by silhouettes of people crossing in front of the camera, getting up to go to the loo.'

'When officers got into the flat, they found racks of VHS recorders set up to produce copies, but no tapes. Nothing. Place had been cleaned out.'

'The people he owed?' I hazarded a guess. 'Taking goods to the value of?'

'So why not take the equipment?' Jack frowned. 'That was worth more than the tapes.'

'Anyone arrested?'

'No. The estate went as quiet as a mouse. Couldn't get anyone to talk. It was the sort of thing Hannah *should* have been all over.'

'But he wasn't?'

Jack shook his head. 'Turned up at the scene, went through the motions, but nothing came of it. The *Express* ran an article, but it was a skim job, and Hannah never really dug for it. That was one I suspected he'd been warned off. Case was still open when I retired.'

'Think he took payouts?'

'Nothing you could say was illegal. Immoral maybe. Not cash, perks. Meals in expensive restaurants. Holidays in the Costa del Crime. He'd give us information when it suited him – so he kept the cops on side. I bought him a few rounds in the pub during the Relay Killer investigation, to see if he'd heard anything on the grapevine.'

'And did he? Give you anything?'

'No. Got more information from the big players in the city at the time, to be honest. Even the worst crooks in the parish wanted that killer caught. Those crimes were an abomination to "honest" villains. Besides, it was bad for business having so many cops on the streets. Think they were as happy as we were when Malecki got banged up. But Hannah was obsessed with the case back then – not in a healthy way.'

I reflected back on my own fascination at the time and shifted uncomfortably.

'Unhealthy, how?'

'More salacious, somehow. Got off on the details a bit too much. Something about him . . .' He shook his head. 'He wanted access to the investigation, in return for anything he might hear. The team held him at arm's length. Most of them thought he was a bit of a weirdo, to be honest. Can't say I was surprised when he brought out the book. He was a real fan of Malecki.'

'A *fan*?' That piqued my interest.

'Was surprised when I heard they had a falling-out in the last couple of years.'

'Over what?'

'No idea. They were thick as thieves when the book came out. Then things changed. A mate of mine has a son in the prison service – was at Wakefield for a while. Said Malecki began refusing all Hannah's requests for a visit.'

200

'Interesting.'

'If this copycat *is* someone Malecki knows, or has known in the past, Hannah might have heard about it.'

I made a note.

'*This* new killer,' Jack said as he watched me write, 'does he take trophies?'

'No. Why?'

'Because that was one of the things that bothered me back then. Family of some victims mentioned things had gone missing and you'd said in your profile, the killer *would* take souvenirs. Instinct told me you were right. We never found any trophies when his place was searched.'

'Suppose once you had an arrest, potential trophies weren't a priority.'

'You were right about his notebooks though. I found one on Dennis Haverley when I searched the car. We never found notes on any of the others. But there would have been some – without a doubt.' His gaze was intense. 'So, where the hell did he keep them, and why have they never been found?'

'Maybe that's something he'll tell us now,' I said, almost to myself.

'Well, if that sadistic bastard is in a sharing mood, ask him where Michelle is. Recovering her body is still something that haunts those of us who were involved at the time.' He stared past me as he recalled those times. His voice was barely a whisper as he added, 'The things he did . . . still give me bloody nightmares.'

Chapter Thirty-Five

The call from Fordley Police Station came as I was driving back from Jack Halton's place. Supt. Warner wanted to see me.

It was evident from the tone of the summons that it wasn't going to be pleasant.

Nothing new there then.

I put in a call to Jen, to tell her I'd be delayed.

'I'm not happy about you visiting Malecki again. I know it's what we do . . . Dealing with people like him.' Her disembodied voice came over the car speakers.

'But?'

'He's probably the most dangerous you've ever dealt with . . .'

I thought back over the last couple of years. 'Not sure about that one, Jen.'

'Well, OK . . . The most dangerous one who's still alive, then.'

She had a point. I'd encountered some of the most depraved offenders in the criminal justice system, but most had either been killed or died in prison.

'I'm worried about you getting involved,' she was saying. 'I am allowed to care, aren't I?'

'Glad someone does.' Something tugged deep inside when I thought about Callum. He'd cared once.

'Not least, because of what happened to Kath, and Geoff. It feels a bit too close to home.'

'Do you think they'd be letting me anywhere near this, if there was a choice?'

'There's always a choice . . . Doesn't have to be you.'

'Malecki won't talk to anyone else.'

'But that means you have to get inside his head.' I could almost hear her shudder.

'That's the job, Jen.'

She blew out a breath in frustration. 'Well, I've been doing the research you asked for. Everything on him since his transfer to Wakefield.'

'How much more can there be? He doesn't exactly get out much.'

'No, but he's still reported on quite often.'

'Oh?'

'His charity, Rebuild, has been in the news, after the tsunami in Indonesia – they made a big donation. But it's his paintings that crop up more than anything.'

I frowned as I negotiated traffic. 'The governor said his last exhibition was a flop.'

'True,' Jen agreed, 'people turned up, ate the cheese and drank the wine, but didn't buy much. But critics were gushing about some of the pieces.'

'Malecki's been painting more, recently.'

'Probably because they're planning a new exhibition. There was an article on it in the *Telegraph* and *Argus*.'

'When?'

'Dates not released yet. But apparently his art is being considered as part of a new educational pathway programme at the prison, accredited by Manchester University.'

Malecki the educator. Part of his rehabilitation, no doubt.

* * *

Warner was pacing in front of her office window, hands clasped behind her back. I felt like a kid dragged into the headmistress's office.

'You should have told me, Jo.'

'I was going to call you later today.'

'You *should* have informed us, as soon as you got Malecki's VO.' She rounded on me, resting her hands on the back of her chair. 'Or did you think the prison liaison officer would forget to keep us in the loop and your trip to Wakefield might go unnoticed?'

'No, but—'

'No "buts", Jo.' She dropped down into the chair behind her desk. 'This is the *second* time you've gone off on your own during a live investigation. You're not behaving like a team player.'

'I'm no longer *on* the team, am I?'

'You *are* as far as I'm concerned, but you're not making my life easy.'

I suddenly felt bone-weary. 'I got the VO on Friday, same day I got your email, saying you didn't need me for anything else. The visit was Saturday—'

'We *do* work weekends.'

I ran a hand across my eyes, trying to ward off a headache. 'I decided to see what Malecki wanted first. If it wasn't a waste of your time and resources, I fully intended to pass it on. Jen is writing up the notes. You should get her email this afternoon.'

'I don't have time to wait. So, I'll have the edited highlights now, if it's all the same.'

I told her everything – from my conversation with the governor, to meeting Malecki and that I'd just visited Jack Halton.

When I finished, she sat back and regarded me across the desk.

'Do you think Malecki's done prison time with this copycat?'

'Possibly. Or the killer is an admirer on the outside.'

She began jotting notes for herself. 'Not happy that he said he'll only talk to you.'

'Not thrilled about it myself.'

'Think he's got anything worth telling us?'

I shrugged. 'He's not doing it to be a good citizen, that's for sure. But there's only one way to find out.' I met her gaze. 'We can stop anytime. But if we *don't* engage and it turns out he knows something useful . . .' I let the inference dangle.

She nodded. 'OK. But this has got to be done under strict guidelines, Jo. No more going off half-cocked.' She stopped and her eyes seemed to bore into my head. 'So, with that in mind . . . is there anything else you want to tell me?'

I told her about Tom Hannah.

After listening, she nodded slowly. 'If an experienced officer like Jack Halton had a bad feeling about Hannah, that's good enough for me. The passage of time can change allegiances. Especially as they've had a falling-out. Hannah could have a name of someone he suspects. I'll call a briefing to bring everyone up to speed. As for your next meeting with Malecki, it has to be recorded, that's none negotiable, Jo.'

I'd expected her to tell me one of the SIOs would take my place – I said as much.

'You and I both know Malecki won't agree. He's made it clear he'll only speak to you. Besides, you understand his psychology, as much as anyone can. You're the only person who can get close enough to play mind games with him.'

Even as I agreed, that quiet, insistent voice was whispering in the dark recesses of my mind.

Damaged psyches have serrated edges. Get too close and they'll cut you to pieces.

Chapter Thirty-Six

Monday Afternoon, Fordley Police Station

Warner sat at the head of the table in the major incident room, flanked by Callum and DI Wardman. Some members of the joint investigation teams were there. The rest were out following up hundreds of actions generated by the enquiry.

'What's your impression of Malecki, Jo?' Warner asked.

Where to start?

'Malecki has two identifiable personality disorders. Narcissism and psychopathy. Among other character traits, that means he has an exaggerated sense of self, a lack of fear and empathy for others and feels no remorse. He's been diagnosed as a malignant psychopath, and they're cold, calculating and manipulative.'

'He's manipulating *you*.' Wardman pinned me with a look he hoped was intimidating. 'Clicking his fingers, so you go running. Hinting that he can help, when all he's really doing is getting his jollies, being at the centre of a major investigation.'

Warner cut in before I could reply. 'We've covered that, Philip. If it proves fruitless, we won't waste the resources. I've authorised Jo to visit again, then we can make a judgement call.' She looked to me. 'Jo?'

'Malecki's so narcissistic, he thinks we should be grateful to have his offer of help. He wants us to appreciate the insight he can give us into his craft.'

'*Craft?*' DS Morgan snorted. 'Bloody hell!'

'That's how he sees it.'

I knew how bizarre it appeared. The way monsters like Malecki considered themselves and their crimes. Perhaps I'd worked with killers and sexual deviants for so long that their twisted logic no longer surprised me. Seeing the reaction of others served as a stark reminder.

'He says he's changed, that he genuinely wants to help as a way of "paying back".'

'So, we let a mentally deranged nutter call the shots?' Wardman said.

'Psychopathy isn't classified as a mental illness. Malecki – horrific as he is – doesn't satisfy the legal criteria for insanity. While it might be comforting to explain his crimes as the act of a lunatic, he isn't one. Writing him off as a madman is to seriously underestimate him.'

'So, if he isn't mad,' Warner said, 'why did he do what he did?'

'He liked it,' I said simply.

'He's offering to tell us how our copycat thinks, the moves he might make. And you believe he'll do that?' Wardman sounded less than convinced.

'There's precedent for it.' Callum suddenly spoke, drawing everyone's attention. 'Ted Bundy offered to help detectives catch the Green River Killer, in the States. He predicted the killer was returning to the victims' graves, and advised police to stake out any new site they found. Bundy was right. If police had acted on his information, Gary Ridgway would have been caught sooner and fewer women would have died.'

'Bundy was jealous of the attention the Green River Killer was getting,' I added – grateful for Callum's unexpected support on this one. 'Much the same as Malecki is annoyed at being copied by a killer he sees as inferior.'

'Bundy wanted a role for himself as some kind of consultant to the FBI,' Callum went on. 'Thought if he could show he was useful to them, it might give him a stay of execution – literally.'

'Bundy also did it to demonstrate some kind of remorse,' I added. 'Repentance for his crimes. Malecki is claiming the same thing.'

Wardman shot me a look of utter contempt. 'Repentance, my arse! There are just as many instances of criminals offering help that led precisely nowhere. So, just how long are you going to indulge him?'

'Until he shits or gets off the pot!' I said bluntly, gratified by the look of revulsion on Wardman's face. DI Heslopp choked back a snigger. 'We give him one more meeting – see if he delivers.'

'Agreed.' Warner's tone was final. 'We can't afford to ignore the possibility that he could come up with a lead. In the meantime, you've all seen the notes from Jo's visit.'

'Team are pulling together a list of prisons he's been in,' DS Ian Drummond said. 'Looking at anyone he seemed close to who's subsequently been released.'

'That'll be a bloody long list,' Wardman said. 'After twenty-odd years inside.'

'Shorter than you think,' Ian countered. 'He's been in solitary for most of it – apart from Broadmoor. Had more socialisation time there. But most of his fellow inmates are either dead or still inside. Not *that* many fit the criteria of having a pulse and being out.'

'Good,' Warner said. 'If he *does* provide a name, we won't have to waste time tracking them down.'

'Then there are his admirers on the outside,' I added.

'Prison are sending over a list of his most regular correspondents and a dip-sample of the fan mail.' Callum read from his notes.

'*Fans?*' Wardman was incredulous. 'Seriously?'

'He gets love letters,' DC Shah Akhtar said.

'Not just from women, either,' I added.

Wardman's face was a picture. 'What is wrong with these people?'

'Hybristophilia,' I said simply.

'Hybrid—what?' asked Heslopp.

I glanced at the curmudgeonly DI. 'A sexual attraction to someone who's committed an outrageous crime – usually rape or murder. Used to be called "Bonnie and Clyde syndrome". Bonnie Parker suffered from it and that's why she was drawn to dangerous men – like Clyde Barrow.'

'I don't get it.' DS Morgan frowned. 'It's sick.'

'In nature, the females of the species mate with the strongest alpha males. It's a survival thing,' I said.

'We're talking about humans here, not animals in the zoo,' Wardman said.

I thought about all the sadistic things I'd seen one human being do to another and I knew people were closer to their primeval ancestors than we'd like to think.

Heslopp cleared his throat. 'So, these women who marry killers on death row? That's this hybristo-whatsit?'

'Predominantly women, but men too.' I looked up, to see Callum watching me. I held his gaze as I added, 'And at least you know where they are every night.'

'That's a given,' Heslopp said with a grim smile. 'On death row.'

'Others who get involved in this type of "prison romance" have a saviour complex,' I went on. 'Believing they can change a man as dangerous as a serial killer.'

'The thrill, I suppose,' Warner mused. 'Being close to an apex predator. Someone who might want to kill you, but knowing he's contained . . . can't get to you.'

'The human equivalent of being lowered into the sea in a shark cage,' I said, thinking back to Malecki on the other side of that perspex screen. 'Watching a great white shark biting the bars – trying to find a way in to you.'

'Is that how it felt?' Callum asked, his voice low, as if we were the only two people in the room.

I looked at him, caught by the question – and the concerned tone in his voice, which was totally unexpected.

'Yes,' I said quietly. 'That's exactly how it felt.'

The moment between us was broken as Warner turned to Callum.

'What do we know about this journalist, Tom Hannah?'

'Obviously not a journalist now, ma'am, but still has contacts in the press and, some say, in the underworld too. He's actually in the system.'

'For what?'

'Accusations of domestic violence in the nineties. His marriage was a volatile one. They both drank and sometimes things would escalate. His wife called us out more than once. He'd get locked up for the night, but then she'd refuse to press charges, so it never came to court. Living off benefits and a scant pension. He writes articles for some true crime magazines these days, but that's about it. Prison Liaison provided some interesting info.' He glanced at his iPad. 'While they were writing the book, Hannah was a regular visitor to Malecki. Then their relationship broke down for some reason and there was no contact until six months ago – when, out of the blue, Malecki sent the journalist a VO.'

'Did Hannah go?' I asked.

'Like a shot. Then went again two weeks later. Hannah sent numerous requests after that, but Malecki refused them all.'

I thought back to my conversation with the governor. 'Six months ago was when Malecki started painting seriously again. Getting pieces ready for a new exhibition.'

'The two things aren't related,' Wardman said dismissively.

'Maybe not.' I couldn't muster the energy to argue with some-one who was determined to take an opposite stance to anything I had to say – just because I'd said it.

Callum read from the file. 'I've put in a request for the prison's visitors log covering the period from six months ago until now.'

Wardman shot him a look. 'Why wasn't I informed?'

'I'm telling you now.' Callum's expression flashed an unmistakable warning the other man couldn't miss. Wardman opened his mouth to say something, then thought better of it.

'In the meantime,' Warner said, 'I want Jo to visit Hannah with one of your team, Callum. See what he can tell us.'

'I can take that one, boss,' Ian piped up. 'I know Hannah from my days on the beat.'

'Know him well?'

'Not really. He knew everything on the manor worth know-ing. Had his ear to the ground, but never gave us much. But I'm a face he'll know. Might make breaking the ice a bit easier.'

'OK. You take it.'

People were more reticent in the presence of a police officer. They were guarded about what they said or how they said it. Nothing was ever 'off the record' when a cop was in the room. It made my job of reading them even more tricky. But given the situation, I really couldn't object.

Warner gathered her notes. 'After that, we need you to visit Malecki again, see if he can give us a list. Ready for that, Jo?'

I nodded. Not sure that I was ready for that at all.

Chapter Thirty-Seven

Monday Evening, Fordley

Tom Hannah lived in a small, pre-war terrace house, a mile from Fordley town centre. An area that had once housed workers in the textile mills, now one of the least desirable postcodes in the city.

Cheap housing had attracted landlords who rented to students or those on the lowest incomes. Maximising profit for minimum investment meant the area had become run-down and neglected.

Rows of identical terraces were separated by ginnels and cobbled backstreets where kids played football or cricket, safe in the knowledge that their makeshift sportsground was too narrow to be a cut-through for traffic.

Most backyards still had the original stone outhouses – called 'middens' by the older generation. People like my maternal grandmother, who could remember having to brave the cold to use an outdoor toilet before government grants financed the luxury of indoor bathrooms.

Gone were the women of a post-war generation, who took pride in scrubbing the front steps, sweeping the cobbles and bleaching their net curtains. Now, the inhabitants of these streets, with a few resilient exceptions, seemed more inclined to use the backyards as dumping grounds for their junk. The old stone privies were home to broken washing machines, torn sofas and weather-soaked mattresses.

Hannah's house was no exception. Despite being forewarned about our visit, he cautiously cracked open the front door and peered at us through the inch-wide gap, dissected by a security chain. Finally giving a disgruntled nod as he recognised Ian Drummond.

'Tom, this is Jo Mc—'

'I know who she is,' Hannah cut across him as he slipped the chain to let us in.

'Pleased to meet you, Mr Hannah.' I smiled, refusing to be offended as he turned his back on me and walked into the house.

The hall carpet felt sticky under the soles of my boots as we followed him down a dimly lit corridor to the kitchen. I stood at the back door, looking through the grimy glass into the yard, with its overflowing wheelie bin surrounded by black bin bags. Some torn by the wind, or maybe by urban foxes that claimed the streets at night.

An inch of frozen snow gave a temporarily pristine covering to the detritus that poked through in places. The whole scene made me feel depressed suddenly.

I was half listening to the small talk between the two men as Hannah went through the ritual of boiling the kettle.

'Don't have any tea,' he said, after asking me if I wanted a brew. 'I only drink coffee.'

Glancing at the unwashed pots stacked in the sink, I felt a sense of reprieve.

'Coffee's fine for me, Tom,' Drummond said breezily.

'Lucky for you, I've got sugar,' Hannah grunted over his shoulder. 'No milk though.'

'Just as it comes then.'

With the formalities over, we followed him into the small front lounge.

Old articles from the *Express* were framed and hung on the walls. Each one had Tom Hannah's byline prominently highlighted.

They reminded me of Jack Halton's Wailing Wall of commendations, but far more salacious. Mug shots of infamous murderers stared out from some. Others had grainy black and white shots of drug seizures or triumphant police officers standing on the steps of the Crown Court. Malecki and his crimes were conspicuous by their absence. The only reference was a framed image of the cover of Hannah's book.

Hannah took one of the two armchairs beside the hearth and leaned forward, staring into the orange glow of the fake-coal gas fire. Cradling the coffee mug in both hands.

Ian indicated for me to take the other chair, but I declined with a half-shake of my head and went to stand by the window. Hannah didn't even glance my way, which suited me fine. My job was even easier if I didn't have to interact with the man. Ian settled himself in the other chair.

I stood with my back to the window, making myself a silhouette. Impossible for him to read my face or see my eyes.

The recent murders were headline news. There was no point beating about the bush.

'We want to speak to you about Jacob Malecki,' Ian said.

'Of course, you do.' Hannah snorted. 'Who else? All over the bloody news right now, isn't he? Loving every minute of it.'

'You know him, Tom, better than most.'

'Not anymore.' Hannah's bitterness was obvious.

'You used to be close. Then he refused your visit requests. Why was that?'

'You'll have to ask him.'

'He won't say.'

Hannah shot him a look. 'I don't believe that.'

'Why not?'

'Because Jacob has an opinion about everything, and he usually can't resist sharing it.'

'What happened?' Ian pressed.

Hannah's eyes never left the fire. 'It's no secret, the book didn't sell like we'd hoped.'

'That didn't cause the falling out between you ... What did?'

Hannah looked at the detective then, his eyes as cold as the ice on the window. 'My publishers wanted a sequel. Offered a big advance, if I could get Jacob to reveal more ... An exclusive.' His voice faltered and he took a breath. 'But the bastard wouldn't agree. Even when I told him that a production company were in discussions about a documentary, but only if there was a second book.'

'And only if it had new material?' Ian said.

'Not new ... explosive.'

'Like what?'

'What really happened between him and Michelle Hatfield.' Hannah put his cup down on the hearth. 'Over the years, Jacob's given various accounts. Even claimed she'd dated him, but that wasn't true. He'd asked her out, when she worked in the pub. But she turned him down, then humiliated him. His ego couldn't stand that. That's why he killed her.'

'And you wanted an exposé?'

'She was his first victim,' Hannah murmured. 'That's where it all started, where he got a taste for it. We wanted the full story. And the rest.'

'The rest?'

'Documentary-makers wanted to know what he'd done with her body.'

'And he refused?' I spoke for the first time.

He looked at me and slowly nodded. 'He knew I needed it. I was struggling financially. He could have turned everything around. On the back of the documentary, the production company were planning a true crime series – with me fronting the episodes.' He looked around the room, as if seeing it for the first time. 'I use to have a detached house in a good part of Fordley. Nice car. When the money dried up, so did the wife. She couldn't get out fast enough.' He sneered at the memory. 'The split left me potless. The book, the TV, could have changed everything. Instead, I ended up in this shithole.'

'And that's what you argued about?' I asked.

'He would have benefitted too,' Hannah snapped. 'It would have been dynamite. Every newspaper and TV station would run that story if he'd give up her body.'

A memory flashed through my mind from 1986. Watching the news with my parents. Shaky images taken from a helicopter, hovering above Saddleworth Moor, north-west England, as Myra Hindley, surrounded by police, led a search for the burial sites of two victims, killed by her and Ian Brady two decades earlier.

There was a public outcry, at what was seen by many as an expensive publicity stunt. Compounded months later, when Brady was taken to the moors for the same purpose.

Mercifully, one victim was recovered and her body returned to her grieving family. The other – Keith Bennett – never was. Despite his desperate mother's fight, until her death, to get his killers to reveal where her son was buried. Saddleworth Moor was keeping its grim secrets to this day.

I'd seen the fallout of brutal deaths, up close. Witnessed the destruction of grieving families, denied the peace of knowing what had happened to their loved ones. I understood only too well what giving up that secret would mean to Michelle's parents. Understood too, the power and control Malecki wielded by not cooperating.

A malicious last defiance. Cruel and calculating. To hold on to information and take pleasure in watching people like Hannah fawn around him in an attempt to get him to oblige.

'Six months ago, he finally sent you a VO,' I said. 'Why?'

'Just wanted to jerk my lead.'

'What did he want?' Ian asked.

'Same question I asked.' Hannah sat back in his chair. 'He just made small talk. Waited for him to get to the point, but it was all bollocks.'

'You didn't ask him outright why he wanted to see you?' I asked.

'Of course, I bloody did.' Hannah rounded on me. 'Have you ever tried getting Jacob Malecki to tell you more than he wants? He said he was "checking on me" – his exact words. Like a parent, summoning a child.' He blew out his cheeks. 'Bloody patronising bastard. I told him if he was playing games, he could get stuffed. I asked him again about the book, or speaking to the TV company, and he flatly refused.'

'So why did you go back two weeks later?' Ian asked.

'He said he might reconsider.'

'And?'

'He made a show of thinking about it. But in the end, dismissed the idea, and me with it.' In a burst of frustrated energy, Hannah suddenly stood up and paced in front of the hearth. 'He was just ringing a bell to make me salivate – like Pavlov's dog.'

Something was nagging at me.

Words.

'When you said Malecki was "checking on" you, what did he say, exactly?'

Hannah frowned, not seeing the relevance.

'It was his usual philosophical bullshit. He goes off on these rambling monologues about human nature and the way people think. His own potted psychology. Then throws out questions that make you feel like you're being tested in some kind of bizarre quiz.'

'What kind of questions?'

'His specialist subject. Killing. Could I do it? What would drive me to it? All the time, implying he knows you, better than you know yourself.' He shot me a disdainful look. 'Like some shrink analysing you from across the room.'

'And how did you answer?' I asked, refusing to be baited.

Hannah shrugged. 'I played along. It was a subject we'd covered before.'

'And did you say you could kill?' I pressed.

For some reason, he couldn't meet my eyes. Directed his remarks to Ian. 'I said I thought anybody could – given the right provocation.'

The DS regarded the journalist over the rim of his mug as he took a mouthful of coffee. 'We think this copycat might be someone he spent time with in prison, or who writes to him. Can you think of anyone?'

'There are plenty who write.'

'Anybody stand out?' Ian asked.

'Mostly damaged women – sad old cows, who kid themselves they're in a relationship with him.'

'What about people who've served time with him?' I asked.

'There was someone in Broadmoor. Young guy Jacob called his "protégé". Was in for killing his mother and sister. Hero-worshipped Jacob.'

'Name?' Ian was suddenly interested.

'Daren Wallace.'

'Do you know if he's still inside?'

218

'Not sure. The staff didn't like the effect Jacob was having on the kid, so they separated them. That's why Jacob killed the doctor and ended up getting shipped to Wakefield.'

'OK. We'll check him out.'

Hannah ran a hand across his unshaven chin. 'The seriously weird ones are on the fan sites. That's where you find the real sickos. If I were you, I'd start there.'

Chapter Thirty-Eight

Monday Evening, Fordley Police Station

I stared at the screen in disbelief. An officer from the cyber unit, introduced to me as Lee, scrolled through an internet site.

'Are these legitimate?' I was incredulous.

'They're genuine, if that's what you mean,' he said, not looking up, 'but a lot of their content is illegal. This is the dark web. If they were in the open, they'd be taken down.'

The pages looked like any you might find for fans of the latest pop idols, but dealing in far darker subjects. Dedicated to serial killers, like Ted Bundy and Jeffrey Dahmer, the cannibal killer.

The officer tapped the screen. 'This one for Dahmer is called "McDahmer's", like the fast food –'

'Yes.' I held up a hand in disgust. 'I get it.'

'There's even merchandise,' my guide said, leading the way on our bizarre tour. I stared, at locks of hair; signed photographs; even worn underwear, sent by prisoners to their ardent fans, who then sold them online. Like a macabre version of eBay.

But it was the discussion forums I was interested in. 'Can we get into those?' I asked.

At the click of a button, we were plunged into conversations that would be the stuff of most people's nightmares.

Some were almost academic by those who seemed fascinated to understand what made these people 'tick'.

The majority though were far more disturbing, with memes mocking the victims or their families. Graphic crime scene photographs, in shocking detail, with captions that generated a sickening humour on the forums.

'Here's Malecki's.' Lee said.

Mainly women, but men too, talking about their sexual attraction to Malecki and his 'film star' looks. One man even posting a tattoo of Malecki's face, inked across his entire back.

'I'm tracking the ones who've written to Malecki or visited him in prison,' the officer said.

'Are there many?'

He shrugged. 'Lots of letter writers. We're concentrating on those who've had regular correspondence in the last couple of years. There are only a few who've actually visited him.'

I knew the plan was for the team to compare those lists with the prison logs.

'Can you also get a list of people who are trading in Malecki souvenirs – maybe track who they're selling to as well?'

'Already on it.'

Chapter Thirty-Nine

Tuesday Morning, Wakefield Prison

It was almost two weeks since Callum had called me about Barbara Thorpe's murder. It already felt like I hadn't thought about anything else, for decades. In some ways, perhaps that was true.

I was waiting down in the segregation unit of the Monster Mansion. In the same room I'd been in just a few days before. Same, but different, because this time I didn't feel totally alone.

There was a voice recorder on the table beside me. The governor informed Malecki that recording the session was a non-negotiable condition and, much to my surprise, he'd agreed.

My thoughts were interrupted by the sound of keys rattling in the lock. The heavy metal door swung open and Malecki was led in. The prison officer waited until his charge was seated and, with a quick glance in my direction, left us, closing and locking the door behind him.

'Good to see you again, Doctor.' Malecki smiled. He looked relaxed. Almost sociable, as if we were meeting for afternoon tea.

'You have something for me?' I didn't want to engage in pleasantries.

'Why so brusque, Doctor? Does the recorder make you uncomfortable?'

'Not at all.'

'Then perhaps it's what I said ... about your father?' He frowned slightly. 'If that's the case, I'm sorry. I didn't reveal those things to upset you. Just to prove how candid I was prepared to be.'

My abruptness was a defence mechanism. An attempt to keep him at arm's length. His disclosure had thrown me and I'd found myself re-evaluating Malecki. My perception of him shifting, despite myself. This time, I had to be more detached.

'You said you could provide names.' My tone was professional. 'This has to be my last visit, unless you deliver what you promised.'

He leaned back and folded his arms. 'I don't recall actually *promising* anything. But I'm delighted you *are* willing to come back.'

I waited.

'Yes,' he finally said, 'I have names.'

He pulled a sheet of paper from the pocket of his tracksuit bottoms carefully unfolding it as he spoke. 'Ordinarily, I wouldn't be allowed to bring anything into these interviews.' He smoothed the paper out on the desk. 'No pen permitted though. So, if I need to make any amendments, you'll need to commit them to memory, I'm afraid.'

'Didn't think you'd ever admit to making mistakes.'

'Everyone makes occasional errors. Even Caravaggio, the classical master I admire the most, made alterations while creating his masterpieces.' He smiled.

I nodded to the digital recorder. 'We have an aide-memoire this time.'

'I'm old school myself. Paper and ink.'

He held the paper up and pressed it to the glass. I leaned forward to get a better look. There were half a dozen names on the list, none of which I recognised, until I came to the last one.

'Tom Hannah?'

'You seem surprised. Do you know him?'

I looked at the eyes regarding me over the top of the notepaper. 'What makes you think Hannah could be the copycat?'

He slid the paper down the glass, leaving it face up on the table between us.

'Because he relished my craft. There was hunger in his eyes when he questioned me about my victims.'

'You began refusing his visits – why?'

'The book didn't do well and he blamed me because I wouldn't discuss the killings. It was a biography. I refuse to dwell on my crimes. I wanted people to appreciate my work as an architect, a painter. To know I regretted those terrible years. I want to publicise my charity work and the money I've raised.'

'And he wanted more?'

'He'd been offered a TV series. There was a lot of money in the offing, not to mention a revival for his flagging career.'

'And yours.' I couldn't resist it. 'Publicity isn't something you're averse to, is it? So why didn't you agree?'

'Because they wanted all the gory details. Can you imagine what that would do to the families? They've gone through enough. I didn't see the point in torturing them further, just to turn a profit for Hannah.'

'It could give them closure. If you're serious about repentance?'

'That's why I want to work with you, Doctor. Once we have this copycat, I'll give you the whereabouts of Michelle's body. But I want that to come through you. Not some shocking exposé, giving Tom Hannah the scoop of a lifetime.'

'Will you give me other information – as a gesture of goodwill?'

'Of course.'

'She disappeared on Wednesday fifteenth of July.'

Keeping my eyes on his and using my peripheral vision, I checked the steady rise and fall of his broad chest beneath the grey sweatshirt. His breathing was slow, rhythmic. Showing no signs of stress. To calibrate it, I matched his breathing with my own, falling into the same gentle rhythm.

'Three days before your nineteenth birthday,' I continued.

He simply nodded.

'Did Michelle die the same night she disappeared?' I asked.

Suddenly our breathing was out of sync. He'd held it on the in-breath – for just a fraction of a second.

'Yes,' he lied.

'Your birthday wasn't until three days later.'

'I always killed on the *day*, not the date, of my birth.'

'So, what did you do on your actual birthday?'

'I visited my parents. Drove there on Thursday and came back the following Monday. They had a party for me.'

'In Kent?'

He shot me a curious look, furrowing his brow. 'Kent?'

'That's where they lived, wasn't it?'

He hesitated for a moment. Unsure whether this was some kind of trick question. Now it was my turn to be confused.

'Originally, yes. But my mother's work meant she spent a lot of time in the north. Eventually, she took a consultancy at the Manchester Art Gallery and bought a place up there. My father stayed in Kent. They visited each other often and came together for family events – the arrangement suited them both.'

'And the party was at your mother's place in Manchester?'

'Yes.'

'I don't recall reading that in Hannah's book.'

'Because it wasn't mentioned.' He glanced down. 'When I was arrested, my parents went through hell. They drifted apart. My mother didn't want the press to know where she lived. Not many people even knew they had separate homes. They never divorced. The police protected their privacy, as much as possible.'

'So, you disposed of Michelle's body *before* travelling to Manchester?'

'Yes.' He didn't miss a beat, but a micro-expression flitted across his face. Barely noticeable. Another lie.

'You said you would share information as a token of trust.'

'But not Michelle's whereabouts. Not yet. Hannah pushed too hard,' he said pointedly. 'That's why I cut him off.'

'Is that why you've put him on your list as a possible copycat . . . Because he annoyed you?'

He looked genuinely hurt at the accusation. 'He savoured my kills in a way that was unusual. His interest was unhealthy. You of all people understand that deviance recognises itself in others.'

I glanced at the recorder to check it was working. When I looked up, he was watching me with a focused attention that was unnerving.

'You need to give me more than that.'

'He wants to bask in my reflected celebrity. Writing the first book gave him a taste for that, but not enough. He wants more. We even discussed it, during his visits.'

'Discussed what?' Even though I already knew, I needed Malecki to confirm what Hannah had said.

'Whether everyone is capable of killing. I told him I believed so – given the right motivation. To protect the ones they love perhaps? Everyone has a button. It's just a case of pushing the right one.'

I thought about my son, Alex, now living and working in London. The things I knew I was capable of doing to protect him. Of the things I *had* done. Things that now lay precariously dormant between me and Callum.

I shifted uncomfortably as I dragged my attention back.

'And Hannah agreed?'

'More than that – he said he *knew* he could kill. Easily. Not in such a noble cause as the defence of others, either. That he had actually fantasised, from adolescence, about killing a stranger. Wondering how it would feel, to cross that line.'

'Why would he cross it now?'

'Anger; envy; greed. The things that drive evil. He's devoured by them all. Plus, my rejection of him. Who knows, perhaps he believes the existence of a copycat might persuade me to agree to the book and the documentary? It's certainly put me back in the spotlight. Useful for someone who wants to capitalise on my crimes, wouldn't you say?'

I looked at the list of names – upside down on his side of the screen.

'And the others?'

'None of the people from my time in prison are alive or free.' He pushed the paper around with his index finger. 'I gave all my admirers on the outside serious consideration. These are the most likely. And they've all visited me. Now that I've upheld my side of the bargain, it's time for you to do the same.'

'What bargain?'

He raised his eyebrows. 'That you would share details of the case, so that I can help.'

'I never actually agreed to that.'

'I never thought you'd go back on an agreement.'

'I'll live with it.'

He leaned towards the partition, elbows resting on his knees. 'But can you live with the escalating body count, Jo? Because I couldn't. Please . . . let me help. You know I can.'

Emotional manipulation. Guilt-tripping. All part of the narcissist's armoury.

I regarded him for a moment. Remembering that I had to elicit as much information as I could and the clock was ticking.

'I'll think about it. In the meantime, you said you could give us an insight into how he would think, what his next move might be?'

He pursed his lips in thought. 'He's wanting attention. Given that, I think he'll make a statement with the next victim.'

'What kind of "statement"?'

'If it were me?' He spread his hands, palms up, like a magician revealing a trick. 'I'd go for something . . . *dramatic*.'

Chapter Forty

Wednesday Afternoon, Fordley Town Centre

McNamara's was quiet. Just a few people at tables near the window, eating late lunches and watching the world go by.

I was sitting with Finn in a quiet corner, as he nursed a mug of tea, digesting what I'd just told him.

'So, this bastard said he followed your da, all those years ago?'

I nodded. 'Said he was at the next table, listening to you talk.'

He pursed his lips, slowly shaking his head. 'It's possible, but I can't remember seeing him misself. Though to be fair, after his arrest, one or two of the staff said they recognised his face from the news. Said they thought he'd been in here.'

'So, there could be some truth in it?'

Finn shrugged his huge shoulders. 'Sure, but when a high-profile killer gets caught, everyone has a story about bumping into them in a pub.'

I was trying to unsee images of Jacob Malecki stalking my parents. Almost more terrifying than thinking he'd done the same to me.

'I was hoping it wasn't true,' I said quietly.

'Then believe it isn't,' Finn said simply. 'None of us can know for sure.'

'But how else would he know about this place? Or that Dad came in here every Saturday afternoon to see you?'

'OK, so if it *is* true, what difference does that make to anything? Your da came to no harm and, thank the Lord, neither did you. That's all that matters now.'

'He said he killed Kath, instead of me.'

'Bastard!' He reached over and covered my hand with his calloused palm, like a bear's paw. 'You can't let that thought live rent-free in your head, girl. The things that bastard did, he did for his own reasons and you're not to blame.'

I tried to muster a smile. 'I know that, Finn. But still—'

'Still nothin', lass. Here, I'll be getting us some colcannon and rashers.' He patted my hand as he got up from the table. 'You'll feel better after you've eaten.'

* * *

I pushed my plate away, amazed I'd managed to polish off the lot, when I hadn't felt hungry.

'There now, didn't I say?' Finn smiled. 'Nothing to distract the mind from troubles, like home cooking.'

He began to stack the plates, when another thought occurred to me.

'You've been here a long time . . . know everyone.'

'Well, not everyone, lass, just everyone worth knowing.' He winked and laughed.

'Tom Hannah?'

'Aye – worked at the *Express*.'

'What do you know about him?'

'Not much. Used to drink in here. Thought he was a bit of a weasel. I never had any dealings with him.'

'Word is, he was in the pay of criminals?'

'Wouldn't be more than one criminal.'

'What do you mean?'

'If someone in Fordley was on the take in those days, there was only one paymaster.' He gestured for one of the staff to

230

come and clear the table. When they'd gone, he leaned forward, conspiratorially. 'Old Man McGarry and his brothers had this city tied up tighter than a duck's arse.'

'Ever hear of Hannah taking pay-offs from the old man?'

'Not in so many words, but it was a given. Wasn't the sort of question you asked, unless you wanted your windows put through or your place burned down.'

'Speaking of burning,' I said, recalling what Jack Halton had said, 'there was a fire, 1993. Guy called Dave Finch got killed?'

His eyes narrowed slightly, becoming cautious. 'What of it?'

'Hear anything at the time?'

'What I heard and what can be proved are two different things.'

'Finn, it's me you're talking to, not counsel for the prosecution.'

But his demeanour had changed, becoming more closed down.

'Bad business – when a man gets killed. Even if it was low-life scum like Finch.'

'Thought he just ran pirate children's videos off a market stall?'

'Those weren't the only types of kiddie films he traded in.' His face hardened. 'Finch was a nonce, but he never got done for that. Plod just had him for shifting dodgy Disney films.'

'I heard Finch owed money. Was it to McGarry? Is that why his place got torched?'

Finn shifted uncomfortably in his seat, looking around as if he imagined we might be overheard.

'The McGarrys were old school. No way would they have made money off child pornography. They hated Finch's sort. Didn't do business with him, I can stake my life on that.'

'I also heard that Hannah was warned off the story.'

'You seem to hear a lot, so why ask me?'

I'd never seen Finn like this. Not with me at least. He was treating me like a cop asking too many questions. And it had all changed with mention of Hannah and Finch.

'Come on, Finn . . .'

His lips pressed together in a thin line. His reticence *really* had me intrigued.

'If McGarry hated Finch, why would he protect him by warning Hannah away from the story?'

Finn's gaze slid away from me, staring at a spot on the floor. I couldn't leave it alone.

'Were the McGarrys responsible? For the fire?'

'No!' Finn's head shot up and he stared at me, shaking his head. 'I told you, Old Man McGarry might have been on the wrong side of the law, but he earned a lot of respect in this city. His business might not have been that holy, but to my thinking, he was a good man. Generous to those who needed it. Good to good people. He didn't kill Finch . . .' He hesitated, the muscles working in his jaw as he struggled with whether to tell me something he'd obviously kept to himself for decades. 'But he knew who did.'

'Who?'

Finn shook his head. 'That I don't know. All I heard was that the old man did a decent family a favour. No one shed a tear for Finch. But good people were involved and the McGarry brothers saw to it that they walked away from the mess.' He looked me in the eye, his voice low. 'Things might be ancient history to some, but to others it's still dangerous ground, if you know what I mean, girl?'

'Surely not now? McGarry's dead and his brothers are old men.'

'But some who were involved then are in important places now.' He hesitated for just a heartbeat. 'And closer to home than you might be comfortable with.'

He couldn't look at me. A shocking coldness settled around us. It felt like something was dying.

I reached out and touched his arm. 'What does *that* mean?'

He slowly shook his head, concentrating on a spot on the polished table.

'Finn,' I pressed, 'look at me . . . please?'

He raised his head, and for the first time, I couldn't fathom the look in his eyes.

'Was someone close to *me* involved?'

'Your job, lass, puts you too close to people who won't want you asking questions.'

'Police?'

Finn was suddenly still. His eyes staring over my shoulder at a past I couldn't see.

'The McGarrys had a lot of people in their pocket, lass. Lawyers, councillors . . . aye, and police – probably most of all. And they're *not* locked up or dead.'

'You can't just leave it there.'

'I don't know any names. So no good you pushing me on that. And you didn't hear any of this from me – understand? If anyone asks, I'll deny this conversation ever happened. I just heard that some that were involved in that mess are in the job, and they won't thank you for poking around in what's dead and gone. Some things are best left alone.'

Chapter Forty-One

Thursday Morning, Kingsberry Farm

Malecki had predicted something dramatic, but no one could have foreseen this.

'Paxton Pits,' Supt. Warner was saying, 'a nature reserve in Cambridgeshire, three miles from where he lived in St Neots.'

Mark Lutner, Michelle's boyfriend at the time of her disappearance, had been found in a birdwatching hide, with his throat cut and a human toe in his mouth.

'One of the park rangers found him when he checked the hides at seven this morning.' I could hear the rustling of paperwork. 'Another twitcher, or whatever they're called, saw Lutner about six last night. They'd been there most nights trying to spot a rare eagle owl. No other sightings of him by anyone after that. The nature reserve is accessible twenty-four hours, but this time of year, it's mostly deserted once it gets dark.'

'Time of death?'

'Not clear until the post-mortem report is in – obviously between six yesterday and seven this morning.'

'Can bet all the pension I haven't got that it'll be between six and midnight – making the kill fall on Wednesday if our man is true to form,' I said.

'First job is to confirm that it's Barbara Thorpe's toe.'

'Amputation on Lutner?'

'Yes, index finger of his right hand.'

I glanced at the clock above the Aga. It was just after ten.

'You've listened to the recording from my interview with Malecki yesterday?'

'Played it to the team at yesterday's briefing.' She hesitated for just a second and then . . . 'That reference to your father . . . What did he mean?'

I told her what Malecki had said about researching me and my family, before killing Kath.

She listened in silence before saying, 'It may not be true.'

'How could he know about my dad's routine though?'

We both fell silent as possibilities were considered. Then she said, 'I'd totally understand if you want to pull out, Jo?'

'No.' I was emphatic. 'Sitting on the outside, wondering what's happening, would be worse.'

'If you change your mind . . .'

'I won't.'

'Malecki predicted something dramatic,' she said. 'Certainly ticks that box.'

Something was beginning to nag, like an insistent itch I couldn't quite reach. Something about the victimology that didn't sit right.

'And the killer obviously went to the trouble of tracking Lutner down,' Warner was saying.

'At the risk of stating the obvious,' I said, about to do just that, 'Lutner isn't a common name. Wouldn't be hard to find him.'

'True.'

'What do you need from me?'

'We've got the visitors log and fan mail from the prison. Intelligence is going through the list of names Malecki gave us and digging up everything we can on those people. Would be useful to have your input. See if anyone flags up.'

'OK.'

'I need all the time you can give us on this, Jo. With other forces getting involved, we need to throw all our resources at it. Hope you haven't got any holidays planned?'

'What's a holiday?'

'I'll let the team know you're coming in.'

Chapter Forty-Two

Thursday Morning, Fordley Police Station

As I walked into the office, the massive scale of the investigation was evident.

The major incident team now occupied the top two floors of Fordley Police Station. Every square inch was filled as officers had been drafted in from other regions and all leave had been cancelled.

'Jo,' a voice shouted above the din and I spotted Beth waving to me from across the room. I weaved between the extra desks and followed her into an adjoining office.

DC Shah Akhtar smiled a weary greeting. 'I'd get a brew – you're going to need it.'

Beth was already on it. 'I'll do the honours.'

There were stacks of letters, photographs and cards.

Shah dropped a letter on to a pile. 'Considering maximum security prisons limit them to four sides of A5, people cram a lot in.'

'Does the prison open all his letters?'

'Yeah. All mail sent to a supermax facility is opened. They used to test the paper in case it was impregnated with drugs. But it's too time-consuming. Now, they photocopy them. Prisoner gets the copy and the originals are destroyed.'

'Are they read?'

The stack was just a sample from Malecki's pen pals. I could only imagine the task when multiplied by 751 inmates.

'In theory. But they don't always have the time or the manpower. So, it's just dip-sampled.'

Beth was back with the tea. 'It's vending machine crap, I'm afraid.'

For me, bad coffee is drinkable, but bad tea isn't. I made a mental note to opt for coffee next time.

Beth nodded to a figure over in a corner with his back to the room. 'Lee, from Cybercrimes, has been seconded to us for the duration. Collating lists of letters and the visitors log, with the fandom sites.'

'That sounds simpler than it probably is,' I said, pulling a face as I tasted the tea.

'Not helped by the fact that most people on the forums go by usernames.' She nodded towards Lee. 'Typical geek. Not much conversation, but great at what he does.'

'Wouldn't want his job,' I said. My technophobia was a standing joke among the team.

'He loves it, all that data crunching. Very anal,' Beth said.

'Anal tension is an understatement.' Shah grinned. 'If you shoved a piece of coal up his arse, he'd shit a diamond.'

'Well, as long as he shits a few diamonds over this case, I'll buy him a pint.' Beth pulled up a chair. 'There's a briefing this afternoon, Jo. Hopefully will have tracked some of these down by then. T.I.E.'

Trace, Interview, Eliminate.

'Simples,' she concluded.

* * *

Thursday Afternoon, Fordley Police Station Briefing Room

Predictably, things were anything but simple.

Nursing a vending machine coffee, which was almost as disgusting as the tea, I listened as Callum went through the latest updates.

'We tracked down the name Hannah gave Ian Drummond,' he was saying. 'Daren Wallace. Befriended Malecki in Broadmoor. Dead end – literally.' He raked fingers through his hair, in that way he had when he was tired or frustrated. 'Daren killed himself, just after Malecki got transferred to Wakefield.'

'What about the names Malecki provided?' Warner asked.

'Of the six – one's dead. One emigrated to Canada last year. Of the three traced and interviewed, we've eliminated two. The last one, we're still trying to track down. Peter Randall. He's served time for assault, robbery with violence and various burglary charges. He started writing to Malecki five years ago and has visited several times.'

'OK. He's a priority,' Warner agreed. 'Randall's in the system, Jo. Take a look at his history, see what you think? That leaves us with Hannah.' Warner tapped her notes. 'Jack Halton said Hannah had an unhealthy fascination with the Relay Killer back in the day. Then he becomes his official biographer, and now, Malecki puts him in the frame as a possible copycat. What was your impression of him, Jo?'

'He's bitter. That much is obvious. Blames Malecki for his situation now.'

'Which is?'

'He's on the bones of his arse,' Ian chipped in. 'Wife took him to the cleaners in the divorce. He was pinning his hopes on Malecki to turn his finances around.'

'This copycat putting Malecki back in the spotlight is good news for Hannah then,' Callum said. 'Think he could be capable of these killings, Jo?'

'It's hardly a deep analysis – spending half an hour in the man's lounge.' I knew I was hedging. On something this important, I wasn't about to speculate just to fit a theory.

'But what's your reading of him?' Warner pushed.

'He's got a history of domestic violence, so he's capable of physical aggression and Malecki said that Hannah confessed to fantasising, as a teenager, about killing a stranger and getting away with it.'

'And you believe the word of a psycho?' Wardman snorted.

'When I asked Hannah, he didn't deny it. In fact, he couldn't look me in the eye. Said he thought anyone was capable, given the right circumstances.'

'Is being financially ruined, bitter, angry and desperate, motivation enough?' Callum asked.

'All of those are enough on their own. You know that,' I said. 'Malecki thinks Hannah might kill, just to prove he's his equal.'

'His name keeps cropping up too often,' Warner said. 'We should pull him in. Callum, get someone round to his place. Let's see where he was on the dates in question. At the very least, we can tell him that Malecki's put him in the frame. See how he reacts to that.' She glanced at her iPad. 'We have an update from Cambridgeshire police. They've fast-tracked the toe for DNA. Should get that back by tomorrow. Assuming it *is* Barbara's, we'll have officers from Cambridgeshire joining the team.' She glanced round the cramped space. 'So, make room and play nice.'

DI Wardman cleared his throat, drawing everyone's attention. 'Latest on the white van sighted near the Stephen Jones scene. No registration to go on and no CCTV around the allotment. We've got an image from a camera in a pub on the main road.' He flicked a remote and a grainy image flashed up on the large TV.

'This was the night of Stephen's murder. The vehicle's travelling away from the allotment. It's just a split second as it passes the pub.' He paused the image and everyone strained to make it out.

'Blimey, could be an ice cream van or a bloody ambulance,' Heslopp snorted.

Wardman put a close-up on screen. 'We've sent the image over to the Forensic Science Service. From the description, they think it's a small Ford. They're working on the model.'

Callum picked it up from there. 'Wakefield nick have come up trumps. As well as visitor records, they've sent footage of Malecki's visits from CCTV in the visitors' hall. Let's see if Randall is on here – along with anyone Malecki *didn't* mention.' He nodded to DS Morgan from his team. 'Tony, you're our Spielberg, I'll let you plough through that lot.'

'Thanks, boss.' He sounded less than grateful.

'Jo,' Callum added, 'watch with him – see if you spot anything. There's no audio, but you're the expert on non-verbal communication.'

Tony gave me a double thumbs up.

'What exactly are we looking for?' I asked.

'Not sure,' Callum said, without looking up. 'Like most of what we do. It's one of those, "you'll know it when you see it" things.'

241

Chapter Forty-Three

Thursday Night, Fordley Police Station

It was almost midnight, but there were still a few people at their desks. The team were putting in all the hours. Missing kids nativity plays and parties. The clock was ticking and Christmas didn't exist.

Tony Morgan was sitting opposite me, straining to watch the CCTV images he'd been poring over for hours. I'd watched it through with him earlier, but broke off to look at Peter Randall's record. Callum needed my notes on him for the next briefing.

'Bloody hell.' Tony yawned, stretching back to ease knotted shoulders. 'Remind me next time to wait for the box set.'

I smiled at him. 'You look like I feel.'

'Got some other names to look into.' He tapped his notepad. 'Couple of regular visitors on the CCTV. Cross-referenced with the visitors log.' He squinted at his own handwriting. 'Gerald Carter, Malecki's art agent, and a woman, Jill Neatley, his assistant or something. Anyway, I'll follow it up tomorrow. I'm not effective anymore.' He stood up and reached for the jacket on the back of his chair. 'Going to call it a night . . . or is it morning?' He nodded to the notepad next to me. 'How you getting on with Randall?'

I chewed my pencil as I looked at the screen, where a picture of a shaven-headed man with dark eyes gazed back at me from the PNC, Police National Computer.

'Been in the system since he was a teenager,' I said. 'Troubled family life. Social services involved almost from birth. Left home at fifteen. The usual litany of adolescent offending. Burglary and robbery with violence became his thing.'

Tony looked at the screen over my shoulder as he shrugged on his jacket.

'He fits your profile. Right age range. Thirty-eight. Self-employed plumber . . .'

'So, he'll probably own a van,' I added. 'Makes carrying a pre-prepared kit easy if he's a tradesman.'

'Being self-employed, he doesn't have to justify his whereabouts to an employer. Valid reason to be in an area at odd hours. Where's he from?'

'Fordley, but travelled for his job. Committed his offences throughout West Yorkshire.'

'He's ticking all the boxes so far.'

I couldn't disagree. His prison record described someone who was physically fit, trained in the gym. A hardman who commanded respect from others on the wing. And his previous criminal history gave him all the attributes he'd need to break into homes and overpower his victims.

'Some assaults were serious. Nothing on the scale of our copycat though.' I was thinking out loud.

'But they develop over time, you said so yourself. Maybe he's graduated to the big leagues?'

'Maybe.'

'Need to see if the DVLA have any vehicles registered to him, then cross-reference with any plates flagged up on ANPR around the crime scenes. If we get a hit, that could be our break.'

'Is it ever that easy?'

His smile was weary. 'Sometimes the patron saint of bobbies smiles down on us.'

'I'm staying for a bit, to run through the CCTV from the prison again.'

'You'll need plenty of popcorn.' He laughed. 'I won't give any spoilers, but the ending sucks.'

* * *

I woke with a start, and for a second, didn't know where I was. I tilted my head to look at the bedside clock – confused to see a stack of files instead.

'Morning.' The deep rumble of Callum's voice only added to the confusion.

He put a steaming mug on the desk beside me.

'Jesus.' The crick in my neck felt permanent as I tried to straighten my shoulders. The office was deserted.

'We don't get five stars on Tripadvisor then?' The fresh scent of Callum's cologne triggered a tug somewhere deep inside.

'Depends how good the tea is?' I tried to smile as I sipped from the mug. 'What time is it?'

'Four a.m. We've all done it, Jo, but this isn't proper rest.'

The usual familiar warmth wasn't there. His concern was the same he'd have for any of his team. Not personal. Not like a lover. It stung, but I tried not to let it show.

'How come you look so fresh?' I rubbed my eyes back into focus.

'Went home for a couple of hours' kip. Shower and a fresh shirt always does the trick.' He sat on the corner of the desk and picked up my notes. 'Get anywhere?'

I stretched. 'Randall *could* be a possible. His record fits. I also read through the psyche reports the judge requested at his trial.'

'And?'

'It was a particularly violent attack on a home-owner who disturbed him when he broke in. Aggression above and beyond what was necessary. The psychologist concluded that he enjoyed inflicting the injuries on his victim. Once he started torturing the poor man, he couldn't stop. Prolonged the attack just for the hell of it. Left him tied to a kitchen chair, in a pool of his own blood. When police broke in, he'd been there twenty-four hours. Randall was lucky he wasn't facing a murder charge.'

'Echoes of Malecki's MO.'

'Hmm.' I rolled my shoulders and winced. 'Randall's on the prison CCTV, visiting Malecki.'

'And?'

I took another sip of tea, starting to feel the welcome kick of caffeine. 'They have a definite rapport. Beyond ordinary friendship.'

'Shame there's no audio.' Callum dropped my notes back on the desk and got up to go.

'What did Hannah have to say when you brought him in?' I asked, reluctant to see him walk away. Despite his coldness towards me over the last few weeks, I hated to admit, even to myself, that I missed him. I found myself reaching for the closeness we used to have, even though I knew it was pointless.

'Nothing – he wasn't at home when officers went to bring him in.' He spoke over his shoulder as he left. 'Go home, get some sleep. We'll get everyone up to speed at the 7 a.m. briefing.'

Chapter Forty-Four

Friday, 7 a.m.

It was hardly worth going home, but Harvey had been on his own too long and needed letting out, plus I needed a decent cup of tea.

Taking Callum's tip, I showered and changed into fresh clothes, before heading straight back to the incident room.

The briefing kicked off with an introduction to the two officers from Cambridgeshire police. A young DC and an older DS, whose names I'd already forgotten, such was my sleep and food deprivation.

'Forensics confirm the toe in Lutner's mouth is from Barbara Thorpe,' the DS said. He glanced at his DC, who took his cue.

'I've got CCTV footage from Paxton Pits. Got a bit of a technical glitch getting your screen to talk to our laptop, though.'

Callum nodded. 'OK. While you set that up, Jo, what have you got?'

I summarised Peter Randall's police record and psyche report, with comparisons to my initial profile of the copycat. 'So, he ticks a lot of our boxes,' I finished.

'Plus, he's in the wind, which makes him a person of interest. You said he appears on the prison CCTV too?' Callum said.

I nodded to Tony, who had been helping the young DC trying to sort out the tech. The screen flickered to life with footage from Peter Randall's visits. I provided the commentary.

'Their greeting is warm – man-hugs on arrival each time, despite being told to break apart by prison officers. They have an immediate rapport as soon as they sit down.'

Everyone in the room studied the screen.

'Look beneath the table.' I pointed to their legs. 'Neither man can see what the other is doing, and yet, they mirror the exact same position of their legs.'

At one point, Malecki sat back in his chair and crossed his ankles under the table. A fraction of a second later, Randall did the same.

'Eh?' Tony Morgan said. 'How does that work?'

'It's called "limbic synchrony". Done intentionally, it's a powerful way to connect with someone and build rapport. But what you're seeing here is "nonconscious mimicry". When it's this unconscious, "mirror neurons" in the brain are firing. Which means these two people have a very strong bond.'

'Wouldn't you see that just among mates?' Beth asked.

'Yes, but the more unconscious the synchrony, the stronger the relationship. And, something else.' I turned back to the screen. 'Malecki has the power and influence in this relationship.'

'How do you know?' Wardman finally piped up.

'Because he makes the posture changes first and Randall follows a fraction of a second later. That makes Malecki "rapport leader".' I paused the screen and rewound – stopping just before a posture change. In each case, Malecki moved first, followed by Randall.

'Anything else?' Callum asked.

'Found a couple of other visitors, boss,' Tony said. 'Gerald Carter, Malecki's art agent, and Jill Neatley. She works at the gallery. Apart from the ones on Malecki's list, these two are his only other visitors.'

'OK.' Callum jotted a note. 'Let's talk to them. Frank, you pick that up – take Jo with you.'

'Right, boss.'

'I've got something.' Everyone turned to the unexpected voice from a corner of the room. Lee, from the cyber unit, cleared his throat.

'I've been studying the Malecki fandom sites. Because they all have user names, I've been looking for corresponding personal details on other social media platforms to identify them. A lot have tattoos, which they're happy to post pictures of. I downloaded the images and circulated them to tattoo parlours throughout the county.'

'Any joy?' Callum asked, with the tone of someone who expected none.

'I got a hit on this one.' He held up the enlarged photo of Malecki's face I'd seen earlier, covering the back and shoulders of the anonymous fan. 'His username is "Wednesdays62".'

'Nineteen sixty-two – the year Malecki was born,' I supplied to no one in particular.

'It was done by a tattoo artist in Wakefield.' Lee's monotone didn't hint at any sense of victory or excitement. 'Artist remembered it, because . . . well, not many people want to see Malecki's face when they look over their shoulder.'

'Get a name?' Callum asked.

'Peter Randall.'

Callum sat up straighter. 'Being on a fandom site of a serial killer isn't a crime, neither is crap taste in tattoos, but added to everything else, Randall goes to the top of the list.' He looked at the two detectives from Cambridgeshire who had finally managed to get the tech working in their favour.

'All we need now is for him to appear on your footage from Paxton Pits, and we can all have Christmas off.'

* * *

248

'This is from the camera at the entrance to the reserve,' the young DC was saying.

He fast-forwarded the footage and we all watched a stream of vehicles entering and leaving the car park.

'Four vehicles go in between 9 p.m. Wednesday and 4 a.m. Thursday. After that, the only vehicle to arrive is the park ranger who found the body. The registrations of those four vehicles are all on the system. They've previously been arrested for engaging in sex in a public place.'

'That's "dogging" to you and me,' Heslopp said.

The DC pretended not to have heard. 'They've been interviewed and eliminated.'

His DS took over. 'We got the registration numbers of all vehicles entering and leaving the park for twenty-four hours and ran them through the database.'

Details of the index plates were coming up on the screen.

'None of the other index plates were in the system. But we've listed all the registered keepers, so it's just a case of tracing them.'

'I know that one.' All eyes turned to an officer at the back of the room. I recognised him as one of the traffic team. 'We've just had a marker put on that.'

'Who's it registered to?' Callum asked.

Everyone seemed to hold a collective breath.

'Tom Hannah.'

'Blimey.' Heslopp hitched his trousers over his huge belly. 'Suspects are getting like buses. None, then two come along at once.'

Chapter Forty-Five

Friday Morning, Fordley Town Centre

I sat at a table in the window of The Munch Bunch and felt my shoulders drop as I relaxed into the familiar atmosphere of one of my favourite haunts.

The café was in the heart of Little Italy. The fabric of the area and its architecture had changed little. A fact that was creating first-world problems for a young girl on her way to work, as she delicately negotiated the ancient cobbles in her impossibly high heels.

'Jo. Didn't expect you this morning.'

I smiled at Domino, the waitress who was hovering at my elbow.

'Just left a briefing at Fordley nick.' I rubbed tired eyes. 'Arranged to meet someone, and this was an easy walk from there.'

'Oh, charmin' and here's me thinking you just liked my company.'

'That too.'

'OK. Pot of tea for you.' She smiled at her own prediction. 'And . . . what for your friend?'

'Coffee, black no sugar. But wait until he gets here – he likes it mouth-scalding hot.'

'Hmm, that kind of friend?' She wiggled her eyebrows suggestively.

'What?'

'If you know how he likes his coffee – he must be a very special "friend"?' She drew speech marks in the air.

An image of Joshua Weston, Chris McGarry's solicitor, with his thick horn-rimmed glasses and balding head. He reminded me of Penfold from *Danger Mouse*.

'Er . . . no. Not like that.'

'OK, if you say so.' She quickly wiped the already pristine tabletop with a cloth. 'Anything to eat?'

I was about to say no, but my stomach reminded me I hadn't eaten since yesterday.

'Got any current teacakes?'

She raised her eyebrows. 'Does the King have horses? Coming right up.'

The breakfast rush had gone and the place was quiet. The hiss of the coffee machine, a gently familiar sound, triggered feelings of warmth and respite. This was one of the few places I could truly relax outside of my home.

As I watched the street, a familiar figure came out of Chapel Mills apartments opposite and walked towards the café. A moment later, the old-fashioned bell above the door chimed and a small, grey-haired woman in an immaculate tweed overcoat stepped inside.

'Morning, Mary.' Domino smiled brightly. 'Your bread order's here. Arrived fresh this morning.'

'Thank you, m'dear.'

In the reflection of the window, I could see Domino nod in my direction. 'Look who the cat dragged in.'

'Jo.' She beamed. 'How *are* you?'

'I'm good.' I stood up into her outstretched arms for a tight hug. 'How are things at Chapel Mills?'

'She glanced over at the building where her late son had lived. 'Do you know – moving into Leo's apartment has been the best thing I've ever done.' Her gentle smile was tinged with sadness.

251

I'd met Mary the previous year, when the family had called me in to review her artist son's death. Despite the unhappy reason we'd met, it was the start of a fond friendship.

'How's Charles?' I almost didn't want to bring up the domineering husband, who tried pressuring her into selling their son's penthouse after his death. But I'd always enjoyed kicking elephants in rooms.

'He's happier too.' Mary's spine straightened and her chin jutted defiantly. 'Old fool never thought I'd actually move out. Anyway, he can get on with his golf in peace now.'

'And how are you spending your time?'

'I've been cataloguing Leo's art. His agent in London has arranged an exhibition in the spring. There has been such a lot of interest in his work since he . . .' Her voice tailed off, shying away from the horror of his death. 'You must come over to see the pieces before they get shipped.' She patted my arm and I couldn't resist the enthusiasm shining out of those pale eyes. 'I'll cook us something nice and we can catch up properly.'

*　*　*

Mary left, as Joshua arrived. He came straight over, peeling off thick leather gloves and a heavy scarf.

'Bloody freezing.' He shivered, shrugging off his coat.

Domino appeared beside us, delivering my tea and toast and Joshua's mug of coffee.

'Scalding hot – just how you like it.' She grinned at him and went back behind the counter.

Joshua looked impressed. 'Blimey, that's what I call service. So, what's so secretive that you couldn't tell me over the phone?'

'Not secretive, exactly.' I suddenly didn't know how to start. 'I need some information.'

'Okaaay. Like what?'

'That's the problem – I'm not sure.'

'Well, that narrows it down.'

'This stays between us, right?'

'Jo . . .' He looked genuinely offended.

'Sorry. But I've already been warned to leave this alone – that the implications might have a long reach.'

He took a sip of coffee, regarding me over the rim. 'That applies to just about everything I do. Go on . . .'

'I want information that I think Chris McGarry, or one of his uncles might have.'

'He's put your number on his approved list—'

'But as a category A prisoner, his calls are recorded.'

'And it's not something you'd want anyone listening to?'

'Are any of his uncles on the outside?'

'No.' He took a sip of coffee. 'I'm working on getting Chris transferred. They sent him to Belmarsh.'

If they want to be bastards about it, could be the Isle of Wight.

Belmarsh in south-east London wasn't much better.

'His little boy, Mikey, is ill,' Joshua said. 'Suspected cancer.'

'God, every parent's worst nightmare.'

'There's a decent case for moving him closer to home.'

'Are you going to be seeing him?'

'I'm doing most things over the phone.' His smile was thin. 'I don't want to be schlepping two hundred and fifty miles, if I can avoid it.'

I didn't feel as though I could ask that of him, so I nodded and stirred the teapot.

'I could arrange a private visit for you to see him? As his psychologist.'

Finn's warning rang in my ears. If there was a bent cop in the mix, I couldn't risk news of a visit getting out.

Echoes of what Ron Wallis, the young crime reporter, had said.

Fordley nick's got more holes in it than a leaky colander.

'No. Don't think that would be safe either.'

He raised a curious eyebrow. 'Safe?'

'I don't know who I can trust right now.'

'My calls to Chris *aren't* recorded.' He was choosing his words carefully. 'That would violate legal privilege.' His gaze held mine across the table. 'So, I could ask the questions for you?'

I took a long breath. 'Could be risky.'

He waved my objections away with his hand. 'Tell me and I'll decide.'

So, I told him.

Chapter Forty-Six

Friday Afternoon, Saltaire

The Victorian village of Saltaire, four miles from Fordley, was named after the industrialist who built it and the river, which ran through it.

Sir Titus Salt built the village on the River Aire for his workers. In addition to the rows of terraced, stone-built cottages, there's a library, school, church and bath-house. Quite a philanthropic idea in its day, when a few miles away, Fordley's mill workers often lived in abject poverty.

Salts Mill had been a working factory until 1986. Now it was filled with cafés, restaurants and small arty shops. The whole top floor had, for as long as I could remember, been home to the David Hockney art exhibition.

Voted as one of the most beautiful villages in the UK it became a magnate for tourists, even on a cold, grey December morning like today.

'Parking's a bloody nightmare,' Frank Heslopp grumbled as he squeezed his car past a tour bus, before finding a space on Victoria Road.

Gerald Carter's art gallery, unimaginatively named Picture This, was an unassuming shop next to a trendy café. In the window, there were two large framed oil paintings displayed on wooden easels. Neither had a price tag.

'If you have to ask, you can't afford it,' Heslopp said as he held the door open for me.

The interior was welcomingly warm and smelled of wood polish.

A tall, slim man in his mid-sixties appeared from the dark interior of the shop. He was sporting an open-necked shirt and silk cravat, like a thirties caricature of what an art expert should look like.

'Detective Heslopp?' He extended his hand to me.

'Er, no,' Frank said over my shoulder. 'That would be me.'

'Oh, apologies.' Gerald Carter's smile seemed genuine, as he shook Frank's hand. 'You must be Doctor McCready then?' It obviously never occurred to him a doctor would be female. 'The police rang to say you'd be coming.' He extended an arm. 'My office is at the back.'

We walked past a centre table with a huge vase of oriental lilies, their bowed trumpets filling the space with a heavy scent that bordered on overpowering.

'Jill,' he called, 'can you watch the shop, please?'

There were sounds of movement from an area at the back and a woman I guessed to be in her forties appeared, wearing jeans, a crumpled off-white T-shirt and trainers stained with paint.

'Jill's our art conservator,' he said, as if he needed to explain her appearance. 'She's usually in the workshop.'

Carter's office was a windowless room, lit by discreetly placed antique lamps. The walls were adorned with expensive-looking paintings. He gestured to a leather sofa to one side of a large knee-hole desk and took the armchair opposite.

'Would you like any tea . . . coffee?'

'No, thanks.' Heslopp spoke for both of us. 'We're here to talk to you about Jacob Malecki.' Carter nodded, pursing his lips as he waited. 'He's still painting in prison.' It was a statement, rather than a question, but the pause was Carter's opening to offer something.

'Yes. He's working on a new collection.'

'For the exhibition?' I asked.

'Yes, it's in the New Year. We're hoping to generate a lot of interest – particularly in view of Jacob being in the news recently.'

I was surprised he'd openly admitted that the renewed interest in his serial killer client might actually help sell his paintings.

'All the proceeds will go to Rebuild?' Heslopp asked.

Carter nodded. 'After our commission, of course.'

'How long have you been Malecki's agent?' Heslopp asked, although it was in his notes.

'Since the beginning. We met at one of his auctions, when he was an architect. He was gaining quite a reputation. I was working in a gallery in London as a junior partner and was sent along, to see whether we could offer on any of the pieces. In the end, my gallery didn't buy. But I met Jacob and we got on. There are just a few years between us and I was impressed by how much he'd achieved. I told him he could make a very good living as an artist. His work was exceptional.'

'So, how did you become his agent?'

'I set up on my own and moved here. Jacob was the first person I contacted and it went from there.'

'A lot of people dropped Malecki when he was convicted. Didn't it concern you?' I asked.

Carter seemed to consider me, with a look bordering on disgust. 'My feelings for Jacob have never changed. His imprisonment makes no difference.'

Heslopp raised his eyebrows, but said nothing.

'What exactly *are* your feelings towards him?' I asked.

'I admire the man and his work. Nothing will diminish that.'

'What he did would make a difference to most people,' I pressed.

'I'm not most people,' he said simply. 'We became very close before his . . . arrest. I won't devalue that time by abandoning him. He's still the man I . . .' he caught himself '. . . believed in then. For me, what he did doesn't define him.'

The same words Malecki had used.

'How close was your relationship, exactly?' Heslopp took the question by the scruff.

Carter shifted in his chair. 'That depends on what you mean.'

'Was it sexual?'

Good old Heslopp – direct as ever.

Carter glanced from the DI to me and back again. 'Do I have to answer that?'

'You're helping us voluntarily, Mr Carter, but this *is* a murder enquiry.'

He sighed. 'We were young. Both single. Homosexuality isn't a crime.'

'I didn't know Malecki was homosexual,' Heslopp said.

'Jacob was pansexual even before it had a name,' Carter snapped. 'He's not restrained by gender identity. In fact, Jacob was never confined by society's rules – in anything he did.'

Ain't that the truth.

'That's what I admire about him,' he added, with a note of defiance.

'You've been a regular visitor to the prison?' Heslopp changed tack.

'Of course.'

'You know him probably better than most. Has he ever mentioned anyone that you think could be emulating him?'

'These copycat killings?' Carter curled his lip in distaste. 'There are so-called "fans". People who write to him. There are even websites, so I'm told. But, to answer your question – no.'

'And Jacob has never talked to you about anyone he's particularly close to who may have been in prison with him?'

Carter's eyebrows raised even more. 'No.' He was obviously upset at the thought of anyone higher in Malecki's affections than himself.

'If that's everything, I have work to do.' He stood, signalling an end to the conversation.

'Before we go,' Heslopp said, 'I'd like to speak with Jill.'

'What on earth for?' Carter seemed genuinely surprised.

'If you can spare her for a few minutes?'

Carter walked past us and into the gallery. 'Jill,' he called out. 'The police would like a word.'

* * *

Jill Neatley sat on the edge of a workbench in her studio. The slim figure, with short-cropped dark hair and thin, angular features, reminded me of a pixie.

One glance around the workshop told me a lot.

It was obsessively tidy. Tools and brushes all efficiently stored. A bookshelf, arranged in alphabetical order. A mug and spoon, laid side by side on the worktop by the immaculately clean sink.

She was sitting perfectly still. Her legs weren't swinging, as most people do when they perch on a desk. Hands clasped in her lap. A study in concentration. The light glinted on a small, coloured glass cross dangling from a thin, silver chain around her neck.

259

Neatley by name, neatly by nature.

'How long have you worked here, Jill?' Heslopp asked.

'Started as an apprentice. The conservator here wanted to retire, so they took me on. I was eighteen. Been here ever since.'

'What year was that?'

'Nineteen ninety-two.'

'Straight from school?'

'Bunked out of school at fifteen.' She pulled a face. 'You could do that then. Was a typical "lost" teenager. Rebelled against the system – didn't know what I wanted to do. Eventually went backpacking with a friend.'

'So how did you end up here?' Heslopp was asking.

'Art was the only thing I was ever any good at. Had some vague idea about being an artist. When I was travelling through Paris, I had to fund myself. Didn't fancy working in a bar so I got some casual labour working in a place selling artist supplies. But it ignited something in me, you know? Got to know the local street artists along the Seine. Tried my hand at it and wasn't bad. Became part of the arty bohemian community. But eventually ran out of money, so came back here and started looking for a job. The art college had a board up, with job opportunities and . . .' She indicated the room with a wave of her arm. 'Here I am.'

'What about qualifications?'

'Gerald was great. He said he would rather recruit someone with a love for art, then teach the rest. Did day-release at college. Took the exams I *should* have got first-time round. Did a foundation course and then went on to Fordley Art College.'

'Impressive.'

Her smile was self-effacing. 'It's all about finding a passion in life, isn't it? A circuitous route, but I got there in the end.'

'You weren't tempted to get a job in a museum or bigger gallery? It strikes me, with your qualifications, you could earn far more than here, in Saltaire.'

'It might only be a small gallery, but we do a lot of art conservation for some of the museums and private collectors. It brings in more revenue than the pieces we sell. That's reflected in my salary – so I do OK. Anyway, it's all about loyalty,' she said simply. 'Gerald had faith in me, when no one else did. He funded everything. I'd never had people believe in me before then.'

'And Jacob Malecki?' I asked. 'His crimes didn't change anything for you?'

She shook her head. 'Gerald introduced me to him when I was just eighteen. I admired his art. His architecture too was *amazing*. I'd never met a talent like him. What came after . . . well, it is what it is. I don't know why he did those things, but, to be honest, all I'm interested in is his art.'

'You accompanied Gerald on his visits to Wakefield Prison?' Heslopp made a show of glancing at his notes, as if to check the fact, but I knew what was coming.

'Yes.'

'Were the visits social?'

'Business, whenever I went.'

'What kind of business?'

'What frames Jacob wanted. What code-signatures he would use. How best to display various pieces for an exhibition.'

'Code-signatures?' I asked.

'When Jacob was an architect, he did portraits of the celebrities who commissioned him. They were commanding high prices at auction, so provenance was crucial.'

'So that buyers could be sure they were genuine?' Heslopp asked.

261

'Yes. A couple of forgeries appeared on the market, but they'd been spotted and never went into circulation. Jacob paints by putting the image down in layers. In between the layers, he adds watermarks, which you can only see in certain light or at certain angles. The same way they create images on banknotes. It makes it very difficult to forge. After that, for extra security, Jacob began putting a signature on the back of the canvas – where it's stretched over the wooden frame. He altered each one by adding a symbol and number, and only we would know which "code-signature" was on each painting. When they came in here for framing, we'd log it. Once I've framed the piece, the signature's hidden. Gerald keeps the log with all the codes in his safe.'

'But if a buyer wanted to check,' Heslopp said, 'they'd have to remove the frame – wouldn't that risk damaging the painting?'

'No. You see, Jacob uses a type of paint for the signature that shows up when subjected to infrared reflectography. Most auction houses have the equipment. If it matches the code we have registered here, they know it's genuine.'

'How do you get the paintings here, from the prison?' I couldn't imagine HMP arranging transport.

'Gerald uses a courier to move all our pieces. Not just Jacob's. That way it's all insured.'

'You never visited Malecki alone?' Heslopp changed tack.

She began playing with the glass cross. It was the first animated gesture I'd seen.

'No. Gerald has to sign off on everything. So, we always went together.'

'We have the visitors logs from the prison,' Heslopp said. 'That show you visited six months ago. Alone.'

She began playing with the cross again. That habit was a 'tell'.

'Oh, yes. I'd forgotten about that.'

262

'Was that a social visit?' I asked.

'It's . . . er, awkward.' She glanced at the door as if she expected Gerald Carter to spring into the room and catch her out.

'We don't need to tell Gerald,' Heslopp reassured her.

She paced over to her workbench. Finally turning to lean back on it as she faced us.

'Jacob wasn't happy with some of the decisions about his upcoming exhibition. Gerald vetoed some of my choices. Jacob wanted to discuss it with me, before he tackled him about it. He sent me a VO.'

'And Gerald doesn't know about the visit?'

She shook her head, distractedly picking up a small chisel and then putting it down again.

'How would you describe your relationship with Jacob?' I asked.

'He respects my work and my opinion. We've always got along.'

'Not close then?'

'Professional – not close.'

'Has he ever mentioned any fans to you?' Heslopp cut to the heart of it. 'People who write to him, or visit him?'

'No.' She shook her head. 'He wouldn't discuss things like that with me.'

* * *

'What do you think?' Heslopp asked, as he pulled out into traffic.

'Of Carter?'

He opened the driver's side window to allow the smoke from his cigarette to blow outside. Annoyingly, it didn't.

'And the "Rebel without a Clue".' He grinned at his own pun. 'I think she's gay.'

263

I shot him a look. 'What makes you think that?'

He shrugged, dropping ash into his lap. 'Just looks it.'

'Even if she is, what's that got to do with anything?'

'Nothing. She just seems the sort – you know. Arty, bohemian leftie.'

I regarded his profile. 'You were off on the day they ran the diversity course, then?'

'Oh, come on, you've got to admit, she's a typical feminist type?'

'And all women who stand up for equal rights are lesbians?'

He shot me a look, realising his Neanderthal views were actually being challenged. 'Well, not *all . . .*'

'If I didn't know you better, I'd think you were winding me up.' I cracked my own window open an inch, to try and let in some fresh air. 'Listen to yourself.'

Thankfully, the conversation was interrupted as a call came in.

'Frank.' Callum's voice came over the Bluetooth. 'Where are you?'

'On the way back, boss.'

'Good. There's been a development ... Tom Hannah just handed himself in.'

Chapter Forty-Seven

Saturday Morning, Kingsberry Farm

I was sitting at my desk, but wasn't being very productive. Harvey was snoring contentedly on the Chinese rug – after our three-mile walk over the snow-covered moors early that morning.

Unlike him, my lack of motivation had less to do with aching muscles, than it did with the knots I was trying to unravel in this case.

I wanted to know what Hannah had to say after he'd unexpectedly handed himself in. I was about to call Supt. Warner, when my mobile rang. Caller ID flashed up 'Elle Richardson'.

'Jo? Where are you?'

'At home. Why?'

'Got something you might find interesting. Want to come to my office?'

'Whoever *wants* to visit a morgue?'

She laughed. 'They're called mortuaries these days, darling.'

'Always be a morgue to me.'

'At least my customers are dead quiet – although they might give you the cold shoulder.'

'Very funny.'

'I can magic up a sticky bun, if that helps?'

'I couldn't think of anything worse than eating surrounded by cadavers.'

'Your loss. How long will you be?'

I glanced at the clock. 'Give me an hour.'

'OK,' she said cheerfully. 'See you then.'

* * *

The mortuary was in a low-level building, at the back of Fordley Royal Infirmary. The unblinking eye of a security camera monitored my progress as I pressed the intercom.

'Hi, Doc,' Gus said cheerily, as a 'buzz' and metallic click unlocked the door.

I went through an entrance hall and into an echoing white-tiled corridor.

Gus's head popped out of the staffroom. 'Got a brew on, Jo.'

A kettle was as much a part of standard equipment as Stryker saws and scalpels.

Despite the impression most people have of a place that deals exclusively in death, the atmosphere here was unfailingly warm and friendly.

Coldness was reserved for the steel fridges that lined the end of the corridor. Each one holding six bodies, in neat rows of sliding metal shelves.

Gus was whistling tunelessly as he made the tea.

'There you go.' He thrust a mug into my hand. 'Get your laughing gear round that.'

'Thanks.' I cradled the cup, to defrost my fingers. 'Where's Elle?'

'Her office.' He gave me another cup. 'Take that to her, will you?'

'Did she mention that I wanted you to check the log for me?' I tried to make it sound casual.

'Oh yeah. The Barbara Thorpe post-mortem. You needed the name of the police officer who attended? I'll check before you go.'

My boots echoed in the hollow stillness of a place that usually bustled with the business of the dead.

Today, no trolleys clattered down to the fridges and the thrumming sound of water running into stainless-steel sinks was absent.

I found Elle at her desk – auburn hair glinting in a pool of light from an anglepoise lamp.

'Thanks for coming, Jo. Short notice, but I wanted to take advantage of the lull.'

I pulled up a chair. 'What's up – no one dying today?'

'Don't jinx it. Doesn't happen often.' She pulled a file from the top of a lopsided stack. 'Remember I said the knife used in both your cases had an unusual shape?'

'Yes.'

'It's not something I've seen before, which bothered me.'

'Why? You can't be expected to know the shape of every knife out there.'

She looked at me, as if I'd just declared the earth was flat.

'I'll have you know, I can identify most bladed weapons from the wounds they leave. It's a specialty of mine.' She sniffed indignantly. 'From a Stanley knife, to a hacksaw. If it can cut into human flesh, I've seen it before.'

'But not this?' I peered at the photograph she had on the computer screen. It was a close-up of the wound on Barbara's throat.

'The entry point. This mark here.' She traced it with an elegant finger. 'The cutting edge is curved, but there are serrations above the handle, leaving a jagged edge on the skin. The profile's similar to some zombie knives I've come across, but not identical.'

'A what?'

She pulled up images of ornate knives, the size of machetes. All had vicious serrated edges and were decorated with symbols.

'Inspired by zombie movies and video games. Weapon of choice for street gangs. Bloody horrendous. Your offender is using something about the size of a large kitchen knife. Zombie blades come in all sizes. It's their serrations that are unusual.' She pointed to the castellated edges on some of the pictures. 'Typically, they're like the square teeth you'd find on a chainsaw.'

'And that's what you're seeing here?'

'Yes. These weapons have been banned in the UK since about twenty sixteen. Difficult to get hold of. Illegal to own or sell.'

'People who use these aren't likely to hand them in during a knife amnesty,' I said.

'True. There are plenty out there. I see the end results in here on a regular basis.'

'Think that's what we're looking for?'

She pursed her lips and slowly shook her head. 'I said the profile is *similar*, because of square edge to the serrated teeth. That's the closest I can liken it to – but not exactly the same. Your man is using something unique, I'd say.'

'Custom-made?'

'Probably.' She took a sip of her coffee. 'I'll trawl through the database and see if I can find anything. If not, it could be a one-off.'

'A unique weapon might be easier to find.'

'Simpler to identify as the murder weapon, once you have it. Unlike a bread knife – found in everyone's kitchen drawer. It ties the owner to the crime.'

'Have you told the team?'

'I'm about to.' She smiled. 'Just wanted to give you a heads-up, in case the Boy Scout doesn't share.'

'Thanks – appreciate it.'

As I was leaving, Gus stuck his head round the door. 'Checked the log for you, Jo.'

'And?'

'The cop who attended Barbara Thorpe's post-mortem was Beth Hastings.'

Chapter Forty-Eight

Saturday Afternoon

Despite the freezing temperatures outside, Tom Hannah was sweating.

I was watching a recording of his interview from the previous day, when he'd walked into Fordley Police Station, saying he believed the police wanted to talk to him.

The team were still waiting for forensics from the Lutner murder scene. They'd arrange for CSIs to go over Hannah's car, which was conveniently in the police car park. He'd given permission, but they'd arranged a warrant anyway. He'd thrown the clothes he'd been wearing on Wednesday and Thursday into the washing machine. But they'd be retrieved and tested.

Heslopp was the senior interviewing officer, assisted by Beth. Hannah had refused a solicitor.

A patina of sweat glistened across Hannah's forehead as he sat opposite the detectives. His shoulders slumped and his eyes ringed by dark shadows, he hardly looked like a man who'd have the brass neck to walk into a police station and hand himself in.

'Paxton Pits is a three-hour drive from where you live.' Heslopp glanced at his notes. 'And that's without stopping for a brew or a pee – so it probably took you longer than that. Want to tell us why you went there?'

'I've already been through this. I got a call from someone saying they had information about the copycat killings. An exclusive.'

'And he wouldn't go into detail over the phone?'

'No.'

'So, just like that,' Heslopp said, 'you jump in your car and drive a hundred and fifty miles? For someone who wouldn't give their name?'

'Yes.' His breath left him in a gust of frustration. 'I get anonymous tip-offs all the time, for the true crime magazine. Sometimes they pay off, sometimes they don't, but I can't afford to ignore them.'

'So how do you know it's not a wild goose chase?' Beth asked.

'I *do* try to qualify the lead.' He glared at her with contempt. 'In this case, he gave me information that's not been released to the public.'

'The signature on the letter to the *Express*?' Beth read from Hannah's initial account.

Since then, he'd been given a break so the team could verify what he'd said. This was round two – to check for consistency in the face of new information they were about to confront him with.

'No one knew what F.O.W. meant. My source said it was "Full of Woe", like the nursery rhyme.'

'Full marks to you on that one,' Callum said. He was standing next to me, watching the same recording.

'Thanks,' I muttered.

'And how did your caller say he'd come into possession of information about the copycat?' It was Heslopp again.

'He said he'd met the guy years before, at work.'

'Did he give the name of the company?'

'No, just said it was a plumbing place – they'd trained there as apprentices.'

'Randall's a plumber,' Callum muttered.

'Been friends ever since,' Hannah was saying. 'But lately his friend had become obsessed with the copycat murders. He was a Malecki fan. Had pictures of him all over the house. He claimed

270

to have irrefutable evidence that his mate was the copycat. Said to meet him in the car park at six o'clock.'

'You were visited by one of our officers on Monday. You never mentioned this call.'

'I've *told* you.' Hannah slapped the table with the flat of his hand. 'How many times?'

Until they're sure you're not making it up as you go along, I thought, chewing the end of my pencil.

'Tell us again.' Beth's voice was quiet, encouraging.

'I didn't get the call until Tuesday night – *after* Ian Drummond and that shrink came to see me.'

'You got down to Cambridgeshire at what time?' Heslopp asked.

'About half five. Parked up and waited. I rang the number he'd called me from, but it was unavailable. I waited until eight-ish. By then it was obvious he wasn't coming.'

'What did you do then?'

'Left. But I was freezing and hungry. Visitors centre shuts at four, so I went to the Shell station on the Great North Road. Used the loo, bought a coffee and some food and filled up for the journey back.'

'You didn't return home that night – why not?'

'I pulled off the road, to have my sandwich and the coffee. It started snowing and visibility was bad. I was knackered and didn't fancy driving in that. So, decided to have a kip before I carried on.'

'Where did you pull off?'

'About twenty minutes' drive from the garage.'

'Did you see anyone?'

'No. It was dark. It was just a gateway to a field.'

'Then what?'

'Slept longer than I intended. When I woke up it was nearly midnight. Snow was getting worse. Bloody car was stuck. Just had to sit it out. Kept the engine running on and off to keep the heater on. The gritters appeared about seven in the morning and it had started raining, so I could get out.'

'Then what?'

'Drove to a services further north. Got some food and read the paper. I wasn't in a rush. Kipped in the car for a bit. Left at lunchtime. Got into Fordley about four.'

'Officers called at your place Thursday afternoon. You weren't there.' Heslopp's tone was deceptively casual.

'I didn't go straight home. Had to go shopping for food. Then went to my local. If ever I needed a beer, it was then.'

'Which pub?' Beth asked, though they already knew.

'Red Lion,' he said wearily. 'The landlord knows me. He'll remember.'

Heslopp nodded. 'You say you finally got home about ten that night?'

'Yes. Just went straight to bed.'

'And you say you learned about the incident at Paxton Pits the next morning?'

'Yes, I heard that a body had been found.'

'On the news?'

'Yes.'

Heslopp sat back in his chair, tucking his overstretched shirt into the waistband of his trousers, frowning in confusion.

'You see, Tom, this is where we have a bit of a problem with your story.'

Hannah ran a hand through his hair. 'Like what?'

'Mark Lutner's body was discovered early on Thursday morning. But nothing went out on the media that day. There was a news blackout.' When Heslopp smiled, it always looked more like a baring of teeth.

272

I watched Hannah's body language. He was starting to leak unconscious stress signals.

Heslopp continued, 'We never want the victim's family to find out from the news that their loved one's been murdered. We have to verify their identity and inform next of kin and until that's done, we don't give anything to the press.'

'I heard about it on Friday morning, I told you,' Hannah insisted. Beneath the table, I could see his knee beginning to bounce with nervous energy that had nowhere to go.

'The first news about a body being found was broadcast five minutes before you handed yourself in.' Heslopp paused, letting that fact percolate.

Hannah's breathing was becoming more rapid as his heart rate soared. 'I . . . Well, I don't understand that.'

'No, Tom. Neither do we. It's a good twenty-minute drive from your house to the station. You must have already been on your way here, when the news went out.'

Again, the silence.

Hannah rubbed his eyes with the heel of his hand. 'Er . . . Yes, that's it. I remember now . . .'

'Go on,' Beth encouraged again.

'I was driving to visit my mum at the nursing home. It came on the car radio, so I turned round and drove here instead. Yes, that's how it happened.'

'How'd you know we'd be wanting to speak to you?' Heslopp asked.

'I knew you'd be checking cars that'd been in the area at the time. Wanted to eliminate myself. I *do* know how these things work.'

Chapter Forty-Nine

Saturday Afternoon, Incident Room

'Like he says,' Callum ran his fingers through his hair. 'He does know how these things work.'

'Meaning he'll know how to create a narrative to explain why he was in Cambridgeshire at the time of the murder,' Beth concluded.

'Everything he says checks out, boss.' Shah was at his desk. 'CCTV shows him entering and leaving the car park at the beauty spot, when he said he did.'

'There's the gap, when he says he was parked in that gateway.' Callum paced the front of the room. 'The gritter driver remembers seeing a car there at seven, but couldn't remember what make or model.'

'Got him confirmed at the service station on the A1,' Shah said. 'Till receipts for the food and newspaper and CCTV shows him leaving around the time he says. Only thing he forgot to mention was that he also bought a half-bottle of vodka. We found the empty in the back of his car.'

'Explains why he stayed at the services longer,' Callum said, rubbing the faint stubble on his chin. 'Wanted to sleep it off before getting back on the road.'

'The landlord at the Red Lion in Fordley confirms he was there until about ten on Thursday night,' Shah finished.

'We know Lutner died between six and midnight, if we're running with Jo's theory that our copycat would make the killing fall on a Wednesday,' Callum said.

'He was,' I said, certain.

'Hannah can't account for his whereabouts between eight that night and seven the next morning. Plenty of time to leave the car in the gateway and walk back to the park. Lots of ways to get in without being seen, if you're on foot. He could kill Lutner, then hoof it back to his car and say he was sleeping there until the next morning.'

'But why would he drive into the car park at six in the evening, knowing he'd be picked up on the cameras?' All eyes turned to me. 'Why not park out of the way and walk into the park after dark?'

'Because he knows his car will be picked up by any number of ANPR and CCTV cameras between Fordley and Cambridgeshire,' Beth said. 'He's said it himself – he knows how we operate. Might as well come up with a plausible alibi, to fit the evidence he knows we'll find.'

Somehow that just didn't feel right to me.

'What about his source saying that the copycat was a plumber?' Beth said. 'Hannah can't know we're looking for Randall, can he?'

Callum sat on the corner of a desk. 'He's close enough to Malecki to know about him. Easy enough to mention that fact, to add veracity.'

Frankly, I didn't think Hannah had the smarts to come up with something as elaborate as all this. I was just about to say so, when Tony Morgan walked into the room, slightly out of breath.

'We've been through Hannah's phone, boss.'

'And?'

'A number, ending 091, called his phone on Tuesday at 10.05 p.m. It's a burner. We can see he tried calling it back on

Wednesday at six and then again just after eight. But it didn't connect. The number's unavailable.'

'Matches what Hannah said.' Callum couldn't hide his disappointment.

'But here's the thing—' Tony waved the printout in his hand '—*another* unidentified number called Hannah at nine on Friday morning. Call lasted just under a minute.'

'Forty minutes before Hannah turned up here,' Shah said.

'Before radio news broke the story.' Callum tapped a pen against his thigh as the cogs turned. 'Someone tipping him off that we're looking for him?'

Finn McNamara's words echoed through my mind.

Some who were involved then are in important places now . . . and closer to home . . .

Was a cop tipping Hannah off? Was that how he knew about Randall?

Tony nodded. 'Looks like that's a burner too and it's disconnected now.'

'Our Tom gets a lot of calls from people using burner phones,' Callum said, almost to himself. 'We need to be asking him who he spoke to yesterday morning.'

Chapter Fifty

Sunday Morning, Kingsberry Farm

'A cop?' Jen was incredulous. 'On Callum's team?'

'Or DI Wardman's.' I gazed out of my office window as I spoke to her over the phone.

Snow covered the moors in a thick, downy blanket. Unmarked. Pristine and inviting. Like the still surface of an empty swimming pool that tempts you to dive in.

'Surely Callum's team would be too young to have been involved with the McGarrys, or Hannah when Finch died in . . . what year was it?'

'Nineteen ninety-three.'

Jen was struggling to get her head round the implications as much as I was.

'When did Frank Heslopp join?'

'He's the right age, but he moved up to Yorkshire from the Met.'

'What year though?'

'No idea and no way of asking, without raising suspicions.' Another thought occurred. 'Finn implied they were in the job *now*. Doesn't mean they were back then.'

'But he wouldn't say who?'

'Said he didn't know and I believe him.'

'So, we're looking for someone involved with the McGarrys *and* Hannah back in the day . . . and now?'

'Hannah's the key to it.' I was thinking out loud.

Harvey sat in front of me, with sad eyes that said I hadn't been paying him enough attention. He put his jowls on my knee and made a huffing sound.

'Someone tipped Hannah off that the police were looking for him. Probably advised him to turn himself in voluntarily.'

'Well, that narrows it down. Who else would know that?'

'We're back to the investigations teams.'

'You going to tell Callum . . . or Supt. Warner?'

'I want to,' I admitted, 'but I don't know who to trust.'

'You thought someone was briefing Callum about your movements. Maybe you're not paranoid after all?'

'Not sure which is worse,' I said. 'Being paranoid, or being right.'

'Maybe take comfort knowing you're rattling someone.'

'"Some that were involved . . . are in the job, and they won't thank you for poking around in what's dead and gone",' I murmured.

'What?'

'The last thing Finn said to me.'

'So, what are you going to do?'

'Poke around in what's dead and gone.'

* * *

As soon as I'd hung up, the phone rang again. It was Callum.

'Just wanted to update you on the latest.' He was brusque.

'OK.'

'You sound surprised.'

'Maybe because I am.'

'Look, I know things are not . . . great between us, but you're still part of the team and I need you to be as up to speed as everyone else.'

'Well, that's good.' Was all I could think to say.

'We've had initial results back from Cambridgeshire. So far, nothing connects Hannah to the scene. No trace fibres, blood – nothing.'

'What about his car?'

278

'Same. They've recovered his clothes, but I'm not holding my breath. Especially as they've been through the wash.'

'Blood traces have been found on washed clothing—'

'I know.' He cut me off. 'But if he'd killed Lutner, then gone back to the car, there would be some transfer there. But there's nothing. Decision's been taken to release him under investigation. We can't hold him without something more concrete.'

'What did he say about the number that rang him on Friday morning?'

'Said it was a source. Some guff about a story for the true crime rag he writes for.'

'But wouldn't give a name?'

I knew he was shaking his head. 'Says he doesn't know. That same number's come up twice in the last few months. He says it's someone giving him info for his articles and they're anonymous. There are two other numbers that the Telephony team say are burners. They've rung frequently over the last few weeks. He says the people who give him the leads usually use burners. There's nothing unusual in that and he's happy to take the information without knowing their identities.'

'And a good journalist never reveals his sources.'

'Yeah, some such bollocks.'

There was a silence and for an aching moment I wanted to tell him about the suggestion of a cop on the team leaking information. But something held me back. I really didn't have enough to go on yet. And I still didn't know who to trust. Even Callum.

That thought shocked me, even as it entered my head, but I couldn't shake it.

'You can watch the interview tape when you're in,' he was saying. 'There was an interesting moment when we told him Malecki had put his name forward as the possible copycat.'

'How did he react?'

'Went ballistic. Said Malecki was just being a vindictive bastard. Giving us the runaround and causing him trouble into the bargain.'

'So, it's a massive coincidence, that he ends up at the next murder scene?'

'Don't believe in coincidences ... Especially ones as big as that. Besides, Malecki's not the only one to mention Hannah. Jack Halton did too. Obviously, Hannah doesn't know that.'

Something occurred to me. 'Could I get copies of the prison CCTV? I want to go through the visitors footage again.'

'No problem. There's an early morning briefing tomorrow – usual time, if you want to attend?'

'OK.'

'Meantime, I want you to look again at Randall. Need more of an insight into his character.'

'I could do with the psych report that was done for his trial,' I said.

'I'll get that to you, and, Jo ...'

'What?'

'I *do* value your input. Despite how things might be right now ... thanks.'

Chapter Fifty-One

Early hours, Monday Morning, Kingsberry Farm

For a second, I thought the alarm had gone off. I'd set it for sparrow's fart – 5.30 a.m. – to get to Fordley in time for the briefing. Whatever had woken me from a dead sleep, the red glow of my bedside clock said 2 a.m.

Confused, I propped up on one elbow, then fumbled for my phone when it rang again.

'McCready,' I mumbled.

'Jo?' A familiar voice, that in the fog of half-sleep I couldn't quite place. 'Belmarsh calling.' He laughed softly.

I sat bolt upright.

Chris McGarry.

I pushed the hair out of my eyes and leaned back against the headboard.

'Obviously not through the prison switchboard?'

'Er, no. You know how it works, Jo, you're not *that* naive.'

'You're taking a hell of a chance, Chris.'

'Getting the phone smuggled in was easy. It was the charger that made my pal's eyes water.' He laughed again. 'Wasn't just for you, I need it for business.'

'But if you get caught . . .'

'You're worse than the missus – stop worrying. Listen, I've heard from Joshua about Hannah. Thought it was safer to speak to you directly.'

'There's been a development.'

'Like what?'

'Hannah's been arrested.'

'For what?'

I hesitated.

'Oh, come on, Jo. If you don't trust me, I can't help.'

'What does it say about me that right now, I trust a man serving time in Belmarsh more than I trust the police?'

'That you've got great instincts.' I could hear his grin.

'The copycat killings.'

There was a low whistle down the phone. 'Fuck me. Didn't think the little weed had it in him.'

'That's just it. Neither do I. But he was at the scene, at the exact time of the latest murder.'

'There's me thinking we would be talking about Dirty Dave Finch.'

'Still need to. What do you know about that?'

'Personally, not a lot. I was just nine years old when he became a crispy critter, but I remember the talk on the estate. My uncle was Dad's right hand back then. He's doing time in Wandsworth. I've spoken to him and he's told me what I think you want to know.'

'I was told Hannah was on your dad's payroll.'

'True.'

'And that your dad warned him away from covering the story?'

'Also true.'

I waited, but emptiness crackled down the line.

Chris was far from his ebullient self. But then, we'd never before had a conversation that touched at the heart of his family business – or his family loyalties.

'Is this how you want to play it?' I asked.

'Keep going.'

I took a long breath. 'OK. Is Hannah still in your pocket?'

'No.'

'I was told your father wasn't involved in Finch's death, but he knew who was?'

'Correct.'

'That a local family was responsible and your father covered up their involvement?'

'Yes.'

'Were other people paid off in the cover-up?'

'Yes.'

'Who?'

Another empty silence, and then, 'Some police.'

'Names?'

'Sorry, Jo. No can do.'

'Because they're still serving?'

'Actually, the two I know of are both dead now. Of natural causes before you ask.'

'Then why not give me their names?'

'It's something we don't do,' he said simply. 'Even after they're retired or dead. If word got out that we did, no plod would ever work with us again.'

'Which means you've got police on your payroll now?'

'Like I said, you're not naive.'

'If I give a name, will you confirm it?'

'No.'

There goes that plan.

'Was Finch trading in child pornography?'

'Yes.'

'And that's why the local family were involved?'

'Yes. Their little girl – five at the time – was groomed by Finch. He made videos of her being abused by himself and his sick mates. The family found out. You can fill in the rest.'

'Can you give me the name of the family?'

'No. My father went to a lot of trouble to protect them. Not to mention the kid involved. If I give you their name, it was all for nothing. There's no expiry date on a murder charge, Jo. Wouldn't want to see it all come out now.'

'Was someone in that family a cop?'

'Not sure whether they were a family member. But someone involved then is a cop now. And before you ask, I don't have a name.'

'Would your uncle know?'

'Says he doesn't. Think that died with my old man. All he knows is that they're in the job, or at least they were last time he was on the outside.'

'Which was how long ago?'

'Five years.'

'Can you tell me where they were serving?'

'Somewhere in the West Yorkshire force.'

'Are they protecting Hannah . . . from inside the force?'

'Word is they may be. Hannah found out what the family had done. My old man warned him to keep his mouth shut. As far as I know, he has done ever since.'

'Do you think Hannah's involved in these killings?'

'Personally, I wouldn't have thought he'd have the balls-to-brains ratio for it. He's a self-absorbed worm, that much I *do* know. Used to beat up on his missus, especially if he'd had a few too many. He can be a violent bastard, but only with women. Cowardly shit. Drink is his weakness – always was. He's approached me a few times, with offers of running exposés on rivals – to get them out of the game. But I won't touch him. Too unreliable. Besides, it's not the way we do things these days.'

'Might have been better than your last solution.'

He laughed. 'Yeah, probably. But you know how it is when family's threatened, Jo? Wouldn't trust anyone else to take care of it.'

'Speaking of family, how's your little boy?'

'Not great. He's in Fordley Royal Infirmary, but they're transferring him to Jimmy's.'

Saint James's Hospital in Leeds.

'It's a brain tumour – malignant.'

'Oh, Chris.' As a mother, I couldn't help but imagine my own son Alex and how I'd feel. 'I'm so sorry.'

His voice caught and the thought of a man like Chris choking with emotion made my own eyes fill up.

'It's operable though – so . . . you know.'

'And your application for transfer?'

'Joshua's on it.'

'Let me know if there's anything I can do.' I meant it.

'I've opened a tab for this one, Jo . . . just so you know.'

Of course he had. I wasn't fool enough to think his help was gratis.

'And, Jo . . .'

'What?'

'Be careful. I mean it. The people you're dealing with play for keeps . . . Watch your back.'

Chapter Fifty-Two

Monday Morning, Incident Room, Fordley Police Station

There was no point sugaring things up, so Callum didn't.

'We've got nothing to link Hannah to the murder scene.' He launched straight into it. 'Not on him, his clothes or his car and nothing in the birdwatching hide. We've spun his house and his phone. No point holding him and running the clock down, so he was released under investigation over the weekend. If Intel turn up anything on those burner phones or the other numbers, we can always pull him in again.'

'Forensic Science Service have come back on the images of the white van,' DI Wardman said. 'They're pretty certain it's a Ford Connect.'

'Without a registration to go on,' Heslopp muttered, 'cohort of owners could run into thousands.'

'Until we get a break that narrows it down, we go through those thousands and eliminate them, if that's what we have to do,' Callum said.

Wardman tapped his notes. 'They've confirmed it's white . . .'

'White van man,' Ian Drummond muttered, just loud enough. 'Can't be many of those around.'

'With marks on the side they think are from a decal being removed,' Wardman ploughed on regardless.

It was something, but not much. And I knew the results could still run into thousands of vehicles around the country. Elimination would take time. Something the team didn't have.

'The good news is . . .' all eyes turned to Tony Morgan '. . . DVLA have got a vehicle registered to Peter Randall.' He paused for dramatic effect. 'A white Ford Connect.'

'I'd like to say "bingo",' Heslopp said, 'but I'd hate to jinx it.'

'Too much to hope that it's at his registered address?' Callum said, taking a drink of coffee.

'He's not been there for months,' a traffic cop chipped in. 'Van's not been seen by neighbours in as long, either. Got a marker out on it. If it moves, we'll pick it up.'

'If Hannah's telling the truth,' Callum said, looking at the whiteboard for Paxton Pits, 'and he *didn't* kill Lutner.' He tapped a mugshot. 'Randall is in pole position.'

'Hannah's anonymous caller said his mate was a plumber,' Heslopp supplied. 'His van fits the one near Jones's place and he loves Malecki enough to have his chops inked across his back.'

'And he's on the fan sites,' Ian added.

'Lee said he'd got something important on those.' Callum scanned the room. 'Where is he, anyway?'

As if he'd conjured him up, the door flew open and in an uncharacteristic burst of energy, Lee almost fell into the room.

'Afternoon,' Heslopp said. 'Glad you could join us.'

Lee's face was flushed. 'I've been tracking fans on the Malecki site. Following those who seem the most radical. One who goes under the username WednesdaysChild is trading in unusual Malecki merchandise.'

'Unusual, how?' Callum asked.

'Because they claim it's stuff from the original murder scenes.'

'Trophies,' I said, suddenly feeling my innards tighten.

'They must be fake,' Wardman said dismissively. 'Malecki never took trophies – except for body parts.'

287

'He did.' I shot him a look. 'Family members said things had gone missing.'

'Well, before we get carried away,' Callum interjected, 'we need to verify it. With no way for buyers to authenticate these, it could be just a scam. Dark web isn't exactly an Amazon website. Show us what you've got, Lee.'

* * *

We all studied the images on screen. A distinctive Montblanc pen and a single silver earring.

Callum looked to me. 'You studied the original crimes longer than anyone, Jo. These look familiar?'

'Not the earring,' I admitted, 'but the pen. I've seen that in a photo. Press article, if I remember.' I bit my bottom lip as I thought back. 'Graham Hirst, maybe?'

Beth was busy at her computer.

'Got it.' She turned the screen to show an image of Graham Hirst, with the distinctive white top of the pen in his top pocket.

'Beth, go through all the records for the original victims,' Callum directed. 'See if you can find mention of the earring. Lee, get everything you can on WednesdaysChild. Whoever it is, has access to stuff only Malecki knew about. We need to find out where they're getting it.'

'On it, boss.'

Chapter Fifty-Three

Monday, Late Morning

I'd decided to work from the farm.

After the kitchen, my office was probably the place I spent the most time. It was my sanctuary. A space filled with things I loved. It smelled of wood polish and leather-bound books, from the wall of bookcases that held volumes covering every conceivable aspect of murder or murderers past and present, as well as photographs and souvenirs from my travels.

The lamp's honey-coloured glow made the room feel even cosier against the freezing weather outside.

Jen was making a brew, while I watched the CCTV from the prison visiting hall.

I'd trawled through hours of it. Even as I closed my eyes, I could see the images playing across my darkened eyelids.

I tried to refocus. Switching from the film footage to read my profile of our copycat.

Profiles were organic. Rarely fixed. Growing and shifting with each new piece of information as investigations unfolded.

There was something niggling at me that I couldn't shake. A feeling that what we were seeing was not all it appeared to be. It was a gut instinct. One that had served me well, but I knew wasn't enough to take to the investigating team.

Jen put my mug on the desk.

'Penny for them?'

'Not worth that much.' I took a welcome sip of scalding tea.

She settled herself at the desk across the room. 'I've been doing some digging into possible ways to ID a cop who could have been involved with the McGarrys or Hannah around 1993.'

Now she had my full attention.

'Go on.'

'It was a local family on the estate where Finch lived who were involved in his death.'

'Yes.'

'And someone involved with what happened then is in the police now. So, I went through the census records for the estate from those years and pulled up the list of family names.' She glanced at me over the top of her reading glasses. 'If you go through it, there might be a name you recognise.'

'You never cease to amaze me, Jen.'

'Is this a good time to ask for a pay rise?'

I scrolled down the names and slowly shook my head. 'I don't recognise any of them.'

She shrugged. 'No bonus for me then.'

'Just because I don't recognise the name, doesn't mean it's not there. I don't know everyone. Could be any officer in West Yorkshire . . . or even further afield by now.'

'But to check, you'd have to compare that list with a database of police officers,' she said.

'Don't have access to that. And can't ask without raising suspicion.'

We both fell silent for a minute, until Jen broached a subject I knew she would, eventually.

'Heard any more from the lovely Eduardo?'

'Few WhatsApp messages.'

'He seems nice . . .'

Her tone flagged up a silent concern. I shot her a look. 'But?'

'Too nice . . . ?' Her grey eyes were anxious.

'Know what you mean,' I conceded. 'But just because the job has made us cynical, doesn't mean there aren't genuinely nice people out there.'

'Call me a suspicious old cow, but perfection like that makes me nervous.'

'You're a suspicious old cow.' I grinned.

She shrugged. 'Well, if he turns out to be a mad axe murderer, don't say I didn't warn you.' Her tone was only half-joking. 'What do we do about the Finch case?' She brought us back to work.

'Need to get some fresh air. Try to clear my thinking.' I stood up and Harvey, who'd been snoring loudly on the rug, was immediately on his feet. Long tail swishing in anticipation. 'Yes, you heard.' I ruffled his silky ears. 'Time for a walk.'

* * *

My boots crunched over the frost-hardened, tufted grass as I followed Harvey across the moorland. He ran ahead, having to bounce over the snow that was almost up to his chest.

I took a long ice-cold breath, enjoying the crisp freshness, and pulled up the collar on my coat. My father, who loved trekking these uplands, always maintained there was no such thing as bad weather, only the wrong clothes. I smiled as I remembered him – wishing we could have one more walk together. One more conversation.

As I followed aimlessly along, I thought about the threads I was struggling with.

When I looked at these scenes, I saw no rage and certainly no sexual sadism, all of which were present in the original series.

This copycat seemed to want the opposite of that. No prolonged time spent with the victim. A blitz attack, from behind – according to Elle.

The victimology was the main factor that was prodding me to think about this whole case differently. That's why I'd asked for the CCTV footage, so that I could look for evidence confirming my own fledgling theory.

After hours of studying the film, I'd run it at twelve times normal speed. Watching the people moving in fast time, like an old Charlie Chaplin movie. It was helpful, because it highlighted patterns in proxemics and body language that can be missed when watching in real time.

I always found this a good place to think. Away from the noise of traffic and hubbub of the modern world, time slipped away. My thoughts only accompanied by the occasional bleat of sheep and the cry of a bird of prey, wheeling overhead.

Ahead of us, the landscape rose up to meet a charcoal-grey sky that promised more heavy weather.

Harvey bounded over to me with a stick he'd dug out of the snow. I launched it for him then leaned on the dry-stone wall. Resting my arms along the top to look over into the adjoining field.

A movement caught my eye. A second later, a red fox appeared, cautiously sniffing the air. I glanced over my shoulder at Harvey, thankfully occupied with his stick.

I rested my chin on my arms and watched as a second, younger, fox appeared. Staying in the shadow of his companion. They stood for a moment then, feeling safe, began to trot across the snow, which was hardened to a thick crust.

The leader stopped suddenly – tilting his head to one side as he stared intently at the snow beneath him. The younger halted in his tracks, watching this masterclass in the hunt.

Tutor fox suddenly jumped straight up in the air – at least three feet – then plunged head first into the snow, with jaws wide open. Emerging, shaking his head, with a small mouse in his teeth.

Behind me, Harvey barked at his stick and the two predators darted away. I stared at Harvey, as the pieces finally fell together.

Chapter Fifty-Four

Monday Evening

Back at the farm, I placed a call to someone I thought might be able to help Jen with her research into the census. Then grabbed my files and jumped in the car, calling Callum on my way in to Fordley to say I needed to speak to him as soon as I got there.

When I arrived, I collared Tony Morgan. To demonstrate my theory, I'd asked if he could create a layout for the CCTV footage that would show rows of images – like a split-screen.

As expected, Callum was in his office.

'Most of the team are in,' he said, barely glancing up from his laptop. 'Your mate, Dr Richardson, called an hour ago to say she's found something. We've set up a team Zoom call.'

'Bloody hate Zoom,' I said, dumping my case on the floor.

'I know, but she says we need to see post-mortem photos. She's too busy to come in and we can't all traipse down there.' He stood up and began to shrug on his suit jacket. 'Whatever it is you want to tell me, you might as well brief the team at the same time.' He hesitated, with one arm in a sleeve. 'Unless it's private?'

'Not private, exactly.' He slowly slid the other arm in. 'But I'd rather run this past you first, before going public.'

'OK.' He sat back down.

'I don't believe we're dealing with a copycat.'

'You don't?'

I shook my head.

'What then?'

'A disciple.'

* * *

Callum glanced at his watch.

'OK, everyone. We've got fifteen minutes before the Zoom call with Dr Richardson.' He gestured me to the front. 'Jo's got a theory about our killer. If she's right, it changes the way we need to tackle this.'

I faced a sea of faces.

'Looking at the MO and the victimology, I no longer believe our killer's a copycat.' That was greeted with an uncharacteristic silence. No smart remarks. No jokes. Just an expectant stillness.

'I think we're dealing with a disciple.'

'A what?' asked a young PC at the back.

'Someone who kills at the request of their leader.' The PC looked like he wished he'd never asked.

'So, in *this* case,' Heslopp ventured, 'that "leader" would be Malecki?'

I nodded.

'What makes you think Malecki's directing all this?' Callum gave me my cue.

I hadn't told him that my thoughts crystallised while watching an old fox teach a young one how to hunt. He'd probably have me certified.

'This killer's MO and victim selection have bothered me from the start,' I confessed. 'Copycats choose a series to replicate for a reason and stick as close to the original as possible.'

'These killings are identical to Malecki's,' Wardman interrupted. 'Leaving a body part in the mouth of each victim, cutting their throats . . . all the same.'

'The "how" is the same,' I conceded, 'but the "why" isn't.'

'Explain that.'

'A copycat is attracted to a series that tap into their own fantasies. Malecki was a sexual sadist. The main event is the terror of the victim. The pleading. The look in their eyes when they realise

295

what's about to happen to them. Malecki enjoyed torturing his prey. I don't see that here.'

I tapped the images of Stephen Jones, Barbara Thorpe and Mark Lutner.

'According to Dr Richardson, the attacks were from behind. That's a major departure from Malecki's MO. No looking the victim in the eye as they die. No savouring the terror. All the body parts were amputated post-mortem. None of the paraphilia I'd expect to see in someone aroused enough by Malecki's crimes to copy him. This is Malecki-by-numbers.'

'That covers the MO,' Callum said. 'What about the victimology?'

'Malecki entered busy homes, confident in his ability to overpower and control his victims. This killer is deliberately targeting single occupants, all over fifty—'

'So far.' Wardman cut across me.

'They all lived solitary lives—'

'Lutner didn't,' Wardman persisted.

'I agree – he's an outlier. He was chosen because Malecki wanted him dead. Malecki said the next murder would be "dramatic". He wasn't guessing, he already *knew*. Lutner was killed in an isolated place and vulnerable and from behind,' I ploughed on. 'This offender is either physically or psychologically incapable of dealing with a head-on kill.'

As Wardman opened his mouth to say more, Callum unexpectedly came to the rescue. 'If these *are* disciple killings, what other characteristics would you expect to see?'

'The leader chooses their followers carefully. To be sure they'll "follow through" and cross that ultimate line. They'll often "test" them, by initiating discussions around rape or murder, or even involving them in a "lower-level" crime, to see how committed their devotees will be.'

'Hannah said Malecki's favourite topic was whether he could commit murder,' Ian said.

'He's probably had those same conversations with Peter Randall and others, too.' I looked at Tony. 'Have you got the footage lined up?'

'Yep.'

'This is a collection of CCTV from the prison visits by Peter Randall, Tom Hannah, Gerald Carter and Jill Neatley.' I pressed the remote. 'The screens across the top are from a year ago or more. The bottom ones are the most recent.'

In the top row, the visitors were animated, laughing, smiling. Engaging in two-way conversation.

The bottom screens showed something very different.

The people sitting opposite Malecki were hardly moving. Their backs were straighter, their expressions more serious. Malecki was doing most of the talking, with just occasional comments and slight nods from his visitors.

'Recent visits look more subdued,' Tony said.

'These aren't social visits,' I said.

'What then?' Wardman asked.

'Interviews.'

That statement rattled around a still room.

'Malecki's auditioning for a disciple?' Callum said.

'Yes, and that process began six months ago.'

'Sorry—' Wardman sounded exasperated '—but before we go down this rabbit hole, can I just be clear. You're asking us to believe that someone would kill, just because their "idol"—' he rolled his eyes at the last word '—tells them to?'

I sat on the edge of the desk. 'You don't have to take my word for it.'

'I wasn't about to.'

'Murder-history is full of examples. Myra Hindley under the direction of Ian Brady. The most famous are the Charles Manson murders in the USA.'

'Isn't he a singer?' a young PC asked.

'That's Marilyn Manson, you pillock,' his mate said, digging him in the ribs as laughter rippled round the room.

'Charles Manson,' I explained, 'led a cult – The Manson Family – in sixties America. Twenty or so members. Men and women. On Manson's instruction, they killed the actress Sharon Tate and four other people, in her home in LA. Manson wasn't present, but was found guilty as he'd ordered the murders.'

'Is this hybristo—thing?' Shah asked.

'Hybristophilia, yes. Disciples are in love with the leader – to the point they'll do anything for them. Even murder. It's the ultimate folie à deux – "madness of two". The irony is that if these two people had never come together to feed this thing, the murders might not have happened. Hindley wouldn't have committed murder if she'd never met Brady.'

'So, the disciple is more likely to be a woman?'

'Not necessarily. Manson had male disciples.'

'Gerald Carter had a sexual relationship with Malecki,' Heslopp said, scratching his chin.

'And,' I added, 'he's still in love with Malecki.'

'Does a disciple ever turn on their idol?' Shah asked.

'Only once the bond is broken. Usually after they've been caught and start to blame one another,' I said. 'Hindley and Brady turned on each other, but it took decades in prison. The disciple needs the acceptance of their partner in order to feel whole. It takes a lot to break that. The dominant one will more often discard a disciple, once they've tired of them. Then move on to find another person to manipulate.'

'So, what happens to the disciple they've dumped?'

'It's usually their body that gets dumped,' I said without humour. 'The best way for two people to keep a secret like that is to kill one of them.'

'Anything else, Doc?' Heslopp asked.

'Yes. Probably the most important element in our case.'

'What's that?'

'Victim selection is *always* done by the leader.'

Chapter Fifty-Five

Monday Evening, Briefing Room, Fordley Police Station

It was time to take Elle's Zoom call.

Her face filled the screen at the front of the room.

'I told you about the unique profile of the knife used in the Jones and Thorpe cases.' She was saying. 'Cambridgeshire's results are in. Same weapon used on Mark Lutner – so that ties your killings together.'

'Every little helps.' Callum smiled.

'I went through the database to look for anything similar.'

'OK,' Callum said.

'But I found something I didn't expect.'

He looked up, but said nothing. Elle clicked some keys. 'These are post-mortem pictures from victims who've all had their throats cut.'

We stared at seven close-up images no one really wants to see before going to dinner.

'All have the same wounds.'

'Same knife?' Callum asked.

'I'd stake my pension on it.'

'Who are they?' he asked.

'The first four are the Ledlaw family, in 1987. The other three were Malecki's victims from 1987 to 1989.'

There was a stunned silence.

'What about Malecki's victims prior to 1987?' Callum finally asked.

'All those were killed with a standard, straight-edged blade, which has never been recovered. Victims who came *after* these seven – the Gordons and Kath Hutchinson – were matched to the knife that was found in Malecki's car, when he was arrested.'

'Just for clarity,' Callum said hesitantly. 'Malecki used *three* different weapons in his killing career?'

'Correct.'

'And in the middle period, he switched to a custom-made blade?'

'Yes. I can't find anything like it on the mass market. And I've included banned weapons and exotic items we sometimes see coming in from abroad.'

'And this unique knife is being used in the latest murders?'

Elle nodded, pushing fingers through her red curls. 'I'll keep looking. I've got colleagues in the UK and round the world. I'll circulate a description and see if anything similar turns up.'

'OK. Thanks, Doctor.'

The screen went blank, and for a moment, no one spoke. Then Heslopp cleared his throat.

'How does a knife that Malecki used nearly thirty years ago get into the hands of our killer?'

'If our copycat is on the fandom sites,' Lee said, 'he could have bought it.'

'Or, if I'm right,' I said, more certain than ever that I was, 'Malecki could have given the knife to his disciple.'

'He's in prison.' Wardman stated the obvious. 'How can he have kept a knife for three decades, to give to someone now?'

A few in the room rolled their eyes, but Wardman was too busy glaring at me to notice.

'He's told them where to find it,' I said. 'Along with his notebooks.'

'Notebooks?' Wardman frowned.

'Malecki kept meticulous notes on each of his "projects". Those books, along with the trophies I always believed he took, have never been found.'

'And you believe he kept this custom-made knife in that stash?'

'Yes – which brings me back to the victims we're seeing now.'

'What do you mean?'

'I think our victims were ones Malecki was stalking during the time he was killing. Malecki has given his disciple access to his notebooks and his knife, and told them to complete his original kill list.'

Chapter Fifty-Six

Monday Night

'I wanted to speak to you alone.' Callum's voice came through the Bluetooth as I drove out of Fordley. 'But you'd gone when I finished with the team.'

'Sorry. I need to get back. The snow's getting heavier. Weather warnings for a bad storm coming in.'

'I just want to run through some things.'

'OK.'

'Your thinking about our victims being on Malecki's kill list?'

My reflection in the darkening windscreen nodded at me. 'All older – solitary people who, with the exception of Lutner, have lived at the same address since the eighties or nineties.'

I hated doing things on-the-fly, preferring to put my theories down on paper. I said as much.

'I know.' Callum's sigh was loud down the phone. 'But right now, I don't have time. So, humour me.'

'Joan Rigby got me thinking. She said Barbara had lived there since the estate was built. She was habitual, especially her routine with the cat. She never deviated from it. Those were the type of people Malecki zeroed in on. Their habits made them vulnerable. Easy prey.'

'And Jones?'

'Lived in that house since 1991. Malecki was arrested in 1993. Jones could have been one of his "projects". But he never got to follow through with it, because he got caught.'

'I'm listening.'

'Lutner bothered me,' I admitted.

'Why?'

'Too random for a copycat. It made a connection to Michelle Hatfield. Which didn't sit right with me. I couldn't see a modern-day copycat wanting to forge his own legend, going after him. Plus, geographically it didn't fit the profile. So far, he's stuck to West Yorkshire. To deviate from that and travel a hundred and fifty miles away . . .'

We'd used a 'spatial profiling' expert a few years ago. He told us offenders had a defined spatial range. Some did commit offences over longer distances, but usually that was part of an established route – such as a lorry driver, like Peter Sutcliffe, the Yorkshire Ripper. I believed our killer's base was West Yorkshire.

'That distance makes Lutner an outlier, literally, *and* in the victimology. If we were dealing with a copycat that would be a really unusual deviation.'

'Unless . . . ?'

'Unless he's acting on instructions. Lutner makes more sense if Malecki's directing things. It's the way his mind works. Picking someone connected to the one murder victim that's never been found. The one everyone wants to know about.'

'Stretching resources across multiple police forces,' Callum agreed. 'Certainly, gives us the runaround. But why now?'

I slowed down to concentrate. The snow was thick and heavy. Coming down in soft pillowy flakes that were sticking to the unlit country road, making driving more perilous.

'He started "interviewing" for his disciple six months ago. The same time he began painting more for his exhibition. He's fallen out of the popular imagination. What better way to put his work back in the spotlight again? And complete his *real* life's work into the bargain. The challenge he set himself and the thing that *truly* inspires him.'

'What if you're wrong?'

That thought had been keeping me awake at night.

'We both know the direction of the investigation isn't dictated by a profile, Cal. It's just one tool in the box. Besides, it doesn't change the suspect list you've already got.'

'What are your thoughts on Gerald Carter and Jill Neatley?'

'If it had been a copycat, I would rule them both out. Carter is devoted to Malecki, but he hasn't got what it takes to initiate this on his own.'

'But as a disciple?'

'He ticks the boxes. He's in love with Malecki and will do anything to keep that. He's too weak for a face-on confrontation with the victims. Blitz attacks from behind would be just his style.'

'And Neatley?'

'Jury's still out,' I admitted. 'I'd need more time with her. She's difficult to read.'

'Even for you?'

'I'm not an infallible polygraph. Some people get past my radar. But what I can tell you is that Hannah's definitely *not* your killer.'

'His hatred for Malecki could be an act,' Callum said, 'to throw us off the scent.'

'No one's that good an actor.' I shook my head. 'It's not Hannah, Cal. His drinking's a major weakness and would lead to stupid mistakes. I'm not seeing anything so disorganised. Our killer has far more self-control and discipline than Hannah. I think he was set up. And if Malecki's behind things that makes perfect sense.'

'Think Malecki's using the burner 091?'

'Could be the anonymous male caller,' I speculated.

'No way to know though.' He sounded as weary as I knew he was.

'Unless we ask him.'

'You think he'd be honest?'

'Not if he wants us to believe we're chasing a copycat.'

'If we tell him we know it's a disciple, how do you think he'll react?'

'Only one way to find out.'

Chapter Fifty-Seven

Tuesday, Wakefield Prison

Callum shifted on the leather sofa next to me as we waited in the governor's office.

We both turned as Rob Harding came in – his expression less relaxed than when I last saw him.

'Sorry,' he said as he sat. 'Too many tasks, not enough day. My secretary told me the reason for your visit. I have to say, I'm surprised.'

'That we think Malecki might have an illegal phone?' Callum said.

'Smuggled contraband is a serious issue, Chief Inspector. Especially phones. The damage they can cause on the outside is incalculable. We pride ourselves on the level of security here.'

I thought about Chris McGarry's late-night call and hoped the discomfort didn't show on my face.

'Use of illegal mobiles is usually by drugs or organised crime gangs,' Harding went on. 'Jacob has never been involved in anything like that.'

'There's a first time for everything.' Callum's smile lacked humour.

'He's subject to regular security searches, but he's never been found in possession of anything.'

Callum's tone was conciliatory. 'Governor, we believe there's a serious threat to life and we need to be sure Malecki isn't communicating with people on the outside. I can only do my job, with your cooperation.'

The police couldn't just demand what they wanted in a situation like this. Contrary to popular belief, within the prison estate, the governor held ultimate authority.

'You have reliable intelligence for this?' Harding asked.

Callum shot me a look. 'I believe so.'

'What do you need?'

'While Dr McCready is interviewing Malecki, I want his cell turned over. But I don't want the search carried out by officers on his wing.'

Harding regarded him steadily. 'It wouldn't be. I'll authorise a search by the specialist security team.'

'I also want him to be subject to a full body search.'

Harding nodded. 'I'll have that done down in the segregation unit, when he leaves Dr McCready.'

'Would it be possible for Malecki to be held down there for the time being?' Callum asked. 'We could do with him being incommunicado for a while.'

'That's not possible, I'm afraid. Unless he's broken prison regulations, he can't be punished by being put into solitary.'

'Don't tell me—' I couldn't stay quiet '—that would breach his human rights?'

Harding's eyes met mine. 'Yes, Doctor. Exactly that.'

'What about the rights of people who might die if Malecki *isn't* segregated?' I was incredulous.

'You haven't given me any hard evidence that's the case.' Harding's composure in the face of such potential risk was staggering to me. 'We haven't searched Jacob's cell yet and until and unless anything is found, I'm not committing myself to any course of action.'

'If you find a phone?' I pressed. 'Or any illegal contraband? He would be in breach of prison regulation then, wouldn't he?'

'Yes. And in that case, he would be punished by being sent to the segregation unit. But until then . . .'

Callum said, 'If he's allowed back to the wing, I want all his calls recorded and all interactions with other prisoners watched by wing staff. Anything unusual gets reported to my team, and I want recordings of any phone calls to be sent directly to the incident room.'

Harding quirked an eyebrow. 'Anything else, while we're at it?'

'If I think of anything, I'll let you know.'

*   *   *

We'd planned a strategy for the way I would interview Malecki, but there were too many variables for it to be scripted.

I glanced at the digital recorder. The light blinked from the screen, reassuring me that it was working.

Malecki was already sitting on his side of the security screen, regarding me with an expression that veered from curious to bemused.

'The police have gone through your list,' I said simply. It wasn't a question, but I gave him the silence to answer.

He crossed his legs. 'With what result?'

'Four of the six names have been eliminated.'

'And the other two?'

The team had agreed that I should tell him – just to gauge his reaction.

'Tom Hannah and Peter Randall.'

'What did they have to say?'

'The police are still looking for Randall. Any idea where he might be?'

'Beyond his usual address?' He shook his head.

'And Tom Hannah has been arrested.'

His expression remained impassive, apart from a slightly raised eyebrow. 'Because I put his name forward?'

His whole demeanour was carefully controlled, giving nothing away. If I was right about his having a disciple, this was a masterclass in masking behaviour.

'He was at the scene of the latest murder.'

'Lutner.' He nodded. 'I saw that on the news.'

'You don't seem surprised.'

He shrugged. 'Nothing surprises me these days.'

'You predicted something dramatic.'

'Indeed.'

I made a show of glancing at my notes. Then asked a question the team had supplied.

'According to the visitors log, Gerald Carter and Jill Neatley visit regularly.'

'Yes. Gerald's a friend. He brings Miss Neatley only when we have to discuss technical things. What of it?'

'Jill Neatley came to see you on her own, in the summer. Why was that?'

'Gerald was going against some of my choices for the exhibition. I asked to see her to get her side of it, without the pressure of her boss being there.'

'You asked her not to tell Carter about the meeting?'

'It would have made things awkward for her if he found out. I didn't want that.'

'Do you think either of them would be able to commit these murders?'

He laughed. 'You can't be serious?'

'That's not an answer.'

I watched him, calibrating his body language. But he was giving me nothing.

'Gerald carries spiders out of the house, rather than kill them. As for Miss Neatley, I really don't know her that well, but Gerald tells me she's a bleeding-heart liberal, who spends her spare time working for charities. She doesn't strike me as the killer type. Randall and Hannah on the other hand . . .'

He paused, waiting for me to say something. I let the silence stretch out between us. He spoke first.

'Has Hannah been charged with murder?'

I feigned surprise at the question.

'Not yet. You see there's nothing linking him to it. No forensic evidence whatsoever.'

'Unusual,' he said quietly. 'But not impossible to achieve.'

Time for the big reveal.

'He's innocent. Well, off this at least. But then, you know that, don't you?'

His breathing rate increased, ever so slightly.

'Barbara Thorpe and Stephen Jones were two of your projects, weren't they?'

His eyes narrowed slightly, becoming cautious. There was a tension in his body that hadn't been there before.

He stayed uncharacteristically silent.

Sometimes I read what was between the lines. That blurred mirage of truth that shimmers between what is said and unsaid. Stare directly at it and it evaporates, but let it hover just outside the peripheral vision of my instinctive eye and I see it.

I could see it in Malecki now. In his body language. His silence.

Any doubts I may have had about a disciple were dispelled in that instant.

'You kept notes on them, as you did with all your potential victims. Some you followed through on. Others you kept back until the time was right. You told me yourself, everything had to be perfect, didn't it?'

Those intensely dark eyes seemed to bore into my skull, trying to see my very thoughts. His lips lightened in colour as he pressed them together. The tension he was holding inside was palpable.

I leaned closer to the glass. 'The time's perfect now, isn't it, Malecki?'

'You're deluded.' He spoke so quietly, I could barely hear him. His eyes were as hard as obsidian.

'You have a disciple. Picking up where you left off.' I held Malecki's intense gaze with one of my own. 'You began interviewing for them six months ago. How am I doing so far?'

He clasped his hands around a knee, and rocked back in his chair, trying to look relaxed. But I could tell, he was scrabbling to regain his composure.

'I'm surprised at your flawed logic.'

'Really?'

'If I had a disciple, I would need to communicate with them.' He opened his arms to encompass his surroundings. 'From in here?'

'Mobile phones are easy enough to get in prison.'

A micro-expression flitted across his face. Hidden in an instant, but not before I'd read it.

Relief.

The tension left him and he sat back.

'A mobile phone? Not my style, Doctor.' He was regarding me with amusement now. 'Search my cell – you'll find nothing.' Then his eyes widened in sudden realisation. 'Ah, but that's what's happening right now, isn't it? While I'm here with you.'

I wanted to puncture his bravado.

'And your trophies? We've tracked those being sold on the dark web.'

He became suddenly very still.

His previous benign demeanour was gone. Replaced now by the side of his character I suspected only his victims ever saw.

The mask slipped and something reptilian moved behind his eyes.

I drove home my advantage. 'A foolish move for a disciple, wouldn't you say? Have they gone against your instructions and used their own initiative on that one?'

His jaw tightened as he gritted his teeth. He sucked in a breath, as if I'd punched him in the solar plexus. Then he simply rose from his chair and went to bang on the cell door. 'Our time together is over, Doctor,' he said without turning to look at me.

The door opened, and he paused. Confused by the sight of three officers from the security team waiting for him on the other side.

'Oh, forgot to mention,' I said. 'We've arranged for you to have a cavity search.' He shot me a look over his shoulder.

'You're welcome,' I called, as they led him away.

* * *

Callum was quiet as we drove out of Wakefield.

'You OK?' I stuck my head in the lion's mouth.

'Security team didn't find anything in his cell, or inside him.'

'No.'

He took his eyes from the road to glance at me. 'You don't sound surprised.'

'When I told him about the disciple, I knew from his body language we were right. But the minute I mentioned a mobile phone, he was relieved. He knew we were wrong about that. When he said we should search his cell, he *knew* we wouldn't find anything. Like he said, not his style.'

'So, what *is* his style? He has to communicate with the person on the outside somehow.'

'Any more from the prison phone logs?'

He shook his head. 'He makes fewer calls than just about any other prisoner in there. He doesn't have anyone to call. Estranged from his mother. Father dead. No close friends . . .'

'Except Gerald Carter.'

'You still think he's likely?'

'Yes.'

'Randall?'

'If I had to choose between the two, my money would be on him. I looked at the full psyche report you sent over. He fits, in too many ways to ignore.'

I stared out of the passenger window, watching pedestrians huddled against the bitter wind and flurrying snow.

'Tomorrow is Wednesday,' I said, almost to myself.

'I know.' Callum ran a hand across his eyes. 'Press Office is inundated with update requests. People are screaming for a more visible police presence on the streets. Trouble is, we don't know where he'll strike next.'

'It'll be in West Yorkshire,' I said quietly, still looking out of my window.

'Care to narrow it down for me?'

'Probably Fordley. A woman, over fifty, who lives alone.'

I risked a glance at his profile, seeing the muscles bunch in his jaw.

'Copycat or a disciple,' he said tightly. 'I don't care about the "why" – just the "who". We need to catch this bastard, before anyone else dies.'

Chapter Fifty-Eight

Tuesday Late Afternoon, Kingsberry Farm

When I walked into my kitchen, I was greeted by the last thing I ever expected to see.

My mother, complete with apron and wooden spoon, standing at the Aga, stirring a bubbling pan. Beside her, Eduardo Mazzarelli, helpfully chopping herbs. They both glanced up as I came in.

'Ah, Phina,' Mamma gushed, bustling over to give me a one-armed hug as she held the spoon in her other hand, dripping tomato sauce onto my stone floor. 'This is Eduardo.' She beamed at him.

'I know who he is, Mamma. But what are *you* doing here?'

Visits from my mother were a rare occurrence. Especially unannounced and never without it being a family occasion.

'Jen told me you were ill, Phina.' Mamma was busy stirring the pan again. 'I came making meatballs,' she explained in her heavily Italian-accented English. 'You don't eat when you're poorly. Don't look after yourself.'

I stared at the pair of them.

'Phina?' Ed asked, grinning at me.

'Short for Josephine.' I pulled a face. 'But if you call me it, I won't answer.'

'She no like it,' Mamma huffed. 'No like feminine name, no like feminine job . . .'

Jen walked in, with an armful of paperwork that she dumped on the kitchen table.

'Oh, you're back.'

I nodded towards Mamma, with a 'is this down to you?' look.

At least she had the decency to look sheepish. She pushed her glasses into her hair on top of her head. 'Mamma rang, but you were out. I told her the reason she hadn't heard from you this week was because you'd not been well . . . you know, with the throat and everything.'

I rolled my eyes at her and she mouthed a silent 'sorry'. Then busied herself with the post.

'How did you get here, Mamma?' I shrugged out of my jacket. My mother didn't drive and I knew taxis wouldn't come along the unmade track to the farm in the snow.

'Taxi left me at end of your lane. I would have to walk rest of the way, but this nice boy was driving here and stop for me.' She smiled at Ed.

'Luckily, just on my way here to help Jen with that stuff you rang me about, when I saw this lovely lady.'

'Told him he must stay for dinner,' Mamma said. 'He says he's a friend of yours, so I invite him.'

'It's OK,' Ed said quickly. 'I have to go back this evening.'

'You staying, Mamma?' I asked. Warming my hands over the hotplate.

'No. Got a Christmas dinner tonight with the bowls club.' She tapped the spoon against the side of the pan and put it on a saucer on the counter. Wiping her hands on my apron. 'Maybe this nice boy give me a lift back, eh?'

I opened my mouth, but Ed waved my objection away before I could make it. 'No problem. My pleasure.'

I peered into the pan, at meatballs bubbling in thick sauce. 'Thanks, Mamma. I really appreciate it . . . but you didn't need to.'

316

'Yes, I did.' She was looking at Ed as she spoke. 'She has terrible job.' She shook her head. 'No job for a woman, dealing with killers and rapists. All the hours, with no time for good home cooking.' She gave me one of her looks. 'I keep telling her, she's going to die lonely. Why you can't get a proper job, eh?'

'In an office – yes, I know, Mamma.'

'Tell her, Eduardo.' She stared up at him. 'Nice boy like you, wouldn't want a woman like that.'

'Oh, I don't know . . .' He was struggling to contain the grin.

I was used to this. The surreptitious criticism, wrapped up to look like motherly concern. Relentless since childhood and just as biting as ever.

'You're too strong-willed, Phina.' She began to unfasten the strings of the apron. 'Men don't like that. Don't like a woman with too many brains, either. I warn your papa when he insist on your education. A girl don't need that. When a man gets to know you, they'll leave you. And look . . .' She waved her arms around. 'Here you are, all alone – no husband. Men like a woman who makes a home. You're so stubborn—'

'Not stubborn,' I said weary of this same conversation. 'Just independent.'

'Stubborn.' She almost spat the word. 'And too clever to take your mamma's advice. It makes you unlovable.' She nudged Ed. 'Tell her.'

He grinned at me over the top of Mamma's head and winked. 'Yeah, I like my woman chained to the kitchen sink. Having my tea ready when I get in at night.'

'You see!' Mamma shot me a victorious look.

'OK.' I held my hands up. 'I'm leaving you to it, while I drop this lot in the office.'

317

'What time do you need to get back?' I heard Ed asking Mamma as I walked down the corridor.

'Can we go now?'

Jen hurried down behind me.

I dumped my files on the desk. 'Did you two get anywhere?'

'Massively.' She glanced back towards the kitchen. 'Left Mamma cooking and got a lot done, but then she commandeered him as her sous-chef.'

When I walked back into the kitchen, Mamma was struggling into her winter coat. Ed leaned back against the Aga, his long legs stretched out in front of him. He suppressed a laugh and rolled his eyes at Mamma's back.

'Want me to come back, later?' he whispered, looking over at the pan. 'And help you eat this lot.'

'Definitely.'

Chapter Fifty-Nine

Tuesday Evening, Kingsberry Farm

With the dishes cleared away, we'd taken our wine down to the office. Harvey, full of leftover pasta, snored contentedly on the rug.

Earlier in the day, Jen and Ed had cleared space on Jen's desk for his laptops. Plural. Three of them, linked together with lines of cables, which to my untrained eye resembled Mamma's spaghetti.

'Jen's idea to go through the census was a good one, but it had limitations,' Ed was saying as his fingers moved over the keys. He didn't tap them, like me. It was more of a hovering touch that seemed to miraculously type at lightning speed.

I took a sip of Malbec, watching as rows of text filled the screen.

'Instead of looking for the cop,' he was saying, 'I thought we might identify the family.' He took a sip from his own glass and turned his laptop towards me. 'The family's five-year-old daughter was abused by Dave Finch.'

'Yes.'

'So, I explored census records for families with daughters that age.'

I scanned the list. 'Don't recognise any of the names.'

He shrugged. 'Didn't think it'd be that easy.' He smiled, pulling up more pages. 'Someone *involved* with the family is a cop now. Could be male or female. So, I looked for uncles, aunts, cousins et cetera.'

I watched the names appear on the screen. 'Wow. That's more than I would have thought.'

'Had to trace maternal and paternal sides of all the families. Plus, they moved around and settled all over the country. I've created a programme to cross-reference these with other criteria that might help narrow it down,' he said, not looking up from the screens.

I watched his profile for a moment. 'You're really in your element, aren't you?'

He grinned. 'Love it. Especially the sneaky stuff.'

'Err, how sneaky, exactly? I don't want you doing anything that'll get you in trouble.'

'We need to know if any of the names on here joined the police.'

I frowned, suddenly worried about what I might have started. 'But that's—'

He waved away my objections with his hand. 'Think it's best if we operate a "don't ask, don't tell" policy.'

'But, Ed, your laptop can be traced – your IP or whatever. My internet . . .'

'Chill.' He grinned at me. 'Anyone looking at this right now thinks I'm operating out of Singapore. In five minutes, the location will shift to Belarus. It's not my first time, Jo.'

'I know, I just—'

'Just nothing.' His hand covered mine and gave it a gentle squeeze. 'I'll be in and out of these databases before anyone knows the door's even been opened. Won't leave a trace. Trust me.'

* * *

Wednesday Morning, Kingsberry Farm

I felt his warm breath against my cheek, even before I opened my eyes. I rolled over and looked into dark brown eyes, an inch from my own.

Then he licked my face.

'Harvey!' I tried to push six stone of boxer dog off me, but he was having none of it. He licked me again, panting in that way that made him look like he was laughing.

I struggled to sit up on the couch and looked round my empty office, with a vague memory of going to sit on the sofa in the early hours, while Ed carried on working.

There was a blanket over me that I didn't remember getting. As I swung my feet onto the floor, the office door opened and Ed appeared, carrying two mugs.

'Morning, campers.' He sounded far brighter than he had any right to.

'What time is it?' I took the cup.

'Seven thirty.'

'Sorry, I must have fallen asleep.'

'That's OK. You nodded off, so I covered you up and carried on till five-ish.'

'You must be shattered.'

'Nah. Used to it. Besides, me and Harvey took the sofa in the lounge. Caught a couple of hours in there.'

I took a welcome sip of tea. First cup – best of the day.

'Feel bad you spent the whole night working.'

He fussed Harvey, who was loving the attention. 'Could have stopped if I'd wanted to, but got into it.'

'Find anything?'

'None of the people we listed, or their extended family, joined the police, or took civilian jobs with the force.'

I couldn't help worrying about breaching confidential databases.

'I just hope you were careful.'

He shot me a look that said, *not that again*.

'OK.' I held up my hands. 'Just nervous about this, that's all.'

He sat in the armchair. 'Some of those on the list have moved abroad and one or two ended up in prison.'

'How could you find . . .'

He held up a hand. 'Don't ask, don't tell, remember?'

I sighed and nodded.

'Good news is, I may have found the family.'

He had my full attention. 'Who?'

'The Sheridans lived on the same estate as Finch. They had a five-year-old-daughter in 1993.'

'So did half a dozen others you found.'

'Bridget, the daughter, killed herself in 2005.'

'When she was seventeen.'

'Hmmm.' He took another gulp of coffee. 'Not an exact science, but her death certificate shows the place of death was Westwood Park psychiatric hospital in Fordley.'

'Know it well.'

'You were head of forensic psychology there, weren't you?'

'A thousand years ago.' I put my cup on the table and stretched cramped muscles. 'You think if she was the same girl who'd been abused by a paedophile, it might account for her stay in a psychiatric unit, as a teenager?'

'And the manner of her death. Like I say, not an exact science, but worth following up.' He got up and began to pull cables from his laptops. 'Right now, I have to get back to the day job.'

Chapter Sixty

Wednesday Morning, Kingsberry Farm

Jen and I were working in companionable silence in the office. The landscape outside my huge arched window looked like a winter wonderland.

'Keep your eye on the weather, Jen. You don't want to get stuck up here.'

'Oh, I don't know. Can think of worse places. Besides, Henry might appreciate me more if he had to fend for himself for a while.'

My mobile rang. It was Elle.

'Just calling with the info you asked me about.' She launched straight into it. 'Post-mortem report on Dave Finch?'

I grabbed a pen. 'Thanks, Elle.'

'Want to tell me why you're revisiting a death from 1993?'

'Just following an instinct.'

'Good enough for me. Well, although his flat was torched, the arsonist didn't do a good enough job. Finch's body was recovered with minimal fire damage.' I could hear the rustling of paperwork. 'He had dozens of bruises and abrasions over his torso. Consistent with taking a beating, but he actually died from severe brain trauma.'

'Caused how?'

'A severed artery caused by a heavy blow.'

'He was hit over the head?'

'No. He had a broken jaw.'

'Sorry, I'm being slow on the uptake.'

'Looks like the kind of injury we see in a "one-punch death".'

'A blow to the jaw can kill?'

'Yep. I've seen a few single-punch deaths in my career. Usually drunken lads in pub brawls. It's either caused by the punch knocking the victim down and they hit their head on a hard surface. Or, as it looks in this case, the blow is so severe, the brain bounces round inside the skull, like jelly in a bowl. The trauma causes a bleed on the brain. In Finch's case, it tore the artery.'

I was scribbling notes.

'Got a meeting, need to love you and leave you.'

I thanked her and hung up, just as my office phone rang.

'Jo?' It was Supt. Warner. 'The team listened to the recording from your interview with Malecki. In light of his reaction, and what happened after you left, looks like you're right about a disciple.'

'What happened after I left?'

'Once he was back on the wing, he made a call to one of the numbers on his PIN. The call was recorded and sent to the team. I can't go into it over the phone, rather you came in to hear it for yourself. The techies can explain the rest.'

'OK. When do you want me?'

'Now would be good.'

Chapter Sixty-One

Wednesday Afternoon, Fordley Police Station

This close to Christmas, Fordley town centre would normally be packed with shoppers. But today, it was almost empty.

Despite requests from the police, the press whipped up feelings of foreboding, as every Wednesday approached, and a sense of barely subdued fear pulsed through the city.

News items reinforced the fear by reporting the soaring sales of home security systems and asking people not to panic, which predictably had the opposite effect.

CCTV companies were doing a roaring trade. Even the RSPCA were getting involved, as they reported a rising demand for big dogs. Especially Rottweilers and Alsatians.

People were staying indoors. Despite the reality that this killer usually targeted people in their own homes. They'd probably have been safer at the Christmas market, which this year complained that takings were down as the public stayed away.

When I finally got into the station, the place was humming with the frenetic energy of a fast-moving enquiry.

As the body count had risen, so had the number of officers involved, including those brought in from other forces. The major incident rooms now occupied two floors of the station, with every inch of space taken.

Supt. Warner was in a huddle with Callum and DI Wardman.

'Recording from the prison is in here.' She ushered me into an office. A young officer I didn't recognise was sitting at the table, with the digital recorder.

'This is DS Charlie Thompson from our specialist telephony team.' Supt. Warner made the introductions. 'He'll explain how this call was made.'

Callum took a seat. Wardman hovered at the door, before saying, 'I've already heard all this, ma'am, so I'll get back to the team if that's OK?'

She nodded, without looking at him, as DS Thompson cued up the recording.

'As you'll know,' he began, 'prisoners are given a PIN to make telephone calls.'

I was on more than a few prisoners' PINs myself, including Chris McGarry's.

'Malecki only had four personal numbers listed and eight professional ones,' Charlie was saying. 'All of the latter were for members of his legal team or specialists they called on. His firm used non-geographic numbers, with the prefix 03.'

'Why a non-geographic number?' I asked.

'Malecki's solicitors had offices around the UK. It allows calls to be redirected to virtually any landline or mobile. The numbers were also diverted to out-of-hours answering services.'

'OK.'

'This firm rented a bundle. Each one was assigned to one of their offices and the answering service would route the calls.' He passed me a sheet that I recognised as a prison phone list. 'When Malecki was sent to Wakefield, his numbers were verified and they've never changed. The last time he called his legal team was five years ago, when they were launching an appeal against his transfer. It failed and he never called them again.'

'Until yesterday.' I ventured a guess.

Callum said, 'We checked the number. It was the solicitors' branch in Hull.'

'And?' I was struggling to see where this was going.

'That practice closed four years ago and the number was never reassigned.'

'So, how could he have spoken to anyone?'

'It's still registered with the answering service,' Charlie said. 'After the office closed, the solicitors stopped putting the number on their ads and stationery. It was sitting there as a spare.'

'So, who did they route his call to?' I was feeling slow on the uptake.

'A pay-as-you-go mobile that was discontinued as soon as the call ended. A burner phone.'

I glanced from Callum, to Charlie and back again. 'But how is that possible?'

'I sent officers round to the answering service,' Supt. Warner said. 'Woke a magistrate up to get a warrant to look at their records. Apparently when the Hull office closed, the service was issued with this mobile number and told to route any calls there. The request was sent via email from the head office of the solicitors, which as an existing account wasn't unusual. It looked authentic. But our techies have checked and it's a cloned email. From an IP address that was bounced round a dozen servers worldwide. Untraceable now.'

'This number is the 091 burner that called Hannah with the anonymous tip, to go to Paxton Pits,' Callum added. 'Play the recording, Charlie.'

We all listened as the phone dialled. Whoever answered didn't speak. There was a crackle on the line, before Malecki's unmistakable voice filled the room.

'QRM,' was all he said. Then he hung up.

'That's it?'

Warner and Callum both nodded.

Before I could ask the obvious question, Charlie supplied the answer.

'It's "Q" code,' he said, as if that explained everything.

'Which is what exactly?'

'A standardised collection of three-letter codes that each start with the letter "Q". An operating signal initially developed for commercial radiotelegraphy. I recognised it because I'm a radio ham,' he added rather sheepishly.

'Why would he use that?' I frowned. 'If he knows the burner will be discontinued as soon as they ended the call, he could have spoken normally.'

Charlie shrugged. 'Malecki would know that his calls are recorded. Whoever answered was briefed not to speak – meaning we don't have a record of their voice. By using a prearranged code, if the call was compromised, and it was someone else on the other end, they wouldn't understand the message.'

'So, what does it mean?' I asked.

'The literal definition is, "I'm being interfered with." A more usual interpretation is that communications are suffering from interference or interception.'

'So, he's telling whoever he spoke to that we're on to them?'

'We wanted to see how he'd react if we told him about our disciple theory,' Callum said.

'And now we know,' Supt. Warner said. 'He's broken cover and communicated with his accomplice on the outside.'

'He could be telling them to abandon the plan. Go to ground,' Callum said thoughtfully.

'Let's hope so,' I said, though I already had my doubts. 'That way, no one else dies.'

Callum stood suddenly and paced the room.

'Damn Rob Harding and his prisoners' rights. How can we catch this bastard when Malecki's free to make calls whenever he bloody well feels like it?'

'We've double-checked the other numbers on his list and they're all legitimate.' Warner's tone was conciliatory.

'What's to stop him having other prisoners make calls like that for him?' Callum persisted. 'Not possible to check every number of every prisoner's PIN. It'd run into thousands and even if we had the resources, we haven't got time. Harding should have agreed to put Malecki in solitary.'

'I called him,' Warner said. 'Asked if this was enough to put Malecki in the Seg? He declined. Said he'd have him put on basic – have his privileges removed. But he didn't feel it warranted anything more severe.'

'He plays by the rules,' I said, thoughtfully.

Callum's breath left him in a gust of anger. 'And *we* have to play by the same shit rules, but Malecki doesn't, and because of that, innocent people are going to die! He needs to be shut down, so he can't communicate inside or out.'

'Well, unfortunately that's not possible.' Warner gathered up her notes. 'So, we'll have to work with what we've got.'

* * *

Warner asked Callum to bring me up to speed, and left us to it.

'Remember the number from the burner phone that called Hannah the morning he handed himself in?'

'You suspected it was someone tipping him off?'

He nodded. 'Two other numbers called him nine times in the last few weeks. All from the same IMEI.' He saw the look on my face. 'International Mobile Equipment Identity. It's like your phone's unique fingerprint.'

'You mean, all from the same handset?'

'Yep. Whoever owns it is swapping SIM cards. Each SIM shows up as a different number.'

'Hannah must know it's the same person.'

'Which is why we're pulling him in.. Confront him with the new evidence and see what he says.'

'Any way to trace the owner?'

He shook his head. 'It's still a burner. Probably bought for cash. Phone carriers and manufacturers share IMEI numbers to enable tracking of stolen phones. It's a long shot, but we've put in a request to see how many SIMs are going through that handset.'

'Does the rest of the team know all this?'

'Yes.' His eyes held mine. 'Why?'

Because if there is a cop protecting Hannah, that number could be theirs.

He knew me too well. 'Jo . . .?'

If he was involved, he wouldn't have shared the information he just had.

I took a long breath and told him about the possibility of someone inside the force protecting Hannah and compromising his investigation.

When I'd finished, he stared at me for what seemed like an eternity. Finally, washing a hand across his eyes.

'This all started when you spoke to Jack Halton?'

'He told me about Dave Finch.'

His gaze held mine with an intensity that bordered on uncomfortable. 'And Old Man McGarry – covering for whoever killed Finch? You heard that where exactly?'

I thought about Chris McGarry's illegal burner phone and the fact the Finn had said he would deny our conversation, if asked.

I couldn't betray those sources. Finn especially – he was my godfather and friend. If the police questioned him that would end our relationship forever. As for Chris, the consequences for him in prison, revealing this information, were too terrible to contemplate.

'Just rumour.' It took effort to look him straight in the eye. 'Random bits of info I picked up.'

He pursed his lips in thought and I knew he was debating how far to push.

'Dave Finch's murder is still an open case, Jo. If you know who killed—'

'I don't,' I said honestly.

'The family who were involved. Do you know who they are?'

'Not for certain . . .'

'Stop hedging, Jo. You're in too deep now not to tell me everything.'

'It could be the Sheridan family.' I told him about their daughter, Bridget, and the manner of her death. 'It's tenuous at best, Cal.'

I held my breath, hoping he wouldn't push for more. No way would I be able to tell him about Eduardo's involvement.

He nodded. 'And you think someone involved with that family, and the cover-up of Finch's murder, is in the police now?'

'Or working in a civilian capacity.' I nodded. 'I was told people close to my job wouldn't want me digging around and that I should leave it alone.'

'And we all know the best way to get you to do anything is to warn you not to.'

'Look, Cal, I hesitated to say anything, because it's all unsubstantiated. But once you told me about the burner phone calling Hannah before he handed himself in . . . I couldn't keep it from you. It could be someone on the team.'

He nodded and sat back in his chair.

'If it is, then they'll know we've traced the SIM cards to the same handset.'

'So, if they suddenly ditch it . . . ?'

'Not conclusive proof, but it'd be one hell of a coincidence.'

He needed this like a hole in the head.

'What happens now?' I almost daren't ask.

'We can't suspend the investigation. But I'll have everyone on the team washed through ACU.'

'Anti-Corruption Unit? Can it be done without them knowing?'

He nodded. 'But if they can't find anything to corroborate your intel, then realistically there's not a lot we can do. What you've given me so far is third party hearsay.' He leaned forward, resting elbows on his knees, so our faces were just inches apart. His breath was warm against my face. 'Unless you can get your sources to come up with something more tangible?' he said quietly.

'I'll try.' But even as I said it, I knew I couldn't.

'OK,' he said with a sense of finality. 'I'll have to pass this on to Supt. Warner. And it stays strictly between the three of us.'

* * *

On the drive home, I rang Joshua Weston and asked if he could get Chris McGarry to call me – privately. He didn't ask what I meant by 'private', so, I assumed he knew, but neither of us would admit to that on an open phoneline.

Chapter Sixty-Two

Thursday Morning

I'd just got back to the farm after an early morning walk with Harvey when Callum called.

I was acutely aware, along with the rest of the country, that today was Thursday, and as his name flashed up on my phone, my stomach lurched.

'I hope this call isn't what I think it is?' I said without preamble.

'Unfortunately, yes.'

Another body.

'Who is she?'

'Not a she.'

I stopped dead in my tracks. 'What? But that's not . . .'

'I know.'

'You're sure it's the same killer?' Even as I asked, I knew it was a stupid question.

'Unless there's someone else who could leave Mark Lutner's finger in the victim's mouth.'

'Got an ID on the victim?'

'Oh yes, we know who he is.'

Something bad was coming.

'Who?'

'Dennis Haverley.'

* * *

'Looks like, "the one who got away", finally didn't,' DI Heslopp said without humour, as the team crammed into the briefing room.

I looked at the crime scene photo, added to the whiteboard with the rest of the dead.

I'd never seen Dennis Haverley in the flesh. No one had, apart from the original investigating team, three decades earlier.

His identity had been kept a closely guarded secret at the time. A fact that Callum was imparting to the team, as I stared at the image of a man I now knew to be seventy-three years old.

His throat had been cut as he sat in his chair, in a lounge that you would call cosy, if it wasn't for blood spatters across the furniture and up the walls.

'Haverley wanted to remain anonymous,' Callum was saying. 'He didn't appear in court, and during the trial, he was referred to as Victim X. The whole thing unhinged him.'

'Especially as Malecki tried for him twice,' Heslopp added helpfully.

'Haverley moved out of town,' Callum went on. 'He didn't need to change his name or hide his identity, because none of that was public knowledge, but he couldn't stay in the same house, knowing he'd been stalked there. He went to a remote cottage, up on the moors just outside the village of Oldfield, Keighley. Which is where his carer found him when she went this morning to give him breakfast.'

'Poor bastard,' someone muttered.

'This proves it's a disciple,' Callum was saying. 'Only Malecki could know about Haverley.'

'Why go after him now, boss? It breaks the pattern,' a young PC on the team asked.

'Jo said Malecki's true motive was to complete his "projects". Now we know it's a disciple, he can drop the pretence.'

'We believe the call Malecki made on Tuesday evening was to tell his disciple we were on to them,' Warner added. 'Once he delivered that message, they'd probably prearranged a change of plan.' She looked at me. 'Jo?'

I walked to the front. My attention was on the image on the board. A man whose death I felt was down to me.

I said to the picture on the board, 'Malecki would have a built-in contingency for being compromised. That's what we're seeing now. If we hadn't worked it out, I think he intended to let this play out as a copycat. We would never know the first three victims were on his original list. They would just look like random choices. The irony is, if it had gone the way he intended, Dennis Haverley would have been safe. To go after him would have given the game away. The "Q" code means the gloves came off. They switch to an alternative plan to speed things up before we can stop them. No need to conceal the victims' true identities.' I turned to face the room. 'When I told Malecki we knew it was a disciple, he was angry. He wanted to lash out and prove that he's still a force to be reckoned with, even from inside the Monster Mansion.'

I looked back at the picture on the board.

'When I confronted him, I condemned Dennis Haverley to death.'

* * *

The briefing continued, but most of it floated somewhere above my head.

I was aware of people speaking, but their voices sounded muffled, as if they were coming from the bottom of a deep ocean.

I couldn't take my eyes off Dennis Haverley's photograph. His eyes, wide and rheumy. Staring at me accusingly, from the other side of life.

'Jo?' Beth's whispered words finally penetrated. Her eyes were concerned. 'You OK?'

I nodded, even though I felt like a spectator in a dream. I forced my attention back into the room, just as Callum was calling on Lee from the cyber unit.

He flicked on the TV, to show screenshots of his searches.

'Wednesdayschild is trading in Malecki items. We've found a Montblanc pen that belonged to Hirst, the first known victim.' He glanced at Beth.

'I was tasked with the silver earring,' she said. 'No one alive to confirm it, but I found photos of Irene Gordon wearing a pair that look identical.'

'I created a profile and joined the Malecki fan site,' Lee said. 'Gave it a history to look like the account's been established for over a year. Trying to get alongside Wednesdayschild and pose as a potential buyer.'

'So, how much does this stuff go for?' a young PC asked.

Lee shrugged. 'Depends on provenance. Few years ago, a shirt he wore came up. There was a photo from an Italian news article of him wearing it, covered in paint – so it could be authenticated. It went for ten thousand euros.'

'Fuck me.' Heslopp nearly spat out his coffee.

Lee ignored the interruption. 'I've gone back as far as the origins of this site and I can't find any mention of a custom-made knife belonging to Malecki. No weapons attributed to him have ever come on the market. Whoever's using that knife now didn't buy it on here.'

As the briefing ended, I was still looking at Haverley's photo. I became aware of someone standing beside me. I followed the suited legs upward, to see Callum.

'You OK?'

'Be lying if I said I was.'

336

His eyes followed mine to the whiteboard, as he took the seat beside me. 'Not your fault, Jo.'

'Isn't it?'

I felt his hand on my arm, squeezing gently. 'We all agreed what you should tell Malecki.'

I slowly shook my head. 'I know. But if I'd thought it through . . .'

'It's not all on you,' he persisted. 'No one could have foreseen this.'

'*I* should have.'

'You're too hard on yourself.'

'That's what I do, isn't it?' The words caught in my throat. 'Think like they do. Try to anticipate.'

'But not—'

'I should have realised . . .' I heard my volume go up and was thankful the room was empty. 'That if anyone was unfinished business for Malecki, it would be Haverley.'

'Any one of the team could have made that leap. But we didn't either.'

'How many more, Cal?' I could feel the prickle of unshed tears and tried not to blink and have them spilling down my cheeks. 'How many more can he get to, before you stop him?'

He opened his mouth to say something, just as Heslopp appeared in the doorway.

'Boss, governor from Wakefield Prison on the phone. Says it's urgent.'

I followed Callum to his office.

He snatched up the phone. 'Yes.'

I studied his face, as he listened.

'Like I said, there's a first time for everything. OK. How long for?' He nodded at the answer. 'Thanks for letting me know.' He hung up.

337

Heslopp was standing between us, hands on hips. 'Well? Don't tell me, Malecki wants another meeting.'

'Better than that.' It was the first time I'd seen Callum smile in what seemed like forever. 'During a routine security search on the wing, they found a shiv hidden in Malecki's cell.'

'Shiv' – a knife made by prisoners, often by melting a razor blade into the plastic handle of a toothbrush. Simple, but devastatingly effective.

'He swears it's not his.' Callum couldn't conceal his pleasure. 'Was taken before the governor for adjudication and pleaded not guilty, but couldn't explain how it'd got there. He's been banged up in the segregation unit. Three weeks punishment.'

Heslopp grinned. 'Result.'

* * *

The drive back to Kingsberry was more treacherous than ever.

I had an old Land Rover Defender, which I'd inherited a few years before, from a neighbouring farmer when he'd died. It lived in the barn at the back of my house and was rarely used.

It had none of the mod cons I was used to, but when the weather made the roads almost impassable, it was a godsend. I was thinking about digging it out when an incoming call interrupted my thoughts.

'McCready,' I answered, distractedly.

'Jo?' Chris McGarry was speaking in a whisper.

'You're taking a risk, calling during the day.'

'Worth it. After speaking to you last night, I wanted to know how it went?'

'Just as you said.'

'Great stuff.' I could hear the grin in his voice.

'I hope a prisoner didn't—'

'Not a prisoner,' he interrupted, 'a screw. Been in my uncle's pocket for years. He owed us a favour – I called it in.' He laughed softly. 'They really should get paid more, then they might not be so tempted to break their own rules.'

Callum had talked about rules.

We *have to play by the same shit rules, but Malecki doesn't . . . he needs to be shut down.*

'Thanks, Chris.'

'Anytime.' There was a pause, then. 'Actually, Jo, there is something you can do for me.'

I have a tab open for this one, Jo . . .

'What?'

'It's Sarah. She's really struggling. Mikey's getting the best care, but the stress is getting to her. GP's put her on antidepressants. They help a bit, but they've said she needs to see someone. I want her to have the best . . .'

'Of course.' I didn't need to think about it.

'I'll give her your number. Owe you one, Jo.'

'Think that ship's sailed,' I muttered. Under no illusion that, in Chris's world, this was how working off a debt began.

Chapter Sixty-Three

Friday Morning, Kingsberry Farm

I was beyond tired. My bones ached with exhaustion and not just because I hadn't slept.

I was strung out and weary. After all these years, I thought my armour was impermeable to trauma fatigue. But occasionally the pain and misery of the things I dealt with seeped around the edges of my professional defences and permeated my soul.

'Soul destroying' was a term people used all too easily to describe everyday events. But I'd seen souls destroyed for real. It had a look, which once seen, you could never forget.

A look in the eyes of victims who'd survived the most unspeakable horrors. A look that said they'd never trust anyone again. That their faith in human nature was gone – broken forever.

In the eyes of children who'd been robbed of their innocence, or families who'd lost loved ones.

Most of the time, walking over the secluded moors with Harvey was enough to restore my equilibrium. A decompression that evened out the troughs of a bad day. But it wasn't cutting it this time and I knew I wasn't immune to the burnout I'd seen so many times in others.

The weather battered the windows and howled around my walls. I flipped the lid on the Aga and put the kettle on the hotplate. Jen was working from home today, not wanting to drive in the worsening weather.

Harvey curled on his bed in front of the oven, snoring contentedly, showing no interest in braving the weather either.

As I prepared the teapot, I decided to give myself the day off. Curled up on the sofa in front of a log fire.

We both jumped when the bell above the Aga clanged as the office phone rang. I ran down the corridor to catch it before the caller rang off.

I grabbed the phone. 'McCready.'

'Jo.' Supt. Warner sounded weary. 'I need you to come in.'

'Now?' I looked out at the snow. 'There's a storm forecast . . . it's getting bad up here.'

'Callum reported what you'd told him. ACU are involved. They need to speak to you and so do I.'

Inwardly, I groaned. Wishing, not for the first time, that I'd kept my mouth shut.

'I've got to change vehicles first. My TT can't manage in this.'

'Fine.' She sounded brusque. 'I'm not going anywhere.'

Chapter Sixty-Four

Friday Afternoon, Fordley Police Station

Callum held the door for me as we left Warner's office. It had been an uncomfortable thirty minutes, but I'd managed to substantiate what I'd told Callum, without compromising Chris McGarry or Finn.

Officers from ACU had spoken to Jack Halton, who was more than happy to confirm what he'd told me.

'ACU haven't come up with anything, yet,' Callum said quietly as we walked down the carpeted corridor to the lifts. 'They've looked at Dave Finch and the Sheridan family. No one from any of the joint investigation teams has any familial connection.'

'Have they interviewed the family?'

'No one to interview,' he said grimly. 'Father died years ago. Mother's in a home with advanced dementia. There was an older brother – Nick Sheridan. He was in the army when Finch died.'

'Where's he now?'

'Killed. Motorbike accident in Northern Ireland in 1995.'

'Then all we have left is rumour. What did Hannah say when you questioned him about the phone calls?'

Callum punched the button for the lift.

'He's lawyered up, which was predictable. Went "no comment" on us.'

'So, what now?'

'Unless something turns up, there's nothing to hold him on.'

The doors slid open and we stepped into the lift.

'At least we got one lucky break,' he said, to our reflections in the mirrored wall. 'Malecki getting chucked into solitary.'

'Yes.' I kept my expression impassive. 'Lucky.'

As we stepped out of the lift, Frank Heslopp collared us in the corridor.

'There you are, boss.' He sounded out of breath.

Callum followed him towards the incident room, with Heslopp moving faster than I thought he could.

'Tony's been scouring CCTV from the time of Haverley's murder. You need to see this.'

A group huddled around a computer screen.

'Boss,' Tony said when he saw Callum. 'No cameras along the road through Oldfield, to Haverley's cottage. So, we looked at the main routes in and out. Picked up a white van going past a row of shops in Keighley, heading in the right direction, but it was a side shot.'

Everyone leaned forward to get a better look. The side of the van had some kind of outline on it.

'Where a decal's been removed,' Heslopp supplied helpfully.

Tony put the end of his pencil on the screen. 'Right at this point, a bus comes the other way. All city buses have dashcams, so I thought it might have caught the registration as it passed. The bus company sent us the footage.'

The image showed the front of a white Ford Connect, head on as the path of the two vehicles crossed. The registration number was clear. Everyone recognised it instantly; it was burned into our collective memory.

Peter Randall's van.

* * *

343

Supt. Warner called Callum, DI Wardman, Heslopp and me into her office.

'Jacob Malecki's screaming blue murder,' she said without the hint of a smile.

Heslopp snorted. 'My heart bleeds.'

'Well, that's as maybe,' she said tightly, 'but while it's good that he's off the grid, it still leaves us with an existing issue.' She turned to me. 'You said when you mentioned the mobile phone, Malecki was relieved?'

'He knew the cell search wouldn't find anything.'

'If he's not using a mobile to communicate with the outside, then how?'

'He used the public phone on Tuesday,' Wardman said.

Callum shook his head. 'That's the only time in over two years. Any letters he's written have been photocopied by the prison and kept. It's over a year since he wrote to anyone.'

'He's been in touch with his disciple more recently than that,' Warner mused.

'Maybe he doesn't have to,' Heslopp said, 'now that he's set them off on a pre-prepared plan with the "Q" code.'

'But he *was* communicating with them before,' I said. 'Until he realised we were on to him.'

'The only way to reach the outside is through visits.' Heslopp said. 'Phone or letters – how else?'

Callum looked at me as the same thought hit us both.

'His paintings,' we said in unison.

Chapter Sixty-Five

Friday Night, Kingsberry Farm

Callum had obtained a warrant to seize Malecki's paintings.

According to Gerald Carter, everything his client had produced for the past six months was destined for the new exhibition. If Malecki *was* somehow getting messages out of the prison in his paintings, we'd only have to look at the most recent works.

There was nothing I could add to the proceedings, so I'd come back to the farm. But not before I'd asked Warner for the archived files on Malecki's arrest and the transcripts of his interviews from 1994.

'What are you looking for?' she'd asked, even as she was authorising my access.

'Not sure. Fishing expedition, if I'm honest.'

'There are hundreds of files. Not sure where you'd start.'

'Me neither. But what else do I have to do on a Friday night, this close to Christmas?'

* * *

I sat in my office at the farm, with brown cardboard storage boxes stacked either side of me. A small sample from a choice of hundreds.

I'd chosen the ones I thought most relevant, but they could be the wrong haystacks for hunting my particular needle.

I was currently reading through Jack Halton's early reports.

Much like the Yorkshire Ripper hunt in the late seventies, the same names kept coming up. But leads were missed, in a tsunami of data which, before the use of computers, relied on handwritten index cards to store information. Cross-referencing was almost impossible as the investigation sprawled across fifteen long years and Malecki continually slipped through the net.

Something Jack said had stayed with me. I trawled through Manilla folders, until I found what I was looking for.

Records from the car hire company, when Malecki travelled home for his birthday.

He'd picked the car up from Cambridge. The mileage was recorded on collection and return.

Just as Jack said, Malecki had gone over the agreed limit and his father had to pay the difference. According to the log, it had been an extra thirty-nine miles.

Not a huge amount, considering how much it cost to hire the car in the first place. Presumably, that's why his father had kicked off about it.

I opened Google Maps and put in his mother's address in Manchester. Then studied the surrounding area. Where would that extra thirty-nine miles have taken Malecki?

Malecki kidnapped Michelle Hatfield on Wednesday night.

I thought back to the moment in the Seg, when I'd asked the question.

. . . *you disposed of Michelle's body* before *travelling to Manchester?*

Yes.

I'd seen the micro-expression that flitted across his face as he'd answered. He'd lied.

Just a few miles from his mother's house in Old Trafford was leafy Cheshire. Acres of open spaces, farms and country walks and the Manchester Ship Canal. Plenty of places to dispose of Michelle's body, on his way home.

Jack Halton's voice echoed back to me . . .

Said she was a birthday present to himself.

Malecki was precise about everything. Including language. Words.

'Not an *early* present,' I muttered to myself. 'A present . . . on your *actual* birthday. Three days later. Saturday eighteenth of July.'

His nineteenth birthday.

His first kill.

His first mistake.

Chapter Sixty-Six

Saturday Morning, Kingsberry Farm

'What time is it?' Callum's voice was thick with sleep.

'Just gone six – sorry.'

'Bloody hell, Jo. I only got to bed at half four.'

'I haven't been to bed at all.' I scanned the notes I'd made in the early hours. 'Couldn't sleep once I'd found this. Thought you'd be on your way to the office.'

'In a couple of hours,' he said, irritated.

I could hear movement and imagined him swinging his feet out of bed. 'But as you think sleep is overrated, what is it that couldn't wait?'

'I've been studying the records from Malecki's arrest.'

'No wonder you can't sleep.'

'Michelle Hatfield was his first kill. The mistakes he made then informed his MO in the future. That's why he began obsessively planning.'

'OK.' I could hear him filling the kettle.

'He hired a car on the afternoon Michelle disappeared. He told me he killed her and disposed of her body before he drove to Manchester the next day.'

'But you don't think so?'

I shook my head. 'We can only guess what he did with her that night, but I'm certain that she was still alive – probably in the boot of the car when he went north the next day.'

'What makes you think so?'

'He said killing her was a birthday present. I think he killed her on his *actual* birthday. The Saturday.'

'So, what did he do with her until then? Ask his mum to put her up in the spare room?'

'You're not funny.'

I told him about the mileage discrepancy.

'On that journey from Cambridge, he could have come off route at any point and dumped Michelle's body,' Callum was saying as cups and spoons rattled in the background. 'What makes you think those extra thirty-nine miles were in a radius of his mother's house?'

'Because I've read the police interviews with his parents. On Saturday morning, Malecki left the house, saying he had errands to run. His father was annoyed, because he was late back. Missed the start of his own party at two in the afternoon. He never accounted for his whereabouts and by the time police were asking the questions, it was thirteen years later. No way to check and they'd made their arrest, so they didn't sweat the minor details.'

'This coffee hasn't kicked in yet,' he said wearily, 'give me the edited highlights.'

'When Malecki drove north, Michelle was alive. He took her somewhere close to his mother's house. Left her there until Saturday morning, then went back to have his fun with her, which doesn't bear thinking about. He cut off her finger, then killed her. His birthday present.'

The silence on the other end of the phone stretched out for so long, I thought he'd gone.

'Hello?'

'I'm still here.'

I waited, but he didn't say anything, so I pushed on, speaking fast to get my theory out, before he cut the legs from under me.

'Malecki told me he'd studied the mistakes of other killers and knew he wouldn't fall into those same traps. His first kill

349

was on his birthday. Afterwards, he knew that was an identifiable signature. One that could give too much away. But his ego meant that he couldn't resist making future kills relevant. So, from then on, he killed on the day and not the date. He also never made the mistake of keeping a victim alive after that. He realised it posed too many complications. Not least finding a deposition site for the body. Ever since Michelle, he's left them at the murder scene.'

'Not many places he could hold her, alive, for almost three days, without anyone seeing or hearing anything. Not to mention coming and going unnoticed.' But I could hear him considering the possibilities.

'Lots of rural areas just a short drive from Trafford. In 1981, plenty of empty farms, outbuildings.'

'Even if you're right, we don't have the resources, Jo. It doesn't form part of the current investigation—'

'It *does* though, Cal. Malecki's always refused to say what he did with Michelle's body. Why? Because I believe, wherever it was is the same place he stored his notebooks and trophies. Throughout his killing years, he visited his mother regularly. Killers who take trophies like to return to them . . . often. And in his later years, he moved permanently to the north.'

'You think the disciple's been there – to get Malecki's custom-made knife and notebooks?'

'Yes. And the trophies that are appearing for sale.'

'A thirty-nine-mile radius is a hell of a search area. I haven't got the manpower for that, or the budget. We're stretched as it is and frankly, your theory's not enough to justify it. I'd never get it past the powers that be.'

'I could keep looking, in my own time?'

'As long as you don't bill me, it's your time to waste.'

Chapter Sixty-Seven

Saturday Morning, Kingsberry Farm

'Have you got the time to waste, though?' I asked, as Ed set up his row of monitors across Jen's desk.

'Firstly, it's *not* a waste, and secondly, I enjoy the challenge. Besides, I'm officially out of the office for the next few months, so no one's going to miss me for a few hours here and there.'

My curiosity was piqued. 'Taking leave?'

'Hardly.' His voice was muffled as he crawled under the desk. 'Volunteered my expertise to work alongside DICE.' His head popped up from the other side. Clocking my expression, he added, 'Dark Web Intelligence, Collection and Exploitation. They work in partnership with the National Crime Agency and Regional Cyber Crime Units.'

He crawled out and stood up, brushing dust off his jeans. I made an embarrassed note-to-self to vacuum under the desks more thoroughly.

'Sounds impressive.'

'I *can* multitask. Especially if I'm supplied with endless cups of coffee.'

I returned his infectious smile. 'OK. I'll take the hint.'

Harvey followed me as I went down to the kitchen, just as my mobile rang.

'Just wanted to bring you up to date,' Callum said. 'We recovered Malecki's paintings from the gallery in Saltaire, this morning.'

'Bet Gerald Carter wasn't best pleased?'

'You can only imagine. Threatened to sue, if any damage is done. We also seized the log book from his safe, with the code numbers and signatures for authentication. The techies will be checking those against the canvasses at the lab.' I could hear him taking a drink, which I knew would be strong coffee. 'There were two canvasses not accounted for at the gallery.'

'Did you trace them?' I poured boiling water into a cafetière. The closest it came to 'good ground coffee' in my house.

'They're at Wakefield Prison. The final pieces for the exhibition. So, another interesting conversation was had with Rob Harding.'

'Don't tell me, he complained it would violate his prisoner's rights?'

'Surprisingly, no. Agreed to their collection, good as gold. Didn't realise how big some of these paintings are though. One of them is eight feet tall. No wonder they can't store them in Malecki's cell.'

'So, what's next?'

'Forensics inspect the frames and canvasses, using infrared reflectography.'

'Will you call me when you get the results?'

'It should be immediate. They'll either see something or they won't.'

'Anything I can do in the meantime?'

'Actually, there is.' I heard him rifling through some papers. 'Lee in Cyber has got a list of trophies being sold. He has no idea whether they're genuine. Be helpful if you could take a look?'

'No problem.'

'I'll email it. Oh, meant to tell you . . . the handset we traced through IMEI?'

'What about it?'

352

'Went dead. Same day as our team briefing.'

'Coincidence?'

'What do you think?'

*　　*　　*

Ed turned one of the monitors towards me. 'I haven't forgotten about the Sheridan family. I'll carry on looking into them, at the same time as this geographical stuff.'

'The Sheridans might be a dead end.'

I told him about my conversation with Callum.

'Once he started tracking the burner phone, I had to tell him what I knew. He said no one had a familial connection to anyone in the force.'

'If you want to stop at family, I'd agree, but—'

Whatever he was about to say was interrupted by my mobile. Caller ID said Mary Fielding, my friend from Chapel Mills, who'd invited me to see her son's paintings. Seeing her name made me realised what I'd done.

'Oh, God, sorry, Mary.' I launched straight into my apology. 'I completely forgot. I've been so busy.'

She'd texted the date to my phone and I'd not put it in the diary.

'Want to make it lunch tomorrow, instead?' she said, with no hint of disappointment.

'Yes, lovely. Sorry again, Mary.'

I hung up, then rolled my eyes at Ed. 'Too many plates spinning.'

'Know what you mean.' He was already engrossed in a programme he was running.

*　　*　　*

353

I read the email Callum had sent. Lee had added a note:

Interesting, the alleged trophies began to appear one
week after Stephen Jones' murder.

These things popping up now wasn't a coincidence. I knew
beyond doubt that Malecki had trusted his disciple with the
whereabouts of his grim collection, and that was the source.

There were several items of jewellery, which the vendor said
belonged to Malecki's victims. Looking back at old news reports
and photographs was one way to check.

Most people kept mementos and camping gear in their lofts.
Mine was also crammed with box files on cases I'd been involved
in over the years.

I'd pushed through bags of Christmas decorations that I still
hadn't even thought about putting up until I found the Malecki
files I'd kept from my student days.

Ed helped lift them down, dumping them in my office before
going back to his row of monitors.

Now, I was sitting cross-legged on the floor, surrounded by
old, yellowed newspaper clippings.

I began studying the photographs and early accounts from
those who knew the victims. Occasionally stopping to compare
them with Lee's screenshots.

The companionable silence was shattered when Callum rang.

'News?' I blurted – anxious for a result.

'Nothing from the paintings.' He couldn't hide his disappointment.

'I was sure that was it.'

'Me too. Infrared showed the signatures, but that was all. No
"Dear Disciple" messages. And nothing found in the frames.

The framing is done in the gallery, though, after leaving the prison. So, that was a long shot. But we checked anyway.' His breath gusted down the phone. 'If the paintings *had* been his way of communicating, it would have narrowed down our field of suspects to anyone who had access to them.'

I sat back on my haunches in a sea of paper. 'What now?'

'We keep looking. Speaking of which, Lee's found some more items. They only went up this morning. I've emailed them.'

'Thanks.'

Almost as an afterthought, he added, 'How're you getting on?'

I glanced at Ed, with his back to me. 'Nothing yet.'

'Keep me posted.'

My laptop pinged as the call ended. I went to my desk to look at the latest from Lee. As I opened the message, my heart froze.

Almost sensing it, Ed turned in his chair. 'What's up?'

I stared at the screen, unable to speak.

He came to stand behind me. I could feel his breath on my neck as we both stared at the picture of a paperweight.

A glass dome with snowdrops inside it.

'Kath's,' I breathed.

He squeezed my shoulders. 'God, I'm sorry, Jo.'

* * *

After telling Callum about the paperweight, I'd debated calling Geoff Perrett. But I just didn't have the words.

How to tell him that one of his wife's treasured possessions had come up for sale, on a sick site dedicated to the man who'd killed her?

My energy seemed to sap, leaving me weary and unable to concentrate.

'It's getting late,' Ed said as we sat together on the sofa. 'I should go. You didn't sleep last night – you must be shattered.'

'I'd prefer the company,' I said, staring into the flames licking round crackling dry logs. 'Not sure I'd sleep anyway, now.'

His arm tightened round my shoulders. 'Want me to go out for takeaway?'

'God, hadn't thought about food. Sorry. You must be starving. I'll throw something together.' I got up and went into the kitchen. 'If you're happy with fruits of the fridge?'

'Good job it's not *my* fridge. Be interested to see what you'd do with a piece of mouldy cheese and a can of Stella.'

Harvey followed us and I let him out. A gust of freezing wind, laced with stinging hailstones, smacked my face.

'Second thoughts,' Ed said from the lounge door, 'glad I'm not going out in that. Fruits of the fridge sounds perfect.'

As I cooked, Ed towelled Harvey down and set the table. In less than an hour, I was serving the food.

'Wow!' Ed looked impressed.

'Pollo Milanese, with spaghetti pomodoro. One chicken breast, hammered thin, to make enough for two, tinned tomatoes and dried spaghetti . . . oh, and breadcrumbs. I always have those in the freezer from leftover bread. Jen told me it was bad to feed it to the birds, so . . .'

He raised his glass of water. 'Cheers to the chef. If the day job doesn't work out, I can always get you in at Gino's restaurant.'

He reached for the bottle of wine and poured some into my glass.

'You not having any?'

He took my hand across the table. 'Can't . . . if I'm driving back later.'

I took the bottle and filled his glass. 'Then don't.'

356

Chapter Sixty-Eight

Sunday Lunchtime, Chapel Mills, Fordley

The view from the penthouse at Chapel Mills was stunning. I stood at the huge window overlooking the city and marvelled at how snowfall could make even the bleakest town look like a fairy-tale landscape.

Little had changed since I'd been here the previous year, with the small addition of Mary's personal belongings dotted around.

'You've made the space your own.' I looked down at the crown of grey curls and gave her a hug.

'I take comfort from being in the place Leo loved.'

'Good.' I gave her a squeeze.

'Come on.' She walked down the corridor to Leo's studio. 'Let me show you these paintings.'

As she pushed open the double doors, the familiar scent of oil paint and linseed wafted over us.

The room was flooded with natural light. Gone were the heavy wooden shutters over the windows. A feature Leo had installed, when he feared he was being stalked. A fear that became a terrifying reality.

She went to a stack of canvasses propped against the wall. 'I've just finished cataloguing these.'

There was a sketch on a workbench.

'What's this?'

She came to stand beside me. 'An underdrawing. We found it when we were clearing out the old canvasses.'

'We?'

'Max – Leo's agent,' she explained. 'He comes up from London to help me with everything.'

The image had been done with watered-down black paint.

'Leo obviously started the underdrawing, then abandoned the idea,' Mary was saying.

It was a moorland scene of a place I recognised. Top Withens, a ruined farmhouse high on the moors above Haworth. Said to be Emily Brontë's inspiration for *Wuthering Heights*.

'It's stunning,' I murmured, marvelling at the detail that could be imparted with broad, almost careless strokes.

'They're all going to the States. But I'm keeping this one,' she said wistfully. 'Makes me feel like I'm looking over his shoulder while he's working. Of course, everything has to be authenticated. That's why it's taken so long to get organised.'

'What does that involve?' I asked, walking around the studio.

'Verification by independent experts. Max takes care of all that. But because Leo always made an underdrawing, it's easier to prove these are originals.'

'How so?'

'Someone copying a painting would stick to the original composition exactly. There would be no changes.'

'Whereas, the original artist *does* deviate from the underdrawing?'

'All the time. It's only a guide. Leo often changed his mind.'

She went to a file on the table.

'All the paintings were X-rayed and subject to infrared, as part of the authentication report.' She pulled out an X-ray and took it over to a portrait.

'The X-ray shows the underdrawing Leo did, before painting over it in oils. See here? The man's hand is in his lap on the X-ray. But when you look at the finished painting—' she traced it with her finger '—Leo's changed his mind, and painted the hand on the man's thigh.'

She put the X-ray back in the file. 'So, you see why the existence of pentimenti in a painting is evidence of its originality.'

I froze as her words triggered a memory. A conversation in the bowels of the Monster Mansion.

Why you want to help?

Pentimento.

'What did you just say?'

She looked at me, quizzically. 'Sorry, dear?'

'"Pentimenti"?'

'Yes. It's an Italian word, used in the artworld. It means "repentance". You know, because the artist has made an amendment.'

I stared at this woman who had no idea of the monumental significance of what she'd just said.

'They're commonly seen in works by Old Masters.' Mary was happily chattering, as my thoughts tumbled. 'Caravaggio composed directly onto canvas, so he changed his mind a lot. There are more pentimenti found in his work than most of the classical painters.'

Words.

Malecki's voice, echoing . . . mocking me, now that I realised the significance.

Everyone makes occasional errors. Even Caravaggio . . .

Mary stopped and looked at me.

'Are you all right, dear?'

'I need to speak to this agent, Max.'

'He's coming next week.'

'No, Mary . . . Now!'

Chapter Sixty-Nine

Sunday Afternoon

When I got into the Defender to ring Callum, there were text messages from Ed.

That morning, after the awkwardness of waking up beside each other, we'd quickly dressed and taken Harvey for a walk.

The blizzard of the previous night had blown itself out, and the morning was sunny and bitterly cold. The kind of winter morning I usually loved to lose myself in. But there was a tension radiating from Ed that was borderline uncomfortable.

After walking in silence for half an hour, he eventually stopped.

I braced myself for what I thought was coming.

'About last night . . .' he started.

'It's OK.' I pre-empted. 'If you're going to say it was a mistake, and you'd rather we pretended it never happened, I'm fine with it.'

He looked shocked. 'Well, I'm not.'

'You're not?'

'Don't sound so surprised.' Then his face became suddenly more serious. 'Unless that's how you feel?'

'Of course not.'

He pulled me to him. 'Thank God for that. Been bricking it all morning.'

Now, as I sat in the Defender, I quickly read his messages.

Hope you're OK?
How's your lunch going?
Missing you. Xx

All this felt a little strange, after having no 'significant other' in my life for so long. And Callum had never been the sort to send me messages – unless they were work-related.

Thankfully, I didn't have time to dwell on it. The cold was already seeping through my bones, so I switched on the engine, to get some warmth from the ancient heater.

I dialled Callum, surprised when a woman answered.

'DCI Ferguson's phone.'

'Beth?'

'Hi, Jo. The boss is tied up – it's gone mental here. Located Randall, at his girlfriend's house. Crash team kicked his door in at the crack of dawn. He's in custody.'

'That's brilliant news.'

'Better still, the white Ford van was parked on the bloody drive! Can you believe that?'

'They're not all criminal masterminds.' But even as I said it, a doubt was starting to bubble at the back of my mind.

'He's certainly not.' She snorted. 'Anyway, van's with Forensics and we're getting ready to interview Randall. Anything I can help with?'

I told her about my conversations with Mary and the phone call I'd had with Max.

'Blimey.' She'd been taking notes. 'You'd better come in.'

* * *

Sunday Afternoon, Fordley Police Station

'You called Max Andrews?' Callum said, nursing a mug of tepid coffee. DI's Wardman and Heslopp were crammed in the small room with us.

361

'He explained infrared reflectography is limited to how far it can penetrate. If the paint is put down in layers, infrared might not capture everything.'

'But X-ray can?'

I nodded. 'That's why they use both, for authentication.' I told him what Jill Neatley said, about Malecki painting in layers, the way they print banknotes.

'Right.' Callum put his mug down and picked up the phone. 'I'll get onto Forensics.'

'All this because your friend used an Italian word for "repentance".' Wardman's sardonic tone was grating.

'With Malecki, nothing is coincidental.'

'But still?' Wardman's smirk made me grit my teeth.

'You think it's a fluke that he uses a word that just happens to be a technique in art, that shows hidden elements in a painting?' I didn't even try to hide my annoyance. 'Or that he mentioned Caravaggio, whose work provides more examples of pentimento than almost any other?' I stood up, unable to contain my anger. 'He told me he didn't trust technology, that he was "old school". Christ, he's spelling it out for us!' I knew I was raising my voice, but I couldn't help myself.

Wardman opened his mouth, but Heslopp cut him off.

'I'm with the Doc. Her instincts are usually spot on with this stuff.'

I shot him a surprised look. Testimonials from him were rare. Appreciation for me, rarer still. He gave me a half-smile.

'So how does this disciple—' Wardman drew quotation marks in the air '—read these messages – if they're there at all? Hump the paintings down to Fordley Royal Infirmary's fracture clinic, to borrow their X-ray machine?'

'God, you're really starting to get on my ti—' I started.

'Pretty sure the gallery doesn't have an X-ray machine,' Heslopp cut in before things got messy, 'but we'll search it.'

'I asked Max where they took Leo's paintings,' I said tightly, resisting the urge to staple Wardman's tongue to his tie. 'He said they used the facility at Fordley university's art department.'

Callum, still holding on the phone, looked at DI Heslopp. 'Frank, can you . . .?'

'On it, boss.'

* * *

Late Sunday Afternoon

I sat in an observation room, watching on screen the interview taking place with Peter Randall.

A DI from the joint investigation team was leading the interview, with Beth in a supporting role.

Randall sat sullenly beside the young female duty solicitor appointed to him.

I'd missed the beginning, but it was obvious they'd covered the basics and were getting to the heart of things.

Callum sat beside me, arms folded. 'At least he's not gone "no comment",' he murmured.

It was obvious his young solicitor would have much preferred a silent interview. But Randall seemed only too happy to help.

'You say you were working on this contract for the last four months?' The DI checked his notes.

'Yep.' Randall stretched his legs out in front of him in an exaggerated display of nonchalance. 'You can check with the customer, he'll confirm it. So will the other lads on site.'

'And while you were on this job, in Cumbria,' the DI went on, 'where *exactly* was your van?'

'My client has already provided that information,' the solicitor interrupted.

'We just need to clarify the details.' The DI smiled. 'If you don't mind telling me again, Peter?'

'Kept it in the compound, with the other site vehicles.'

'And it never moved, in four months?'

'No. We lived on site. If we went out, we shared a works van. Boss paid the petrol, so it was sweet.'

'And you never came back to Yorkshire in that time? Not to visit your girlfriend . . . family?'

'We've covered this.' The solicitor sounded exasperated.

'But you see our problem?' The DI turned his iPad towards Randall, showing the image from the bus dashcam. 'We have your van, captured here on the Oakworth Road, last Wednesday. Less than five miles from Dennis Haverley's cottage. On the night he was murdered.'

Randall leaned forward to study the picture.

He slowly shook his head. 'What can I tell you? It's not my van, mate.'

'That's your registration number?'

'Looks like it.'

'And the marks where you removed an old logo from the side are the same.'

'Seems so.'

'But you've no idea how it could be there . . . on that night?'

Randall sat back in his chair. 'Not a scooby.'

'My client has cooperated fully with your investigation, Detective Inspector,' the solicitor said. 'You've found no forensic evidence in his van to connect him with this offence. Nor on any of the clothes he's willingly handed over.'

'Not yet,' the DI said tightly.

'And if you had any forensic evidence linking Mr Randall to the crime scene, we'd be having a very different conversation. So, I assume you haven't – despite my client providing a DNA sample.'

'Not that we needed it.' Callum huffed quietly beside me. 'The scrote's already in the system.'

The solicitor was getting into her stride.

'I've requested the expense forms Mr Randall supplied to his client in Cumbria. They show his mileage on leaving Yorkshire on the thirtieth of August and his current mileage. It proves his van hasn't been making extra journeys up and down the M6.'

'I've got an alibi for last Wednesday anyway.' Randall smirked. 'Told you, we was in a pub in Penrith, till closing time. Then I went back to the digs with the lads.' He sat back, with a decisive nod, as if he'd more than made his point.

'Cocky little shit,' Callum grunted.

'I agree,' I said. 'Not looking good, is it?'

He took a long breath, shaking his head. 'If all this checks out, it proves Randall was in Cumbria, but not his van. Someone else could have used it. He could still be involved.'

I looked back at the man in the interview room. 'Have they asked him about Malecki?'

'He doesn't deny being a friend, or that he's on the fandom sites and that he's visited him in prison. None of which are against the law . . . Unfortunately. Says he hasn't heard from him for months.'

I turned my attention to the interview.

'He's not leaking any stress signals,' I said.

'It's not his first time in the chair,' Callum said quietly.

I studied his body language. His demeanour and that illusive ingredient I could see and understand, but could never quantify to others.

'His energy's all wrong.'

'Energy?' Callum shot me a look.

'Not *physical* energy.' I tried to explain what I could see with my 'third eye'. 'Emotional energy.'

'And what's it telling you?'

'That he's enjoying himself.'

'He's a fan of a serial killer. With a portrait of a monster tattooed across his back. Of course, he's enjoying himself. This is the kind of attention nutters like him just love. Unfortunately, I can't charge him with being in possession of an offensive attitude.'

'If you can't tie him to it, with forensics, what then?'

His eyes never left the screen. 'We keep digging.'

As I was about to leave, there was a knock on the door and Lee from Cyber poked his head in.

'Boss . . . you free?'

'Yep.'

'You asked me to pose as a buyer for that paperweight on the DNM?'

'DNM?' I asked.

Lee looked at me, as if humouring the hard of thinking. 'Dark Net Marketplace.'

'What about it?' Callum said impatiently.

'Wednesdayschild's accepted our bid late last night.'

'Hope you haggled,' Callum said. 'Would look suspicious if we just agreed fifteen hundred quid straight off.'

'Fifteen hundred pounds!' I was staggered.

'No way to verify its authenticity,' Lee went on, unfazed. 'So got it for nine hundred pounds.'

'Any closer to identifying Wednesdayschild?' Callum asked.

'I've identified their bitcoin wallet, but that doesn't give us an individual ID. Transactions go through a Bitcoin escrow account, held in Argentina. But that's encrypted to hell and back.'

'You lost me at bitcoin wallet,' I admitted.

'Me too.' Callum grimaced.

'All you need to know,' Lee said in a tone of someone used to explaining his geek world to non-geeks, 'is that following the money isn't an option in the time we've got.'

'Any suggestions?' Callum's patience wearing thin.

'Now we've bought the item, it has to be delivered. To do that, the seller has to crawl out of the darknet and come into daylight. We've given an address in Fordley for the delivery.'

Callum nodded. 'OK.'

'They usually move goods via courier. Once we know which parcel service it is, we track it backwards, to where the package was picked up. With any luck, that'll lead us to them.'

We both looked at each other and I knew we were thinking the same thing. This was all taking time and the clock was ticking down on someone else's life.

Chapter Seventy

Monday Morning, Kingsberry Farm

It often went like this. Nothing for weeks, then everything happens at once.

The first thing to happen was a call from Callum, as I was working alone in my office.

'Result.' Was all he said.

'With the X-ray?'

I automatically glanced over to Jen's desk. She'd be the first person I'd share with. But she'd called to say she'd picked up the sore throat I'd had and was staying home.

'It's some kind of code,' Callum was saying. 'Ones and zeros – like binary.'

'Malecki was never going to make it easy.'

'Cyber techies are working on it. The two paintings we collected from the prison are being X-rayed today, but I'm sure we'll find the same on those. Three or four lines of noughts and ones across the bottom of the canvas.'

'The only person those messages could be for is someone who comes into contact with the canvasses . . .'

'And has access to an X-ray machine,' Callum added. 'Frank spoke to the university. Carter's gallery never used their facility. They use an auction house in York. Anyone can buy a portable machine though. They range from the size of a photocopier, for a couple of thousand pounds, plus, there's an X-ray scanner in Wakefield prison. Which widens the field more than I'd like.'

'What happened with Randall?'

'Site manager in Cumbria confirms Randall was there for the whole four months. Security cameras on the compound show Randall's van hasn't moved.'

'How can the same van be on Oakworth Road last week then?'

'Cloned,' he said simply. 'Someone's got the same make and model vehicle and put Randall's number plate on it.'

'And the marks on the side?'

'Easy enough to replicate. It's only a black outline of the original signage.'

'Someone's going to a lot of trouble to make Randall look guilty.'

'The disciple,' Callum said simply. 'Malecki puts Randall and Hannah on the list and the disciple does the work to make us believe they're suspects.'

'Luring Hannah to Paxton Pits,' I said. 'Then cloning Randall's van.'

'Looks like we haven't got enough to hold Randall. We'll probably have to release him under investigation.'

'Like Hannah,' I said, almost to myself.

'Gerald Carter's still in the frame . . . no pun intended. You said he fits the profile as a disciple?'

'And he has access to the canvasses.' I thought about it for a moment, before adding, 'So does Jill Neatley.'

'But she admitted she scans the canvasses when they come into the gallery. Not sure she'd be so forthcoming if she was involved. She just used infrared to check the signatures,' Callum said. 'No X-ray machine at the gallery and the binary code doesn't show up with reflectography. If Carter *is* involved, Jill Neatley's in a dangerous position. She could be at risk.' I could hear him shuffling paperwork. 'I'm not ready to let Hannah off the hook just yet either. He's still up to his neck and Carter knows more than he's saying.'

'I said in my profile, the offender's looking for weak targets. Doesn't want a house with multiple occupants, because they're not confident of being able to control them.'

'Which could mean, not physically strong?'

'Which would apply to Carter or Hannah.'

'The only suspect we have who's built like a weightlifter is Randall.'

'When Elle ... Dr Richardson told me they were attacked from behind that raised a flag for me.'

'Why?'

'Attacking from behind minimises the chance of confrontation. A physically weaker assailant would want to avoid that.'

I thought back to my conversation with Elle in McNamara's bar. *Inflicted with some force in the case of Stephen Jones. The wound went down to the vertebrae ...*

'Barbara Thorpe wasn't attacked with the same ferocity as Jones. The knife was applied with more pressure in his case – almost decapitated him. A physically weaker killer would attack a male more aggressively to make damn sure he didn't put up a fight.'

'If we do eliminate Randall,' Callum said, 'Carter and Hannah are neck and neck on the suspects list.'

'Is that another sick pun?'

He ignored that, before saying, 'We need a surveillance team.'

* * *

The next thing to happen was an unexpected visit from Ed.

I heard the growling engine of his four-by-four a minute before he knocked on the door. Harvey bounded ahead as I went down the corridor to the kitchen.

'This is a surprise,' I said, letting him into the porch, where he stood, knocking snow from his boots.

He had a cardboard tube under his arm. 'Wanted to bring you this.'

'What is it?'

'Surprise,' he said mysteriously.

He followed me into the kitchen.

'Brew?'

'Always.' He slipped off his jacket, hanging it on the back of a chair, then came up behind me and slipped his arms round my waist.

He kissed the back of my neck. 'I've missed you.'

I wriggled out of his arms, 'Easy, tiger. Some of us have to work today.'

He brandished the cardboard tube like the spoils of war. 'Ah, well, that's where this comes in. Mind if I take it into the office?'

'Knock yourself out.'

Harvey, fickle as usual, followed his new friend, leaving me to the domestic chores.

When I walked into the office, Harvey was sitting on the rug, watching curiously as Ed tacked poster-sized printouts on to the wall.

I handed him his coffee.

The posters joined up like jigsaw pieces. A mix of satellite images and aerial photography, creating a 3D image.

'Google Earth?' I hazarded a guess.

'Yep. Of the area I calculated we need to be looking at, for Malecki's hidey-hole. Easier than trying to make sense of multiple images on a computer screen.'

We were looking at a rural area, much smaller than the thirty-nine-mile radius we'd started with.

'How did you narrow it down?'

He leaned back against my desk, nursing his mug.

'If Malecki visited the site on the morning of his birthday, I reckoned the thirty-nine miles were made up of three journeys. On the night he travelled north, let's assume he left Michelle somewhere on the route to his parents' house.'

'OK.'

'On the morning of his birthday, he travels from his parents' place to the site and back again. I plotted the area for us to consider on that basis.' He took a mouthful of coffee. 'Good coffee, by the way.'

'Thanks.'

'If you're right about this location being visited by the disciple then we can rule out areas that have been built on since 1981.'

He pushed away from the desk and went to maps he'd tacked up on the right-hand side.

'These are plans from a geological survey that was done in 1983. It shows what the area was like, around the time Michelle went missing. I compared it to the present day, and blocked out areas that have been built on. What we're left with on these maps ...' He tapped the ones on the left. 'Are places that are still accessible.'

The 3D provided amazing detail. Farms, buildings, fields and forest areas.

'Wow! I'm impressed.'

'Aww shucks, it was nothing, ma'am.' He grinned, finishing his coffee. 'Anyway, got to get back.'

I stepped into his open arms, relishing the feel of him – the taste of his lips, before reluctantly pulling away.

'Think you'd better go, before I change my mind about working today.'

'Spoilsport.'

* * *

372

An hour after Ed left, I was standing in front of the maps, pencil in hand, putting myself into Malecki's mindset almost three decades earlier, when my phone rang.

It was Supt. Warner.

'Can you come in, Jo?'

'The weather's closing in up here. Can't we do it over the phone?'

'Not really.' The hesitation in her voice told me she was holding something back. 'It's rather sensitive.'

Chapter Seventy-One

Monday Afternoon, Fordley Police Station

Callum, DI Wardman and myself were in Supt. Warner's less-than-spacious office.

'Initially the call went to the SIO.' Warner indicated Callum. 'But obviously, got escalated to me. I contacted the manager at Fordley Mental Health Crisis Team and, with their client's permission, had her records sent over.'

I scanned the client assessment form. 'Who's Sylvie Roberts?'

'You'll know her as Sophie Adams,' Callum said.

'The seven-year-old, who witnessed the Gordons' murder?'

He nodded. 'Her parents gave evidence at the trial and the film of Sophie, picking Malecki out of an ID parade, was shown. After the trauma it caused the family, they requested Protected Persons status.'

The Protected Persons Service – called 'witness protection' on TV crime dramas – meant that people were given new identities and moved to a different part of the country, to rebuild their lives.

Warner picked up the story. 'The Roberts family, as they became, relocated to France.'

'So, how come she's back here?'

'The scheme's voluntary,' Warner explained. 'She kept her new identity, but opted out of the scheme a few years ago.'

'Why on earth would she want to come back to Fordley?' I asked.

'Her brother, Harry,' Callum said.

The baby. Born in a snowstorm, on the night of the Gordons'
murder.

'He's thirty now, Sylvie's thirty-seven,' Callum was saying.
'He got a job over here four years ago. Sylvie came with him. It
was Harry who called us.'

'The parents divorced in France,' Warner said. 'The family
fractured over the years. Just Harry and Sylvie now.'

I looked again at her patient record. Sylvie had suffered from
crippling anxiety throughout her teenage years, resulting in
periods in and out of psychiatric units.

'Says here that since returning to the UK, she's developed
severe agoraphobia.'

'Hasn't been out of the house in two years,' Warner added.
'Harry's her main support.'

'Malecki appearing in the news triggered severe PTSD,'
Callum said.

'Hardly surprising,' Wardman piped up, from somewhere
behind me.

'When Haverley's murder went public,' Callum explained,
'Sylvie's condition deteriorated. The mental health team obviously didn't understand why, but Sylvie and Harry don't want to
tell them, because that would mean revealing her real identity.'

'She'd know the significance of Haverley, where no one else
would,' I said, to no one in particular. 'Even though they were only
young, their parents will have told them about the case and the
trial. The fact that Malecki was caught on his way to kill Haverley.'

Warner nodded. 'And that Jack Halton took a closer look at
Malecki's car, because of Sophie's . . . Sylvie's photofit. The evidence she gave about hearing him say his name was "Jake" and
the ID parade. The part she played was pivotal to his conviction,
despite her age.'

Warner scanned her notes. 'Harry called to assess how realistic Sylvie's fears were. Get some kind of reassurance.'

'I'm going to visit them,' Callum said. 'As SIO, it'll show we're taking their concerns seriously.'

'In view of Sylvie's fragile state,' Supt. Warner added, 'I want you to go too, Jo. Having a psychologist attending demonstrates we're handling this with the care it deserves.'

* * *

Monday, Sylvie Roberts' House, Fordley

It was hard to reconcile the image of a cute seven-year-old to the woman sitting on the sofa in front of us.

Her painfully skinny frame, with jutting collar bones, hinted at an eating disorder. The impression compounded by her sallow complexion and the dark bruise-like shadows under her eyes. She hugged an oversized jumper around herself, in an effort to conceal her body.

She still had long, blonde hair, tied with an elastic band, but thin patches, where her scalp showed through, were evidence of hair loss. Her fingernails were bitten down to the quick.

Ever since we'd arrived at the neat, end-terraced house and been ushered into the small lounge by her brother, Sylvie had almost huddled into the corner of the sofa, chain-smoking her way through Callum's introductions.

I watched as she lit another cigarette from the stub of the last. Despite the rest of the room being clean and tidy, the ashtray on the glass coffee table between us was overflowing.

Sylvie's knee bounced with nervous energy and her dark eyes constantly darted to the doors and windows.

Hypervigilance.

A common symptom of PTSD. An unrelenting, adrenaline-fuelled state where perceived threat is seen in every shadow; every sudden sound; every human encounter.

Heightened awareness the human body was never designed to maintain for longer than a moment of actual danger. To constantly be like this was unbearable and completely exhausting. Like running the engine of a car at a hundred miles an hour, in first gear – day in, day out.

'You have a different identity,' Callum was saying. 'And having lived in France under the Protected Persons Service, for decades, we don't believe Malecki, or anyone he might be connected to, would know how to find you.'

Sylvie stared at some spot over his shoulder. She hadn't uttered a word since we'd arrived.

Her brother sat on the sofa beside her, with his arm around her shoulders.

'The Chief Inspector's right, Syl. There's no reason to be scared. They're going to protect you.' He looked to Callum. 'I mean … you'll have someone here with her, until this nutter's caught, right?'

'I can arrange to have a marked police car drive past, every evening.'

Harry gawped at Callum. 'That's it?'

'No one knows your new identity, or where you live. We believe you're safe. I understand your concerns, Harry, but of everyone who might be at risk, we believe Sylvie has the least to worry about. We've evaluated the threat levels as very low.'

'No one knew Dennis Haverley's name either,' Harry cut across him, his voice rising. 'But he's just as dead! You couldn't protect him, could you?'

'Investigating officers and Jacob Malecki knew Haverley's identity and he didn't change his name or move far after the case. No one knows your new name – even we weren't aware when you called.'

Harry was in no mood to listen. 'After everything she went through as a kid, to help put that bastard away, that's the best you can do?'

'I appreciate how this must feel.' Callum's tone was mollifying. 'We *do* have a duty of care, which is why we're here to reassure—'

'You.' Harry turned to me, his tone caustic. 'You're a shrink – you of all people must know what this is doing to her? Tell him!' he shouted.

Sylvie visibly jumped, drawing her legs up, almost curling into a ball on the sofa.

'Do you live here with Sylvie?' I asked gently.

He shook his head. 'Did when we first came back. But I had to get my own place.'

I understood.

He wouldn't want to verbalise it, but Harry was only young. He had his own life to live and much as he loved his sister, caring for someone with such severe mental health issues took its toll. Not just on his mental well-being, but on his freedom and social life. When loved ones became carers, their lives could shrink, as much as that of the person they cared for.

'I live just down the road,' he was saying. 'Five minutes' walk.' I nodded and smiled, in a way that said, I wasn't judging. 'I come before work and then on my way home.' He still felt the need to explain. 'Do her shopping and everything. But I have to work.'

I reached out and lightly touched his arm. 'It's OK. It can't be easy.'

Sylvie stared at a spot on the carpet. There was no sign she was aware of the conversation going on around her.

I moved into Sylvie's eye-line.

'Sylvie,' I said quietly, 'I'm Dr McCready.' Her gaze never moved from the floor. 'I've come to check on you. Make sure you're OK?'

Her eyes flickered, but she couldn't meet my gaze.

'I know you're scared, Sylvie . . . I understand.' The silence stretched out to the point of being painful.

Callum shot me a look and lightly shrugged his shoulders. I turned back to the woman huddled on the couch.

'The police will keep you safe, but they can't have someone in the house with you all the time.' There was an imperceptible lift of her chin. I knew she was listening. 'I don't think you would want that, though, would you? A stranger in your home all day?'

She looked at me then. Her dark eyes brimming with unshed tears. Slowly, she shook her head.

For someone with her conditions, having a stranger in her safe space would be too stressful. It would feel like a violation.

'But you have Harry.' I glanced at Callum. 'And DCI Ferguson will leave a number you can call if you see or hear anything out of the ordinary.' Callum nodded his agreement. 'Plus, the police car driving past too. Would all of that help?'

Her slight nod was barely noticeable. But it was something.

Then Callum spoke, his voice sounding suddenly loud.

'One of the things I came to discuss with you was the possibility of moving out? Stay with relatives or friends somewhere outside of Yorkshire? Just until this is over.'

Harry was vigorously shaking his head, but before he could speak, a hoarse voice drew all our attention.

'No.' Sylvie shook her head. 'I won't leave here . . . you can't make me go out.' She dug her fingers into the cushion, like claws hanging on for dear life.

'It's OK, Sylvie,' I said quickly, moving my face nearer, so that she had to meet my eyes. 'No one is going to make you leave here if you don't want to.'

Her eyes met mine, almost pleading. 'I can't.' She shook her head. 'I can't go outside . . . I can't!'

Harry leaned over and scooped her into his arms, stroking her hair and rocking her, like a child.

'It's all right, Syl . . . hush, it's all right.' He looked at us over the top of her head. 'I'll move in with her, for the time being. Just leave that number, and make bloody sure that car patrols past every day.'

* * *

Callum's BMW was crap in the snow. A fact that I would once have enjoyed ribbing him about. But given his mood since we'd left Sylvie and Harry, I wasn't inclined to mention it.

'That went well,' he said grimly.

I spoke to the passenger window, as I looked out at people sliding their way across icy pavements.

'What did you expect?' My breath created a small patch of mist on the glass.

I saw him shrug in the reflection. 'I'm not used to that, I suppose.'

'What?'

'Someone as unravelled as her. You're used to it, I'm not.'

'You never get used to it,' I said quietly.

'To be like that though. Not a life, is it? I mean, what the hell has she got? Never leaves the house. Never feels the sun on her face. Couldn't ever have a relationship, could she? Not when she's so broken. She might as well . . .'

380

'Be dead,' I finished for him.

'I didn't mean . . .'

'She's another of Malecki's victims. He took her life as surely as if he'd cut her throat.'

'We have no idea who's next,' he said. 'But like Haverley, anyone involved in the earlier case might be a target.' He shot me a look. 'You were on his list . . . as a student.'

'But he changed his mind,' I said with a conviction I didn't quite feel.

'Didn't kill Haverley the first time round either.'

'It's not the same.'

'Isn't it?'

'No! He *still* intended to kill Haverley. That's why he tried again. But he decided to leave me in the game.'

'That was before you pissed him off.' Something in his tone sent a trickle of apprehension down my spine. 'You're the one who put us onto this disciple, Jo. Think he's going to let that go?'

The silence stretched as I struggled to come up with an answer I actually believed.

'What was it you said, when Haverley was killed?' Callum replayed my own words back to me. '"Malecki wants to lash out and prove that he's still a force to be reckoned with, even from inside the Monster Mansion".'

'But—'

'I've got a duty of care, Jo.'

I leaped ahead of him. 'You're not saying . . .'

'You need to be moved, to a place of safety.'

Chapter Seventy-Two

Monday Afternoon, Fordley Police Station

'Surely I'm safe enough at the farm? There's a snowstorm coming in – it's almost inaccessible on the moors in bad weather.' I was trying to plead my case, in front of Callum and Supt. Warner.

'Doesn't hurt to take precautions.' Warner's expression brooked no argument.

'But I didn't own the place when Malecki was arrested,' I persisted.

'Haverley was at a new address,' Callum countered. 'So was Lutner. We can't take the chance, Jo.'

'Everyone on the periphery of the original case is being visited,' Supt. Warner said. 'Even jurors and solicitors from his trial. Anyone still alive from the original enquiry. They're all being advised to be vigilant and to call the number we've given them if they see anything suspicious. Or, better still, go away for Christmas.' She perched on the edge of the desk, already distracted by something on her iPad.

'This request, for a surveillance team,' she said to Callum. 'It's doesn't cover our whole suspect list, I hope?'

'No, ma'am, we're restricting it to Gerald Carter and Jill Neatley, for now.'

She shot him a look. 'Never mind "for now". The cost of keeping two people under twenty-four-hour surveillance might just bust my budget. Why Neatley?'

'Carter has access to the paintings and he was the only one who used the X-ray facility at the auction house in York.'

'But never on Malecki's canvasses,' Warner pointed out. 'Only on the ones they were commissioned to evaluate.'

'As far as we know. We're checking to see if he could have had an opportunity to scan Malecki's paintings.'

'Same question,' she persisted. 'Why Neatley?'

'I believe she could be at risk from Carter. If this code *is* the way Malecki's communicating with his disciple, Carter might want to tie up loose ends. Or, she could be an accomplice. We need to eliminate that possibility by keeping tabs on what she does and where she goes.'

'And if the binary sequences on those paintings is just Malecki playing games – another red herring to have us disappearing up our own arses? I'll have to answer to the assistant chief constable for deploying a team to watch Carter and Neatley do their Tesco shopping.'

'Appreciate that, ma'am.'

She sighed. 'The request will have to go to an independent authorising officer, unconnected to our investigation. I'll submit it to headquarters.'

She turned her attention back to me.

'I know you don't like it, Jo. But of all the civilians involved in this, you're the most at risk.'

'But still—'

She waved a hand to cut me off. 'Malecki's focus has changed, Jo. That "Q" signal set off a prearranged plan, which can only result in more killing. We have to identify this disciple and get ahead of them before someone else dies. In the meantime, I have to minimise risk and harm to anyone we think might be a target. And, like it or not, you *are*. Probably more than most.' She slipped off the desk and gathered her notes, signalling an end to this discussion. 'Make the arrangements, Callum.'

'Yes, ma'am.'

I rounded on him as soon as we were alone. 'You can't be serious?'

He just raised an eyebrow.

I gasped in frustration. 'Where would I go?'

'Take a Christmas break. Stay in a hotel.'

'What about Harvey?'

'Put him in kennels.'

'Not bloody likely! He's never been kennelled.'

'Well, you can't get Jen to move in and look after him, like you usually do.' He ground on with annoying logic. 'Assuming Malecki's accomplice *does* know where the farm is, anyone there would be at risk.'

'Oh, for God's sake.' I slammed my notebook on the desk. 'This is ridiculous. The next victim could be one of his original "projects". Someone we can only identify if we crack that code. He might not be deviating from his original plan.'

'Tell that to Haverley.'

Whatever was coming was cut short, as Heslopp stuck his head round the door.

'What is it, Frank?' Callum sounded grateful for the interruption.

'Just wanted to bring you up to speed with my visit to Fordley University.'

Callum went to the eternal coffee percolator on his bookcase and poured a steaming mug.

'There's a mobile X-ray machine, shared by different departments,' Heslopp read from his notes. 'When Max took Leo Fielding's paintings, they were X-rayed in the art department. The professor there is an expert in authentication and conservation . . .'

'I don't need the man's CV. Frank, just get to the good bit.'

'I know Wardman was being a prick when he made that remark about taking them to an A & E department. But he wasn't far wrong. In order to scan canvasses this size, the machine needs to be a pretty big bastard. Not something your average person is going to be able to afford so we can eliminate mobile machines kept in someone's spare room. They also said, Carter's gallery never used their machine.'

My mobile rang. Seeing it was Ed, I stepped into the corridor to take the call.

'How's it going?' Hearing his voice somehow lifted my spirits, which had begun to feel decidedly gloomy.

'OK . . .'

'Doesn't sound it.'

'How can you tell, from one word?' He was already making me smile.

'I'm getting to know you.'

I told him about the police saying I should move out of the farm. The minute I'd said it, I knew I'd created another complication for myself.

'Stay at mine.' Was his predictable response, one I'd struggle to answer without upsetting him.

It felt unwise to be locked down for the foreseeable at his home – a place I'd never visited, and virtually living together, for God knew how long. I'd lived alone for so long, I wasn't sure I could share someone's intimate space. I was becoming fond of him, but certainly wasn't as emotionally involved as he obviously was. Agreeing to move in with him, for whatever reason, was likely to send him signals I wasn't ready for just yet.

'It's lovely of you to offer, but . . .'

'It's no bother.'

I leaned back against the wall and closed my eyes. I was exhausted and couldn't remember the last time I'd eaten.

'Please don't be offended, Ed. It's just . . . too soon.'

385

There was an uncomfortable pause, before he finally said, 'It's fine.'

'Doesn't sound it.' I mimicked his own words.

'Touché.' He laughed. 'I'd be lying if I said I wasn't disappointed. But I respect your feelings. You want to move slowly . . . right?'

'Right.'

'As long as you still want to keep moving . . . I can deal with that.'

'God, you're so needy,' I teased, knowing he could hear the smile in my voice.

'When are you moving out? And if not to mine, then where?'

I chewed my bottom lip as I thought through my options. Dismayed at how limited they actually were. 'It can't be anyone obvious, like Jen . . .'

'Or Mamma?'

'God forbid.' I shuddered. 'I'd rather take my chances with a serial killer.'

He laughed, before thankfully changing tack. 'I was actually calling with information on the Sheridan family. The more I look at it, the more certain I am they were involved in Finch's murder.'

'Go on.'

'The older brother, Nick Sheridan, was in the Royal Signals, deployed to Northern Ireland. A week before Finch's death, he was given leave and travelled back to the UK.'

'You think he confronted Finch about what happened to his sister?'

'It's possible. Your friend Finn said the family found out and that's why Finch was killed. What I can tell you is, the day after the fire, Nick Sheridan went back to Belfast.'

'And died over there . . .'

'Poor sod was dodging bombs and bullets and ends up getting killed in a traffic accident.'

'Anything else?'

'Not yet. I'll email what I found so far. You get anywhere with the geographical stuff on Malecki's hiding place?'

I had to admit that I hadn't. 'But wherever I end up staying, I can take the work with me.'

As I ended the call, Tony almost bumped into me as he rounded the corner.

'Hi, Jo. Didn't expect you in tonight.'

'Me neither.' I sounded as weary as I felt.

'What do you think about this binary code then?' he asked as we walked into the incident room.

I washed a hand across my eyes. 'Haven't seen it yet.'

'Take a look.' He turned his monitor towards me and I stared at rows of noughts and ones. They'd been photographed from the X-rays and looked like silver-grey negatives.

I jotted down the rows in my notebook, wondering when I'd last seen binary. Maths was my worst subject at school and I was eternally grateful, I'd never had to use a quadratic equation since the day I'd left.

'There's a briefing tonight,' Tony was saying. 'With any luck, the geeks might have worked it out.'

My mobile vibrated across the desk as it rang. I read the caller ID.

'Hi, Elle.'

'Hope I haven't disturbed anything fun?'

'Hardly. I'm at Fordley nick, waiting for a briefing.'

'Glad I'm not the only sad cow, working late at Christmas.'

She made me smile, despite how I felt. 'What can I do you for?'

'More what I can do for you, sweet cheeks.' She exhaled loudly and I knew she was smoking.

'Remember I circulated the wound pattern from your unusual knife?'

'Hmm.'

'I got a hit – from an unexpected source.'

'Oh?'

'Friend of my parents. Retired now, but was a top forensic pathologist in his day. I mentioned it to him at a dinner party the other night. He said it rang a bell and asked me to send the pictures over. He just got back to me.'

'And?'

'Said he'd seen wounds just like it, years ago. Killer was never caught and the weapon never recovered.'

'When?'

'August 1986. He was working in Europe at the time.'

'Where?' My heart began to thud just a little harder.

'Italy.'

A thousand thoughts clashed in my head. Dates, locations. Disjointed facts jostling for attention. I made hastily scribbled notes, so I wouldn't lose the tenuous threads.

'I'm emailing the details to the Boy Scout. It's not relevant to his current enquiry, but proves the knife was around in the eighties, possibly used abroad,' she was saying. 'Listen, if it's not too late after your briefing, fancy grabbing something to eat, seeing as we're both in town?'

'Absolutely.'

'Jo,' Callum called from the doorway, tapping his watch. 'Briefing.'

'Got to go,' I said. 'I'll call when I'm out.'

Chapter Seventy-Three

Monday Evening, Fordley Police Station

The joint SIOs had brought everyone up to speed with developments.

Randall and Hannah had been 'released under investigation'. Forensics had found nothing in Randall's van, house or clothing and there was nothing incriminating on his phone.

'We're monitoring Randall and Hannah's phones,' Heslopp said, 'and doing drive pasts of their haunts. So far, they're sticking to their routines.'

The team had been told about Sylvie Roberts, and our visit to her and Harry.

'Everyone connected to the earlier case and Malecki's trial has been put on notice,' Warner told them. 'Anyone we feel is at particular risk is being advised to break their routine and change location, if possible.' She shot me a knowing look, which wasn't lost on the team, then handed back to Callum before dashing off to another meeting.

'Supt. Warner and myself met with the ACC, to put our case for surveillance,' Callum said. 'We had to justify why we're not simply arresting Carter. But what we've got is circumstantial at best. Plus, once we pull him in, we show our hand and if he is the disciple and we don't have enough to satisfy the CPS, he could walk out of here and break off his activities. Which leads us precisely nowhere.'

Ian spoke up. 'If we keep him in play, isn't there a risk to potential victims? Especially as we don't know who's next.'

'Yes,' Callum agreed. 'If we lose him, there's a chance he'll get to the next target.' He sat on the edge of the table. 'Which is why that can't happen. We've got his phone monitored on live cell site.'

A PC raised his hand. 'Why surveillance on Carter and not Randall as well?'

'Only a few people have access to the binary code on the paintings. Randall and Hannah don't, but they're still persons of interest.'

'What about people at the prison? Or at the university?' the PC persisted.

He had a point. Callum was playing the odds.

'There's that possibility,' Callum conceded. 'But we have to narrow our focus of attention.'

'Do we know for certain that the code *is* instructing the killer?' someone at the back asked.

'Malecki put it there for a reason, and never expected it to be found,' Callum said.

'Or wants us to think that.' Wardman couldn't help himself, then he caught the look Callum shot him and clamped his mouth shut.

'Which is why we have to crack this code.' Callum handed over to a techie.

The young man took his place at the front. I thought, he looked about twelve – or did that mean I was getting older?

He slid his glasses further up the bridge of his nose, with his index finger, before flicking the remote that brought the rows of code up on screen.

'The binary system is a mathematical expression that uses only two symbols, those being zero and one. Each digit is referred to as a "bit", or binary digit. Assuming the binary code represents text, we must translate it by first converting each letter to its decimal equivalent. Where the capital letter "A" is represented by the number sixty-five, each subsequent letter is one number higher than its predecessor . . .'

'For fuck's sake,' someone muttered, just loud enough.

'You don't need to explain *how* it's done,' Callum finally interrupted, raking fingers through his hair, 'just whether you deciphered it?'

'Er, using an ASCII chart, we input the binary numbers—'

'And?' Callum snapped.

'It's indecipherable.' The lad blinked, like a rabbit caught in the headlights.

'You mean you couldn't make head nor fucking tail of it?' Heslopp growled.

'It doesn't convert to meaningful text, if that's what you mean?' The young man's cheeks flushed. He turned back to the screen. 'We then converted it to numerals. But we can't find a correlation between the numbers and anything relevant such as dates, page numbers, or map grid references.'

'It's just gobbledygook?' Heslopp said what others were thinking, but wouldn't dare vocalise.

'Potentially,' the analyst said. 'We've sent it to Fordley University. They have a cryptanalyst there.'

'OK,' Callum said. 'Keep working on it.'

As the young man left, the briefing rolled on.

'If that code *doesn't* mean anything—' Wardman was trying to redeem himself '—then it's just Malecki playing games. Wasting our time.'

Callum pinned him with a stare that stilled the room. 'And if we finally establish that to my satisfaction, we'll move on. But we can't ignore it.'

Lee raised his hand, diffusing the tension.

'We've bought the paperweight from Wednesdayschild. It's going to be delivered tomorrow.'

Callum looked at his DC. 'Beth, I'm putting you on the courier service. Find out where they collected it.'

'Right, boss.'

'Everyone else, you've got your tasks allocated.'

As the briefing ended, I gathered my things. Stopping short when Callum appeared at my elbow.

'What are your plans?' He was brusque.

'Getting something to eat – if that's OK with you?'

'You know what I mean. Moving out?'

I held up a hand in defeat – I didn't have the energy to argue. 'I will, but I have to decide what to do with Harvey, not to mention packing.'

'Let us know your location. But sooner rather than later.'

'I have to make arrangements with Jen, tell Mamma . . .'

'Saying where you're going defeats the object. Don't tell them – full stop.'

I glared at him. 'What, you think Jen or Mamma are going to call Malecki and tell him?'

He exhaled, exasperated. 'Do you have to be so stubborn?'

'Independent.'

'Bloody-minded.'

'It gets results.'

'It could get you dead!' he snapped, walking away.

Chapter Seventy-Four

Monday Evening, McNamara's, Fordley

Elle pushed her plate away and sat back, replete. Finn wasn't in and the place was quiet, with staff outnumbering the few late diners.

'I agree – too early to move in with Ed.' After I'd explained about having to relocate. 'Depending on how you feel about him, of course?'

I toyed with the stem of my glass. 'I like him. He makes me feel . . .' I struggled with the words.

'Special?'

'Yes, and valued. Something Callum hasn't managed lately.'

'But, he's in far deeper than you are, right now?'

I nodded. Ed had made his feelings about me clear. But I wasn't there yet. Maybe I never would be. Not just with Ed, but any man, now.

'If I move to his place, I worry he'll take that as a sign of commitment that I'm not ready for just yet.'

'Come to mine,' she said. 'It's a no-brainer.'

It made sense. Although we were friends, not many people would include Elle in the close circle of people in my life and although I'd visited her place a couple of times, I'd never stayed there.

'As long as you don't mind being there on your own?'

She'd already explained, they were visiting Rina's family in Scotland, to make up for not spending Christmas there.

'We have to leave tomorrow as I'm rostered for leave until Monday.' She rolled her eyes. 'On call between Christmas and New Year, though.'

'I don't mind. You sure it's OK to bring Harvey?'

'Absolutely. Anyway, you're doing me a favour. I was paying a local farmer to look after Butch and Sundance. Don't have to if you're staying. Long as you don't mind mucking out and doing the feeds?'

'I'd enjoy it.' I'd worked at the local stables when I was a teenager. That's where I'd learned to ride. Looking after horses again would be a pleasant distraction.

'I'll pack tonight and come to yours in the morning. You can show me the routine before you leave.'

She nodded, savouring the wine. We'd limited ourselves to one glass as we were both driving.

'For once, I actually agree with the Boy Scout.'

'About what?'

'Not telling anyone where you're staying.'

'I know,' I conceded. 'Just the way he said it, like a command. Got my back up.'

'You'd think he'd know better.' She swirled the wine thoughtfully. 'Interesting – that knife being used in Italy. You had a chance to look at the stuff I emailed the team?'

'Not yet.'

'The shape of that blade reminded me of something. Couldn't place it, until Italy was mentioned. Now I can't get the similarity out of my mind.'

'Similarity to what?'

She took a pen and began drawing on her napkin. I watched as she sketched a blade, with a wide curve and six small serrations from the base of the blade to the handle. She pushed the napkin across the table.

394

'*Ferro*,' she said, simply.

I stared at it, my brain crawling through its database of words and terms.

'Italian word for "iron"?'

She smiled. 'Try again.'

I googled it on my phone. It brought up a list of companies. Then images of Porto Ferro beach and Murano glass.

'Try *fèrro*,' she hinted, enigmatically.

And there it was.

The ornament on the front of Venetian gondolas.

A counterweight to the gondolier at the back. Originally made from iron, but more often stainless steel these days. The wide curved top signifying the doge's cap – the six teeth representing the six districts of Venice.

'You've sent this to Callum?'

She nodded. 'Only relevant if he finds the knife. But now he knows what it might look like.'

* * *

As I walked across town, my mind was full of lists. Things I'd need to take so I could carry on working from Elle's place.

The car park was full when I'd arrived earlier, so I'd parked the Land Rover in a side street behind the police station.

As I turned the corner, I saw Beth, leaning against a wall. She was engrossed in a phone call, and didn't see me. She ended the call and then slipped the small mobile into her boot.

I stopped in the shadow of the building and watched.

She pulled another phone out of her pocket – her usual mobile – and began thumbing a message.

As I stepped out to cross the road, she looked startled as she recognised me.

'Jo. What're you doing here?'

I nodded to the Defender. 'Going to my car.'

Her gaze followed mine. 'Oh . . . the Landie?'

'TT's no good in this weather.'

'I just nipped out to phone home.' She couldn't have looked more guilty if she'd tried. 'Anyway, got to get back to the coalface.'

I watched her go as I fished car keys out of my bag. The car door was stiff with a ream of ice round the edge, and I had to lean back and yank it open. Sliding into the driver's seat, my breath plumed into the freezing air. I turned the ignition.

Nothing.

I tried again. A click . . . then nothing.

'Shit!' I slammed my hands against the steering wheel. 'Don't do this to me . . . not now.'

'Got a problem?'

I jumped.

Ian Drummond was beside my driver's window, his neck buried in a thick scarf, hands jammed into the pockets of his North Face jacket.

I opened the driver's door. 'Bloody thing won't start.'

'Want me to take a look?'

He walked to the front, signalling for me to pop the lid. I watched as he stuck his head inside, fiddling with some wires, before looking round the edge of the raised bonnet.

'Try it now?'

I turned the key.

Nothing.

He dropped the lid with a thud.

'I'm no expert.' He blew on his cupped hands, stamping his feet against the bitter cold. 'But sounds like the starter motor's knackered.'

'Bugger!' I looked at my watch. It was after eleven. 'Got to get home. Need to pack.'

'No taxis would go up there in this weather. Better come back to the station – see what we can sort out.'

* * *

Callum looked surprised as I walked into the office.

'Thought you'd left?'

'Tried to.' I fell into the nearest seat. 'Bloody Land Rover won't start.'

I told him about meeting Elle and her offer.

'I'll see if anyone from traffic's available with an X5. Get you home. But then they'll have to take you to Elle's tonight. Can't guarantee there'll be anyone available in the morning.'

'I don't mind driving her, boss,' Ian offered. 'If I can borrow one of the X5s?'

'Thought you'd clocked off?'

'Was going for my train when I saw this damsel in distress.'

Callum shook his head. 'Nice offer, Ian, but you've not slept. I need you on your game.'

'Is Dr Richardson's place far?' Ian asked.

'On the moor above Turnhole Clough,' I said.

'Didn't know there were houses up there.'

'House – singular. Ferndean. Used to be a farm.'

'Can see why you'll need a four-by-four. Bloody inaccessible in this weather.'

'No bad thing,' Callum said. 'Makes it even safer – now you've finally taken the advice to relocate.'

I ignored the dig. 'I'll call Elle.'

Callum walked back to his office as I looked for my phone.

Several people walked into the incident room and exchanged greetings and banter with some of the team.

One woman in particular drew my attention.

I collared Beth as she walked past. 'Who're they?'

'Surveillance team, in for initial briefing.'

'Know her?'

'Name's Abbie, I think.'

I looked again at the slim blonde. The same one I'd seen getting into Callum's car.

I followed her eyes. She was watching Callum in his office doorway. They exchanged a look and both smiled. Then she turned back to her colleagues.

Callum glanced my way. Our eyes locked for just a second, before he went inside and closed the door.

Chapter Seventy-Five

Tuesday Morning

We stood in Elle's hallway surrounded by bags and boxes. Harvey was outside excitedly exploring.

'Blimey, you don't travel light.' Rina, Elle's partner, laughed as she sipped a coffee.

'In my defence, this is from my office. I've only brought one bag of clothes.'

The traffic officer who'd taken me home the previous night had been less than impressed when he'd seen the archive boxes from the Malecki case.

'If it's any consolation,' she said, rubbing a hand over her short-cropped hair, 'Elle can pack this much in shoes.'

'I heard that.' Elle appeared in the doorway, dressed for the stables.

'Right.' Rina grinned. 'If you two are going out to the nags, I'm off to finish packing.'

Elle handed me a waxed jacket and wellies. 'Help yourself to anything you need from the boot room.' She fussed Harvey as he thundered back in, dancing round her legs. 'All the outdoor gear's in there.'

'"Boot room" – very *Downton Abbey*,' I teased.

'Be nice if it was heated, then it would be posh. It's an original part of the house, so the windows in there aren't double glazed. It's like a meat locker in winter. The only reason I have it is because it came with the house. To be fair, the only reason I have a kitchen is because that came with the house too.'

For someone so adept at wielding knives in the autopsy suite, Elle was renowned for her lack of culinary skills. 'You sleep, OK?' she asked as I fell in step beside her.

'Yes. Sorry it was so late when I arrived last night.'

'No problem. Gave you time to get your bearings.'

The four-bedroomed farmhouse was nestled into the hillside, almost hidden by trees on three sides. The rooms were low-beamed and cosy, filled with country-style furniture.

Overlooking a valley dedicated to rearing sheep, the darkstone house sat on the stunningly beautiful border between Yorkshire and Lancashire. The rolling moorland, wild and pristine under its blanket of snow, led the eyes to brooding Pendle Hill in the distance. The silence only broken by the distant bleating of sheep and the rustle of wind in the trees.

'Remember we have no landline at the house and the mobile's patchy. You might get a signal once you're out of the dip and up on the tops, but it's rubbish in the house.' Elle slid the bolt on the stable block. 'The internet is good though, so we use WhatsApp to make calls. I've left a note with internet login and anything else you'll need.'

As she swung open the door, we were greeted by a waft of warm air, which smelled of horses and hay. It was a comforting scent, taking me back to a more carefree time, when my days were filled with horses and country hacks. Long walks across the moors with my father, and swimming in the remote, high moorland tarns.

Butch and Sundance snickered and tossed their heads, excited to see us.

I picked two apples from a bucket and fed them as Elle filled the nets with fresh hay.

'Oh, by the way,' she said over her shoulder, 'Gus asked me to pass on a message.'

'Oh?'

'The night of Barbara Thorpe's post-mortem – you asked which officer attended?'

'He said Beth Hastings.'

'It was, but an exhibits officer was sent. We were busy that night. He was registered at reception, but not the log. Gus realised the error when he filed the notes.'

I stroked Butch's nose. 'Who?'

'DS Ian Drummond.'

Chapter Seventy-Six

Tuesday Morning, Ferndean House

I'd set myself up in Elle's office. A small, cosy room off the large kitchen. She'd lit the wood burner and I watched the flames curling around logs.

I'd sent a message to Ed and Jen, explaining there was no phone signal, but I'd been told not to divulge my location and they could use WhatsApp for calls and messages.

Now, sitting here, I felt suddenly distanced from the enquiry. The thing that had dominated my days and permeated my previous life for what seemed an eternity.

I wanted to know whether the team had managed to get anything from the courier company who'd delivered the trophy.

Would that lead them straight back to Wednesdayschild? Maybe too much to hope for. Whoever it was, they had access to trophies Malecki had never admitted taking.

Tomorrow was Wednesday.

I shuddered. There was already a victim in the killer's sights. A plan already in motion. Would it be tomorrow? Next week?

I felt helpless – impotent to halt a deadly machine that seemed to grind on despite all efforts to stop it.

I pictured Malecki, pacing his small, cold cell in the Seg at the Monster Mansion, and hoped he was suffering. At least I could take satisfaction from knowing I'd sent him there – with a little help.

Harvey padded into the room and came to me for a fuss. I stroked his silky ears and patted his huge chest, until he went to flop in front of the crackling fire.

Then I began unpacking the boxes. Tacking up the posters Ed had printed, until one wall looked like a satellite view of the Cheshire countryside.

Tea was the next priority. Carrying the brew back into the office, I looked up Callum's number on WhatsApp. My thumb hovered over the icon, as images of the blonde from the surveillance team went through my mind. Whatever had happened between us, business was business and I needed to speak to him.

He answered almost immediately.

'Everything OK up there? Why you calling on WhatsApp?' he asked.

'It's the rural idyll. No landline or mobile signal.'

'You got everything you need?'

'Apart from a vehicle,' I said, suddenly feeling totally isolated. 'Feel stuck up here.'

'The more inaccessible you are the better.'

'From the killer's perspective, or yours?' That sounded more acerbic than I'd intended.

'I'm not doing this now, Jo.' Irritated.

I gave myself a mental slap. It wasn't like me to be bitter, or jealous.

'Fine. I'm actually ringing about the ACU investigation.'

'Just a minute.' The office noise faded as he went somewhere more private. 'Go on.'

'Last night, just before eleven, I saw Beth in the street. She was on a phone – not her usual one.'

'People do have more than one phone.'

'But they don't keep it in their boots.'

'What?'

I explained what I'd seen.

There was a long pause.

'We're monitoring Hannah's phone. Watching all the numbers that called him from burners, in case any of them were switched back on.'

'And?'

'The handset that was swapping SIM cards hasn't been used since we revealed it at the briefing. But 091, that called Hannah to set up the meeting at Paxton Pits, was used last night.'

'From where?'

'It pinged from a mast in Fordley centre – the one nearest the police station.'

'What time?'

'Ten fifty-five.'

My stomach churned. 'Beth?'

'The timing's right.' He exhaled, slowly. 'I'll have to pass it to ACU.'

'Is there anything I can do?'

I mentally kicked myself for slipping into that well-worn, but meaningless phrase people use when they know there is absolutely *nothing* to be done.

'Not until we see what they find.' Then in that way he had, of reading my mind, he added, 'And before you go beating yourself up for telling me – don't. If Beth is the leak, I need to know. You've done the right thing.'

'Thanks.'

'I haven't got long, is there anything else?'

'Any news on the paperweight?'

'For once, we got a break. The courier is a local business – not one of the big boys. Turns out, head of security is ex-job. Only retired a couple of years ago. So, we didn't need the hassle of getting a warrant for their records.'

'Suppose it's too much to hope you got an address for Wednesdayschild?'

'Never that easy.' I heard him shuffling paperwork. 'The parcel was dropped at a village shop in the Dales on the B6265 near Cracoe. They run a pick-up-and-drop-off parcel service. Courier picked it up from there. Old couple run it. There's no CCTV and they couldn't remember who dropped it off.'

'Elle told you about the custom-made knife. Possibly from Italy?'

'Helps to know what it looks like. But Malecki can't serve any more time, even if we do link a murder in Italy to him.'

'No, but it gives closure to the victim's family.'

'That's something to consider later. Right now, we've got enough to be getting on with. Surveillance team have been deployed. For what it's costing let's hope it pays off.'

* * *

After my call with Callum, I felt restless and unaccountably angry. I slammed around the house, unpacking my belongings, until Harvey stopped me on the upstairs landing.

'What?'

He tilted his head, but as I impatiently went to walk round him, he moved, blocking my path. Then sitting down, he reached out a paw, whining softly.

Unexpected tears pricked my eyelids as I knelt down and hugged him.

He gently licked my cheek.

'You're right, we need to walk.'

I left my clothes strewn on the bed and ventured into Elle's impressively stocked boot room. Choosing a heavy coat and long yard boots, we walked out into a winter landscape that took my breath away.

I was used to the spectacular moorland around Kingsberry, especially in winter. But this scenery was new to me and, despite the bitter wind and the dullness of the day, utterly stunning.

My boots crunched over snow that was beginning to freeze. Ice forming a crystalline crust that sparkled like diamonds scattered across the landscape.

The lane to the house was just a farm track, lost now under the white duvet of snow that drifted almost to the top of the drystone walls marking the boundary.

Harvey was in his element. Dashing in mad circles as his nose picked up new scents and exciting tracks to follow. I threw him a snowball. He leaped, catching it in his jaws, then looked confused as it exploded into nothing.

We walked to the bottom of the valley and looked up at the Atom Panopticon on the hill opposite. Its granite-coloured surface reflecting the fading pewter grey light, like some alien spaceship had landed in Narnia.

Huge feathery flakes started to fall, drifting gently from a dove-grey sky that promised more to come.

I called Harvey and turned to climb back up the hill to the house. The light was fading fast and the bitter cold was beginning to bite.

Chapter Seventy-Seven

Tuesday Evening, Ferndean House

All I could do was concentrate on the other loose ends, most of which were connected to Malecki's earlier crimes. A feeling I'd carried since my student days and never been able to shake – that there were other victims we didn't know about.

I carried a glass of wine from the kitchen and stepped over Harvey, who hadn't moved from his spot in front of the fire since we'd come back from our walk.

The lights suddenly flickered. I went to the window and parted the curtain. Cupping my hands against the dark glass, I could see the snow falling thick and fast. The lights flickered again – for longer this time.

Power outages were something anyone living in the sticks became used to, especially in bad weather.

I went back to the kitchen, and got a torch and some candles from under the sink. I didn't have far to look before finding vintage candle holders and even a heavy silver candelabra in the dining room.

'Very *Downton Abbey*,' I muttered – smiling, as I carried my haul back to the office.

I began to unpack the archive boxes from the Malecki enquiry. Somewhere would be a snippet, overlooked or not logged – like the unaccounted-for mileage – that might give us a lead.

When the lights finally went out, it took me a second to register what had happened, because the flickering log burner continued to light the room with an almost romantic glow.

Typical, when you're on your own, McCready.

I lit the candelabra, putting it down next to me so I could keep working.

There was one box I hadn't opened. The cardboard was the faded yellow of old parchment and the label had peeled off. I cut the tape around the edges and lifted the lid. It had the familiar scent of old paper. That smell you get when you open a vintage volume in an old-fashioned bookshop.

I pulled out books on architecture and design, exam awards and a birth certificate in Malecki's name.

The things we all keep in a dusty box at the back of a wardrobe. Documents and keepsakes, too important to discard, which we might need to produce one day. I assumed they'd been taken from Malecki's house after his arrest, when police seized everything.

There was a shoebox in the bottom, containing handwritten notes and cards, from Malecki's student days. I flicked through the messages, mostly from women.

The irony that I was reading love letters by candlelight wasn't lost on me. Nor the fact that the subject of such devotion was a cold-blooded serial killer.

The wind howled down the chimney and I shuddered at the thought of women falling in love with a monster like Malecki. I didn't have the stomach to keep reading. I dropped the letters and picked out the books.

Why keep textbooks in a box of important documents?

As I opened the first volume, I found the answer.

There was a dedication, dated on Malecki's graduation, and signed by his father, with a reference to a song, or music. I assumed it was the kind of 'in-joke' families have. A shorthand way of referencing things only they understand.

In Tom Hannah's book, Malecki talked about how close he had tried to be to his father. A stern man, with standards Malecki felt he never lived up to.

He portrayed himself as the emotionally tortured child of a detached and intractable father and an overbearing mother.

A veiled attempt to explain why Malecki had turned out the way he had. Striving to attain a perfection he never could – feeling like a failure despite his outward successes. Indulged by a mother whose devotion left him with a superior sense of entitlement that fed his narcissism.

I moved the candelabra to the desk, and without thinking opened my laptop, confused for a millisecond when it didn't switch on.

Duh – no electricity and the battery's not charged.

How automatically we use things without thinking, expecting them to always be on tap.

I opened my notebook instead, glad I'd copied down the lines of binary code in longhand.

Studying the rows of zeros and ones, I imagined Malecki painting them onto his canvas – sure no one but his devotee would ever see them.

'No good finding them, if we don't know what they mean,' I muttered to myself. Harvey lifted his head to watch me.

'Come on, fella.' I stood and stretched aching muscles. 'Late one last night and I'm shattered.'

He lazily uncurled from his warm spot and followed me.

The wind made a high-pitched howling, as it blew through the frozen branches of the surrounding trees and battered the windows. I held the candelabra out in front of us, to light the way upstairs – feeling like the madwoman in the attic in *Jane Eyre*.

Chapter Seventy-Eight

Ferndean House

Malecki was laughing at me.

I sat on a couch in his cell, my arm draped over the side, as he'd instructed, while he painted me. He turned from the canvas, wielding the paintbrush that dripped with red paint. No. Not a brush, it was a knife!

I jumped up and ran for the door – his laughter bounced off the stone walls as he took the three paces that would close the distance between us and end my life. I desperately pressed the panic button, triggering the alarm that screamed through the cell block. A red light, strobing in time with the pounding heartbeat of the siren.

I sat bolt upright, and for a moment, I didn't know where I was.

I looked round an unfamiliar room, which glowed with the flashing light that had chased me out of sleep.

On the bedside table, the crimson digits of the screeching alarm clock projected four pulsing zeros across the walls.

The electricity was back on.

I leaned against the pillows and hugged myself, watching the illuminated numerals dance across the curtains, seeming to develop a rhythm all their own.

Like music.

I stared in to the middle distance as my subconscious served up a miscellany of disparate facts that now made sense.

I slapped the alarm into silence, found a dressing gown, then ran down stairs. The analogue clock on the wall in the kitchen said 2 a.m.

The office was still warm from the glowing embers in the log burner. I opened my laptop and plugged it in, then knelt among the papers scattered across the rug, finding the book, with its dedication from Malecki's father.

Beneath his copperplate signature, what I'd taken to be a description of someone humming a melody:

dah dah di di di di di di dah dah

Google gave me the diagram I was looking for. I got my notebook and studied the rows of binary – checking them against the internet chart. My heart was hammering so hard, it made my writing tremble, as I scribbled letters beneath the code.

I stared at the row I'd deciphered. Then checked it again, more carefully this time. Like a disbelieving gambler checking a jackpot-winning lottery ticket.

'Holy shit!'

I dialled a familiar number. It rang out endlessly and just when I expected it to go to voicemail, Callum answered.

'Hello?' His voice was thick with sleep.

'It's me.'

'Huh?' I could hear movement and imagined him struggling to wake up.

'What is it?' A female voice, in the background.

I froze.

'It's OK,' Callum said, but he wasn't speaking to me. Then, 'Jo?'

'Has the cryptologist looked at the code?'

'Not yet. Why?'

'It's Morse.'

The excitement of my discovery evaporated. Adrenaline drained away, leaving me feeling unexpectedly hollow.

'Go on?' He was awake now.

'Zeros are dots. Ones are dashes. Morse code.' I sounded flat, as if I was reciting a shopping list.

'How do you know?'

'Malecki's father wrote a dedication in a book, in Morse. He was a naval officer. Malecki was a cadet.'

'What did the note say?'

'Seventy-three.'

'What?'

'It's morse abbreviation. It means "fondest regards".'

'Have you checked Morse against the binary lines?'

'No!' I snapped, as the supressed anger bubbled up. 'I just called you on a whim. Of course, I bloody well checked. So, if Goldilocks there has a pen and paper handy, she can write down what it says.'

'It's OK,' he replied – icy-cold as his anger matched mine, 'I'll remember it.'

I blew out my breath. 'The code on the oldest painting translates to: "SJ, BK17". The next line on the same canvas is: "BT, BK22".'

'SJ, Stephen Jones. BT, Barbara Thorpe,' Callum said.

'I think he numbered the notebooks he kept on his projects,' I said.

'"BK" . . . books seventeen and twenty-two?'

'Yes. On another canvas, it says "Lutner" – in full. But no book reference. I don't think he had him as a project in the eighties. He probably discussed with his disciple before they embarked on this murder spree that they'd include Lutner.'

'If they discussed it, why would he write it on a painting?'

'Because he sent the paintings out of the prison, in the order he wanted the victims to be killed. There are no dates for the killings, just book references and initials.'

412

'What about Haverley?'

'Nothing referencing him that I can see.'

He thought for a moment. 'The "Q" code. That was the signal to switch targets and change strategy.'

'Probably.' I felt suddenly very weary.

'Right . . . thanks.' Was all he said before hanging up.

I stared at the phone in my hand, barely resisting the urge to throw it across the room.

Chapter Seventy-Nine

Wednesday, 8 a.m., Ferndean House

'Why so upset?' Elle was saying. 'You're seeing the gorgeous Eduardo.'

The same question I'd been asking myself since my call with Callum.

'At least I waited until I knew we were over.' I was trying to rationalise it to myself. 'He was seeing her while he was with me.'

'Well, you know what they say, darling?' I could hear the noises of a busy street. Someone was playing bagpipes. She exhaled as she smoked. 'The best way to get over someone is to get under someone.' She laughed at her own joke.

'How is Edinburgh, anyway?' I wasn't feeling the humour.

'Oh, you know . . . typically tartan.' She sounded bubbly and relaxed, and suddenly I felt bad pissing on her parade.

'I'm glad you're having a good time. You deserve the break.'

'Thank you, darling.' I could hear Rina saying something. 'Anyway, was calling to make sure you're OK and my boys are behaving themselves?'

'Mucked out and fed this morning. They're good as gold.'

'Excellent. Anyway, must dash. Rina wants breakfast, she gets "hangry" if she doesn't eat on the hour.'

* * *

I'd been staring out of the window, watching the blizzard outside. Over the hills, crackling fingers of lightning fractured the sky, followed a few seconds later by muffled rumbles of thunder.

'Thunder snow'. A rare phenomenon, when warm air, rising from the bottom of the valley, hits cold air from above. I'd only witnessed it once before and although it was spectacular, it meant worse weather to come.

I'd spent the morning trying to make sense of the rest of the binary code. No doubt the university would confirm it was Morse, when they finally got back to the team.

I'd found more initials and book numbers. Who they referred to was anyone's guess. People who had notebooks on them. The next victims. If we hadn't tumbled to the disciple, Malecki would have carried on completing his 'kill list'.

But the 'Q' code changed the plan, and we had absolutely no idea where they would strike next.

Behind me, my laptop 'pinged', alerting me to an email.

It was Jack Halton.

Had a visit from the police. Told to be on alert. Been trying to call you, but just getting voicemail. You OK? Worried.

I called him via WhatsApp.

'Thank God,' he said. 'The police told me anyone connected to the earlier case should be vigilant. When I couldn't get hold of you, I feared the worst.'

'I've moved out for a while. No phone signal here so internet calls are best. What about you?'

'I'm not going anywhere. Got my lot coming here for Christmas. I'll be all right.' He paused for a second. When he spoke again, his tone had a gravitas we both understood. 'Listen, you look after yourself. Lock the doors, stay put and if there's anything suspicious, triple nine it . . . right?'

'You too, Jack. Take care.'

As soon as I hung up, another call came through. It was Ed.

I told him about the code and my conversation with Callum.

'I'm worried about you,' he said, tenderly.

'I'm fine.'

'Wish I could be with you, but I'm working at the NCA in Manchester for the next few days. At least tell me where you are, so I know you're safe.'

'I've been told not to say. Even Jen doesn't know.'

'This is me, Jo. Surely . . .'

The hurt in his voice decided me.

'I'm at Elle's house. Middle of nowhere. It's blowing a hooley and the whole place is snowed in. No one could get up here without a tractor.' I tried to inject a smile into my voice, but couldn't quite manage it.

'You sound down.' His voice was gentle.

'I'm fine.' I repeated, but with each iteration, it sounded less convincing. I *was* lonely and unaccountably sad.

It was Callum I wanted to care. Him I wanted to call me. Despite everything.

'Feel so helpless.' My words choked. 'Someone out there is on borrowed time and there's nothing I can do.'

'Sounds like you've played a blinder – working out the Morse.'

'It doesn't help now. He's switched plans. All it proves is we were right about the disciple.'

'What're you going to do now?'

'Look at the other stuff we've got.' I told him about Elle's find and the unsolved murder in Italy.

'Was Malecki in Italy then?'

'There was a picture of him in an Italian newspaper at the time. The shirt he was wearing sold on the internet.'

'You sound tired. Give yourself a break. Curl up in front of the fire and read a book or something?'

'Can't remember the last time I did that.'

'Call me every day . . . and stay safe.' There was a pause before he added, 'You're too precious for me to lose now.'

* * *

I did curl up on the sofa with a book – for all of five minutes.

My mind was too busy with all the elements still unresolved.

Elle's main lounge, with its huge, silver Christmas tree, was lovely. But felt too big for just me and Harvey. Besides, one look at the cream upholstery and light rugs, and I decided it was far safer to keep Harvey and his wet paws in the cosy office.

I brewed tea and went back to my laptop. Ed had emailed everything he'd found on the Sheridan family.

It included a link for the local advertiser, carrying ads for business and news stories about the local community.

Ed had highlighted an article, covering Nick Sheridan's passing out parade in 1992. I enlarged the snapshot of proud parents and his little sister, Bridget, surrounding a tall, lanky lad in uniform. In the background, other families stood in groups, hugging their sons and daughters. The names of all the people in the photograph were listed underneath.

I was about to move on, when one name caught my eye.

A quick internet search provided even more details. The more I read, the more pieces began to fall into place. By the time I picked up the phone, I knew who had killed Dave Finch.

Chapter Eighty

Wednesday Morning, Ferndean House

'University called,' Callum said as soon as he picked up. 'You're right – it's Morse code.'

'That's not why I'm ringing.'

The lamps flickered.

'Sorry, lost you then,' he said.

'Power outages,' I explained, 'I keep losing the internet.'

'Right.'

'I'm calling about Dave Finch's murder.'

'Unexpected, but go on.'

'Nick Sheridan had his passing out parade in 1992.'

'So?'

'In the same group of cadets that day was Ian Drummond.'

My bombshell was greeted with silence. I pushed on.

'He told me he wasn't into sports. Said he had two left feet and no coordination. But he was Regimental boxing champion, two years running. Why would he lie about something like that, unless it was relevant?'

'Is it? Relevant?'

A crack of thunder rattled the windows and all the lights dimmed.

'Cal – you there?'

'. . . say again.'

'Finch was killed by a single punch. A bit of digging on the internet brought up pictures of Nick Sheridan with Ian at Regimental events. They were friends.'

'What's your theory?' He sounded reluctant to believe that his DS could be implicated.

'A few days before Finch was killed, Sheridan and Drummond came home on leave. The family had found out about Finch's abuse of Bridget and Sheridan went to confront him. Whatever happened in that flat, Finch ended up dead. The place was torched to cover up the evidence and the day after the fire, the Regiment returned to Belfast.'

I hesitated, but knew I had to tell the rest. 'Old Man McGarry arranged for the flat to be cleared of the videos, so none of the films of Bridget would ever be found. He covered the family's tracks and warned Hannah away from the story.'

'Why?'

'McGarry thought the family had suffered enough. He didn't want to see them implicated in a murder and he hated nonces.'

'You have evidence of McGarry's involvement?'

'Word of mouth – sources I trust.'

'Ian might have known Sheridan ... might even have been friends, but there's nothing to put him in Finch's flat on the night he died.'

'If it *was* Ian who killed him with one punch, that would explain why he's kept his boxing history secret. I'll bet he didn't mention it in his application to join the police ...'

'We can check.'

'You've established no family members have a connection to the police. But what if the connection to the Sheridans was through friendship? Ian wasn't in the police then. But he is now and he was a friend of the family – it all fits, Cal.'

'Anything else?'

'My source says it's possible Hannah found out who killed Finch. That kind of information is useful. Especially if the person is a serving cop.'

419

'Ian said he knew Hannah from his days on the beat.' Callum was thinking out loud.

'Ian volunteered to interview Hannah. He couldn't afford anyone else talking to the person who knew what he'd done. He said he barely knew him, but when the journalist made us a brew, he knew Ian took sugar in his coffee. It didn't register at the time, but came to me last night. How would he know that, or remember it decades later?'

'My leak in the team,' Callum muttered.

'The person who rang Hannah to warn him you were looking for him? The same person who ditched the phone using different SIM cards, as soon as it was revealed in the team briefing.'

'Doesn't explain Beth's secret phone though,' he said.

Another clap of thunder made Harvey jump from his place on the rug and go look out of the window.

'Hello . . . ? You still there?'

'Barely hear you.' His voice was almost drowned out by crackling on the line. '. . . Hannah . . . blackmail Ian.' The connection was breaking up. 'He'll be suspended.'

Was the last thing I heard before the power went out and disconnected the internet.

420

Chapter Eighty-One

Wednesday, Ferndean House

Harvey stood with his huge paws on the windowsill, barking at each clap of thunder.

Between the candelabra and the log burner, we had enough light, but without electricity, I couldn't communicate with anyone. Even my phone's 4G was useless, with no phone signal.

There was a sound outside. I looked out of the window, but despite being early afternoon, it was already dark.

There it was again. As if a door was banging in the wind.

I went into the boot room – stood and listened.

There were windows either side of the outer door. I rubbed the glass with my sleeve and peered outside, cupping my hands against the pane. The noise was coming from the stables.

Harvey rested his paws on the sill of the other window; mimicking me, he looked out too.

The stable door was closed, so that wasn't the source of the sound. The direction of the wind shifted and another sound was carried towards us. Horses, whinnying.

I realised they were kicking their stalls. Probably frightened by the thunder.

I quickly pulled on yard boots and a long, waterproof riding coat. Grabbed a scarf and gloves off a peg.

'Sorry, Harvey. You'll have to stay here. If they're scared, seeing you might not help.'

There was a torch on the bench. The light was dim when I tested it, but good enough to get me across the yard.

As I pulled open the door, it was nearly snatched out of my hand by an icy blast of wind. Harvey took up his post at the window and watched as I crossed the yard. As I got nearer, the sound of panicked horses grew louder.

Lightning scratched the blackened sky, illuminating my way with an electrifying crack.

The stable door was heavy, but swung open easily as I slid the bolt, I cursed as the wind grabbed the door. After struggling to close it, panting and sweating, I leaned against it to get my breath.

Compared to outside, the barn felt warm. I pulled my scarf down and slipped the hood off my hair, letting my eyes adjust to the dark.

Both horses were stamping their hooves against the floor of their stalls, but seemed to calm when they saw me.

'It's OK . . . only the weather,' I said softly.

Sundance was nearest to me. His eyes were wide, ears locked forward as he arched his neck. I pulled my gloves off, standing on tiptoes to reach his flaring nostrils. I let him take the scent of my skin, as he made loud fluttering sounds in his nose. He kicked the door of his stall, banging it against my knees.

Butch didn't seem as distressed. His eyes were calmer, and instead of stamping and kicking, he was stepping around his stall, whinnying softly.

'You're worried about your friend, aren't you, boy?' He lowered his head so I could stroke his forelock, then pushed his head under my arm. I fussed his ears and patted his neck.

Another drumroll of thunder made Sundance rear up on his hind legs, nostrils flaring. He rolled his eyes, showing the whites in his terror. As his front hooves hit the ground, he began kicking the stall.

I leaned in as far as I dare and brushed my hand down the bridge of his nose, gently shushing him. Finally, he began to quieten, his hooves scrapping the ground, rather than pounding. His muscles quivered under my hand, but he leaned his head on my shoulder, becoming calmer the more I stroked and talked to him.

Eventually, the thunder began to move away from us, rolling down the valley. Until the only sound was the howling of the wind and hail.

Sundance was calmer, but still jittery. I debated staying with them longer, but the barn didn't feel quite so warm now. I pulled on my gloves and gave them a final fuss.

The torch finally died and I left it in the barn. The flickering candles in the windows at the house created a golden pool of light on the snow, making it easy to see my way back.

I opened the barn door, just enough to squeeze through, so the wind couldn't slam it and spook Sundance. I smiled. It reminded me of creeping out of my son's bedroom when he was a baby, after finally getting him off to sleep.

The smile died on my lips, when a figure appeared round the corner of the house.

423

Chapter Eighty-Two

Wednesday, Ferndean House

Whoever it was, hadn't seen me. I pressed myself against the side of the barn.

How had they got up here?

Squinting against the sleet and wind, I could make out the shape of a large vehicle on the drive. Maybe a farmer?

The figure walked to the door, the silhouette of their arm reaching for the handle. Harvey barked furiously, butting his nose against the glass, making whoever it was think twice about opening it.

As they walked past the lighted window, I could see it was a man, dressed in dark trousers and jacket, and wearing a black baseball cap. I expected him to knock on the door, but instead, he walked round to the back of the house.

I pushed away from the wall of the barn and headed for the vehicle. As I got nearer, I could make out the blue and yellow Battenberg markings of a police four-by-four.

Thank God for that!

Callum maybe, sending someone to check I was OK?

Then the driver reappeared. He saw me and suddenly stopped, obviously not expecting me to be outside.

I smiled, until I saw who it was.

'Ian!'

As he took a step forward, I took a step back.

He stopped. 'Jo.' He smiled. 'What's wrong?'

'What are you doing here?' The wind tried to snatch my words away.

'The boss sent me to get you.'

I said nothing.

'We've got intelligence,' he shouted. 'You're not safe. I've been sent to move you to a secure location.'

He took another step and I did the same in reverse. There was almost the width of the house between us and I wanted to keep it that way.

'You're lying.' I carried on walking backwards, trying to calculate how many steps it was to the boundary wall.

'What are you talking about?' He frowned as he continued to keep up the smile. 'Come on, Jo. Stop playing silly buggers. Get in the car where we can talk.'

'Why not the house?'

We could both hear Harvey throwing himself against the door, barking like a rabid hound. 'Or don't you want to meet my dog?'

Automatically, his eyes went to the window, where Harvey was almost biting the glass.

'We haven't got time for this, Jo. The boss wants you back in Fordley. Just get in the car and I'll explain.'

Two more steps and I could feel the roughness of the dry-stone wall against the backs of my knees.

'It's too late,' I called. 'Callum knows.'

'Knows what?'

'About Dave Finch.'

He became suddenly still, as if frozen to the ice. The plume of his breath on the cold air stopped, as he held it.

'I don't know what you're—'

'Regimental boxing champion ... was it your single punch that killed Finch? When you went to confront him with Nick Sheridan – about Bridget?'

Those few words, if I was right, would tell him we knew everything.

Despite the dim light, I could see the colour drain from his face. As my words sank in, I could imagine his brain racing to process it.

'Did Tom Hannah send you?'

'No.'

'Who?'

'Not Hannah. I don't know who he is.'

'He' – my thoughts were racing. Could Malecki have a phone? Easy enough to get in prison, but impossible for him to have smuggled one into the Seg.

'Were you sent to kill me?'

'No!' He sounded horrified. 'I wouldn't ... couldn't ...'

'You killed Finch.'

His shoulders slumped. 'That was an accident. None of this is what you think, Jo.'

'What were you told to do when you found me?'

'Drive you to a place. Hand you over, that's all.'

'Hand me over to who?'

'I don't know.' His eyes were almost pleading. 'If I don't deliver, they'll destroy me.'

'They can't hold Finch over you now. You can't be black-mailed anymore.'

'Nick's dead.' His voice had dropped, as if he was talking to himself. 'There's no one else who knows.' He glared at me with eyes as dark and hard as marbles.

'Hannah knows,' I said.

426

He started to walk towards me, slowly shaking his head and a horrific truth hit me.

'Oh God . . . what have you done?'

The wall was behind me and I knew from my walk with Harvey that the six-foot drop on the other side had filled with drifting snow.

Drummond kept coming.

I braced myself and fell backwards over the wall, into the blackness beneath.

My back hit soft snow on the other side and I sank into the drift.

Drummond yelled and I heard his boots crunching across the frozen snow as he ran. I'd have seconds before he closed the distance.

I crawled on all fours, away from the wall and into the black void, towards open moorland.

Behind and above me, I heard his heavy breathing as he reached the spot where I'd gone over.

I crawled frantically until I heard his boots against the rock and knew he was jumping down after me.

He must have landed where I'd already flattened the snow, robbing him of the cushion. He hit solid ground, the breath escaping him with a painful grunt.

Now I lay still, holding my breath.

I guessed I was ten feet away from the wall.

The darkness was absolute. The kind of pitch-black that feels like you have your eyes shut. No matter where I looked, there was nothingness. At this lower level, the house was obscured. No light reaching us from there.

My heart was hammering so hard all I could hear was blood thundering in my ears. I strained to hear beyond my own frantic pulse, to what he might be doing just a few feet away.

He must have been feeling his way, reaching out to find me. Was he crawling, as I had?

The snow by my foot shifted. I stiffened, resisting the impulse to pull my leg away. Another movement, depressing the snow by my boot.

He was here. He'd found me.

Pain shot through my temples as my blood pressure soared off the scale.

'Jo!' His voice thundered into the empty blackness.

The sound was from above.

He was standing over me, right at my feet. I could hear his breathing.

One more step and he would trip over my legs.

Holy Mother of God – don't move.

Then, I felt him ... heard him turn away, his boots sliding into knee-deep snow as he trudged back to the wall.

I stayed still, not daring to believe that he'd simply give up.

The sound of him scrambling up the wall.

A second later, a car door slammed and an arc of light sliced through the blackness, sweeping above my head.

Shit! He'd gone back to the vehicle for a torch.

Before I could move, he appeared on top of the wall, swinging the beam across the field.

A round disc of white illumination moved slowly across the snow towards me, like a malevolent eye.

It stopped at the toe of my boot ... then slowly moved up my legs, until it shone in my eyes, blinding me.

'It's over, Jo. Don't think about running. You know you can't outpace me ... not with that leg of yours, in deep snow.' He jerked the torch. 'Get up and walk towards me.'

A crashing sound made Drummond turn and look behind him, just as he was hit hard by an unseen force that plunged him off the wall, onto his back in the snow.

He cried out in shock, flinging his arms wide in a vain attempt to stay upright, letting go of the torch which landed between us.

In its light, I could see Harvey, straddling Drummond, his bared teeth almost touching the man's face.

I was about to call him off, when Drummond made the mistake of fighting back. He grabbed Harvey's thick neck, trying to push him away, at the same time bringing his leg up hard, to knee my dog in the ribs.

The snarl was primeval, as Harvey sank his teeth into Drummond's forearm, shaking his head from side to side, like ragging a toy.

Drummond screamed. 'Fuck . . . call him off!'

I sat up in the snow, and watched for a moment, just to be sure Harvey had the advantage.

'Harvey – stop!'

Drummond lay panting on the ground, with six stone of solid boxer dog standing on his chest. His left arm was still in Harvey's mouth, but he must have relaxed his bite because the man wasn't screaming anymore.

'If you make one wrong move, Drummond, I'll let him rip your throat out.'

To make the point, Harvey growled, closing his jaws just a fraction.

'OK . . . OK . . . for God's sake, get him off.'

I stood up and walked towards them.

'Drop it, boy.' Harvey reluctantly let the arm go, but stayed on top of Drummond, a low growl rumbling in his chest.

I picked up the torch and swung it over them.

Drummond's jacket was ripped – the padding spilling out, like a teddy bear's intestines. Blood dripped into the snow, seeming even more red against the pristine white.

He groaned, cradling his bloodied arm. 'I never meant things to go this far, you've got to believe that.'

'If killing Finch was an accident, why not go to the police?'

'Nick's family didn't want anyone to know. Bridget had been through enough. They didn't want it in court or in the papers.'

He tried to roll over. Harvey growled louder, baring his teeth.

Drummond stopped moving, but talked faster. 'We were just kids – nineteen. We were going to get all the tapes, give him a kicking and run him off the estate. Community justice – that's how it worked down there.'

'You didn't live on that estate.' I sounded calmer than I felt.

'Nick asked me to go back with him when we got leave, to sort Finch. His dad had told him about Bridget.'

'What went wrong?'

'Finch pulled a knife on Nick. I punched him and he went down. Didn't think I'd hit him that hard. I didn't mean to kill him, it was an accident.'

'And the McGarrys?'

'Nick's dad was a friend – went to school with them. He called them.'

'But Hannah knew and started blackmailing you when you joined the force?'

He grimaced. 'Let me sit up.' He tried to lift himself.

Harvey snarled, revealing his teeth, which he lowered to an inch above Drummond's throat.

'I don't think he wants you to.'

The cold was making my leg ache; I shifted my weight to the other foot. It didn't go unnoticed.

'For Christ's sake, Jo, do we have to do this out here? Let's get out of the weather – we're going to freeze to death.'

'Tell me about Hannah first.'

'Yes, when I came out of the army and joined the force, he came to see me. Told me he knew what me and Nick had done. Nick was gone. Just me to take the blame.'

'He blackmailed you?'

'Not for money – information. Just small stuff, when I was a PC. Tip-offs for his crime reporting. I could live with that. I made sure I never gave him anything big. Never compromised any major enquiries. He went quiet when he wrote the book. I thought it was over, that I wasn't useful to him anymore.'

'When did it start again?'

'When he was trying to get Malecki to do the book and the documentary. He told Malecki, he had a cop in his pocket. Trying to get more influence – impress him.'

I knew how Malecki's mind worked. The insidious way he got inside people's heads. The way he could charm information out of people. A master manipulator.

'Let me guess ... he got Hannah to tell him who you were and what you'd done?'

'Promised Hannah he'd do the documentary in exchange for my identity and the burner number we'd been using. Said it would make his time inside easier if he had a tame cop.'

'Then put Hannah in the frame as the copycat?'

Drummond groaned, gripping his arm tighter as he nodded.

The snow around him was becoming darker red. I tried to estimate how much blood he was losing.

431

'I told him what Malecki had done. I was the one who got him to hand himself in.'

'How did you know he wouldn't tell the team about you?'

'I told him I'd protect him. I'm more useful to him in the game than out of it.' He grimaced; the blood seemed to drip faster. 'Then . . . I started getting calls from a burner – to do more.'

'You were in Malecki's pocket by then?' He nodded. 'Was it him who called?'

'No. Caller was female – couple of times a male.'

'On the 091 number?'

'Yes.'

'What did they want you to do?'

'Discredit you – get you away from the case.'

'You were the one who told Callum about the things I was doing?'

He nodded. 'Wasn't hard – the boss's interest was already somewhere else. He had his own reasons for not wanting you around. If Warner hadn't interfered, he would have cut you out of the investigation.' He closed his eyes, his face rigid with pain. His head was rolling from side to side in the snow.

I relented.

'Harvey – stand.' Harvey looked at me, then back at Drummond. Reluctantly, he got off his chest and came to stand between us – never taking his eyes off the potential threat.

'When that didn't work, Malecki asked to see me in the prison, right?'

He nodded.

A wave of anger punched through my fatigue. 'Did you know what he was planning?'

'No.' His eyes widened and held mine with a sincerity I knew he couldn't fake. 'All I knew was that he didn't want you involved. I didn't know Malecki was behind the killings, that it was a disciple. I thought he either genuinely wanted to help the investigation, or just wanted to get off being at the centre of things – you have to believe that.'

'Keep talking.'

'I said I wanted out – I wasn't going to do anymore.' His head dropped, his chin on his chest. 'The person calling . . . said they wanted to know one last thing . . . then they'd end the black-mail.'

'And you believed that?' I was incredulous. 'Despite every-thing else, you're a cop! You're not that naive?'

'I thought if I tied up the loose ends . . . the only other person who knew what happened . . . it would have to stop.'

'Hannah?'

He ignored the question, but I knew that's what he'd done.

'If Malecki made accusations against me, it would be his word against mine. There would be no one to corroborate it.'

Suddenly a thought struck me.

'Did they call you on Monday night . . . just before I saw you in the street?'

He nodded. So that call wasn't Beth after all. Any sense of relief I might have felt was squashed by the enormity of what Drummond had done.

'You sabotaged my Land Rover?'

He didn't say anything, but his face told me I was right.

'Then you waited for me to return to it. Is that why they called you that night? To find out where I was moving to? Were you planning on driving me there – so you knew where I was?' I remembered how insistent he'd been to take me to Elle's.

'You told me where Elle's place was while we were talking to the boss about getting you home. I'm sorry, Jo.'

'What was it? The thing they wanted to know?' I pressed, sensing he was shutting down. Either through loss of blood, or something else – I was losing him.

'Told me to deliver you to an address tonight.'

'Where?'

He shook his head.

'That's not it – there was something else they wanted to know . . . what?'

'It all ends . . . tomorrow.' Was all he said.

He struggled up, leaning back on his good arm, kneeling in the snow, like a supplicant at confession. Harvey growled and took a step forward. I halted him with my hand.

He was rambling. 'What I did . . . it's gone too far. No one else can die.'

He suddenly swung his good arm forward. I stepped back, but not fast enough to avoid the rock he'd been hiding.

The sound of it hitting my temple seemed to come from somewhere outside my body, as the pain exploded in brightly coloured shards behind my eyes. I felt myself falling backwards, the breath leaving me in a gust as I hit the ground.

A cacophony of sound. Harvey barking. Shouts. Snarling.

The ice against my face momentarily cleared my senses. I struggled up on one elbow, in time to see Drummond coming towards me. Harvey seemed to defy gravity as he leaped forward – all four paws leaving the ground.

Drummond realised his mistake, stumbled backwards to create space between him and Harvey's jaws. Then he turned and ran towards the wall with Harvey right behind him.

Harvey was jumping, rather than running, in snow that was chest-deep on him, slowing him down just enough to give Drummond the advantage. He got to the wall and began to scramble up, hampered by using only one arm.

The heaving boxer dog reached the wall and leaped, his jaws closing round Drummond's shin bone, his hind legs swinging in midair as he hung onto his prey.

Drummond's scream made the hair stand up on the back of my neck. I watched as Harvey clung on, shaking the leg in his mouth, like a shark with a flailing fish.

Drummond managed to hold on to the top of the wall, then kicked at Harvey with his other foot. The well-aimed boot caught my dog on the side of the head and he let go, falling back into the snow as Drummond heaved himself over the wall.

Harvey shook himself, then turned to look for me. He barked and ran towards me as I reached up to feel something warm and sticky running down my face. My fingers were covered in blood. For some reason, I wiped them in the snow, watching as more blood dripped off my chin.

Harvey's body felt warm as he leaned against me, licking my face and whimpering softly.

'I'm OK, boy ... OK ...' was the last thing I said, before the buzzing in my ears drowned everything out, and the world went black.

Chapter Eighty-Three

I don't know how long I lay in the snow. When I finally opened my eyes, Harvey was lying over me, his front paws protectively resting on my chest. I could feel the warmth of his breath on my face. He licked my nose, his long tail beating the snow in relief.

I struggled to sit. My limbs felt heavy and I began to shiver uncontrollably against the gnawing cold, despite the warmth from Harvey's body protecting me from the worst.

Gingerly, I touched the right side of my face, which felt swollen. My right cheekbone was visible in peripheral vision, which wasn't a good sign, and as I stood, a wave of nausea rolled over me.

The world tilted and I stumbled, putting my hand out to feel Harvey's collar. Instinctively, he began walking slowly, while I hung onto him – leading me back to the wall.

There was no way I could climb it, so we followed its line as it curved to the end of the driveway, then slowly, painfully, made our way up to the house. It took longer, but was the best I could do.

The wind had dropped and the stinging hail had become soft feathery flakes drifting lazily from a heavy sky.

The police vehicle had gone and Drummond with it.

The boot-room door opened when I leaned against it, then I saw the shattered window, which Harvey must have jumped through to get to Drummond.

I tried the kitchen light switch in the vain hope the power had come back on. It hadn't.

The candles had all gone out, and I fumbled around, lighting more. Dropping to my knees, to check my dog. He leaned against me as I ran my hands over him, finding a slight cut on his head, I assumed from smashing through the glass. But boxers' skulls are made of granite and it had stopped bleeding already.

His chest, usually white, was a matt of dried blood. I grabbed a cloth from the sink and began gently wiping it away, terrified of what I was going to find. But there was nothing to see: the blood wasn't his.

'Good boy.' I dropped the cloth on the counter. 'With any luck, that bent bastard will bleed to death.'

My phone wasn't in my coat pocket. I'd probably dropped it in the snow, but no time to look for it now. Somehow, I had to warn Callum about Drummond and everything he'd said.

I sat on the floor, thinking through my options. With the power still out and no phone, they were pretty limited.

I heaved myself up from the floor, fighting another wave of nausea. The banging in my head had its own percussion section, and I had to wait for my vision to clear.

Harvey followed me back into the boot room as I stripped off my wet clothes, which were sapping the last of the heat from me. I rubbed my skin with a thick woollen jumper to get some circulation going, before pulling it over my head. Adding more layers and a dry riding coat.

'Come on, fella – we're going back to basics.'

* * *

Sundance whickered and snorted as he looked over the partition between the two stalls, watching me put the bridle on his friend.

I'd considered saddling Butch, but didn't have time. Besides, I knew what we were about to do would take what little strength I had left. I'd learned to ride without a saddle when I was a teenager

437

and I was studiously ignoring that little voice, reminding me just how many decades ago that was.

Harvey walked beside us as I led Butch out of the stables. There was an original stone mounting step beside the barn, which I silently thanked God for.

Butch stood rock still as I swung onto his back, gathering the reins and lightly touched my heels into his sides. The last thing I needed was for him to bolt forward and tip me off.

I debated following the track to the main road, but it was a longer way round.

Going cross country, down the valley and up the other side, to the panopticon was shorter and quicker – provided I could stay mounted over rough ground.

It took a while for me to find my seat without a saddle, but after a few minutes, we'd settled into a steady pace, Butch sensing what I needed from him.

I leaned forward, putting my weight into my knees and let Butch do all the work. The crisp, cold air was helping me and by the time we reached the bottom of the valley, my head wasn't as fuzzy, though the pain still throbbed in my temple.

Harvey was lagging behind in the deep snow, which posed little problem for the horse, but he was still there, a few yards behind.

The wind dropped and we didn't have to battle through a blizzard. Still, the snow found its way down my collar, melting on my skin and trickling down my back. Despite the dry clothes, I was beginning to shiver again. The cold seemed to have seeped into my bones, and was eating its way out from the inside.

My strength was fading. The pain in my left thigh going from its usual dull ache to stabbing shards of electricity shooting into my groin.

438

I laid my face against Butch's neck, grateful for the warmth, urging him on, as he threw his weight forward – going up a gear to pull up the hill.

Covered in a blanket of snow that masked most recognisable landmarks, the landscape was as featureless and unfamiliar to me as the surface of the moon. Thankfully, Butch knew the way. Every hack and bridleway for miles around were routes he'd taken for years. And, as we crested the hill, I recognised the panopticon.

I'd lost all sense of time, but I knew the distinctive sculpture meant we were just minutes away from a farm that would have a landline.

I sat straighter, invigorated by having the end in sight, and steered Butch across the deserted visitors' car park and onto the Lancashire Moor Road. A tractor had obviously gone this way, packing the deep snow into a solid surface, which meant we could pick up the pace.

Harvey was alongside, as Butch stretched out, into the controlled, three-beat gait of an easy canter.

* * *

Harvey barked until the farmer opened the door, to see a horse, ridden by bedraggled woman, with a face like a punched lasagne.

In typical Yorkshire fashion, he didn't miss a beat.

'Blimey, lass, you lost the posse?'

I half slid, half fell off Butch and leaned on the farmer as he took me into the house.

I garbled something about being in an accident and needing to use their phone to call the police.

While the farmer went to take care of Butch and Harvey, his wife showed me into the candlelit sitting room, to use the landline in private.

I called Callum and told him what had happened, as briefly as possible.

'Jesus, Jo, are you OK?'

'Not sure,' I said honestly.

'I'll get uniform to come for you. Bring you in here, where we know you're safe.'

'What about Drummond?'

'If he's in a police vehicle, we can track it.' He went silent as he ran through all the implications. 'He must have known, by taking that car, he was at the end of the line. Especially if he'd managed to get you to go with him. Bastard!' he exploded. 'There's no coming back from this. He'll have to go to ground.'

I listened, but I couldn't think straight. As the adrenaline ebbed away, my body felt heavy and disjointed, as if it'd been taken apart, then put back together all wrong.

'Listen, Cal, I need to get out of these wet clothes and get some painkillers.'

'Sorry. You go. Someone will be there as soon as . . . and, Jo . . .'

'What?'

'I'm glad you're OK.'

After the call, I'd gratefully allowed myself to be looked after – stripping off soaking boots and jacket, and being wrapped in a blanket and installed by the fire with a huge mug of tea.

'If you're freezing, that's a good sign, lass,' the farmer's wife said as she tucked a rug round my legs. 'It's when you don't feel it that hypothermia's setting in.'

'Sure you don't want anything stronger, lass?' the farmer asked when he came back inside.

I could have killed for a brandy, but I'd have to keep my head together for a bit longer. Besides, it probably wouldn't help a suspected concussion. I settled for painkillers – and more tea.

Chapter Eighty-Four

Wednesday, Fordley Police Station

There was a subdued atmosphere in the incident room. The knowledge they had a corrupt officer on their team hit everyone hard. It was the worst kind of betrayal.

I gingerly touched the Steri-Strip stitches the traffic officer had applied to the wound on the side of my forehead.

'How do you feel?' Callum asked.

'Like I've got a New Year's Day hangover but without the fun.'

'You should have agreed to go to Casualty. You've probably got a concussion.'

The thought of sitting in A & E, not knowing what was going on, was worse than the pain in my head.

'I'm fine.'

He didn't look convinced. 'Well, they won't treat you if you refuse, so it's your call.' He perched on the corner of the desk beside me. 'Harvey deserves a meaty bone for that performance.'

The farmer had agreed to look after Harvey and Butch until we could collect them.

'Think he chewed enough on Drummond's tibia,' I said without humour.

'It's been circulated that he's wanted.' He washed a hand over his face. 'Uniform went round to Tom Hannah's place. He's dead.'

'I can't believe it.' Tony Morgan looked crestfallen. 'Ian . . . of all people. Thought he was as straight as it got – bastard!'

'You need to make a statement,' Callum was saying. 'Everything Drummond said.'

His expression softened and he reached out and gently touched my swollen face with his fingertips.

I flinched from his touch, partly because of the pain, but mainly because being reminded of his tenderness would have unravelled me.

'He didn't explicitly say he'd killed Hannah,' I said.

'But he implied it.' Callum's face hardened. 'And Hannah *is* dead. There was no sign of forced entry. Looks like he opened the door to his killer. CSI are at the scene.'

'If it looks like a duck and sounds like a duck,' Tony Morgan said, 'It's a fucking duck.'

'He said if Hannah was dead, the only person who knew for certain what he and Nick Sheridan had done would be gone.'

'Then, presumably, if Malecki put him in the frame for it,' Callum said, 'it would be the word of a convicted serial killer against his. With no solid evidence, he probably thought he'd get the benefit of the doubt.'

'Tying up loose ends, he called it,' I said quietly.

'Once you told him you knew what he'd done, you were going to be another loose end,' Tony said. 'Bastard!'

We all looked up as Heslopp appeared.

'Boss, the old couple who took the parcel, in the shop in Cracoe, called.' He was talking fast. 'The shop doesn't have CCTV. But their neighbour has a camera doorbell and it picked up the person delivering the paperweight. Local uniform just sent the images through.'

We all gathered round a computer screen.

'Thank God it only overwrites every ninety days,' he said, pressing 'play'.

We all strained to get a closer look as a figure, carrying a parcel walked past the gate.

'Bloody hell,' Callum breathed.

It was Gerald Carter.

* * *

'If surveillance had been deployed a day earlier,' Callum was saying, 'they'd have seen him dropping that off.'

'Are you going to arrest him?' I asked, taking a sip of tea, as my stomach churned with nausea.

We were in Callum's office. I'd given my statement and then he'd asked me to see him alone.

Callum shook his head. 'All we'd get him for is selling the trophies on the dark web. Charge would be theft and handling stolen goods. If he's the disciple, that's more important. Warner met with ACC Crime. He's authorised us to let him run, with a surveillance team behind him and Neatley.'

'That's not what you wanted to see me about, is it?'

'No. Wanted to let you know – ACU have finished with Beth. They checked her phones. None of the burner numbers are on there.'

'So, what was she doing with that second phone?'

'An affair,' he said simply.

He didn't look at me as he got up to pour himself a coffee. Talking with his back to me. I liked to think he couldn't meet my eyes as he talked about it, but perhaps I was being too generous.

'She's been living with her boyfriend for a couple of years. He's not in the job.'

'Who's the lover?' I asked, not that it mattered.

'Traffic cop – no accounting for taste, I suppose. She wanted to keep it quiet around here.'

'Let me guess,' I said wearily, 'he's married?'

443

He nodded as he sat back at his desk. 'So, she kept the shag-phone a secret. ACU have checked. It's all been verified. I should have her back at work tonight.'

My head was banging worse than before.

'You OK?' He looked concerned.

'I'm fine,' I lied.

'It's Wednesday.' He stated the obvious.

'We've no way of knowing he was going to strike tonight. I mean, it could be next Wednesday . . . any Wednesday.'

'That's just it, Jo. I think the next killing *was* going to be tonight.' He looked at me steadily, before saying quietly, 'And the victim . . . was you.'

I sat, stunned.

'Drummond was going to deliver you to the disciple.' He was watching me to gauge my reaction. 'That was the final thing Malecki wanted from him. That was the price to end the blackmail.'

'But he said . . . it all ends tomorrow. What does that mean?'

Callum shrugged. 'Kill you tonight – he's off the hook by tomorrow.'

'Boss.' Tony knocked on the door. 'Supt. Warner's in the incident room.'

I followed Callum out of his office.

'Right, listen up.' Warner was addressing the room. 'The ACC wants me and DCI Ferguson over at Laburnum Road.'

West Yorkshire Police's headquarters.

'DI Heslopp, I want you here with DI Wardman to coordinate actions being followed by the team. I want updates on all existing lines of enquiry as they come in.'

'Yes, ma'am.'

'You're with me, Jo. After what happened earlier, I'm not letting you out of my sight.'

Chapter Eighty-Five

Wednesday, Police HQ, Laburnum Road, Wakefield

We stood in the ops room, in front of a bank of screens displaying maps divided into grids, showing where the surveillance cars were. A dedicated surveillance officer, introduced simply as Gareth, was coordinating activity in the room.

A radio was broadcasting communication between the surveillance team, giving us a running commentary on what was going on.

'It's all audio,' Gareth explained. 'Cameras mounted inside the surveillance vehicles, but we track what's happening mainly via comms between the cars. This map here is showing the team deployed on Jill Neatley.' He indicated another. 'This is Gerald Carter.'

'Sit rep?' Supt. Warner asked.

'Neatley left home this morning, usual time. We followed her Mini to the gallery. She opened up, called Gerald Carter. They spoke for a few minutes. Officer deployed on foot in Saltaire, says there's a "closed" sign on the gallery door. Lights are on in the workshop at the back, so looks like she's working on her own. She came out at 13.15 and went to the butty shop. Went back with her lunch and hasn't emerged since.'

'What about Carter?'

'Didn't go in to work,' Gareth said. 'His routine's changed. At 22.35 hours, he took a call from the burner 091 and left the house. Surveillance are following the Jag now.'

'It's a right, right, right.' A voice came over the surveillance channel. 'Onto Manchester Road.'

'Roger that,' came the reply.

'That's Ben Harrigan,' Gareth said, 'operational commander on the ground. He's Bravo 1.'

'Bravo 1, we have eyeball. Target held at lights.'

'Roger that.'

We listed to a stream of clipped instructions, as cars were ordered into different locations, while the lead car with eyes on Carter followed their target out of town.

Cars moved forward, overtook the Jag and slipped a couple of cars ahead of him, while others fell back, making sure no one car was behind him the whole time.

It was almost impossible for me to follow. Like a motorised version of 'find the lady', the sleight of hand and distraction involved was impressive.

The Jag indicated as it approached the roundabout at the top of Manchester Road.

'Where's he going?' Supt. Warner asked nobody in particular.

Gareth studied the map. 'Anywhere from there, ma'am. Once he gets to the roundabout, he could take the M62, or any number of routes.'

'If target takes M62, Bravo 3 to follow. All other units on standby for north and west exits.' Ben Harrigan sounded far more relaxed about this than I was.

We watched as the symbols on the map showed the dance taking place. As the Jag neared the roundabout, I actually held my breath.

'Bravo 3, it's a left, left, left onto Rooley Way.'

'Most likely route from here, ma'am.' Gareth said, 'is one of the housing estates up here.' He tapped the map.

'Who's up there, Callum?' Warner asked.

The team had a list of everyone involved in the original Malecki case and their locations.

Callum went to study the screens.

'Left takes him into the Rigby Wood estate, ma'am. Right leads down Sheepcliffe Lane into the Poplars.'

That got my attention. 'Poplars?'

They both turned to look at me.

'I was visiting there a few weeks ago.'

'Who?' Warner asked.

'Jack Halton,' Callum said.

Chapter Eighty-Six

Wednesday Night, Police HQ, Laburnum Road, Wakefield

'Put that on the air,' Supt. Warner commanded.

Gareth picked up the handset. 'Target vehicle could be headed for the Poplars. Potential victim resident at 28 Poplar Avenue.'

'He's ex-job,' Warner added.

'Roger that.' Ben Harrigan alerted all units to the situation unfolding as Gerald Carter's Jag moved suspiciously close to Jack.

The radio went silent, except for the hiss of an open frequency. Then the surveillance chatter suddenly burst into life.

'It's a right, right, right, into Poplars – all units cover exits from north and east.'

'Shit,' Warner said. 'Why didn't Halton take our advice to move out?'

Callum shot me a look I pretended I hadn't seen. My eyes were glued to the grid.

Ben Harrigan's calm voice came over the air. 'Do you want us to intercept, ma'am?'

Warner's eyes were fixed on the grid.

'Maintain eyeball for now. We've come this far – we need to see what action he commits to before we move.'

She turned to Gareth. 'The arrest team, on the back of surveillance, they're in place?'

'Yes, ma'am.'

'Move them into position at Halton's place.'

Abrupt orders went out, with the screens changing as officers rushed to Jack Halton's sleepy semi-rural estate.

The door opened and a tall man with a military bearing walked in. Everyone's back became a little straighter.

'Sir,' Supt. Warner said.

He acknowledged Callum with a nod, then looked at me. 'This is Dr McCready.' Warner made the introductions. 'Jo, this is ACC Ross Newsome.'

With no time for the pleasantries, we both nodded a greeting before he turned his attention to the screens.

'Sit-rep?'

Warner brought him up to speed.

'Arrest teams and armed backup coming in from the other end of Sheepcliffe Lane.'

'Bravo 1. It's a stop, stop, stop on Poplar Avenue.'

Carter's Jag had parked at the other end of the street from Jack Halton's house.

'Do we let Jack know what's going on?' All eyes turned to me.

'No.' ACC Newsome's eyebrows drew together as he regarded me. 'Last thing we need is him doing something unpredictable.'

Jack Halton was being staked out like a lamb, to lure a tiger.

I stared at the grid, wishing it was a real image.

The radio stayed eerily silent.

'What's he waiting for?' Newsome asked.

I glanced at the clock on the wall – 23.58.

'Midnight,' I said.

Chapter Eighty-Seven

Wednesday Night, Police HQ, Laburnum Road, Wakefield

'Why midnight?' Callum asked.

'Drummond said it all ends tomorrow.' I stared at the grid, then back to the clock. 'Maybe he's waiting for—'

The radio burst into life. 'Subject exiting car. On foot, heading south down Poplar Avenue. Carrying a package. Shoebox size.'

'Stand by all units.' Ben Harrigan's even tone showed no hint of the adrenaline that must have been coursing through his veins.

'Subject approaching target address.'

Suddenly the radio exploded with shouts of 'Stop, armed police . . . stay where you are . . . stand still.'

Updates were coming in so fast and from so many units, I couldn't keep track.

My pounding headache wasn't helping. Eventually, I sat back and let it wash over me.

The main thing was, Jack Halton was safe.

* * *

An hour later, we were back in the incident room in Fordley. Callum was updating the team.

'No weapons found on him. Nothing to indicate he was going equipped to kill Halton.'

'What was in the package?' Heslopp asked.

'A silver ring,' Callum said. 'With a note that said, "To Michelle, with love".'

Callum had an image of the thin silver band on his phone.

'Michelle Hatfield's.' I said, looking at it. 'A present from Mark Lutner. She always wore it on the middle finger of her right hand. The finger that was found in Graham Hirst's mouth.'

'So, how does Carter explain that?' Wardman asked.

'He swears he had no idea what was in the package,' Callum continued. 'Says it was delivered to him, with instructions to take it to an address in the Poplars. It didn't have a name on it. Claims he didn't know who lived there.'

Beth was back. I was glad to see her, though she looked pale and tired and was avoiding eye contact with her colleagues. She'd come to see me as soon as I got back into the office, telling me about her brush with ACU.

'So sorry, Jo,' she'd said, 'don't want you to think badly of me.'

I'd gingerly touched my swollen cheekbone, which was pulsing with pain. 'For what? Having an affair, or a shag phone?'

She gave me a tired smile. 'For not telling you . . . having to be investigated by ACU.' She shrugged. 'I don't know . . . all of it.'

'After what Ian Drummond's been found guilty of, it hardly compares, does it?'

My attention was brought back to the present as Callum raked a hand through his hair. 'We're going from what Carter said at the scene, which was a bit disjointed. He seems to be suffering from shock . . .'

'Hardly surprising, having half a dozen hairy-arsed firearms officers popping out of the bushes.' Heslopp grinned.

'Admits he's been selling trophies since last year. He got an email from Wednesdayschild, saying they'd come into possession of some trophies. They wanted him to be a third party – delivering them to parcel courier services. But he was instructed to deliver this particular one in person. In return, he was paid for his services. We'll go through his bank accounts to verify what he's saying.'

'So, he's not Wednesdayschild?' Beth said.

'We're not taking his word for it, but that's what he's claiming.'

'What about Neatley?' Tony asked.

'She was still at the gallery when we left Wakefield,' Callum said.

'Blimey,' Tony said, 'she puts in longer hours than we do.'

The door opened and a sergeant I recognised from Traffic came in.

'The vehicle DS Drummond stole. It's been found in Fordley town centre, keys still in it.'

'Bloody lucky it wasn't nicked again.' There was a ripple of laughter around the room. Dark humour – even in the most awful situations. The thing that got them through a grim shift.

The sergeant didn't crack a smile. 'Some bits of kit seem to be missing from inside, but we'll do an inventory. A lot of blood on the driver's side, boss.'

'Good old Harvey,' Beth muttered, flashing me a weak smile.

'If he's badly hurt,' Callum said, 'that might limit the distance he can cover now he's on foot.'

After he left, discussions turned to Drummond and what he'd done. How hard it was to believe. That hunting one of their own was as tough as it was distasteful.

I was only half listening. My mind going over again the things Drummond had said.

'. . . Carter looks like a decoy,' Heslopp was saying.

'We've still got surveillance on Neatley,' Callum was saying, 'and I want eyes on Randall.'

'A decoy for what?' Wardman asked.

'Tomorrow,' I murmured.

'What?' Wardman's face was crumpled in that cynical scowl I'd come to loathe.

'Drummond said . . . "It all ends, tomorrow."'

'The disciple always kills on a Wednesday.' Wardman's tone was condescending. 'Tomorrow's Friday.'

I was looking at Callum as I thought out loud.

'Yesterday, he said "It all ends tomorrow."'

'Thursday,' Callum said, watching me carefully. 'What's significant about Thursday . . . today?'

I glanced at Beth, 'What's today's date?'

'December fifteenth.'

My horrified look galvanised Callum even before I uttered the words.

'Harry Roberts' birthday. The Gordons were killed just after midnight on the fifteenth.'

'Sylvie,' he said as he snatched his jacket and made for the door.

453

Chapter Eighty-Eight

'I want eyeball on Peter Randall.' Callum's orders were brusque as he drove at speed towards Sylvie Roberts' house. 'Surveillance on Jill Neatley – she could be at risk . . . or an accomplice. Armed response to this address . . .'

He was calling in the cavalry. Every resource he could throw at it would be heading towards Sylvie's quiet street filled with peaceful terrace houses.

I thought about her mental state and what this would do to her already shredded nerves. I knew that's why he'd brought me along.

What if you're wrong about this?

Even as that critical voice nagged at the back of my mind, I feared I wasn't, but hoped for Sylvie's sake that I might be.

'Thank God it's stopped snowing,' Callum said to me.

'How long?' I didn't need to elaborate. We'd both had our eyes glued to the time, ever since we'd left the station.

'Maybe fifteen minutes.' He gunned the car through a red light, grille lights flashing, but no sirens.

'What made you think of it?' he asked, staring straight ahead.

'Drummond said the anonymous caller wanted to know one last thing then they'd end the blackmail. But he wouldn't tell me what that one thing was. Carter, waiting until midnight before delivering the parcel. That put us into Thursday, and Drummond's remark about "tomorrow" made more sense. Then when I realised the date . . .'

'You think they wanted Sophie Adam's new identity and location, from Drummond?'

'It wasn't me they wanted,' I said. 'It was her.'

If only she'd stayed in the Protected Persons scheme.

The radio crackled to life. It was Gareth in the ops room in Wakefield.

'Update from Ben Harrigan, sir.'

'Go ahead.'

'Alpha 1 is following Neatley. After she left the gallery, she didn't go home. She's heading into Fordley.'

Callum said, 'I'll tune into the surveillance channel on Airwave and follow you on there.'

He adjusted the radio and it came alive, with updates from the surveillance team following Neatley's Mini.

'Alpha 1. It's a stop, stop, stop on the nearside. Suspect decamping.'

'Roger that. Alpha 2, can you get eyeball?'

'Abbie's out of the car. On foot, following suspect.'

'Roger that. Abbie, over to you.'

Abbie – the blonde.

I looked at Callum's profile as he drove. The muscles in his jaw were clenched.

'Abbie. Comms working, reading loud and clear. Got eyeball on suspect. On foot heading into Birchfield Road.'

We listened to transmissions, going back and forth between Abbie and her team.

'It's a right, right, right into Birchfield Park. Got eyeball,' Abbie said.

'All units, cover exits to Birchfield Park.'

'Difficult not to be spotted across those playing fields,' Callum muttered quietly.

We both knew the park. A large open space in the centre of a deprived part of the city. Intended by urban planners as a peaceful area where the local community could relax and enjoy nature.

In reality, it had become the haunt of drug users and prostitutes after dark, though maybe not on a freezing night like this.

During the day, a place law-abiding citizens still avoided, due to the street gangs who congregated there. The children's play area, long ago rusted and broken and littered with discarded drug paraphernalia and used condoms.

'Abbie, checking comms . . .'

The radio hissed . . .

'Abbie? Come in . . .'

'All units, Abbie not responding. Loss of comms. Can anyone deploy on foot?'

'Alpha 2. Bob out of the car. On foot.'

The silence seemed to stretch out forever, until the radio suddenly crackled.

'Code Zero! Officer down . . . repeat Code Zero. South end of Birchfield playing fields.'

Chapter Eighty-Nine

Code Zero, only called in extreme cases, overrode every other operational consideration and the surveillance teams all broke cover, rushing to help.

Units from all over the city responded, and the Airwave was thick with calls.

Callum's knuckles were white as he gripped the steering wheel. He'd stopped in the middle of the road. Thankfully in the early hours of the morning, there was no traffic.

'Cal.' I squeezed his arm.

He turned to me, but his eyes didn't register. Then suddenly a call on the radio snapped him back.

'Ops room, Gareth, sir.'

'Go ahead.' Callum's voice was flat – detached.

'DC Abbie Jensen suffered a stab wound to the neck. Paramedics en route.'

'Any sign of Neatley?'

'No, sir. Units in the area conducting a search. She can't get far on foot.'

'Keep me updated.'

'I'm sorry, Cal,' I said quietly.

He just nodded, his expression unreadable.

I glanced at the clock again. We'd lost valuable minutes, but it wouldn't be helpful to say so.

A minute later, his phone rang.

'Ferguson.'

'Force control, sir.'

'Go ahead.'

'Units dispatched to Sylvie Roberts' address – armed response ETA ten minutes.'

I followed his eyes to the dashboard clock.

'We'll get there before them,' he said.

* * *

Once we came off the main road, the side roads were still thick with snow, which had been shovelled into piles by people clearing their driveways. The ruts had frozen hard.

'Bloody hell,' Callum hissed as the back end of the BMW fishtailed on the ice.

He slid the car into a space by the kerb. 'Come on, better to walk from here. Don't want to take the car into her street and alert whoever might be planning to show up.'

We were two streets away from Sylvie's house.

As I got out of the car, my boots slid on sheet ice that looked like glass covering the pavements.

A full moon in a cloudless sky illuminated the scene with an eerie blue light which shimmered on the crystalline surfaces.

Callum reached for my hand and steadied me as I slid across the path and onto the road. He set off at a jog.

I managed to keep up with him, ignoring the pain in my leg and cursing my laboured breathing. I'd never been built for running, even when I was younger and fitter, but I'd have to pull it out of somewhere tonight.

Callum slowed as we reached Sylvie's street, finally stopping in the shadow of a corner shop a few hundred yards away.

He peered round the edge of the building.

'See anything?' I said from behind him, as I leaned against the darkened shop window, gasping for breath.

'Nothing. Sylvie's place is in darkness,' he whispered.

'Shouldn't we wait for backup?'

He shook his head. 'I'd rather get inside the house and know she's OK. You can keep her calm when the cavalry arrives.' He glanced back at me. 'I don't want her freaking out when a load of armed cops shows up.'

Just as he was about to move, his phone rang – sounding deafening in the unnaturally silent street. He snatched it out of his pocket and pressed the button to silence it.

'Ferguson,' he answered quietly.

I watched him frown. 'Where?' he snapped. Then, 'Any units near enough to intercept?' He nodded. 'Contact the incident room. Tell DI Frank Heslopp what's happening.'

He switched his phone to 'vibrate', so it didn't ring again, and slipped it into his pocket. Then turned to lean back against the shopfront, next to me.

'What?' I asked, quietly.

'Peter Randall's van just tripped an ANPR camera. Looks like he's on the move.'

'I thought you had people watching him?'

He shook his head. 'Surveillance team were on Neatley and Carter. When Abbie . . . when the Code Zero went out, everyone rushed over to Birchfield.'

I looked up at a pale sky, scattered with a constellation of bright stars. It would have seemed beautiful at any other time. Tonight, the galaxy just seemed to make me feel even more insignificant.

'Think he's working with Neatley?' I asked, watching my breath suspended in the cold air.

I felt him look at me. 'We didn't find any evidence they knew each other.'

'Given Drummond's involvement,' I said thoughtfully, 'we can't be sure who knows what anymore.' I looked up at him. 'How far away is Randall's van?'

'Last known location, a couple of minutes from here.'

He pushed away from the shopfront. 'Come on.'

We both headed down the street, staying in the shadow of the buildings on the opposite side to Sylvie's. I offered up a silent prayer that Harry would be with her. But it was his birthday after all – he could have gone out partying.

I caught a sound and tilted my head to listen. I put my hand on Callum's shoulder and squeezed, making him stop. He looked round, raising his eyebrows in a silent question.

A soft 'clacking' sound. There it was again. He heard it too, and we both glanced around, trying to find the source. Then he pointed. I followed his direction, to the bare branches of a tree in the garden opposite. The limbs, covered in a thick sheath of ice, were being blown against each other by the wind, creating a hollow percussion as the branches touched.

I rolled my eyes and mouthed a silent 'sorry'. He began to move, then stopped so suddenly that I walked into the back of him. He put a hand out, to hold me behind him. Then pressed us both further into the shadows.

His hand signal indicated the other end of the street.

Peter Randall's van turned the corner, then stopped.

As we watched, the door opened and someone dressed entirely in black climbed out of the driver's side. They turned and pulled the hoodie tighter around their face, which was covered by a dark scarf.

My heart began to hammer and I held my breath.

The figure walked towards Sylvie's house, rubber-soled boots making no sound as they approached.

Callum tensed; his arm felt like an iron bar under my hand.

His breathing became steadier, while mine became more rapid.

I waited, knowing that any minute, he was going to make his move.

'Police. Stop!'

The shout was deafening.

My mind froze in confusion. The challenge hadn't come from Callum.

A few yards in front of us, under the cover of shadows, a police officer appeared from nowhere. I could see the distinctive white cap of a traffic cop as he ran at the figure, who stopped in surprise.

It was obvious, even to me, that the traffic officer had made his move too soon.

'Shit!' Callum hissed, then leaped forward. 'Police!' he yelled.

The driver, who hadn't got as far as Sylvie's house, turned and began running back towards the van.

Callum half turned to me as he ran. 'Stay there,' he shouted.

The traffic officer tried to intercept the driver, but something was slowing him down.

He tried to catch the suspect's arm but the figure lashed out and the officer yelled in pain. Something clattered on the ground between them. The officer grabbed fresh air, slipping on the ice and falling face down in the road with a sickening thud.

Callum was gaining, but not fast enough. He ran past the officer on the ground, trying to close the distance before the driver could get back to the van.

He reached the vehicle, just as the suspect slammed the driver's door and gunned the engine.

He stood in front of the van, arms stretched wide, as if he could stop it by sheer force of will.

'Callum, NO!' I screamed.

The driver's scarf had slipped down, and as the van jumped forward, we could both see the face.

Jill Neatley.

Callum dived sideways, but was hit by the front offside wing, the blow spinning him round and throwing him into a pile of shovelled snow on the kerb.

The traffic cop was kneeling in the middle of the road, facing the oncoming van.

I stared in horror, as Neatley accelerated.

'No!'

My shout was drowned by the screaming of the engine and the officer on the ground as the van hit him. Neatley didn't even slow – bouncing straight over the kneeling figure, whose head was level with the Ford's grille.

The bile rose in my throat as I watched him disappear underneath the vehicle, which passed me, skidding on the ice as it careered onto the main road.

The empty silence was suddenly deafening.

My entire focus was on Callum, lying on his side against a pile of frozen snow, his back towards me. He wasn't moving.

'Oh, please, no.'

I ran and fell to my knees beside him, sliding the final few inches, until I could put my hands on him and roll him onto his back.

'Cal . . .'

His eyes fluttered open.

462

'Oh, thank God.'

'Neatley.' He groaned, struggling to sit up, grimacing as his hand went to his right shoulder. He looked past me to the body in the middle of the road.

I stood up and slowly walked towards the officer. I didn't need to look too closely to know he was dead.

Thick blood pooled around the remains of his shattered head.

Something in the kerb glittered in the moonlight. I went and crouched over a wide curved blade. The custom-made knife in the shape of a *ferro*.

Walking back to the dead cop, I looked at where his face should have been. There wasn't enough left to identify him. But I already knew who it was.

I could tell by the torn trousers and the bloodstained make-shift dressing around his right shin.

Chapter Ninety

Thursday Afternoon, Fordley Police Station

I sat in the incident room, a cup of cold tea by my elbow, vaguely aware of the team chatting around me, but my attention was on Callum's office door.

I hadn't taken my eyes off it, since Supt. Warner had gone in there.

Reading body language, demeanour and a person's emotional energy were as automatic for me as breathing. But sometimes, I wished I could switch it off.

Now, was one of those times.

I'd known what this was from the minute she came in.

When the door finally opened and Warner stepped out, her expression was grim. She passed through the office without a word.

Heslopp caught my eye. He knew too.

I glanced back at Callum's door. Heslopp followed my gaze, then gently shook his head. His unspoken advice was clear, and for once, I agreed with him.

I was the last person Callum would want to see.

When the cavalry had arrived at the scene, hours earlier, everything had happened in a blur.

Paramedics on scene ignored Callum's protests that he was fine, and had taken him to hospital.

I'd gone with him and given my statement of events to an officer from CID while we waited for the reluctant patient to come out of X-Ray.

Hours later, he'd emerged, with his right arm in a sling to sta-bilise a broken collarbone, which thankfully didn't need surgery.

Refusing to stay at home and rest, he was back in the incident room.

The officer who'd died after being run down by Neatley was identified as Ian Drummond. He'd taken items of uniform from the police vehicle before abandoning it.

'He obviously knew they were going after Sylvie Roberts,' Heslopp said as he briefed me when I'd arrived at the station. 'Must have gone to her home on foot. It's about an hour's walk from where he left the vehicle.'

'Probably took him longer, with the injuries Harvey inflicted.'

I'd recalled what he'd said at Elle's place.

What I did . . . it's gone too far. No one else can die.

'I think he wanted to make amends,' I said. 'After he'd told Neatley where she was, he realised he couldn't have Sylvie Roberts' death on his conscience.'

My thoughts were dragged back to the present, as Callum came out of his office.

He looked pale. His face deliberately expressionless. His jacket was slung over his good arm. He avoided eye contact and walked out of the office.

'Boss, I just need . . .' Tony Morgan called after him.

'Leave it, Tony,' Heslopp said. 'The boss needs some time-out.'

* * *

'You OK, Jo?'

Warner came in as I was making a brew in the staff kitchen.

I shrugged. 'Shit night.'

'Abbie's dead,' she said quietly, leaning against the wall.

465

'I guessed.'

'It'll be announced officially soon. Thought Callum needed the heads-up, before everyone else hears it.'

'How did *you* know about them?'

Even I hadn't known, and I was sleeping with him.

'While he was being treated last night, Callum asked the staff at the hospital if he could see her. He told them they were in a relationship.'

Just hearing those words felt like I'd been kicked in the stomach.

I couldn't bear the scrutiny in her eyes. I took a sip of tea, concentrating on the carpet.

'She was critical when he left her, but they said she might pull through,' she was saying. 'I was there, just now ... when she died.'

I cleared my throat. 'Does she have family?' She paused before adding, 'we're looking to charge Malecki with conspiracy to murder – for all the disciple killings.'

'Her parents – they're with her.'

'Any news on Jill Neatley?'

'The van was found abandoned. It wasn't Randall's. The decal outline on the side of it was painted on.'

'Neatley was an accomplished artist,' I said. 'Easy enough for her to do.'

'Officers went to Randall's last night,' Warner said. 'His van was still on the drive and he was in bed with his girlfriend. They'd been in the pub all night. Plenty of witnesses to corroborate it.'

'So, Neatley was driving the cloned van? The same one near Dennis Haverley's home?'

She nodded. 'Looks like she's been using it all along. Putting Randall in the frame.' She pushed away from the wall.

'We found a row of lock-up garages, on the other side of Birch-field Park. One of them has been rented under a fake name for the last two years. CSI are crawling all over it as we speak.'

'That's why she left the Mini on the far side of the park?' I guessed.

Warner nodded. 'Cut through on foot, to collect the van.'

'And attacked Abbie, when she realised she was being followed?'

'She's been circulated as wanted. Ports and airports notified. We'll find her.'

* * *

'Gerald Carter's still being questioned,' Heslopp was saying to the team. 'Says he didn't know what Neatley was up to.'

'What about Wednesdayschild?' Shah asked.

'Not Carter,' Lee from Cyber said. 'Uniform have searched his apartment. Found packages in the bin, from parcels that were delivered to him, and a note from Wednesdayschild with delivery instructions. We've gone through his computer – no activity on the dark web. In fact, it looks like sending email was as much as he was capable of – techie wise.'

'Know that feeling,' I muttered.

'The fees he says he was paid to deliver,' Lee added, 'are the same amount the items were sold for on the DNM. The vendor wasn't interested in making a profit.'

'It wasn't about the money,' I said wearily, realising I hadn't slept for more hours than I dared count. 'Neatley had access to Malecki's notebooks and trophies. She sold trophies on the darknet, then got Carter to deliver them. It put her at arm's length from the transactions, and if Carter was ever suspected of involvement in the killings, it would add to the weight of evidence against him. She wasn't interested in making money out of it.'

'Did Carter know Neatley was Wednesdayschild?' Beth asked.

'We don't think so,' Heslopp said. 'If they'd been in it together, she wouldn't have needed to post the trophies to him for onward delivery.'

'She would never have wanted him to know, for another reason.' I ran a hand across my eyes, trying to ward off another headache. 'Carter would have been incensed if he'd realised how close Neatley had become to his lover. We weren't the only people she played the relationship down to. Carter never realised she'd visited Malecki without him, or the extent of their previous relationship.'

'Previous?' Heslopp frowned.

'I've had a lot of time to think about it,' I said. 'I don't have all the pieces yet . . . but I think Neatley met Malecki years ago.'

'When?' Heslopp sat on the edge of a desk.

'Italy,' I said simply. 'Malecki was working in Europe between 1985 and 1987. I think he bought the knife in Italy during that time and used it when he came back to England.'

'But then he stopped using it, and went back to an ordinary blade,' Heslopp said.

'Because he gave the Italian knife to Jill Neatley. He was in Europe between 1989 and 1992. Neatley was travelling there in 1990. I think they met then.'

'How old would she be in 1990?' Beth asked.

'Sixteen,' Heslopp supplied.

'Young, impressionable . . . vulnerable in her rebelliousness,' I said. 'She was a bit of a wild child. Disconnected, disengaged with conventional lifestyles and bucking the system. Malecki

468

would have seen that in her and nurtured it. She wanted to be an artist, and there he was. Handsome, famous, talented. She would have been in awe of him. An older man – paying her the kind of attention no one ever had. And, easily moulded into whatever he wanted.'

'She'd hardly run in his circles though?' Shah said. 'Not likely to meet him at an exhibition or cocktail party. I mean scruffy little backpacker, living in communes.'

'She worked in a shop selling art supplies in Paris.' I stifled a yawn. 'Like I said . . . haven't got all the answers, yet.'

The team stared at me in silence. I took a sip of tea, to try to get my tired mind to cooperate.

I looked at Heslopp. 'Remember the necklace Neatley was wearing when we saw her at the gallery?'

'A cross,' he said, 'on a silver chain.'

'Turquoise glass – which is unusual. When I looked up *ferro*, the search brought up articles about Murano glass, from Venice.' I checked off the facts on my fingers. 'The knife shaped like the counter weight on a gondola. An unsolved murder using the same knife in Italy in 1986 when Malecki was there and a Murano glass necklace worn by Neatley. I don't think it's coincidence that they both came back from Europe in 1992, and she just happens to get a job in his gallery in Saltaire.'

'So, they could have been in Europe together for two years?' Beth said.

I nodded. 'I think Malecki started her apprenticeship there.'

'In painting?' Beth asked.

'No . . . in killing.'

469

Chapter Ninety-One

Briefing Room, Fordley Police Station

'We've examined Jill Neatley's phone and laptop,' Lee was saying. 'We can prove she was Wednesdayschild. Accounts, bitcoin transactions . . . everything's there.'

'Burner phone 091,' Heslopp added, 'has been recovered. Dropped in the footwell of the Ford van.'

'Drummond said he'd been called by a man, as well as a woman – who we can assume was Neatley,' I said. 'Who was the man?'

'Carter?' Lee offered.

'He says not.' Heslopp hitched his trousers up. 'We can't find any of the numbers linked to him. No burner found either. More likely Malecki. He's resourceful enough to have a phone smuggled to him.'

I watched the SIOs at the front of the room. Callum had come back to the station for the briefing. He hadn't spoken to anyone except Heslopp and Supt. Warner.

The announcement had been made about Abbie Jensen's death and the whole force was in shock. Thankfully for Callum, their relationship hadn't been public knowledge.

'The Ford van was abandoned at the top of a slip road off the M62,' DI Philip Wardman was saying. 'Heading west. Motorway cameras are being checked, but looks like Neatley took off on foot. It's a rural area, so once off the highway, no CCTV.'

'How far can she get?' someone muttered.

'She's been creative up to now,' Supt. Warner said from her place at the table. 'So, let's not underestimate her. She could have hidden another vehicle, ready to pick up if she was compromised. This has been planned between her and Malecki for a long time. She rented the lock-up and had Randall's van cloned well in advance.'

'Nothing's being left to chance,' Heslopp said. 'Uniform are covering the area, searching farms and outbuildings.'

Every news channel was running the story, with the 'Breaking News' banner scrolling the details on a twenty-four-hour loop. Neatley's face stared out from every screen and newspaper.

Callum's head was lowered over his notes. Physically present, but not really there.

'If we – well, Jo – hadn't tumbled that these were disciple killings, how did they intend this to play out?' Beth asked.

All eyes turned to me.

'They wanted them to look like copycat killings,' I summarised. 'Malecki putting suspects forward to muddy the waters and lead you down blind alleys. Hannah . . . Randall.' I shrugged. 'Then when his kill list was complete—'

'It looks like there were six other victims planned,' Wardman interrupted me. 'From the initials and book references in the binary code.'

'The murders would simply stop,' I continued, 'with the killer never being caught. Malecki's legend would have been revived. His exhibition would have been a sell-out probably, especially if it became known that he'd "helped" the police. That he was a reformed character.' I pinched the bridge of my nose. 'Might have even gone on to do the TV documentary, books . . . whatever.'

'And Neatley?' Beth asked.

'She would get what she wanted. His approval . . . his love.'

'Hybristophilia,' Heslopp said.

'Exactly.' I rewarded his memory with a thin smile. 'But if I'm right about their relationship beginning when she was so young, it would be more than love that drove her.'

'What?' Wardman asked.

'I think Malecki recognised a kindred spirit in her. A protégée.'

Tony Morgan cleared his throat. 'Why get Carter to deliver that ring to Jack Halton, by hand? At midnight?'

'Because once we *did* know it was a disciple, the targets became people who had been involved in Malecki's capture and arrest. The performance on Thursday was the endgame. A grand finale showpiece. Malecki is nothing, if not a showman. He wanted drama. Orchestrating all of it from the Monster Mansion, to show that he could. Halton has been obsessed with finding Michelle Hatfield's body. Delivering her ring to him was a taunt.'

'What he didn't bank on was us finding the code on the canvasses though,' Warner said. 'And when we did, he was in segregation. He didn't even know.'

Being isolated from the game will have driven him demented.

'On that,' Heslopp said, reading from his notes, 'no one at the university remembers any of Malecki's canvasses being taken there for scanning. But we tracked down the old caretaker. Turns out he hadn't retired . . . he'd been sacked.'

'For what?' Shah asked.

'Stealing from the stores. Anyway, turns out he used to let Neatley in, to use the equipment after hours. She told him she was moonlighting from the gallery and didn't want Carter to know.'

'In return for a gratuity,' Warner added.

Heslopp nodded. 'He also said she transported the canvasses in a white Ford van.'

The briefing continued, but my head was thumping. I hadn't slept in so long – I'd come to the end of my reserves. As soon as Warner broke the meeting, I gathered my stuff and made for the door.

She touched my arm as I passed her. 'Thanks, Jo . . . for everything.' She held open the door. 'You look all in.' Her eyes were sympathetic. 'It's a nationwide manhunt for Neatley. Until she's caught, I want a car up at the farm. But if you want to go home, I'll get someone to take you back.'

'No need,' a familiar voice said. 'I'll take her.'

I turned to see Ed's green eyes regarding me with a mixture of concern and relief.

Before I could say anything, he pulled me into a tight hug. 'God,' he said into my hair, 'I've been going out of my mind.'

'I'll leave you to it.' Warner smiled.

Reluctantly, I pulled away and looked up at him. 'How did you even know what . . .?'

'It's all over the news,' he said, taking my files and wrapping his arm round my waist as we walked down the corridor.

'Got finished in Manchester and came straight over here. I wanted to find out where they'd moved you to.' I felt his arm tighten around me.

Callum was ahead of us. He walked into his office and closed the door.

'How is he?' Ed asked.

'Not good. The surveillance officer who was killed – Abbie. They were seeing each other.'

We stopped at the lift and he pulled me to him. 'Shit . . . sorry, Jo. I mean I know you still . . .'

I put my finger against his lips. 'Shush . . . it's OK.' Then buried my head into his shoulder – where he couldn't see my tears.

Chapter Ninety-Two

Three Weeks Later, Manchester

We stood in the corner of the farmer's field, staring at the entrance to the concrete bunker that yawned open at our feet.

Forensics had released the scene a few days earlier and Frank Heslopp had offered to meet us here.

'Built in 1965, during the Cold War, as a nuclear bunker,' he said, jamming his hands into his jacket pocket and stamping his feet against the bitter January wind. 'In the event of an atomic bomb, it would maintain telecommunications with other cities across the UK.'

He walked around the opening, peering down the metal ladder that disappeared into the darkness.

'There's one under Trafford town hall that's connected to these communication outposts. It was designed as part of their civil defence plans in the eighties. Most were being decommissioned then, so it was one of the last built. There was a big stink about it being a waste of money.' He looked at me across the gaping hole. 'Malecki worked with the town hall architect on it when he was a student.'

'Within the thirteen-mile range from his mother's house,' Ed remarked.

'You two came up with the map,' Heslopp said.

'But Jo picked this from the list as the most likely location.' Ed squeezed my shoulder.

Manchester Police had asked us to prioritise possible locations from our geographical research during the hunt for Neatley.

The farmer had always known this was here, in the corner of his field, abandoned and decommissioned. He'd put a fence around it, to prevent anyone inadvertently running machinery over it.

The metal hatch on top could only be fastened from the outside. The interior lock had been removed when it was decommissioned.

I looked at the thick iron hook on the open lid. It looped into a metal ring, like a cabin hook. The lid had to be propped up with the iron pole, to keep it open.

I nudged the hook with my finger. It swung easily.

'Not rusty, or stiff,' I murmured.

'Well, she'd been using it, hadn't she?' Ed said from behind me.

There were three rooms down below, with five-feet thick concrete walls.

When officers had gone down, they'd found the remnants of the communications centre, complete with an old metal filing cabinet and antiquated telecommunications equipment.

The filing cabinet held a selection of maps of various parts of the country – some with notations in Malecki's neat hand-writing. This was obviously where he'd stored his notes and trophies. But they were all missing, presumably taken by Jill Neatley. But they weren't found at her house or the gallery. The police presumed she'd destroyed them.

The most gruesome discovery – apart from Neatley's body – had been the skeletal remains of a young woman. She was missing the middle finger of her right hand.

'Pathologist says Neatley was alive when she was locked in,' Heslopp said, lighting a cigarette. 'No obvious injuries – but the body's been down there three weeks, so a bit juicy. Post-mortem will give us an accurate cause of death. But it could be she simply died from lack of water after being trapped down there.'

I looked along the quiet country lane, two miles from Partington.

'They haven't found a vehicle?' I asked.

Heslopp kicked the edge of the dark-metal hatch. 'Manchester Police scoured the area. No abandoned vehicles found.' He glanced around. 'No CCTV out here either.'

'So, how did she get here?'

He shrugged. 'Maybe she did have transport. Parked it when she went down there and it got nicked?'

'Or someone brought her here.' I thought that was more likely.

'Initial theory is, she went down there and the rod slipped, slamming the hatch. The hook swung into the ring and she was trapped.'

'Like being buried alive.' I shuddered.

'In the pitch-dark, with Michelle Hatfield's skeleton for company,' Ed murmured.

Heslopp walked over to the fence and leaned on it, while he smoked.

I studied the hatch, then kicked the supporting rod away. The lid fell, slamming shut with an echoing clang. The hook swung and glanced off the ring, but didn't slip into place.

Ed heaved the hatch open and I tried again. On the fourth attempt, the hook caught on the ring. Not cleanly, but enough to lock the latch.

Heslopp raised his eyebrows and smiled. 'Just like that.'

I eyed the bunker, not convinced. 'Still doesn't explain how she got out here.'

He dropped the cigarette butt on the frozen field and ground it under his shoe. 'Nope, but it gives me a lot of comfort to think of the long slow death I hope she suffered.'

I knew he was thinking of his two dead colleagues. For police officers, losing their own was a wound that didn't heal easily or well.

Ed walked ahead of us, to get the car.

'How's Callum?' I asked once Ed was out of earshot.

'I haven't seen him since Warner told him to take annual leave, but word is, he's not great. They've been trying to get him to see the occupational psychologist.'

'And?'

Heslopp shook his head. 'Had one session, then wouldn't go back. Says she's a useless navel-gazing hippy.' He stopped and turned to me. 'He really has to see someone, Doc . . . needs the best. But he won't speak to ours.'

'I can't . . . couldn't even if I wanted to,' I said, quietly. 'I'm too involved.'

Heslopp glanced at Ed's back, as he spoke. 'But if you could recommend someone? The boss would value that . . . even after . . . he trusts you.'

I nodded. Already sure that the only person I rated enough to recommend was Geoff Perrett.

'I'll send you some contact details you can pass on.' We started walking again and I finally broached the question that had haunted me. 'How long had he and Abbie been . . . together?'

Heslopp took a long breath. 'Few months. But it's not just that. It'll be the fact that he made the decision to get a surveillance team involved. He'll feel responsible, that's what's tearing him to pieces.'

I knew he was looking at me, but I kept my eyes straight ahead. 'Sorry, Doc,' he said with a gentleness that surprised me. 'Seeing him care for someone else like this must be a kick in the teeth for you?'

I didn't reply as we walked back to our cars.

Chapter Ninety-Three

Five Weeks Later, Wakefield Prison

Now that everything was in the news, there was no longer a need to keep our meetings secret. But my last visit was still to be held down in the bowels of the prison, in the room with the security partition.

'For your own safety, this time,' Rob Harding said grimly, before I was escorted down to the Seg.

I regarded Jacob Malecki on the other side of the screen.

'What did you promise Jill Neatley when you met her?' I asked him.

'I didn't need promises,' he said quietly, his eyes like a cobra watching a mouse. 'Just being with me – a young girl in Paris – was enough.'

'To do this – finish your kill list – she would want more than your approval now.'

'Marriage . . . eventually.'

I raised my eyebrows. 'Prison bride – how romantic.' Then another thought caught up. 'Gerald Carter would never have gone along with that.' What came next was obvious. 'So, before the nuptials, he'd meet a nasty accident no doubt?'

He gave me a smile that looked more predatory than humorous.

'I've done some research.' I filled the silence. 'Two missing girls in Venice at the time you were there.'

He shrugged. 'Girls go missing, every year.'

'In the photographs circulated at the time, one of them is wearing a turquoise glass Murano necklace on a silver chain. Identical to the one worn by Jill Neatley.'

He said nothing, so I pushed home the advantage.

'A limited-edition piece. Only fifty ever made in the summer of 1986. It wasn't with her body in the bunker.'

He'd become very still as he watched me through the partition. 'Perhaps she lost it, when she was on the run.'

'How did she get to the bunker in Warburton, Malecki? Almost forty miles from where she left the van on the M62?'

'She had another vehicle hidden. Just as she had the van in the rented garage.'

'So, why wasn't it found near the bunker?'

He shrugged. 'You're the one with all the answers, Doctor.'

'Did you tell Carter to deliver the trophies?'

'Yes. I told him, I didn't trust anyone else to deliver them and I was entrusting him with that special task.'

'To implicate him?'

'Eventually. People serve their purpose,' he said quietly. 'Until they don't.'

'And the male who called Hannah and Drummond?'

'Phones are easy enough to obtain in prison and fellow inmates are always happy to do favours – for a pay-off. Anything can be hidden in a cell.' He crossed his legs and leaned back in his chair. 'Like the knife they found in mine. How exactly did you organise that?'

'I couldn't have.'

'You're very resourceful, Jo McCready.' His eyes glittered with a reptilian coldness that made my scalp prickle. 'But then, so am I. It would be dangerous to forget that.'

He stood up, signalling an end to the meeting. Walking to the door, he paused and looked back. 'Remember, I have more.'

'More?'

'Disciples, hungry to take Jill's place. You can't stop them all.'

He banged on the door to summon his escort. Then turned to speak to me for the last time.

'I kept you in the game once before – I won't make that mistake again.'

* * *

I followed my escort out of F Wing and through the gates into the main courtyard.

Flashing red lights stopped us from crossing as the huge gates rolled aside and a grey prison van, delivering new arrivals, pulled into the yard.

I watched, distracted – the conversation with Malecki causing a shudder to run through me that had nothing to do with the icy wind that blew across the yard.

A line of prisoners in grey tracksuits was led down the steps, each handcuffed to a prison officer.

The last one to jump down looked across and recognised me.

Our eyes locked in silent communication for just a moment, then Chris McGarry smiled and gave me a lazy salute with his free hand, before being led away.

Chapter Ninety-Four

Elle dropped the paperwork on to a lopsided pile in her in-tray.

'Jill Neatley's cause of death was a heart attack. Brought on by severe dehydration.' She took a sip of coffee and regarded me across her desk. 'I'll save you the science, but looks like she was starved of food and water. Food, you can go without for weeks. Water – or in your case, tea – about three days.'

'No other injuries?'

'Nothing showing at post-mortem. But then the body had started to decompose. Some soft tissue was lost, so bruising wouldn't be evident.'

I looked at the photographs taken at the scene. Neatley's body was found in the same room as Michelle Hatfield's skeleton.

'Suppose that's karma,' I murmured.

Elle pushed the glossy photos around with a finger. 'Broken fingernails, consistent with clawing at the hatch.'

'All the things Michelle Hatfield probably tried, when Malecki left her down there, until he killed her.'

I thought about the five-feet thick concrete walls. Totally soundproofed.

The perfect spot for Malecki to hide Michelle.

'The police still haven't found out how she got there,' I said.

'Maybe they never will – one of those enduring mysteries.'

'Along with the male caller to Hannah and Drummond?'

She raised an elegant eyebrow. 'I thought a prisoner in Malecki's pay was the favourite theory? Or are you thinking she had a male accomplice?'

'Maybe.'

'And why would he kill her?'

'I can think of a few scenarios that would fit. But unless the police find him . . .' I simply shrugged.

She sat back in her chair. 'Have you heard anything from the Boy Scout?'

I shot her a disapproving look. 'Don't.'

'I'm sorry.' She looked contrite. 'How is he?'

'I've heard he's in a bad place. But then he's hardly likely to call me, is he?'

'Why not? He knows how you feel about him. How you've always felt.'

'But he doesn't feel the same.' I took a long breath. 'And I'm never going to get the answers I need, so I'll just have to get over it.'

'Answers like what?' Her tone was gentle, not teasing for once. 'Why he chose to sleep with you, when he was already seeing Abbie?'

I nodded, not trusting myself to speak.

'Because he's a man, darling. It's what they do. The way they're wired.'

I couldn't handle the topic right now. Maybe I wouldn't be able to for a long time.

'Got to get back. I haven't packed yet.'

'Oh yes, your trip to Italy, with the delicious Eduardo.'

'You sure you're happy to look after Harvey while I'm away?'

'Absolutely.' She got up to hug me. 'Butch and Sundance love him to bits, after their adventures.'

'Thanks. I didn't want to drag Jen away from family for so long.'

'Venice, for a month. Fabulous.'

'It *is* work, Elle.'

We were going to look into the unsolved murder Elle had discovered. And the two missing girls.

Besides, I needed time away. Needed to do something different. Be somewhere else, with someone else . . . for a while.

* * *

Ed and I sat in the 1903 lounge at Manchester Airport, sipping drinks and sharing a chocolate muffin.

'You're honoured,' Ed said as he watched me taking a bite. 'I wanted a whole one to myself.'

'I know.' I grinned round a mouthful of cake. 'Tastes better when I pinch a bit.'

'Suppose I'll have to get used to this sharing malarkey then.' He smiled, looking over my shoulder, distracted by the TV on the wall.

'Bloody hell.' His smile evaporated.

'What?' I swivelled round to look.

The sound was muted, but the banner headline said it all:

Jacob Malecki, serial killer serving a whole life tariff, found stabbed to death in Wakefield prison.

'Could you turn that up, please?' Ed called to the waiter behind the bar.

'Prison officials and police are launching an investigation into the killing, which happened when Malecki was supposed to be alone in the shower block. Police are appealing to inmates to come forward with any information.'

'Good luck with that,' Ed snorted as an announcement called our flight for boarding.

* * *

I felt for the first time, in a long time, that I could breathe at last.

As we walked to the gate, my phone vibrated. I looked at a message from the last person I expected.

Callum.

I need to see you.

Ed stopped and looked back. 'Jo? Come on, we'll miss the flight.'

I stared at my phone, but didn't move.

Epilogue

He thinks about locking her in the bunker. Replaying her screams as he dropped the hatch, burying the sound underground.

They'd planned that he would pick her up, from the prearranged spot if anything went wrong. Jacob had told her she could trust him. That he'd take her to the bunker and keep her supplied with everything she'd need, until the time was right to get her safely away.

Her glass cross dangles from his fingers on its silver chain.

He spreads the notebooks out, caressing the covers, stroking the names. Admiring the elegance of Jacob's handwriting – like treasured scripture. Breathing the musky scent of old paper.

He picks one of the books, running his fingers across the name.

'I'll be coming to visit you, Jo McCready,' he says softly. 'But not yet . . . not for a long time. Not until you feel safe again.'

He couldn't prove how, but he knew she was responsible for taking Jacob away from him.

He closes his eyes, picturing the scene. His imagination conjuring up the sound of softly rhythmic breathing. The warm scent of her sleeping.

She might stir, open her eyes in half-sleep, wondering what had woken her.

When she finally realises, it'll be too late.

He'd always dreamed of how he'd kill.

Not the same as Jacob.

Different.

Better.

A knock on the door startles him. He covers the notebooks with the sheaf of papers on his desk, just as his secretary pokes her head in.

'Your next appointment is here, Governor.'

'Thank you, Emma, I'll be along in a moment.'

As the door closes, Rob Harding stands up and slips the notebooks into his desk drawer, making sure it's locked.

He drops the key into his jacket pocket, along with the glass cross on its thin chain. He likes to keep that with him – as a reminder.

Acknowledgements

I would like to thank everyone at RCW Literary Agency. In particular, my brilliant agent Jon Wood for his endless patience and support. His suggestions for the plotline for *A Deadly Likeness*, were brilliant and invaluable. Thanks Jon.

Thank you to the team at Zaffre, for looking after me. Especially, my editor Ben Willis, who works tirelessly to make my work so much better.

Huge thanks to retired Detective Superintendent Stu Spencer, my police advisor, for his work on the procedural aspects of the book. Your ideas and suggestions have made this book far better than the way I first imagined it. I couldn't have pulled this one off without you. Long may we remain partners in crime. Any errors on police procedure, were made in the name of dramatic licence and are entirely down to me.

Details about procedures for handling correspondence within a top security prison, were provided by a prison officer who simply wants to be known as 'Matthew'. You know who you are. Thank you so much for all your help.

I am eternally grateful to the family and friends who encourage me along the way, especially when the going gets tough.

My sons, Adam and Kyle are always on hand when I call with a computer related question. I take it all back – those years you both spent locked in your rooms, staring at computer screens, weren't a waste of time after all. Thanks to Kyle for the crash course in Crypto currency and trading on the Dark Web. I'm afraid to ask how you know the things you know – but I'm glad you do – just don't ever turn to a life of crime.

Adam – credit to you for coming up with the name for our 'Relay Killer'. Thanks too for being my 'frontline support help desk' – when I get stuck with the software and explaining things in a way your technophobe mother can understand.

Thanks to my step-daughter, Katie for helping me brainstorm ideas, and to Charlie, who donated his name to DS Charlie Thompson. Let's hope your fictional character has a long and happy career.

To the good friends, who see my words before I dare share them with the rest of the world and whose honest feedback is invaluable. Maria Sigley, Sharon Beddoes, Graham Bartlett and Alison Barnes. Your constant faith and support, mean the world to me.

I based Harvey on my Boxer dog, Bruce. They're identical in looks, but that's where the similarity ends. Bruce is more Scooby Doo than hero of the hour. He'd never take a bullet for me. A sausage, absolutely but anything more dangerous, forget it.

Last, but by no means least, my best friend and partner Ian, who built me an amazing creative space in which to write. Thank you for all your love and encouragement, especially during the personally challenging events I went through in 2022. It would have been easy to give up and give in, but you kept me going with hugs and endless cups of tea and I simply couldn't have done this without you.